The Golden Key

Cass Geller

The Golden Key is a work of fiction. Any similarity to real persons, living or dead, is coincidental and not intended by the author.

Permission requests can be sent to: wonderlandandwhisky@outlook.com

ISBN (Paperback): 9781739415204

ASIN: B0BWG6KM8X

Editing by Brittany Corley: https://www.thisbitchreads.com/

Cover design by Covers by Jules: https://coversbyjules.crd.co/

AUTHOR'S NOTE

The Golden Key is a new adult fantasy romance containing graphic violence and sexual content including: threat of sexual assault, violence, graphic sexual scenes, abuse (physical and emotional), sexually explicit scenes, self-doubt, anxiety, profanity, mention of alcohol abuse.

The Golden Key is written in British English. Please be mindful of this if you find words that are spelled differently than you are used to. They are not misspelled.

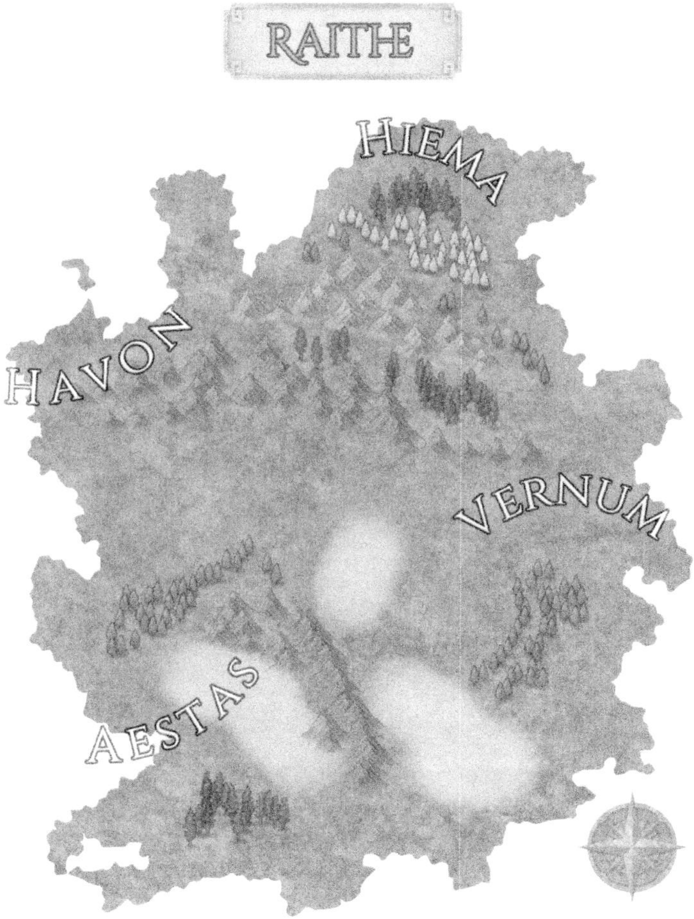
RAITHE
HIEMA
HAVON
VERNUM
AESTAS

Raithe Magic Dichotomy

Elemental

Magic pertaining to the four elements of nature. Most closely associated to the leaders of the seasonal kingdoms.

Fire	Create and manipulate fire of one's own making. Closely associated to Hiema.
Earth	Manipulate earth. Closely associated to Vernum.
Water	Create and manipulate water of one's own making. Closely associated to Aestas.
Air	Manipulate air and wind. Closely associated to Havon.

To everyone healing:
I hope you find the magic in your journey.
Never forget how powerful you are.

Contents

Prologue #

Chapter 1 #

Chapter 2 #

Chapter 3 #

Chapter 4 #

Chapter 5 #

Chapter 6 #

Chapter 7 #

Chapter 8 #

Chapter 9 #

Chapter 10 #

Chapter 11 #

Chapter 12 #

Chapter 13 #

Chapter 14 #

Chapter 15 #

Chapter 16 #
Chapter 17 #
Chapter 18 #
Chapter 19 #
Chapter 20 #
Chapter 21 #
Chapter 22 #
Chapter 23 #
Chapter 24 #
Chapter 25 #
Chapter 26 #
Chapter 27 #
Chapter 28 #
Chapter 29 #
Chapter 30 #
Chapter 31 #
Chapter 32 #
Chapter 33 #
Chapter 34 #
Chapter 35 #
Chapter 36 #
Chapter 37 #

Chapter 38 #

Chapter 39 #

Chapter 40 #

Chapter 41 #

Chapter 42 #

Chapter 43 #

Chapter 44 #

Chapter 45 #

Chapter 46 #

Chapter 47 #

Epilogue #

Acknowledgements #

Prologue

I stabbed him.

I stabbed him in the throat with that beautifully crafted letter opener I'd spotted the first time I was brought to his study.

I didn't even wait to see what the end result was.

Running was the only thought that crossed my mind.

With only the blood splattered engagement dress on my back, I fled.

Into the darkness, I ran.

PART I

THE CURSE

CHAPTER 1

AURELIA

Average looks laced in disgrace. The words my father repeatedly told me for as long as I could remember. My physical appearance came nowhere near the beauty my younger sister exuded, given I was softer around the middle and my smile never fully formed, leaving an air of misery fully etched upon my face. I was not cunning, nor sharp-tongued like my mother, the woman who could charm her way into anyone's good graces with just her words. I was average, at best, and brought nothing to my family name. A name, which had already been effectively disgraced by my father himself.

I couldn't pinpoint the exact moment in which my family began to fall into disrepair. Maybe it was when my elder brother, Archer, went into the woods one day, never to return. It could have also been because my father whittled away the town's money on poor investments and empty promises of a brighter future. Looking back at those early days, our family's ruin was more of a gradual decline, the result casting me in the role of the family and town's scapegoat.

In truth, I'd accepted my fate a long time ago, knowing I would prove nothing extraordinary. My dream of living only a solitary life had died a quick and painful death the day my father decided to transform my title from daughter to tool, awarding me the highest pleasure he could offer — a betrothal to the town's most influential man, Lord Alistair Shelton.

The thoughts of our beginnings in Huxley sifted through my mind as I ran through the dense forest, thankful for the blanket of night. The woods had only ever warranted me with a semblance of peace, and I had hoped they would continue to do so. I had no time to dwell on the fact I'd never been in this deep.

Faster and farther, I ran over the leave-strewn path. My body pumped enough adrenaline to push me over exposed roots and unidentified muck as the musky scent of the earth filtered through my nostrils in a comforting embrace.

The recent rain continued to show itself through the ground as my once white shoes trampled through the continuous mud puddles, splashing who knew what onto the hem of my skirt.

Now wasn't the time to analyse my decision back in Lord Shelton's study. The fear would come for me soon enough. For now, my only focus was to get as far away from the wreckage I wove, in the town I loathed. Huxley had never been a home for me. A thought which often haunted the deepest depths of my mind.

I kept my head steady as I ventured through the woods in a straight line. Or rather, as straight as the unkept path would allow me to. I was conscious to not take any hard turns in case the path brought me back to Lord Shelton. I'd only ever been allowed to explore the outskirts of these woods, and the speed at which my feet and heart hurled me forward created the likelihood that I would turn myself around.

A flash of thick crimson danced across my vision before I shook it off through the continuous panting. Ignoring the strain in my lungs, I pushed forward toward my freedom. The focus wasn't on the burn growing in my legs and chest but instead on being grateful for the change of seasons. Autumn brought a reprieve from the consistent weight of the summer, a season that had always left a foreboding wrapped discomfort deep within my bones.

A small spitting of rain began to drop down through the tree-covered path. The occasional thick, hard drip fell onto my head. I focused on those drops as they slowly travelled down the back of my neck before getting lost in the trellis of my golden locks, a niggling anxiety began to grow. How long had I been running? I cursed myself having not paid any attention nor counting the steps away from Huxley, from Lord Shelton and his 'corrections.' Each one of his lashes, every closed or open fist, he reiterated that he was training me, turning me into a woman worthy of his affections.

The night grew darker, the colours of the forest fading quickly from the tree canopy above me as the lingering streaks of light began to grow dimmer. I would have to slow at some point, my eyes unable to adjust enough to the closing darkness and betraying my need to move deeper into the forest.

The birdsong eased each time my foot landed on the ground in front of me, notifying me the inhabitants of the day forest would soon be turning in for the night, and if I wanted to avoid any potential predators ruling in the darkness, I should too.

The only thing hinting at the length of time I'd ran was the blood coating my wrists. The splatter that sprinkled my skin and dress had hit me immediately after the tip of the letter opener pierced his skin, growing in volume as I pushed the object further. The blood had dried into flakes, tumbling down to the forest floor with ease.

Once I had a moment to think, I knew the panic would set in further, pushing me to remove any memory of the man and what I'd done to escape him. The blood itself wasn't what haunted me, rather the knowledge that I'd murdered my old life, if it could even be called mine, and possibly took Lord Shelton's too. *Not that he deserved to live.*

I dropped to my knees at the bank of a river, ignoring the screaming protests of my aching muscles to dip my hands in. The first order of business was to remove the remaining debris of Lord Shelton's blood. I wanted no physical reminders left of him. The scars littering my skin were another story but those I had accepted. They were part of me. The blood, however, could fuck right off.

The crisp, coolness against my sweat soaked skin pushed a moan from my throat. I let my eyes shut momentarily before I began scrubbing. I wasn't going to use my hands to drink if the bastard's blood still sat against my skin and beneath my fingernails. Given the fading daylight, I couldn't see if the last of it was gone so I continued to scrub until the skin felt raw, picking underneath my nails as best as I could.

Once I was satisfied, I dipped my head, cupping the cold water and bringing it to my lips. My eyes shut as the chilled water coated the burn in my throat. I struggled to take my time as I pulled another handful of the cool liquid to my mouth.

Even though my breathing was still laboured, I welcomed every ache, every breath, and every sensation coursing through my veins. These were the feelings brought on by the beginning of my freedom.

The journey would be long and difficult, but I'd finally taken action. I allowed the pride to sit comfortably in my chest for a few seconds.

I stopped only when the water threatened to crawl back up my throat. I gulped it back down, resisting the urge to vomit. Thankfully it complied. I sat back on my knees taking in the growing darkness around me before prompting myself to move further into the forest.

Rising back to my feet on wobbling legs, the tear in my engagement dress caught on a log, forcing me to rip it further, allowing my legs more room to move. I wanted to claw myself out of the chiffon, delicate blue nightmare I'd been forced to wear. The emotional part of my brain was, thankfully, succumbing to the logical part. I had nothing else to wear and fleeing through the forest naked wasn't high on my list of things to do.

With one long breath, I quickly broke the day's events into pieces, lifting them into their respective crates and boxes before pushing them into the furthest corner of my mind to revisit at a later date. The cellar I'd built in the deepest recesses of my memory was filled with crates, trunks, and various sized receptacles to house the most horrendous memories of my life. Once I was satisfied with my mental packing, I took off across the forest floor once more.

The tree cover grew denser, shielding my path from the rising moonlight. My body and mind fought over reason and need, as my brain tried to warn me of potential night dwelling predators and my affinity for tripping over my own limbs; while my body stayed paralysed in flight mode, needing to get as far from Huxley as my feet would take me.

The rain from the trees above me shifted into mist against my heated cheeks. I tried to savour the welcomed chill against my skin but was interrupted by the image of Lord Shelton and the letter opener, coated in the warmth of his blood oozing down my hand. The slight panic induced by the memory caught me off guard as the toe of my shoe connected with an uplifted root, sending me face first into the forest floor. My body hit the earth with a thud. The blood dripped from the wounds on impact.

Pushing myself up, I shook my hands, fighting with the memory, needing to focus on my next steps. All I could really comprehend was the need to get further into the forest, further away from Huxley, and what would be waiting for me there.

One step forward and my fall was apparent in the new shooting sensations climbing my shins. I looked into the darkness in front of me, the determination to find something or someone grew deeper. Inhaling the lingering rain surrounding me, I took off once more.

The exhaustion hit not long after as my eyes began to sting from concentration and sheer tiredness. I kept moving, promising myself to just get to the next looming oak tree. And then the next.

I knew I wouldn't last much longer without food and more water. I didn't have the relevant skills to hunt or gather myself. I also didn't have any money. A thought I hadn't had until then. I cursed silently. What the hell was I doing? I had nothing. No one. And I thought I could take my freedom so easily? Idiot girl. I knew it was a longshot. I knew my father and Lord Shelton wouldn't give me up without a fight, so my attempted escape may not last long. Unless I'd actually killed Lord Shelton? The thought made the corner of my mouth tip up. The pleasure coating my bones at the thought of murdering a man should've concerned me. But it did the opposite. The only thing I'd regret, if he was dead, was I didn't stick around to watch the life leave his eyes.

I felt the tears build as the realisation of my situation fully sunk in. I was consumed in my own thoughts so deeply that it took me a moment before I could make out the whisper of dawn approaching and the sight in front of me. Picking up my pace, I hobbled toward the looming object. As I came closer, I confirmed it was a building. A cabin. A rather large cabin from what I could make out, and the first form of civilisation I'd seen since I ran from the study the night before.

I moved through a treeline enclosing the property, my sight only focused on the cabin itself. Stopping in front of the large, wrap around porch, a wave of ease washed through my body. I'd never been one to believe in fate, given all I had ever experienced was bad luck, yet I couldn't shake the sense that the cabin in front of me felt....right.

Climbing the stairs, I took in the fine woodwork of the handrail, with small, ornate carvings running all the way up, meeting the post in a flutter of designs I couldn't quite pinpoint.

I reached the top of the porch and hesitated briefly before I moved toward the door. It was possible the people living here would ship me right back to my father. To Huxley and the demise awaiting me. I vowed then only to offer bits of my story, transforming the truth into a believable enough tale.

I knocked three times and waited, listening intently, trying to hear footsteps on the other side. Nothing came. I knocked again. The outlying sounds of the forest life whispered behind me, but no movement could be heard within the house. Frustration began to grow. I could wait on the steps for the owners to return and hope they'd find pity in my circumstances. I wanted to believe a light existed in the darkness, but I knew better. I had no idea how the inhabitants would act toward a scared, dirty woman seeking sanctuary on their property.

I pivoted, about to turn and make my way back down the steps when something flashed in my mind. It was brief but clear as day. My hand, just as it was, dirt beneath my fingernails, as it closed around the doorknob of the building. I focused intently as the vision of my hand twisted the handle and pushed forward.

The illusion dissolved, pushing my chest to move rapidly as my breathing escalated. *What was that?* My mind raced, pumping my veins with… hope. A foreign feeling but also one I knew couldn't be described any other way. An intuition skated through me, encouraging me to follow the actions laid out in front of me.

Open the door.

Turning back towards the front of the cabin, my shaky hand reached for the handle. I closed my fingers around the cool metal, my grip tightening as I turned the knob to the left. Inhaling, I pushed slightly as the door opened with a creak.

Chest rising and falling rapidly, I struggled to catch my breath as I pushed the door in further, pausing slightly to appreciate the muted scent warring with the dew of the morning before scanning the scene before me. The cabin interior was open plan. To my left was a living room, books lining the walls and framing a large, lavish fireplace with a worn couch and plush armchairs surrounding it. The space was warm, inviting. The deep, rich, hues of the interior wood washed a sense of familiarity through me.

Letting my eyes linger on the shelves, I imagined myself pulling out a book and settling down into one of the inviting chairs, allowing my mind to be taken to some fictional world far better than the one I was born into. I shifted my gaze to the right where a wide, curved staircase hugged the wall, leading up to a landing filled with closed doors.

"Hello?" My voice echoed across the space with slight concern.

The door may not have been answered, but it didn't mean no one was inside the cabin. I waited a few moments, no response followed. Swallowing down my fear, I moved inside, shutting the door behind me.

The first sensation that hit me upon the snick of the door was the air itself. A comforting combination of cedar, dwindling fire, and cinnamon danced beneath my nostrils. I closed my eyes briefly, fully appreciating the odd combination before I cautiously decided to make my way through the cabin.

I walked through the living room toward the back of the space, or what I assumed was the back, which revealed another opening that housed a dining area as well as a beautifully laid out kitchen. The kitchen was set out in a square shape, with a wooden island in the centre, where three bowls sat. I could make out a small stream of steam rising from the bowls which told me whoever was here had only left recently.

Gingerly, I shuffled toward the bowls, quickly deciphering it was porridge. I frowned. I hated porridge. The consistency. The lack of flavour, even if you added spices and berries to it. It was disgusting. But not even my aversion to the lumpy food could stop my mouth from watering. It was nearly forty-eight hours since I'd last eaten, forgoing anything in my stomach on my engagement day, knowing it would most likely rise back up at the thought of how Lord Shelton would, in his words, 'finally have me the way he'd always planned.'

I couldn't help myself when I moved closer, lifting one of the bowls in my hands. As luck would have it, three spoons were also set out near the bowls, meaning I didn't have to go snooping through the drawers and cabinets to find one. I sighed. I may be stealing their food but at least I wasn't riffling through their possessions. The logic may not fit but my stomach didn't care to make sense of the situation.

Vowing silently to replace the porridge when I could, I dove in. One skill I did possess was the ability to cook. It was one of the only activities I'd been allowed to learn and do because it meant I could provide properly for my future husband.

The gag came through as soon as the warm, gooey spoonful hit my tongue. I forced myself to swallow, knowing my body needed the sustenance. It may taste like arse, but I would need the strength if I have to run again.

I retched my way through the bowlful, squeezing my eyes shut in the hopes it would help. It didn't. The texture alone contorted my face in a way I'm sure would have been mildly amusing, possibly terrifying if anyone watched me. When the last mouthful pushed down, albeit with a lot of resistance, I walked over to the sink, pumping water into the bowl and cleaning it as best I could. Intruder, yes. That didn't mean I couldn't have manners.

Once I dried the bowl and spoon, I briefly considered eating another helping before I shoved it down, deep. I gagged at the thought. One bowl of mush was plenty for now.

I moved back towards the living room. A tingling settled low in my gut encouraging me to move toward the staircase. The feeling was similar to the one that had urged me to open the door to the cabin, coated in that comfort I couldn't quite explain.

I had no idea how much time I had before the cabin's inhabitants returned, and I was curious to find out more about who lived here.

The smart thing to do would've been to stay outside, on the steps, waiting for the owners to come back. But I couldn't help that I was average at best, and average people didn't always make the right decisions.

Climbing the stairs, I ran my fingers over the bannister as I ascended, noticing similar craftsmanship to the railing out front. It was clear a lot of care had been taken with the design and creation of the building, leaving a layer of affection sifting through the air.

As I reached the top of the stairs, I looked out over the railing. From up here, the space was even more inviting than it was when you were standing in it — the mix of masculine colours, warmth of the wood, and lingering smoke from the fireplace brought me a sense of unexplainable comfort. A smile grew on my face, and not wanting to question why it had appeared, I enjoyed it as it lingered. They were so rare these days — these last ten years. I could count on two hands how many times I'd actually smiled. Now, I smiled in a place I hadn't even been in for ten minutes. The instinct that'd settled inside of me hummed in agreement.

Turning, I counted four doors lining the long hallway. The first three were spaced evenly apart while the fourth sat at the very far end of the landing. Moving to the first door, I opened it to peek in. Lilac tickled my nose, confusing me given the time of year. The room was relatively tidy, a large bed the main focus with a matching wardrobe and chest of drawers on either wall. A considerable size, similar to the cabin itself.

Closing the door, I moved to the next which revealed a beautiful bathroom. A roll top bath hugged the wall on the right while the back left corner housed some sort of — wait, was it a shower? Most of the lords in Huxley had showers recently installed in their homes, a sign of wealth and prestige. I was always curious about the indoor waterfalls. The urge to move towards it and test it out was strong, particularly given the current state I found myself in. I looked down at the torn dress, caked in forest, sweat, and patches of Lord Shelton's dried blood. My hair, no doubt matching. I decided to move on. It would be odd enough for the owners to find a stranger in their house let alone in their shower.

The third door, similar to the first, was another bedroom. Except this one had an air of understanding housed within it. It was difficult to explain just how much the room pulled me in. The first was a standard level of tidy, whereas this one was immaculate. Everything had its place. A hat stand caught my eye where a thick wool jacket hung. Giving in to the urge to be in this room, I walked toward it, letting the fabric run lightly through my fingers. A faint trace of cinnamon filtered through my nose, wrapping me in a warm embrace. I shook myself out of the trance the room had put me in and quickly vacated it, softly letting the door close behind me.

The last door brought me to pause. I couldn't shake the combined awareness of foreboding and curiosity. An odd resistance radiated off the door that only succeeded in pulling me closer. The conundrum pushed my legs to move until I was standing in front of it, my hand on the doorknob. Twisting, a lingering scent of cedar wafted through the barely there crack. I briefly closed my eyes, enjoying the scent.

Pushing the door open further, the hinges creaked as an expansive room came into view. It was almost twice the size of the other two rooms, with a door leading to an adjoining bathroom on the far left, the sliver of the bathtub could be seen from where I stood.

Moving into the centre of the room, the faint cedar scent grew, wrapping its claws around my throat. Not an unwelcome feeling. It'd always been my favourite when I was younger, finding myself in the forest of the majestic giants and allowing it to wrap its magic around me. That's what this room felt like — safety.

I meandered toward the bathroom, finding it almost identical to the one between the first two rooms, including a shower in the back corner. Two showers? Who were these people?

I scanned the room again, noticing the similarities in the three rooms with the masculine design throughout. Did three men live here? Together?

Three large windows spanned across the outer wall with a built-in bench below. What a perfect reading spot. I peered out the windows only momentarily before moving my gaze back to the bed. Out of everything in the house calling to me, the bed itself was the beacon. Piled high with pillows and a thick down blanket, my body groaned with the need to lie down.

Agreeing to at least sit on the bed, a small whimper left my mouth when I met the plush mattress. The connection spurred me to shift slightly, letting my head lean back against the headboard. I knew this was a bad idea. Every thought in my mind screamed I needed to leave, at least go and sit on the steps to wait for the owners, except for the first time in a very long time, my body took control, whispering to continue my descent and enjoy the comfort. It had brought me away from Lord Shelton, my father, Huxley, and it needed to rest. Just for a few minutes, I agreed.

Gently, I let my heavy eyelids move downward, the last thought crossing my mind the exquisite taste of being wrapped in a cedar scented haze.

Chapter 2
Aurelia

"Someone is sleeping in your bed, Mads."

Jolted from sleep by a deep voice, I found myself staring at a dark-haired man. The sleep had been so deep the fogginess was slow to detach. Blinking back as much of the drowsiness as I could, I noticed the makings of a wicked smile growing on his face. *Shit.*

"Hello, darling."

The severity of the situation quickly reared its head. The letter opener covered in Lord Shelton's blood. The race through the woods. The refreshing water against my tongue. Finding the cabin. Breaking into the cabin. Being starved, finding the porridge on the counter, then letting my body give in to the exhaustion by laying down on the bed. Not only was I quite possibly a murderer, but I was also a thief and a trespasser, with no way to defend myself from the man standing directly in front of me.

"What do we have here?" The astonished words of a second male entered the room. Too stunned to take my focus off the first man, I studied him closely. He was handsome, with a boyish-like charm, though the darkness swirling in his blue eyes discredited the potential innocence. The dark mop of hair on his head held a subtle wave, giving the look that he had recently run his fingers through it.

"How in the hell did you get in here?" The second voice cooed in surprise. Not one ounce of aggression could be felt.

Moving my gaze from man number one, careful to keep him in my peripheral, I locked eyes with man number two. Clearly older than the first but radiating a softer energy. His features were somewhat darker, his deep chocolate eyes filled with warmth. Hair colour was similar to the others except his sat just above his shoulders, gentle curls weaving through his locks. I dipped my gaze down to his lips, framed by a sprinkling of facial hair, as the sides of his mouth tipped up, revealing an exceptionally straight smile and a subtle dimple on his left cheek.

The various emotions flooding my head and heart stopped me from digesting the questions. My body quivered with genuine fear as to what these men would do with me. Or to me.

Most of the men in my life had brought only experiences of anger and pain. I had no idea who these two men were, or how they would react to me given I'd broken into their home.

The rise of my heartbeat pounded in my ears. The panic began to claw its way up my spine, triggering another moment of fight or flight. I was no fighter, but if I let the terror grow in my muscles any further, I wouldn't be in a position to flee either.

"Can you hear me?" Man number two took a step closer. My back stiffened, anticipating jumping off the bed and running back down through the cabin. Clumsiness was an inherent part of me, and the mental image of just how the scene would play out involved my foot getting tangled in the sheets, causing me to fall face first on the floor.

Deciding quickly not to go with that escape plan yet, I turned back to the first man, the cocky smile had fully spread across his face, sparking a twinkle in his bright blue eyes. "I didn't mean to break in."

The words tumbled from my mouth without passing through my internal filter. Blue eyes tilted his head back letting out a deep, joyful laugh, no hint of potential sinister thoughts which may have been racing through his head. "You didn't mean to? Yet, you did. So, tell us, thief, what exactly did you mean to do?"

I shifted my gaze back to the second man, digging my heels further into the down quilt, hoping it would bring me a semblance of stability. The dryness in my throat coated my tongue as I did my best to recite the words before they left my lips. "I was lost in the woods, and this is the first place I came across."

From the corner of my eye, I saw the first man cross his arms over his chest, cocking his dark, well-maintained eyebrow in parallel. "What were you doing in the woods to have found yourself so utterly lost?"

I may have killed a man.

I wasn't going to let the words find life. The men in front of me were strangers. For all the evil I knew lived in this world, I couldn't grant them my trust. At least not yet.

"My name is Xavier," the second man interjected my thoughts with a soothing lilt, "and this is Renard. What can we call you?"

I contemplated giving them a false name, ensuring all of my secrets could stay buried for the time being. Except that feeling, the same one I had when I'd discovered the cabin and had then followed me through my exploration, sparked in my belly. A mixture of certainty, safety, and something deeper I couldn't quite describe. The instinct compelled the need to be truthful with these two strangers, as though they were the answer to a puzzle I'd tried to solve for so long.

"Aurelia," I said, my name tumbling from my mouth on a shaky breath. "My name is Aurelia."

The second man's face lit up with a blinding smile, "What a beautiful na — "

"What the fuck?" Anger boomed through the room as a third man stepped in. I whipped my head around to find a very large, similarly dark-haired man, searing with the presence of a predator. I felt my mouth dry instantly at the sight of him. His stature alone should've forced me to cower, yet his intimidating aura wrapped around me like silk. He was beautiful, in the most consuming way. Being in his presence for too long would force me to adhere to any request from his lips. Or simply, succumb to death by beauty.

The first man, Renard, snickered, "The moodiest man in all the land!"

"Shut the fuck up, Fox. Who the hell is this?" He gestured his huge, enigmatic hands towards me. Too ensnared in his power, I couldn't remove my gaze from his that swirled with an autumnal inferno. The beat of my pulse beneath my skin spread across my body, landing deep in my ears to momentarily block out the sounds around me.

Slowly, I let my gaze trail down his well-proportioned face. The exploration halted, briefly, as his jaw clenched in frustration before I visually trailed over his full, partially parted lips. They appeared so pillow soft; I had the immediate urge to trace them with my fingers. *Get it together, Aurelia!*

"This is Aurelia," Xavier politely cut in, saving me from my embarrassing ogling, although I was almost certain man number three didn't even notice it.

"How did she get in here?" The third man practically growled. It took a moment before I realised, he spoke as though I wasn't in mud splattered, ripped clothing, streaked in blood, on top of what I'd deduced to be his bed.

All of my life I was insignificant. On occasion, I put myself in those corners to stave off attention, anger, and abuse. For the most part, it was how others thought I should be. I may not tell them the full truth of why I was here, but I would be damned if these three men would make me feel meaningless. Fleeing Lord Shelton and Huxley meant I had a chance to start fresh, and I would take it. Starting right then.

Straightening my limbs slightly, I pushed my shoulders back in an attempt to show the men I meant business, doing my best to ignore the ever-growing panic. "If you would stop with your caveman bellowing maybe I could catch my breath and we could talk normally?"

Nausea immediately climbed up from the pit of my stomach. It was all well and good for me to make the decision to be a bit more bad arse and less sore arse, but it seems I would also need to allow for a grace period.

The man in front of me could tear me in half, and I wasn't sure if I was scared or excited. Both thoughts I would need to over analyse later. He gave no reaction to my short outburst other than continuing his jaw-clenching marathon.

Xavier took a step sideways towards the third man "What a great idea. Maddox, why don't you put the kettle on, and we will all have a nice chat."

His bewitching tone brought serenity to the tension suffocating the room. I zeroed in on Xavier hoping he could be a potential ally.

Man number three, or Maddox, Xavier had called him, turned on his heel and stalked down the stairs, taking the angry energy with him.

I took a long, deep breath before turning back to the first two men. Xavier offered a quick, calming smile before gesturing after Maddox. I glanced at Renard who looked to be holding back a laugh before gently hopping off the bed and heading down the stairs, thankfully no tripping was involved.

The tremors growing beneath my skin slowed as the deep mahogany floor brought me the grounding that the soft bed linen had lacked. With each step I took, the stability grew back.

Knowing where the kitchen was already, I headed towards the back of the house before quickly glancing behind me to check if the other two men followed. Not a single part of me wanted to be alone with the beast they called Maddox. Well, maybe one part of me did. I decided it was due to the severe dehydration and being covered in bruises. My body could not be trusted.

Maddox stood with his back facing me as I came to the open-plan kitchen. I briefly noted the cogs of his muscles work in unison beneath his loose-fitting white shirt as he fixed the tea.

"Aurelia," the soft, bright voice of Xavier, once again, interrupted my perverted perusal. "Why don't you take a seat here and we'll bring over some refreshments."

"Refreshments? Are we forgetting this criminal broke into our hou —" Renard was silenced by Xavier's hand to the back of his head.

"Ow. That was really unnecessary."

Renard sat down, rubbing the tender spot and casting a suspicious side eye towards his attacker.

"With you, it is always necessary," Xavier countered.

I couldn't stop my legs bouncing beneath the table, not knowing what to expect next. The overabundance of emotions radiating throughout my body and soul had no time to organise themselves, leaving me slightly more anxious than when I woke up to a strange man watching me.

Xavier brought over a plate of what appeared to be small biscuits while Maddox stalked towards the table, practically throwing the tray of tea on top of it before the fourth chair scraped back, punishing our ears. I wasn't able to appreciate the floral scented steam rising from the mug as I was too focused on Maddox as he glared down at me before sitting on the chair, immediately folding his arms over his broad chest. If looks could kill, Maddox would've murdered me within seconds.

Too nervous to make a move myself, I waited for one of the three men in front of me to lead. My gaze briefly swept over the biscuit tray, noticing a small butter knife. Clearly, my dependence on sharp objects had grown rapidly.

Thank the stars for Xavier who broke the silence with his even tone as he picked up the teapot. "Now, Aurelia, why don't you tell us what brought you into our neck of the woo —"

"And breaking into our fucking house."

Maddox's anger was palpable. It was clear both he and Renard weren't pleased with the break-in. Given Xavier was doing his utmost to be polite and welcoming, it couldn't have all been as bad as he portrayed. Or so I hoped.

"Look —" I started, reaching for a biscuit, letting the dehydration and bruises take over my nerves.

"I had to leave my home due to...extraordinary circumstances. I didn't have anywhere to go in town, so I started into the woods. I didn't calculate just how awful my navigational skills are and got severely lost."

No one interrupted. All three of the men had their attention trained directly on me. Taking the sign, I continued, "I found your cabin, and it was the first place I'd seen since early evening yesterday. I hadn't had anything to eat or drink in so long. I was covered in dirt and bruises. I tried to knock. I promise. When I realised the front door wasn't locked, I walked in."

A gruff voice followed my admission, "And just decided to steal our food and —"

"Mads! For fucks sake man. Just let her speak."

Renard's outburst sent a small pang of gratitude through my chest. Offering him a slight smile, I quickly mapped out answering lies to the questions I knew would eventually come before continuing with the truth I could share.

"I'm sorry for eating your food. It was there, looking so warm and inviting. I don't even like porridge so you can imagine how hungry I must've been if I chose to eat it." I chuckled, pausing for what I had hoped would bring a lightness to my present company. It did not.

Sighing, I weaved a few falsities into the next part of my tale. "I was here a few hours, and no one had come home, so I decided to look around to see if I could find out who actually lived here and where you may have gone. I found the bedroom with the bed that looked so inviting that I decided to sit down for a bit until the owners came home. I hadn't slept all night and must have dozed off. The next thing I knew, this guy was staring down at me with a cocky, 'I'm going to eat you,' smile and here we are."

The silence stretched for a few moments before Renard threw his head back in a boastful laugh. "I'm going to eat you smile?"

I didn't let any emotion pass over my face. "Yes. Like the look a predator gets right before it consumes its prey."

Renard's laugh continued to echo through the space before he settled himself. "Believe me, darling, I wouldn't eat you covered in seven layers of forest filth and the stars only know what else."

"Yes, thank you, Fox. Always enlightening the conversation." Xavier leaned forward, placing his elbows on the table before his focus turned to me. "How did you find this house?"

The tone was gentle, yet firm, nothing like Renard's snarky bite or Maddox's anger. The question confused me. How had I found the house? Thinking back through the fog of my exhaustion, nothing particularly abnormal stood out. The only thing I could remember about finding the house was it had felt like a refuge from the darkness brought on by my recent actions combined with my flight through the forest. I wasn't going to mention the unidentifiable sensation it had spurred when it acted as a beacon, guiding me to safety.

"I don't know what you mean?" I asked with curiosity before immediately continuing.

"I was running through the forest all night, when I looked to my left and spotted the cabin. I was enticed by the lights, and I'd just hoped the occupants would be as welcoming as the cabin's energy and offer me temporary sanctuary."

At my last words, I looked directly at Maddox. His stare had not loosened. In fact, if it was possible, it was as though his scowl grew darker. More dangerous.

The silence sat back down between us as Renard leaned over to make his own cup of tea, grabbing a biscuit on the way back upright, shoving it into his face with no semblance of manners or grace.

"And what do you expect from us now that you've broken into our home? What was it you mentioned, sanctuary?" Maddox barked the words at me with a huff on the word 'sanctuary.'

"Why in the hell would we help you?"

Dripping in arrogance and steam, I could only agree it was a fair question. Why would they help me? I came with nothing. After the incident with Lord Shelton, I was nothing. Average at best suddenly seemed like a compliment.

I faced two options; the first, was to come clean with these men, telling them I was on the run because of a murder I'd most likely committed and hoped they would offer me shelter here until I could think of a longer-term plan. The second option, the one I leaned towards most, was to beg. Offer up all I could, which wasn't much outside of my body and no amount of safety on earth would put me in that position. Enough of that was taken against my will already. I had the scars to prove it.

"I just need a place to stay for a little while. I need to figure out what my next steps are, and I can't if I'm starving and freezing to death in the woods."

Eyes on my hands clenched beneath the table, I took one slow breath. Two slow breaths...

"Next move from what? What happened? Don't you have a family?"

I met Renard's eyes, stealing back my spine in the hopes it would fill me with more confidence than I felt. "Not anymore."

Over the years, there were many times I'd wished Archer alive and well. To be by my side through it all. The abuse, the torment, the knowledge I would never be good enough for the Mallory family. At other points, I was glad he hadn't been there to see the despair, the disappointment I'd felt not only in my life, but how I'd never made the choice to change it. I was nothing more than a coward.

"I can cook," the confession left my lips eagerly.

My decision was made. I needed to learn how to keep myself alive before moving on to anywhere else, and the new inclination telling me I was safe pulsed in my abdomen. I needed to throw any potential tool I had in the ring.

"I can clean and help keep the house in order. With winter coming, I'm sure there is plenty for more than three people to do. The only thing I'd ask" — better to get the full list of my demands out now — "in addition to the shelter and food, is you teach me how to fend for myself. I haven't had much outside of traditional schooling, and I want to know how to protect myself, physically and otherwise."

Through glances, the men exchanged a brief, silent conversation. My immediate fate was left in the hands of three strangers. Not just strangers. Men. A sex I'd never had a particular trust in.

The anticipation grew as Maddox studied me, the other two kept silent as the clear leader of the group contemplated. Beneath the table, my fingers caught one of the many rips in my gown, compulsively threading through the frayed edges. I felt the dampness grow in my palms. I should've been thinking about my next move if my request was denied, but I couldn't tear my gaze away from the broad, alluring man in front of me.

Thankfully, we weren't kept waiting too long before Maddox rose from his chair, scraping back in a screech even worse than before. Uncrossing his arms, he looked down at me. "You can stay."

The surliness in his voice was a clear indication he was still conflicted, not knowing if he should actually let me stay. I breathed a quick sigh of relief before jumping from my chair, clutching his arm in my palm as he moved to walk away. His forearm flexed beneath my fingers, sending a jolt of warmth through my body. I wanted to dive deeper into that sensation but instead, crushed it down given the need to deal with more pressing matters.

Maddox turned his head, jaw flexing as the autumnal layers in his eyes caught my own. "Thank you." I all but whispered.

His eyes narrowed, not hiding the deep brown edge filled with flecks of green and gold. How easy it would be to get lost in those depths. Maddox broke the stare to quickly glance up and down my body before a look of disgust spread across his face.

"I'm not doing it for you." His words rumbled from his throat in annoyance.

Before I could question him further, Maddox yanked his arm from my grasp and stormed out of the kitchen, through the living area, and straight out the front door, slamming it for even more of a theatrical effect.

An ominous air seeped through at Maddox's departure. A thick layer of uncertainty settled in my stomach, urging me to follow him, to demand an explanation for his clear hatred of me. This strange man had no idea what I'd been through. All I had sacrificed.

A very real part of me wanted to shout it into his face; however, another very real part of me was covered in the forest, blood, and sweat from the last twenty-four hours.

I had successfully secured the men's agreement to take sanctuary there. The inevitable argument with Maddox would take priority later. I would also need to address the new sensations pulsing through my body and sitting comfortably in my gut. The ones that spurred me into the situation I found myself in. I was grateful for following those instincts, yet I couldn't deny the air of mystery surrounding them. Nor did I want to.

Turning back to Xavier and Renard, I found them locked in a hushed conversation. It took them a few moments before they noticed my attention, subsequently breaking apart. Xavier stood and walked toward me, the gentle smile growing on his face once more. "Let's get you sorted with a shower and some fresh clothes, shall we?"

Trying not to let the excitement of a shower show on my face, I nodded in agreement before turning to follow him. I didn't know what kind of predator's den I'd just stumbled into. All I could think was at least I'd be clean when they devoured me.

Chapter 3
Maddox

How the fuck did she find the cabin?

The years had passed so thoroughly, I'd accepted our fate in this world. Until a golden-haired conundrum woke up in my bed. I couldn't deny her allure, the draw I'd felt as soon as I'd walked back into the cabin. I had *felt* her. Even if she'd been covered in dirt, grime, and what I could only assume were splatters of blood. I could, however, ignore her. I had to. The best and only course of action. Not just for me, for my brothers as well.

Home had become fictitious, with little to no hope left of getting back. It was a fate forced on us. We'd long given up hope of ever returning to Raithe. We'd finally accepted it. Until now. Until that woman found an unfindable house, in a remote wood.

At this point, I had two options. The first and considerably deniable option was to throw her out into the woods to fend for herself. She'd made it a full twenty-four hours in the depths of the Wild Forest, I was almost certain she'd survive long enough to find help elsewhere.

England wasn't rife with woodland predators, especially in these parts. We'd spent years ensuring the Wild Forest was safe from animal and human threats alike.

The problem with option one was I'd already, rashly, agreed she could stay. I couldn't say the exact reason why I made the decision so quickly, without understanding who she was further. It wasn't even my cock doing the talking. I shook my head. I was a lot of things, except never one to go back on my word.

The enigmatic pull toward her grew with each second I spent in her company. Adding in the very real fact that she could see the cabin, when the curse should've ensured no one had that ability. The mystery woman definitely had more to her story, and as much as I wanted to ignore her very presence, I knew we'd have to uncover at least some of her secrets.

The second, and now, only feasible option, was to keep enough of a distance from the woman as humanly possible, not only to protect the little hope I hadn't realised still resided deep within my battered soul, but to quell the heat washing over me when she was near. I would need to enlist both Fox and Xav with option two. My brothers were perfectly capable of pulling out her secrets. They wouldn't need me to build any sort of relationship with her. A brief thought flitted through my mind, what if she fell for Fox? Xav wouldn't be an issue given he wasn't attracted to the female sex, but Fox? He played a dangerous game at the best of times. Having a beautiful woman in such close proximity would be even worse. I would need to set down some ground rules surrounding our new guest, ensuring his cock was left in his trousers no matter how much he wanted to triumph.

Hoping I could avoid her, I walked through the backdoor leading directly into the open kitchen and dining area. The cabin itself was part of our exile, although it was just a dilapidated building when we arrived. We spent some of the initial months here just existing before realising we needed to at least make this place habitable. We'd done more than that. With blood, sweat, and occasional tears, my brothers and I had made the derelict structure into more than just a house. We'd somehow made it more than temporary. It wasn't until five years after the curse was placed upon us that the lingering hatred for the property decreased into a sliver of what it once was. For better or for worse, it was our home.

I found Xav in the kitchen, cleaning up the mostly untouched tea he had insisted we put out for the woman. The brother butler, as we so often loved to tease him, never shied away from an opportunity to entertain, to provide someone safety. The difference in this situation was we hadn't actually had another visitor in the house. Apart from Trix, who was skilled in an art that allowed her into our space. This woman, this golden-haired intruder, had no explanation for why she could see our wooden sanctuary. The mystery deepened the anger already boiling in my blood.

Taking a seat, I crossed my ankles on the top of the table and grabbed a scone before Xav had a chance to snatch them away.

I wanted a reaction from him, but showing frustration wasn't Xav's style.

Swatting my boots out of his way, he dropped a lightness in his tone as he said, "Brother, you certainly made a grand first impression to our guest."

I chuckled at the description. "What the hell did you want me to do? I'm not sunshine and daisies, Xav. It's best she knows that now."

Xav made a noncommittal noise before turning to face me, a hopeful determination settling on his face. "How did she find the house, Mads?"

Relenting, I withdrew my feet from the table, leaning my broad arms against my knees and shoving the rest of the scone in my mouth. I may not be sunshine and daisies, but I wasn't a brute. I hadn't held an ounce of optimism since we'd landed in this hellhole, my mood shifting dark at the faintest of touches. I looked to my brother, a man who had consistently done his best to hold onto a sliver of hope that we would one day get back, break this fucking curse, and be rid of the human realm. I reminded myself that my deplorable mood wasn't the result of anything Xavier did.

"You know I've been asking myself the same thing. It's the only reason I agreed to let the woman stay."

"Aurelia," Xav snapped.

"What?"

"Her name is Aurelia. We don't know how long it will take for us to figure this puzzle out, brother. The least you can do is address her by her name."

I stared him down. The brother with the kindest heart out of the three of us. Even though his cunning was well hidden, his heart never lied. The dark side of me, the one that wanted to squash any of the hope he had left, also couldn't deny his approach. I could keep my distance from her without being a dick. The time when we'd accepted others into our inner circle was so long ago that wouldn't be easy. I also didn't want her to misconstrue any kindness I offered. We couldn't have that.

"Fine. What do you think her story is?"

It wasn't a trick question, Xav's intuition had always been the most trusting of the three of us. I took his observations seriously.

Xav abandoned his tidying to take the seat across from me, leaning his elbows on the table as he ran his fingers over his short beard. "She's definitely known pain. And there's this itch I get when she looks at us with inherent fear. Whatever pain she's known, it came from a man."

I nodded in agreement as my gaze drifted out the dining area window, focusing on the subtle sway of the low hanging branches on the oak trees. Without turning back to Xav, I said, "Broken heart?"

A few beats passed before he answered. He didn't need to. I knew the signs of someone running towards freedom. We'd known enough of them seeking protection back home in our kingdom. We'd always taken them in, no questions asked. So why was this situation grating on me? Was it because of the heat that pooled low in my abdomen every time her blue eyes focused in on me?

"Not a broken heart, Mads." Xav's voice broke me from my reverie. The sight of the inherent breeze left my vision as I turned back to him. I nodded once, not knowing what else I could offer.

Xav leaned back, letting his tone mirror his mellow posture. "Whatever her story is, you agreed to let her stay and that means she is under our protection. I know this goes against your surly man rules, but you can at least be civil to her while she's under our roof."

I grunted, only confirming Xav's judgement of me.

"And there is something more..." Xav's voice trailed off, my head snapping up, needing to know what else he had to say.

"She can see the house. That isn't a coincidence. I don't know the answer to that yet, but we need to earn her trust first. Patience here is going to be key."

My eyes rolled of their own accord. I was not a patient man. I'd used to be back in our kingdom when I was learning how to rule one day. The curse did more than evict us from our home. "What does that mean, Xavier?"

In response, Xav crossed his arms over his chest, settling the seriousness of his statement, "It means, Maddox, that this will take time. Don't go bellowing out questions, demanding answers. She will let us in when she's ready. Clear?"

Xav may have been my younger brother, but he was always the level-headed one. He could put Fox and I in line with just his words and body language. It irritated me, but I also appreciated it. Who knew where we would be if we didn't have Xav's unruffled, logical approach.

I met his stare. "Fine. Where is Fox? I need to speak to him about how he decides to entertain *Aurelia.*"

I wanted her name to grate like sand on my tongue. Wanted it to burn with each syllable. It didn't. The thing danced off my lips, laced with a desire I couldn't and didn't want to acknowledge. It annoyed me. No, annoyed was too tame a word. It infuriated me.

Xav offered me a coy smile, causing me to tense. "Fox is giving Aurelia a tour. Who knows, he may already be fucking her behind the woodshed."

Xav was no stranger on how to push my buttons. He knew I was holding back on what this woman made me feel. My vision blurred in fury at the thought of what Fox may be doing with her. I couldn't let the questions circle my mind because of the high likelihood that Xav was right.

"Fuck." The growl that left my throat surprised me.

I kicked off of the chair with a new type of fire racing through my veins. I really didn't want to have to kill my baby brother today, but if he had so much as laid a finger on the golden-haired mystery, I may have to.

I made quick work of getting back out into the woods, the faint sound of Xavier chuckling followed me. I knew, right then, our quiet, solitary lives were completely turned upside down.

CHAPTER 4

AURELIA

Revelling in the state of my clean body, I dressed in the clothing Xavier had left for me, appreciating the loose cut of men's clothes much more than the suffocating dresses I had to wear back home, before finding Renard, or rather Fox, in the living room as though he was waiting for my arrival.

Making a motion of sniffing the air in front of me, Fox's lips curled into a satisfied smile. "Oh, you smell much better than you did."

I hummed in agreement. "The shower was fantastic."

Xavier was kind, Maddox was not, and Fox, I had yet to figure out where Fox sat.

If I could get him on my side, it would make the temporary living situation much more pleasant.

Fox sauntered over and fell back into the sofa, seamlessly folding one of his legs over his knee, interlacing his fingers through the subtle waves of his dark hair at the back of his head. The unassuming smile grew with a tad more attitude. "So, are you going to tell us your story?"

I took a deep breath, doing my best impression of a relaxed, unafraid, woman, "My story?"

Coy was the only way to play this game, I realised. At least in the beginning.

"Oh, tsk tsk, Goldie. You know you're going to have to spill your secrets at some point."

Leaning slightly forward wrapped in a predator's grace, he continued, "Or we'll take them from you, whether you want us to or not."

His light-hearted lilt was weaved with a more ominous nature.

"Are you trying to scare me? Because I have to be honest, Coyote, I'm already terrified."

"It's Fox." The sliver of darkness in his tone receded promptly, indicating he would play the game. The game itself was unclear, but I quickly established I was willing to bite.

"Coyote, Fox. Same thing."

Chuckling, he studied my face intensely. "I believe we are going to like each other."

I swallowed, doing my best to mask the sound. "Oh, do you? And how are we going to get along?"

"Don't worry, Goldie, not in an intimate manner. There's enough tension between you and Mads to fill an arena. We don't need more around here."

A pang of shock hit my chest. Not wanting to show my discomfort, I leaned against the arm of the sofa attempting to show a relaxed demeanour. "What? Me and Maddox? I barely know the man, and he has a very clear distaste for me."

"Ummhmm. Keep telling yourself that. Enough about my grumpy, eldest brother, tell me more about you."

"Brother?" It made sense. I'd noticed a physical similarity across the three men. A likeness not to be ignored.

"Indeed. Mads is the oldest, Xav is the middle and soft like it too, and I, the most handsome, am the youngest."

I digested the information slowly, as not to startle the fragility of the chaos already sitting in my mind. I would need to tread lightly to get information from these brothers. A feat, they too, would be contemplating.

"Shall I give you a tour of the property?"

Fox's question caught me off guard, triggering a hint of panic I doubt I was able to hide. I hadn't given much thought to my father or Lord Shelton coming after me since I'd taken solace in the cabin, and the thought of going outside where I would be visible shifted my focus back to the task in front of me. Learn how to survive on my own and then get out, as far away as possible.

I didn't want to be obvious in my panic to my present company, especially given I wasn't ready to answer any of the potential questions this might bring, but I could play the safety card, given we were in the middle of a forest. "Is it safe?"

Fox cocked an eyebrow, studying me intently for a few moments before the coy tip of a smile graced his lips again. "Trust me, Goldie, the safest you will ever be in this world is on this property."

I sat silently for a few moments, unable to compose the further questions spinning through my mind. If I gave away too much, the brothers would become even more suspicious of me than they already were. Fox, somehow, sensed my growing apprehension and took one step toward me, letting his voice drop to a level of sincerity I hadn't yet experienced. "I promise you, you're safe here."

Meeting his blue gaze with my own, the awareness in my gut pulsed with belief in his words. Swallowing down my nerves, I nodded in agreement, following Fox outside and hoping to the stars that he was right.

"There are some vegetables over there." Xav pointed towards one of the three countertops already set up with a cutting board and knife. "Why don't you get to chopping those, and I can work on the roast."

I nodded in confirmation before settling into my task. We worked mostly in silence, somehow anticipating each other's movements before they happened. It was peaceful. Comfortable. A calm before a storm. As much as I wanted to question the peculiarity of the situation and why there was such a deep sense of contentment and security, my mind buzzed with too many questions to push yet another one through. I wasn't being naïve; I just didn't have the mental capacity to riffle through every one of the thousands of questions floating through my brain. I had to prioritise and being comfortable after a lifetime of severe discomfort wasn't something I wanted to understand at that moment.

Fox and Maddox stepped into the dining area just as Xavier set the beautifully cooked beef roast on the table, trimmed with various potatoes and vegetables I had happily prepared to accompany it.

Mads had met us at the back end of the property tour with a rage burning in his eyes before snatching Fox away without a word. Neither brother looked worse for wear, yet I couldn't ignore the tension that had settled over the two seeping into the room, filling the meal with an awkward silence.

Xav had tried, a few times, to arouse conversation to at least a companionable level, failing each time. As soon as he was finished with his supper, Mads roughly pushed himself back from the table, leaving the room with the fixated storm cloud following him out.

A few minutes of silence passed before Fox finally broke it. "You said you wanted to learn to fend for yourself, right?"

I caught Fox's eye as the slightly formal tone took me off guard. "I do."

"Good. I'll be running you through some physical training. We can start tomorrow, if you're ready? It will be mostly stretching and breathing. Then you can help Xav with the cooking again."

I swallowed back the slight displeasure of the solemn version of Fox. "That sounds good. Thank you, Fox."

"Morning, thief!" Fox's enthusiasm danced across the breakfast table, forcing a smile on my face given his mood the previous evening.

"Good morning." I'd never been particularly fond of mornings, but his enthusiasm was contagious.

"Are you ready for some training?"

Mouth full, Fox's stare grabbed my attention. "As ready as I'll ever be, coach."

Chuckling, Fox shoved the rest of a potato cake in his mouth before grabbing the mug out of my hand. "Hey! What are you doing?"

Taking a long gulp of the coffee, Fox placed the mug back in my hand before winking, "Tit for tat, thief. Let's go."

Looking down at the now empty mug, I shut my eyes briefly, breathing in the last remnants of the magical black liquid, hoping the smell alone would conjure energy. My stomach grumbled as the lingering scent of breakfast filled the air around us.

"She hasn't eaten anything yet, Fox," Xav shot back.

Fox looked down at me before turning his attention to his brother. "Good. Means she won't throw up."

Xav offered me a smile of apology before promising to have a good lunch ready for us when we were done, and I winced in response, unsure if I was ready for today's training with that ominous warning.

Fox led us to the training ring, babbling on about how I first needed to learn balance and breathing, confirming what we'd be focusing on today. The only part I wasn't concerned about was my breathing, I was at least confident there. However, the balance was another story. Most times, I couldn't tell my left foot from my right, the result of face planting. Often. The scars and bruises that had frequented my body weren't only the result of others. Some of those marks had my name on them too.

Fox pointed to the centre of the ring. "This will be your zone of concentration."

Although his tone insinuated his seriousness at the name, I couldn't help but laugh. Fox shot me an imperceptible glare, waiting for me to compose myself. I clutched my stomach as the words 'zone of concentration' flashed through my mind. After a few beats, I pulled back from my amusement, wiping a lone tear from the crease of my eye before turning my attention back to Fox, as obedient as I could be.

"Can I ask why you find that so funny?" Fox crossed his arms, asking the question in genuine curiosity.

With a low chuckle still echoing through my voice, I said, "It just doesn't roll off the tongue very smoothly."

Fox cocked his eyebrow, the tip of that arrogant smile threatening to break through. "It doesn't have to be smooth, Goldie. All you need to know is that when you are in this circle, you will listen, and you will concentrate. Yes?"

Reminding myself that Fox was doing this for me, I nodded my head in agreement, doing my best to shadow the smirk twitching on my lips.

I followed his pointed finger to the centre of the circle where he verbally instructed me into a general stance, feet shoulder width apart and a slight bend in my knees. When he asked me to relax my shoulders, I found it more difficult than the stance itself. Given my top-heavy build, my shoulders generally leaned forward due to the weight of my chest. When I'd finally managed to tuck my shoulders back, a sense of relief settled in my gut.

"Now, close your eyes." Fox's voice took on a cool, pleasant undertone.

"I want you to breathe in through your nose for a count of four."

Inhaling the freshness of the forest's morning air, I counted...*one, two, three, four.*

"Hold it." The undertone adopted a layer of command, pushing me to obey immediately as I held the air in, a burn beginning to build in my lungs.

"Exhale for a count of four." Fox's voice came from behind me this time, indicating he had shifted around in a circle.

I followed his instruction, the relief in my chest expanded on the exhale.

"Again."

Closing off from the world around me, I only saw the darkness beneath my eyelids. Concentrating on my breathing allowed me to temporarily block out the thousands of memories swirling through my mind at any one time. On my next inhale, I let my lips form the slightest smile, savouring the surrounding nature and infusing my body with its goodness.

We continued this exercise for a few more minutes, before Fox's words brushed my face. "Open your eyes now, Goldie."

My eyelids rose on the last exhale, focusing immediately on Fox. His stance was centred, collected, while the look on his face was difficult to read. Moving to stand next to me, outside of the circle, he raised his arms above his head, reaching toward the treetops above us before rolling his body down towards the ground. "Follow me. Deep breath in on the up and out on the down."

Mirroring his movements, I inhaled as my fingers stretched towards the looming tree above me, the shadows of light peeking through the branches. Before I closed my eyes, I pushed the breath out as I let my body fold over. The tips of my fingers only came to my ankles, the stretch in my spine and burn in my thighs felt, well...good.

Fox moved us into additional stretches, each one more complicated than the last, causing a frustration to counteract the relief I'd felt in the beginning. The biggest issue had been matching my breathing to each of the movements. The more limbs added to the exercise, the more difficult I found to match my inhales and exhales. Fox, seemingly sensing the growing irritation I had toward my body, offered words of encouragement in that cool tone. "It's only the first session, Goldie. The purpose of these exercises is to balance your body, but mostly, to find your physical and mental sweet spot. We want them to work in tandem, not warring on separate sides."

Using his words of encouragement, I internally coached myself to continue my efforts as Fox spent the next two hours doing his best to help me align my body to breath, never once showing a hint of frustration or judgement. At the last of the activities, Fox the instructor faded away, replaced by the Fox I'd initially met. The one with smiles of arrogance and playful words.

"You did good," he added once he advised we were done for the day.

I huffed, "And you are a bad liar."

Fox snickered, "For your first day, you did. Look at it this way, it's your first lesson and it doesn't look like you've had any previous training. I'm giving you some grace. Take it."

I couldn't hide the smile forming on my face. The training, albeit only stretching and breathing, was extremely taxing. Every single part of my body hurt, even my toes, something I never thought possible. Even through all the aches, even the ones to come later, I felt a tiny piece of the blackness inside of me recede. Intentionally focusing on my breathing had given my mind the reprieve it needed.

"Go back to the cabin. Get some lunch. I'm going to train on my own for a bit."

I nodded, turning my sore body towards the path back to the cabin before hesitating. "Fox?"

"Yes, thief?" His blue eyes sparkled.

"Thank you." I was a combination of so many broken pieces. Some of which I hadn't even uncovered yet. All of those containers locked away so tightly in the depths of my mind. Training the last couple hours had given me a semblance of painful peace. Even if nothing further came from the sessions, I would forever be grateful to Fox for showing me how to move my body and the knowledge that, at least physically, I could be stronger.

Clearly thrown off at my genuine gratitude, Fox could only offer back a nod. Smiling, I turned, finding myself on the path back towards the cabin.

"Oh, and Goldie? Make sure you bathe. You smell like the dead."

My smile grew. Fox's layers steadily became visible with each passing minute, and I couldn't deny I would enjoy peeling them back.

The one session of training hadn't fixed me, what it had done was open up a new path. A real chance awaited me now. A chance of freedom. A chance to begin my healing journey, properly. A chance at life.

Lost in my own thoughts, I realised I must've taken the wrong path leading, instead, to the woodshed. Before I could turn around, my vision was captured by a very shirtless, very sweaty Mads. An axe was held above his head, briefly, before it came down on its victim in a swift, strong swoop. Stunned, I couldn't remove my gaze. He was mesmerising. An anger illuminated him I'd only seen briefly the day before. He held so much in his tall, strong frame. My eyes drifted down, captivated by the beads of perspiration rolling down his chest, towards his chiselled abdomen. I had some experience with the male sex, all of which was out of what I felt was necessity rather than pleasure seeking. Then, I'd never fully appreciated the male form. Mads wasn't just any male form, he was comparable to a god, fully captivating me in the need to worship him to the end of my days. *Where the hell did that thought come from?*

"Didn't anyone ever tell you that you'll catch flies with your mouth open like that?"

The playful delivery of his question broke me from my trance immediately. Embarrassment flooded through me, the need to take flight overpowering my very sore muscles. Muttering a very quick apology, I turned on my heel and sprinted back to the cabin, only pausing when I reached the door to confirm he hadn't followed me.

What was I thinking? *I thought he was the most beautiful man I had ever seen.*

Berating myself to focus, not only on the task of survival ahead of me, but also the fact the man surging my body from spark to inferno, actually hated me. No good would come of this attraction, and I resonated that it was best to smash it down, shove it into a tiny little package and then tuck it away in the deepest depths. If only my brain was the part of my body I was warring with.

Without knowing how I got from the door, in a haze of my own indecent thoughts, I found myself in the kitchen with Xav after a thorough shower and fresh clothing. We'd taken to a comfortable routine once again, preparing a lunch of meats and cheeses, chutneys and bread, before Xav excused himself to rally up his brothers.

I had just finished pouring boiling water for the tea when I felt a hard presence at my back, close enough to know he was there but without physical contact. The spice was intoxicating. The sweetness of sweat mixed with the woods of the forest. Paralysed in the aroma, I couldn't turn around, knowing full well who I would find behind me.

"Did you like what you saw?"

Mads' voice was gruff, a welcome contradiction of silk and steel. Adding that to his scent made my knees weaken, and I gripped the countertop, keeping myself upright. My breath grew louder with each exhale. Struggling to compose myself, I slowly turned to Mads' still naked chest in front of me.

He bent down slightly, his nose almost grazing my own. The deep-set anger flashing across his eyes locked on my own. His words were threatening and deep. "Stay away."

Mads reached around me, his chest a breath away from my own, and chuckled. Pulling back, he took a bite of the hunk of ham he'd picked up, then left the kitchen. I felt both relieved and rejected at the loss of his presence. My chest still pumping through the heavy breathing.

What was his problem with me? Xav was more than welcoming, polite. Even Fox had, in his own way, started to accept my presence even if it had only been a day. However, Mads' distaste for me grew at a rapid rate, leaving me more confused and yearning than I wanted to be.

My long-term plan may have not been set in stone, but at least I was committed to staying in this cabin for the foreseeable future. Especially as the kernel of safety continued to grow in my belly, urging me to trust this place and these men.

I could do as Mads said and stay away from him. Avoidance could be my ally. My other option would be to break him. All three of the brothers had layers. What if I could peel back Mads'? An almost impossible task I was sure, except with a higher reward. Stealing my spine, I nodded once to an empty room. It was decided, I was going to force Mads to accept me by any means necessary.

Chapter 5

Aurelia

Xav, Fox, and I quickly fell into a routine; even Mads' consistent avoidance became my new normal. Being with them began to hold a natural aura for which I was eternally grateful. A sense of safety and security was something I'd lived so long without. Not only with what happened with Lord Shelton, but the previous years of abuse from my father that I'd locked away for so long.

Even when most of my time was spent with either Xav or Fox, I found a lot of time to sit in my own head. Both positive and negative. I'd had a hard time confronting all the years of torment I'd so tightly locked away. I wanted to, badly, especially with the new sense of safety I felt with the brothers and the cabin. The physical reminders may always be visible on my skin, but it was the mental scars that haunted me the most. Moving forward in my life, with the freedom I had finally claimed, meant I couldn't keep those memories locked away. I continued to try and release them, convincing myself I was ready to face them, but I'd done such an excellent job of burying them that I struggled to reach them.

Each morning, I assisted Xav with breakfast, then took to the forest floor with Fox for training. Although my muscles had started to strengthen, my clumsiness would get the better of me, which Fox took advantage of by either giving me words of encouragement or laughing hysterically over how often I'd tripped over my limbs. As much as my body ached, I ignored it, keeping up with training and helping around the cabin. I wanted independence to wrap around my bones, giving me a new courage for life now that I was free. Free from Lord Shelton and my father.

At breakfast, Fox had told me our training session was cancelled as the brothers had an errand to take care of. I was free to roam around the property grounds which filled me with a slight apprehension, knowing my father and Shelton could have sent people to look for me. Sensing my trepidation in my lack of response, Fox did his best to assure me I'd be safe given we were in a depth of the forest that people rarely travelled to, and the property was private, meaning any trespassers would, in his words, know their wrath. He left me with a quick reminder of the property boundaries he'd shown me on the first day.

Initially, I had decided to stay in the cabin, not wanting to venture outside and worry I could be found, even with Fox's attempted reassurance. By mid-day, I had completed all of my indoor tasks and attempted to read by the window, failing almost immediately as I became too agitated to sit still.

Abandoning the book, I moved my body into an upright position, letting my palms fall to the tops of my thighs. The breathing techniques I'd practised with Fox were a way to get my mind settled enough that the memories would begin to surface, allowing me to confront them properly.

Drawing in a deep breath of the lingering fire dancing through the air around me, I let my eyes fall closed, silently counting to four before exhaling through my lips audibly. Flashes of memories flitted through, as usual, only letting me see the surface of abuse at the hands of my father and Lord Shelton. Where were the details? I wanted the belt on my thighs to trace through my mind vividly, allowing the anger to seep into my bones, letting me release the fury I knew was buried so deeply.

I repeated the exercise over and over, willing my memory to bring the clarity to the forefront of my mind but only ever getting the small glimpses as I had since arriving in the cabin.

With a frustrated breath, my eyes flew open. Without another thought, I pulled on the boots and coat Xav had given me, my legs then drove me out the front door, down the porch steps, and into the forest.

The solitude of the forest and the blanket of the trees should aid me in opening the deep stores of my mind. The unpacking process would be long and arduous; I was ready to face the memories, if only they'd make themselves known.

Memories of my mother's neglect and hatred of me. Every single issue with my father. My younger sister, ignoring my presence and pain all those years. And my brother? That would take the most time to work through.

I thought about what Archer would say about my current situation. I imagined he'd be furious at our family for the traumatic tornados they'd sent me through. In contrast, he would be warm, kind, and proud of me for putting myself in a safe situation with these brothers— safe, and better than where I'd come from. Archer had been my right hand, and I was never much good with my left.

Furious with myself and my inability to access my memories, I trudged through the forest, not realising how far I'd come until the rushing River Ariana caught my attention. I'd ventured here a few times with Fox in his attempt to teach me how to fish, but never alone.

Making the decision to head a bit further south, I cut right, walking parallel to the river. I did my best to inhale the forest around me, willing the sights, sounds, and myriad of natural aromas to aid me in seeking comfort. Heeding Fox's advice, I wouldn't venture too far south into these woods on my own. Especially not knowing the likelihood that I'd be found.

My boot came down on a buried root I hadn't noticed, cracking beneath my step and sending me sideways. Whirling my arms in a frantic fashion, I caught myself from falling directly on my arse as a small auburn flash caught the corner of my eye, gone before I could pinpoint exactly what it was. Knowing less treacherous beasts lived in the forest, I convinced myself it must have been a squirrel, righted myself fully, and continued on my journey.

The river provided the perfect background music to my voyage, except the serenity of the forest did nothing to abate those damn memories. Before my frustration could grow, I was stopped by a fox. It sat in the middle of the path as if to keep me from moving further forward. He was beautiful. His coat, a glossy, deep auburn, with eyes of the deepest honey, somehow pleading for my attention.

"Hello, sir." It wasn't lost on me that my smooth greeting was directed at an animal.

The fox tilted his head, whiskers twitching. Keeping a healthy distance, I attempted to walk around the fox. The critter, clearly having other plans for me, skittered to block my way once more.

"Look, I just want to walk a little bit further down this path. Is this going to be a problem?"

You really must be losing it, Aurelia.

The fox, appearing intrigued with me, slowly blinked before swishing his tail and turning his head back towards the direction I'd come from.

I felt the profound need to turn around, and I cocked my head at the small creature. It was common knowledge animals could sense much more than humans, having a closer connection to the earth. Was it far-fetched to think this fox had issued me a warning?

Given my new found freedom had only lasted a few weeks, I wasn't ready to give it up to potential death, so I turned back the way I'd come. After a few paces, I turned to find the fox following closely at my back. *Do foxes bite?* Of course they did, except this one didn't seem interested in the taste of my flesh. I shrugged to no one before continuing on.

The fox kept pace with me all the way back to the boundary of trees when it finally decided it had enough and turned in another direction, leaving me on my own once more. What an odd encounter.

The brothers didn't get back to the cabin until after nightfall, by which time I'd already finished the stew for supper, eaten a bowl, then tucked myself into the sofa cocoon in front of the fire, engrossed in one of the books I'd found lining the walls.

Mads walked in the front door, paused momentarily to offer me a low growl before stalking into the kitchen. All three appeared exhausted. Fox, held back from his brothers, choosing instead to saunter over to the sofa where I lay. “No death by forest creatures I see?”

His tone, albeit playful, held a layer of exhaustion.

“Sadly, for you three, I live to see another day.” I turned the page, although I’d lost interest in it as soon as my eyes locked on Mads, that blasted heat immediately building in my centre.

“I did have an odd experience with a fox though,” I admitted, surprisingly.

Closing the book, I set it to the side as Fox raised an eyebrow. “Oh? And what, may I ask, did this fox do?”

“I was heading south along the river when it just appeared and sat in the middle of the path. When I went to walk around it, the fox blocked my way forward, like it didn’t want me to go any further. When I finally turned back, it followed me until I reached the treeline.”

Nodding as though this was nothing out of the ordinary, Fox sat down at my feet, stretching his arm across the back of the sofa. “The fox you met was most likely Rock.”

“Rock?” Surprise filled my voice.

“Yes. He lives with me sometimes.” Fox said matter of fact, as though our conversation about a wild animal was perfectly normal.

Curiosity peaked, so I pushed him. “Your name is Fox and you have a pet fox? A little on the nose, isn’t it?”

He chuckled. “Rock is not my pet. The little bastard showed up one day and refused to leave. He most likely didn’t want you travelling any further on your own.”

Weaving his fingers through the throw draped on my feet, Fox stared into the flames, looking as if he was only half aware of his surroundings. I wanted to ask him why he thought a fox would make a conscious effort of keeping me safe, yet I decided it'd push the conversation from strange to bizarre. Fox's exhaustion shouldn't be pressed.

"Is he friendly?" I urged. Whatever troubled him needed to be vanquished, immediately.

"Friendly enough. He's more of a watchdog, in my opinion." With nothing further to add, Fox stood and walked towards the kitchen, calling over his shoulder, "I'm glad you'll live to see another day."

Stepping out onto the front porch, the warmth of the morning sun kissed my cheeks. I let my eyes fall to relish the sensation. The height of the intense summer heat was now gone, replaced with the crisp autumn winds. I'd always loved the season change, especially when it shifted away from summer.

A shuffling motion had me opening my eyes to find the creature of silky auburn fur, waiting at the bottom of the stairs.

"Good morning, Rock." I stated confidently as though the creature could understand what I said.

Once I passed where he sat, he turned to follow me toward the training ring. Rock trailing after me eased some of the loneliness that lingered deep in my soul.

Arriving in the training ring, Fox was already there, setting out some logs that appeared to form a sort of obstacle course. "I see you've officially made a friend with our little Rock here."

"He was waiting for me when I left the house. Or so I assume he was waiting for me."

Fox confirmed my suspicion that Rock had taken an instant liking to their new house guest and inadvertently adopted me as his own. I couldn't help smiling down at the creature. No living being had ever paid me much attention unless they were looking to take something from me. I highly doubted this fox wanted anything from me apart from companionship. The thought warmed my abandoned heart.

Rock's consistent appearance couldn't have come at a better time given the brothers had increasingly more work or 'errands' taking them away from the cabin. Fox had given me some exercises I could work through on my own when he wasn't there and with Rock by my side, the brothers rarely provided further warnings about the dangers of the forest. When I decided to start letting Rock in the house, I didn't receive any pushback from the brothers apart from a singular snarl I knew had come directly from Mads. My relationships with Fox and Xav began to grow deeper, more open. But with Mads, the distance grew further between us.

One evening, thinking I was alone in the cabin, I took a long shower, donned a tunic and nothing else before waltzing into the kitchen, ready to prepare myself supper for one. One foot inside the kitchen saw me frozen. The ever angry Mads leaned against the stove, steaming mug in his hand, eyes locked on the sight of my long, thick bare legs and generous cleavage on full display from the loose buttons at the top of my shirt.

A sly smile grew across Mads' face, both terrifying and thoroughly seductive. I wanted to eat it. Absolutely mesmerised, I couldn't believe the effect his smile brought to the room. An oddly different person appeared with his grin, contrary to the grim exterior I'd grown accustomed to in the last few weeks.

I stood, motionless, as Mads' eyes grazed my bare legs. I silently thanked the dim lighting in the room, doing the work to cover the scars at the top of my thighs. I couldn't bring myself to turn and leave, the action I probably should've taken. When his gaze found mine once more, the smile had faded much to my disappointment. "I'm sorry," I breathed. "I didn't realise anyone was here."

Mads considered me for a few moments longer before breaking his own silence. "Is this what you do when you're alone? Walk around other people's homes half naked?"

The bite in his accusation shouldn't have brought the hurt it did given my past, my experience being a pawn in other people's games, except coming from him, it did. It hit my deserted heart with a terrifying force. Shoulders back, I established I could fight fire with fire, the foreign sensations this man evoked weren't going to stop me.

"I wasn't aware of the dress code, Your Majesty."

My quip landed in the form of the smirk on Mads' face. He surveyed me, intently, as I sauntered to the cabinet he stood in front of to reach around him and grab a mug. Purposely, I brushed my arm against his, triggering small tingles to spread across my shoulders, creeping up my neck.

"Dress code? Not at all. There is, however, the fact you are in a bear's den," he warned. "And you would do well to remember."

Mads pushed off the counter, making his way towards the living room before I stopped him. "Why do you hate me so much? Besides the small issue of me breaking in here, I'm earning my keep. Xav and Fox seem to have accepted my presence. You just continue to be cold and distant."

Mads stopped. With his back towards me, his shoulders rose and fell with his slow, deep exhale. Faster than should've been possible, he turned and stalked towards me, not stopping until his nose was just about level with my own. "Hate you? I don't hate you, thief. I just don't trust you."

My heartbeat kicked up, immediately wishing I hadn't said anything to the beast of a man taking full use of my personal space. "Everything was going fine. We'd finally accepted our fate, then you walked in — no, you broke into this cabin and into our lives. We didn't ask for you to come here. You shouldn't be here."

I didn't know whether to throw the right hook I'd been working on with Fox or to run away, fast. Instead, I surprised myself. I bit back, finger stabbing into his chest, pushing him slowly away from me. "You were the one who agreed to let me stay. You. Your words landed me here. And just so you are aware, *Maddox,* this isn't exactly the fairy-tale I'd envisioned either. So, we have a couple of options. We can handle this like adults and respect each other's presence. Or you can throw me out into the woods, right now, since it is so hard for you to be around me. You choose."

I crossed my arms over my chest, waiting with bated breath for his response. I knew damn well he could easily pick option two and I'd be right back where I was before I'd found the solace of this cabin. Only this time, with a few more survival skills than I'd had previously, none of which would do me any good in the real world.

Mads considered me for a few moments, jaw clenched, before his throat rumbled the words, "Option one."

He leaned further down, his nose just a hair's breadth away from my own, I was entranced by the greens and golds swirling around his eyes combined with his intoxicating woodsy scent. "But we will uncover your secrets."

Without another word, he stomped toward the back door and disappeared from sight, taking the dense atmosphere with him.

My body felt the force of the interaction as it trembled with an odd mixture of fear and what I could only describe as desire. I let the pride of standing up to him seep through my veins before rushing toward a pair of trousers.

During breakfast the next morning, the most peculiar mood circled around the room as the brothers and I sat at the table. Peace. Or at least a sliver of it. I hid my prideful grin, knowing I'd made a semblance of progress with the eldest brother, even if he'd caught me scantily clad. I wasn't naïve enough to think our brief conversation and agreement had spawned any sort of friendship or romance. *Romance?* Why was I thinking about that? As long as the new plan we'd agreed to made the current living situation more bearable, I felt satisfied.

Given the new peace between us, I decided to take the opportunity at training with Fox to uncover more information to help me win Mads over.

Throwing a jab cross combination Fox had shown me in the air, I called over to him, "Fox, can I ask you a question?"

"You just did." His smug voice travelled through the training ring.

Resisting the urge to roll my eyes, I knew trying to get this information out of Fox as opposed to Xav would be more difficult given his affinity for sarcasm. I also felt Fox would be more honest about his eldest brother rather than a sugar coating from Xav.

"What is the deal with Mads?" I breathed on a jab and an exhale.

"The deal?" Sarcasm laced with sarcasm.

"Yes. Why is he so angry all the time?" I finished my combination before turning to him, my hands on my hips as I breathed deep. I'd been at the cabin for a few weeks, and I rarely saw how Mads interacted with his brothers.

"Mads is.... What I like to call the trifecta."

"Fine. I'll bite. The trifecta?"

"Yes. Trifecta. Moody, broody, and attitudey."

"Attitudey isn't a word, Fox."

"Yes, but it rhymes, therefore, it fits." The saucy yet cheeky smile I'd grown to know so well latched onto his face.

The fact Fox confirmed what I'd suspected of Mads was positive, although it didn't leave me with any ideas on how to break through his tough outer shell.

Fox signalled for me to continue the drill. Right hook, left jab.

"Do you have any helpful advice on how I get past this trifecta?"

Cocking his brow, I immediately regretted asking that particular question. "I can think of a few things."

Taking a deep breath, I had come to know Fox's trickster side indeed loved and included a plethora of sexual innuendos, no matter the subject. None of which bothered me. Thankfully, I'd escaped my main abuser before the force took on a sexual form. Shelton's plan was always to wait until we were wed, or at least, officially engaged. It was the reason I'd snapped that night in his study. So much of my body was already taken against my will. I wasn't going to let him have me completely.

"Maybe something not involving me getting naked or on my knees?" The frustration in my words was hard to ignore, but I'm sure Fox would do a pretty good job of it.

He took a faux pause, as if he was actually thinking of something helpful before, "Nope. Sorry Goldie."

The morning's training session continued without any further interrogation from me. The brothers, although two thirds were somewhat easy to manage, held too many secrets. I needed to be calm and calculated to uncover them.

Walking back from training, Rock at my heels, a plan began to form as I established the individual approaches I would have to take with each brother. Xav would voluntarily give me snippets of their lives, holding back on the more useful information and careful not to give too much away. Fox would lace his information with humour to which I would need to dig past. And Mads? A determination settled low in my gut. The most engaged he'd been was when my words held fire, not the invisible woman I'd tried to be for the first couple of weeks. In order to break past the trifecta, I would have to make him angry and throw the heat straight back at him.

Let the game begin.

CHAPTER 6

MADDOX

"Don't make me beg, Maddox."

Fox's cool delivery wouldn't fool me. Asking me to take over *his* job of training *her* contradicted my plan to keep my distance. I couldn't show any of them how much the woman affected me. I did my best to keep away from her before she decided to saunter into the kitchen, lavish legs and tits on full display causing a number of indecent thoughts to flow through my mind. The combination of distance and indifference hadn't worked. If anything, I thought about our house guest more with each day that passed.

Groaning in frustration, I said, "Can't she train herself? Or take a day off?"

Fox came to stand behind me at the kettle, using his hands to turn me to face him. "You remember our initial training, brother? Were we allowed to take breaks?"

I knew what he was doing, and he did a shit job of it. I chortled, "She's not training to be a soldier, Fox."

Dropping his hands from my biceps, a faint sternness flickered over his face. Fuck. I could never deny my baby brother when he wanted to show emotion. It was so rare, but it always tore straight through my chest, clutching my heart in its claws.

"She needs to be, Mads. For herself. She needs to know she is a warrior, not just physically."

The earnestness in his voice tilted my axis. This wasn't our dynamic, and Fox did a damn good job of pulling my heartstrings. The bastard.

"You know, as do Xav and I, that woman came from something heinous. She's making a lot of progress in training. She still trips over her own feet, but there's a confidence forming in each breath, each right hook. I don't want that to take a pause, brother."

I stepped around him, needing the space from his level-headedness. "Why can't I go to Trix? You can stay here and train her."

Fox laughed at the suggestion, "Because I'm better at charming our dear friend."

It was my turn to laugh. "No you aren't. Out of the three of us, Trix would kill you first."

Holding up his hands in defeat, he stepped toward me once more. "Okay, maybe not, but she does take better to me than she does to your surliness."

I clutched my chest in feigned shock. "I am not surly."

Clapping me on the back, Fox moved toward the front door, not waiting for me to agree to his absurd request.

"We've been focused on introductory hand to hand combinations. Start there, brother."

Fox's defiant tone seeped through the air to slap me across the face. He'd played me. With a sigh of defeat, I made my way toward the training ring.

"Where is Fox?" Aurelia's surprised question slithered up my back, leaving the hairs on my neck at attention.

I'd rarely been alone with the woman, and now that it was just her and I, my body became very attuned to our surroundings. My cock gave a slight twitch at the sound of her angelic voice. *Calm the fuck down.*

I turned to find Aurelia's shock written across her face. "Fox has other things to do today. I insisted we cancel this ridiculous session, but my baby brother is very convincing."

The shock morphed into irritation as her eyes narrowed on the word 'ridiculous.'

Fox may be right about Aurelia needing these sessions. Not just to build her confidence, but to protect herself from whatever monsters she'd known showing up in her future. We'd all assumed it when she broke into the cabin, and yesterday, when I spied the faint lines of the scars on the tops of her thighs, it was confirmed. Those marks had sent me into a rage I hadn't known for a very, very long time. I wanted nothing more than to demand her secrets, pulling at the trauma of her past, before setting it aflame beneath my fingers. I couldn't do that, though. Whatever and whenever she offered us information, we would gladly take it.

I could be patient.

"Great. So, I'm stuck with you?" Her quip didn't land the way she'd envisioned.

Pleasure laced the displeasure of her question that spurred me to bite back.

"Believe me, I'm not happy about it either."

I knew she would detect the lie; I didn't deliver my attempted disgust properly.

"Let's get it over with then." Her huffed response sent a ping of competition through my chest.

"Get it over with? If you aren't going to take this seriously then what is the point?"

With each word I voiced, her irritation settled nervously, evident by her fingers threading through the bottom of her shift.

Her blue gaze widened as her stance centred, rooting her to the spot Fox had ridiculously dubbed the zone of concentration. "The point?"

I smirked at the depth of venom in her words. "The point is I refuse to ever be put in another situation where I can't at least try to defend myself." Her mouth snapped shut at the confession. Her vibrant blue eyes held a hint of fear at the realisation she hadn't meant to let that slip.

Every part of me knew she felt abuse in her past but it still settled like lead in my throat. Eyes narrowing, I refused to break eye contact. "What do you mean 'another'?"

Aurelia's posture shifted, losing the stability it had as she twined her fingers together in agitation, "I just meant a woman should be allowed and able to protect herself."

I didn't buy the lies and I let my gaze reflect that, burning my stare into her own. She was spooked, and I didn't want to force her into the confessions she wasn't ready for. I turned, shifting myself around the ring before I found myself a few feet away from her, "Fox said you've been working on hand to hand. We'll start there. Get into your position."

I studied Aurelia as her feet shifted further apart, leaving a slight bend in her knees as she bent down to test it. Her left fist landed in front of her face while her right sat back in its dominant position. I allowed myself a moment to appreciate the sight of her arms pushing her full chest between them, capturing them in position perfect for me to bury my face in.

Cursing my dick inwardly, I started in slow, calculated circles around her, examining the lines of her body, making small adjustments where necessary with only the lightest of direct touches. The visual worship of her curves never strayed far from my thoughts. When I was satisfied with her posture, I stood in front of her, raising my hands up to use for guidance. "I want two rights and then a left jab."

Obeying my request, Aurelia's fist struck my right palm twice before her left jab struck the other palm. I shook my head. "The jab is too hard."

"Too hard?" She didn't try to hide her frustration. "How can a punch be too hard? That's ridiculous."

Her shoulders dropped, an act that would have earned us a lashing in our own training all those years ago. Silently, I signalled for her to raise her guard again. "This isn't a punch, Aurelia, it's a jab."

It was the first time her name rolled off my tongue in her presence. A warmth beat in my groin as her pupils dilated at the sound. *Fuck. Focus.*

"The punches aren't bad. You need to make sure to lock your elbow at the follow through. Locking your elbow will be harder to block. You don't want to give your opponent an easy opportunity. Give me the combination again."

With no further retort, she obeyed, taking my feedback and softening the jab.

"No. Too soft. You aren't trying to knock someone out with a jab, you at least need it to do some damage. Again."

Aurelia continued the combination at my demand. Her jabs continued to be too hard or too soft, not able to find the balance she desperately needed. Her frustration was evident as her eyes closed over in an anger she failed miserably at hiding. I counted the breaths as I waited for her to give in. A few moments later, she dramatically threw her hands up, letting the irritation get the better of her. "It isn't working."

I read the restlessness in her movements, in the lines of her eyes as they dropped down to stare at the ground. Once her breaths had evened slightly, I let my demeanour soften, hoping it would filter through to my voice as I spoke, "Fighting isn't something you excel at overnight, or in a few weeks. Xav, Fox, and I have been training since we were boys. First, you need to understand your own strength. Dig into that well and you will find the right balance in your movements."

Unknowingly, I had taken a step forward, closing the distance between us. I waited on tenterhooks for her response. After weeks, this was the first time I'd addressed her in a manner filled with compassion instead of resentment. I had to admit, it felt....nice.

Finally, raising her gaze to mine, the vulnerability in those blue depths took my breath away as she whispered another confession, "I'm not strong."

My chest tightened at not only her words, but the defeat behind them. "Strength comes in many shapes. It isn't just the muscles in your body or the determination of your mind. It is the combination of each. Accepting that is a good first step."

Dropping her head once more, she let out a breath, and I studied her body eliciting new emotions: fear, understanding, anger, and hurt. She breathed deeply a few more times as if she worked to hold back tears. To which I was thankful. I may have offered her a sliver of decency, but I didn't think I could handle seeing her cry.

With her gaze fixed on her boots, she let another confession slip. "I'm not strong in any way. Mentally, physically, or emotionally."

The tightness in my chest grew constricting before it was born into a new ache. With my index finger, I gently brought it beneath her chin before slowly tilting her eyes to meet mine, offering a confession of my own. "I don't think that's true at all."

Aurelia wouldn't be with us now if she was weak. Whatever she'd endured, she'd done it with a silent strength deeper than she possibly understood. Wanting to shift my fingers up to cup her cheek in silent support, I forced myself to hold back, dropping my fingers and stepping away from the temptation. "Let's go again."

Without another word, Aurelia positioned herself once more, eyes trained on her target, as her face adopted a determination I hadn't seen in her before. She began. Two punches, jab. Two punches, jab. The combinations continued as a sheen of sweat formed on her brow. Ignoring the beads when they began to drip down, she continued. Two punches, jab. Her breathing escalated as her form stayed strong and her jabs began hitting the right depth. I held back the triumphant smirk dying to break free.

Her eyes transformed with every hit, absorbing each impact. Impressed, I focused on her form and listened intently as her breathing stayed in sync with each movement. Fox had done well with her training. Even though there were aspects of stability she needed to work on, she did have the mental strength she'd convinced herself was fictitious.

I let her continue on, with no need for interruption from me, until her hands dropped to her sides, the beads of sweat dripping through her eyelashes. Her lips twitched, and I wanted nothing more than to know whether they'd move north or south. Giving my head a shake, I decided I'd given her enough of the softer side for one day. I needed distance from her.

"Do your cool down and then you're done for the day." As hard as I'd tried, my voice didn't take the condescending tone I'd envisioned, forcing me to curse inwardly.

Aurelia shifted sideways, letting her eyes close as she took in deep, cleansing breaths. The urge to feel them against my skin grew intense. "Aurelia?"

Opening her eyes, she fixed her gaze on me as if I was the only man on the planet. I let it open my chest further, welcoming the claws as they wrapped around my bruised heart.

"That last round? Those jabs were just right."

The recognition rolled off my tongue before I could think it through. Without letting her respond, I moved around her, holding my breath from her sweet sweat attempting to wreak havoc on my senses.

With steadied movements, I took long strides to the house, focusing on the crunch of my boots over the pebbled path. Clenching my fists, I pulled on every ounce of my restraint to walk away from her. I wanted to blame Fox for the further development of the unwanted feelings unleashing themselves, but I knew the truth. Whatever I'd told myself before today about staying away from the gorgeous, blonde haired, blue eyed, mystery, was a farce. The pull of our bodies, our minds, was magnetic and undeniable. What the fuck was I going to do now?

Aurelia was under my skin, festering away like an incurable disease. The realisation hit me like a ton of bricks as I climbed the first step towards the front of the house — what if I didn't want to be cured?

Chapter 7

Aurelia

The training session with Mads had freed some of the mental and physical confidence I'd buried deep within the confines of my haunted mind. Over the years, I had created various coping mechanisms for myself, but they only pacified the deep self-loathing that always haunted me. The movement of my body, breath, and mind forced me to expand my view on not only myself, but what I could be capable of in the future. The goal now: to accept that I now had a future. One I could own and mould myself.

Not only the result of that session with Mads but also the deep draw I felt toward the eldest brother occupied my mind as I found myself on a solo walk through the Wild Forest. I'd quickly come to appreciate those brief strolls sprinkled with freedom and unintentional healing. The forest, although my relationship with it still in its infancy, brought a reprieve and warmth to my mind.

The fear I'd initially held regarding the likelihood of being found had slowly subsided with each step I took. Fox had occasionally reminded me I shouldn't be disturbed by humans or animals, and I'd finally believed him. The embers of safety I'd felt with the brothers and at the cabin had escalated into a full-blown inferno wrapping me in a secure embrace.

Training continued to gradually raise those ill-gotten memories from the traumatic well my mind had erected for protection all those years ago. The first time Lord Shelton's cane met the back of my knees at the age of seventeen. I can still hear the whistle behind me as the wooden staff flew through the tense air towards my bare thighs. That first lesson was to set me on a path of enlightenment, Lord Shelton had declared. I'd refused to acknowledge my father's request to begin a platonic relationship with the Lord in the hope he would one day take me as his bride.

Every time I practised my breathing exercises, the well released a few of those daunting memories. Each punch or jab I thrust at Fox and Mads' palms was a hope that I would one day use my fists against the men who wronged me. As I stretched my muscles, my composure began to snap back in singular fragments. I may be broken, but I was not forgotten. My mind and body wanted me to overcome my past and focus on the present and potential future. I may have not known what I would do next, but my life was now my own, never to be dictated again by the decisions of others.

The light began to trickle through the past I was so hesitant to face. The level of painful anger was still burrowed deep within me, and I only hoped it wouldn't come crashing down all at once. The focus was to take my healing journey one step at a time. One memory at a time. Similar to those walks in the forest, discovering new elements, some of which were familiar.

Breathing deeply, I focused on the crunch of the ground beneath my boots, the sound quickly became a comfort. A slight breeze wafted through the loose strands of my golden locks, birds providing a faint background vocal to the piece I was so carefully conducting with each step I took.

This particular walk held an air of difference. Generally, I stayed on the path towards the river, Rock on my heels, turning at the point I'd initially met the little auburn creature. He had become a quick companion, having a closer connection with him than any of the three brothers thus far. However, Rock was not with me today. Fox had explained he would venture off, sometimes for days on end, and that it was nothing to worry about. He was, by all means, a wild animal with certain levels of domestication only Rock allowed. If my observations were anything to go by, the brothers were Rock's pets and not the other way around.

A twig snapped. The sound echoed not far behind me.

I paused to assess my surroundings; a wariness began to settle in the pit of my stomach. No other person or creature was within eyesight, which didn't stop me from taking slower, quieter steps as I attempted to control my breathing.

The wariness evolved into a deep sense of foreboding, as though I was being hunted. Once, when I had attended a dinner at Shelton's house, I'd found myself wandering the property, against my father's orders, when I'd stumbled upon a small room housing a surplus of cages. Within the stacked cages were animals — a few rabbits, a small pig, various types of birds, and even a single squirrel. Shelton was known for his brutal experiments on animals as well as his work on, well, me. I remembered the look of sheer terror on each creature's face, and I forced myself not to focus on the cause of fear; instead, opening each cage door with no regards for the chaos I was about to unleash.

The animals had started to squeal, each in their own way, frantically looking for a way out of the room. Moving faster than I'd thought myself capable, I'd thrown open the door, creating a path for them towards freedom. The birds had fluttered away, back to their rightful habitats, each of the ground creatures scurrying off.

A calmness had settled over me then, embracing me for the first time in years. The euphoria was short-lived, as both my father and Lord Shelton had found me as soon as the pig's rear end was out of sight. Afterwards, I'd received the worst punishment of them all, a lashing that lasted so long, I swear I'd felt the whips on my bones and feared that no flesh was left to mar.

Standing there, in the depths of the forest, brought forth the memory of those animals in the cages. Hopeless, scared, with a constant sense of doom. If I had only been better at letting my feelings free, maybe I could be better at predicting danger. I cursed the memories, willing them to shift further so that I could get on with my healing journey and be more at one with my emotions.

Another twig snapped; this time I spun around, coming face to face with my worst nightmare come to life. "Well, well, daughter, where have you been hiding?"

Niall Mallory's voice dripped with disdain and triumph. My father stood ten feet from me, a large dagger in one hand. He was covered in his own sweat, breathing heavily in anger. The panic exploded as true, unaltered fear flooded my veins. How had he found me? The training with Fox wasn't enough to outrun or overpower this man.

And I would rather die in the woods alone than meet whatever fate came at his hand.

"Father. To what do I owe this surprise visit?" It took everything in me to mask the panic in my voice.

Niall took one step closer, provoking me to carefully transition my position into the sprint stance Fox had taught me. He noticed the movement, a cat-like smile spreading across his face. "Now, now, Aurelia. There is no need for your smart mouth. After all, it wasn't I who fled after stabbing a man in his own home. A man, I might add, you are due to marry."

Bile began to rise, and I did my best to clamp it down. I needed to keep him talking; "If you are talking about the man you forced upon me, it was the least he deserved."

I should've bit my tongue, knowing the words would only fuel the fire growing, rather clearly, in my father's eyes. He took another step, lowering the dagger to his side.

"You knew what your duty was. You failed. Did you think you could escape us? It may have taken me a few weeks, but I've found you," he sneered. "We will go home, and *you* will face the consequences of your actions."

A menace grew in my throat that I couldn't quell. "Is he dead?"

The delivery and question caught my father off guard. *Good.*

"No, daughter. You failed at killing him the way you have failed everything else in life. You are worthless. Nothing. And you left the protection of the only family who could've ever provided for you. You ruined the one chance of marriage I could secure."

His face darkened as the words fell between us. "Do you have any idea how hard it was to get Lord Shelton to agree to marry you? We were finally going to be rid of you!"

His bellow shot through the surrounding trees, scaring the nesting birds to flee. I envied their wings, the way they could escape when they sensed fear.

It was no secret how my parents felt about my presence, constantly being told I was the dirt beneath their shoes, a reminder that seeped through me like ice. After the few weeks I'd spent in the cabin, I knew I was more than that. "See, *Father*, now you are rid of me. You can turn around and go home. Pretend like you never saw me and we can both go about our lives."

Niall's answering laugh sent chills down my spine. I had provoked this man enough times in my life to know the foreboding accompanying his manic laughter. Silently, I began to survey my surroundings, doing my best not to draw his attention to my focus on a potential escape route.

"You know I can't do that. You may have paralysed the most powerful man in Huxley. He, nor I," his voice grew a menacing edge as he balled his fist, "will rest until you see the punishment and give us what we've been promised!"

Not wanting to listen to him, I pivoted in the direction I'd come from. I kicked off on my toes and launched into a sprint, immediately tripping over a small root in the ground. Cursing my clumsiness, I made a mental note to push Fox to help me improve my balance if I were to make it out of my current situation. Thankfully, I found my footing quickly, continuing my assault on the ground below. My breathing — rough and deep — made it somewhat difficult to hear my pursuer. Every fibre of my being knew he was there, close on my heels.

What felt like hours were only mere seconds. Making the very poor decision to turn my neck slightly to see where my father was, I tripped again, this time finding the forest floor plastered to the side of my face, a mix of rough bark, leaves, and pebbles digging into the softness of my cheek.

Before I had time to push myself back up, a rough hand wrapped around my ankle, pulling me backwards. My bare skin, assaulted by various stones and twigs, tore open as I twisted around to find my father's back towards me.

Kicking out my free leg, I managed to connect my foot with the back of his knee, causing him to buckle slightly, releasing my ankle. I stood, stopped by my braid catching on a log, halting me from pushing off into another sprint and throwing me back, where I connected with my father's chest with an audible pop. His breath fanned over my skin as he brought the dagger to my cheek, gently grazing it down the side of my face. "Now, that wasn't nice, was it, *daughter?*"

"I am no daughter of yours," I said, ignoring the blade's cooled touch; I ripped my head forward before sending whatever might I possessed as I threw it back to connect with my father's nose. The accompanying crack was followed by a growl of pain wrapped in frustration. The move knocked his stability and I was able to break free into another sprint. The impact of his nose on the back of my skull brought a dizziness that I had no choice but to ignore.

Legs, lungs, and head burning, I kept reciting the same five words in my head — *just get to the cabin.* I had no doubt the brothers would help. As long as they were home. When I'd left on my walk, they were nowhere to be found, meaning I would find myself at the cabin, alone, being pursued by one of the two men I'd like to set on fire. I knew the building wouldn't be enough to keep my father at bay, so I kept with the mental chants — *just get to the cabin.*

As the oak tree boundary came into view, a smile began to form just as pain blinded me, and I collapsed to the earth, landing on the forest's blanket of rocks and leaves. My sight blurred around the edges as I did my best to blink, pushing the threat of unconsciousness as far as I could. My head aching from the impact.

Black boots, scuffed with mud and other foreign substances, came into view with a voice that grated against my skull as it spoke: "You won't win this, girl. You are mine." Niall's words bit with a venom my wounded head refused to process.

A heavy, booted kick connected with my stomach forcing the last of my controlled breaths into a clumsy rhythm. Once. Twice. Three times. The agony meeting my abdomen pushed bile up my throat. My head, still pounding from the bludgeoning, swam further towards the darkness. Fighting it, I twisted to my side, hoping I'd have enough strength to prop myself up.

If I could get into a sitting position, then I may be able to stand, and if I could stand, nothing would stop me from trying to run. The treeline was so close. The best I managed was a slow crawl, my father's laugh taunting me as I dragged my beaten body towards the boundary. A soft glow illuminated through the tree line which could have been a concussion muddling my vision. Whatever it was, I latched onto the unintentional beacon, pulling my body forward.

The nasal sneer of Niall Mallory echoed after me, "Just as we've always known. You're pathetic. I cannot wait to deliver you to Lord Shelton and watch him strip you away, piece by piece."

The words didn't land as all I could focus on was the treeline. My bruised body made its way — closer and closer. And then, a sight of immediate relief: Mads. Just past the treeline.

"Mads —" The plea was barely a squeak, not doing enough to get his attention.

"Who the hell are you talking to? There is no one. No one to help you. No one to save you. You wretched whore!"

Another kick, this time to my kidney, momentarily cutting off my ability to breathe. *Just get to the cabin. Mads will help.* Enduring a beating from my father was part of our history; the difference this time was I had the chance to run. To fight. The difference this time was I knew the world had more to offer; this time was the promise of my continued freedom.

Looking towards my father, I quickly assessed his position. The dumb fucker pulled me behind him, leaving his back exposed. Gathering the last of my physical energy, I kicked my legs out towards his ankles. The impact was immediate as he fell to the ground, cracking his head on a stone. I didn't have time to curse the slight size of the stone as I pulled myself up as quickly as my mangled body allowed. I could breathe later. I would breathe later.

Breaking into what I could only describe as a limping crawl, my body screamed in pain as the more traumatic memories rose to the surface. The visions of how every right was taken from me. The canes, whips, chains, and hands that connected to my body over and over again. In any other situation, those memories would paralyse me with fear. But now? Now, they fuelled my need to push forward, toward Mads and the safety of the cabin.

Finally, around twenty feet away, his eyes focused in my direction. His face contorted after his eyes hardened, showcasing the anger I'd grown to know well. It was palpable. Whether towards me or the wounds, I didn't care much.

"Mads —" I managed to squeak out again. Crossing the tree line, I let my body succumb to the pain. Before I felt the ground beneath me, strong arms engulfed me. Ignoring the shooting pains the connection of our bodies brought, I sunk into his hold, the soothing scent of him easing the ache.

"Aurelia? Who did this?" A fury laced command, not a question.

My breathing, laboured, stalled me from answering in full sentences, the darkness continued to creep in. "Father. Behind. Me. We need… to run."

Mads hefted me up further, slowly turning me towards the path I came from. What was he doing? Why weren't we running? My father would catch up with us quickly. I knew Mads was a trained fighter, but my father was ruthless. He would cut Mads, Xav, and Fox down if they kept me from him.

"Breathe, slowly." He placed his strong hand against my breastbone, pushing me against him, letting the weight of his hold sink into me. His words played with the shell of my ear, filling me with soothing warmth.

"He can't see us."

Confusion clouded my vision as I attempted to turn towards Mads; he halted me as his hand gently turned my face back towards the path. My eyes latched on to my father, who frantically turned as though he couldn't see where I'd gone.

"Where are you? Aurelia! You bitch! I will find you! I will find you and I will break you!"

The ferocity of his rage elicited a wail of frustrated determination that turned every inch of my skin to gooseflesh. Pausing, Niall placed his hand behind his head, finding a spot of blood as he removed it.

Grateful I spilt at least a little of his blood, my mind relaxed but confusion warred with it. "Why can't he see us?"

My words may have been forced on a hush but managing more than a broken sentence felt good, even if my body protested against every second of it.

"Looks like we both have some stories to tell, Goldie," he said, his tone was composed, less demanding than I was used to.

Ever so slowly, he rotated me in his arms, keeping one hand on my hip at all times. When we were face to face, he pushed back a few stray hairs that had plastered themselves across my face in what I could only assume was a combination of dirt, sweat, and blood.

"What did he do to you?" The command in his voice returned, accompanied by something else. Something almost resembling concern.

I stared into his autumnal depths, letting the safety wrap around me.

"He thinks he owns me. And he wants me back."

Mads' brow lowered, as though his thoughts churned through his mind at my confession. Bending down, he lifted my bruised body into his arms, taking one last look at where my father had stood. "Then we need to correct him. Don't we?"

CHAPTER 8

MADDOX

Aurelia's consciousness flickered in and out, unknowingly syncing with the rhythm of my urgent footsteps. To tamp down the rage flooding through my veins, I focused on my hands, one strongly beneath her knees and the other wrapped around her shoulders, careful not to touch the bloodied wound on the side of her head.

Xav and Fox rushed in, both showing similar signs of the alarm I'd felt when I first spotted her, dragging her beaten body towards me. "What the devil happened?"

Fox's panic was evident in his throat, his voice cracking. An emotion I hadn't known him to possess in decades. He moved to the couch to clear the way as I sat down, Aurelia across my lap. I didn't question why not one part of me wanted to let her out of my grasp — or the way her body moulded perfectly to my own.

"Her father." I ground my teeth at the admission, unable to admit to myself, or anyone, that the demons in her past had found her.

Xav disappeared back into the kitchen. No doubt to grab the medical supplies. I looked down at the golden-haired thief. She was in bad shape. And from what I could see, it was mostly the head injury. I needed to keep her conscious. Moving my hand from beneath her legs, I took the sides of her face in my grip, as gently as I could. "Give me your eyes, Aurelia."

My voice was panicked, urgent. I could hear it. I didn't care to mask it with anything else. Carefully, she peeled the lids from her eyes, doing her best to focus on my face.

"You need to stay awake. Do you understand?"

The panic subsided slightly as I stared into those stunning azure depths. Aurelia offered me only a slight nod of her head, enough to squash a bit of the panic.

Fox reached across to softly stroke the top of her head, observing the wound on her left side. "The blow she took to her head looks pretty bad, Mads."

"I know." I could see it for myself, I didn't need him telling me the obvious.

My panic was replaced by rising frustration. "Where the hell is Xav with the kit?"

I needed to keep my heartbeat steady. The last thing she needed was for me to spiral into complete rage as I held her in my arms.

"I'm here you impatient prick. I told you it would take me a bit to gather everything on Trix's list."

Trix. Thank the stars for the goddess of a witch in our lives. I'd never tell her directly, though. Her ego didn't need it.

Aurelia's head rolled towards the back of the sofa; my hand shot out to steady it before it could touch down. Turning her face to lock eyes with mine, I said, "Aurelia, we need you to stay with us." Concern echoed through my words with an underlying feeling I couldn't pinpoint. Fear? I hadn't felt fear in years.

Fox continued his soothing strokes on the top of her head. "Goldie? Let's have a chat while Mads and Xav get you cleaned up. How does that sound?"

Slowly, she tilted her chin back, just enough to find Fox's face, a worrying smile plastered on it. I know I'm not the only one affected by her presence, all three of us were out of our depth.

"Hi." The words stumbled out in more of a croak, rather than the lightness I'd assumed she attempted.

"Well, hello, thief. You've had quite a tumble today, haven't you?"

"My father." The admission sat heavily on her lips.

Fox slowed his strokes as Xav gestured for me to shift her slightly, allowing him access to her head. "I have to be honest with you, Goldie, your father is quite the cunt."

Her body shook slightly beneath my hands, following her attempt at a soft chuckle. I wanted to tighten my hold, to let her know she'd never be without my protection again. It was stupid of us to let her out of the boundaries, especially not knowing what hunter lurked out there for her. She would need to know some things about us now. We were also going to get some answers.

Xav continued to gently remove the earth glued to the head wound, careful not to push too far. I noticed Aurelia wince a few times as she continued to talk to Fox. Each time, I found myself looking for the source of her pain, wanting more than anything to soothe it. As her eyes blinked slowly, and the tip of her tongue drifted out to wet her lips, more than once, it dawned on me that the source of her real pain may not be external at all. Demons weren't always equipped with fiery eyes, horns, and a tail. They come in all shapes and sizes.

Xav handed me a small jar of salve as he turned to Aurelia. "We are going to have to get to some of these wounds, Aurelia. Is that okay?"

Without hesitation, she nodded and I sprang into action. Slowly I began to lift her tunic, revealing a myriad of cuts and fast-sprouting bruises. I ground my jaw at the sight beneath. Not even the fresh, angry wounds could hide the scars already littering her skin. I noticed the slight shake in my hands but urged myself to perform each treatment as deftly as possible.

"We need to clean some of these a bit deeper. A bath or shower will be too intrusive."

Xav outlined his next steps more for her comfort rather than instructions.

"With your permission, we are going to clean you with a cloth. Then, we have a few herbs and salves should speed up the healing process. Can we do that?"

Nodding slightly, Aurelia closed her eyes. None of us knew the full extent of her history, but there were moments where Aurelia would flinch near us that had us question the type of past she had really run from. Approval to touch Aurelia, and any woman for that matter, was something my brothers and I did not take lightly.

"Keep her awake," I commanded Fox.

Xav pulled over one of the armchairs and gently rung out a cloth from a bucket of hot water he'd mixed with some of Trix's herbs. Aurelia hissed when the cloth hit her skin. My brows knitted with concern, ready to push Xav away from her if he only caused her more pain. What the hell?

"It's ok," she breathed. "Feels nice."

Xav proceeded to clean her wounds, offering me only a brief glance when he too noticed the scars. Fox kept her alert by asking short questions, things like her favourite colour and how she liked to take her coffee.

I felt useless just holding her, so I spoke to Xav under my breath, wanting to be of assistance. Xav began handing me jars as he finished cleaning one part of her, instructing me to rub the cream and herb mixtures on each bruise and cut.

I turned to Aurelia, awaiting her silent confirmation before proceeding. She gave it to me quickly. I pushed the salve mixture onto her skin as gently as I could before rubbing my fingers in concise circles over the blossoming injuries. Fox attempted to continue his questioning, noticing Aurelia now solely focused on the balms as they were spread across her torso. When I moved up to touch the side of her face, which was hit with what I could only assume was a branch, she winced. I hated it.

Aurelia opened her eyes to find me staring down at her, no doubt the anger visible in my gaze. Her eyes held a mixture of concern and what I could only pinpoint as vengeance which confirmed my earlier thoughts. This wasn't the first beating Aurelia received from her father. Nor by a man. If I had to guess, she was frequently a punching bag to not one, but many different men throughout her life. She wanted revenge, and I wanted to hand it to her on a silver platter. I would hand her the torch to set them all ablaze.

Leaning forward slightly, I gently traced a line down her cheek with my fingers, never breaking eye contact with her and giving her the only two words I could. "I know."

Her eyes softened, pulling me back into the present, forgetting both of my brothers were there, watching the exchange. Glancing up, I was thankful Fox pretended to be enthralled in pulling the medical kit back together while Xav had disappeared into another room. I definitely wasn't going to hear the end of this.

We sat in silence as I studied her chest rise and fall. The myriad of emotions coursing through my veins was difficult to focus on. All I wanted was to hold her closer, bury my face in the luscious golden locks, and reassure her that she would never have to fight that man again. The other side of me, the one that had decided to never get close to her, reminded me these *feelings* could complicate the future. If she were capable of helping us get home, what would that mean for her? I couldn't open my heart to a future here. I knew that. It was part of the reason I kept my distance. I also couldn't deny the intensity pumping through my chest as my body stayed tightly wrapped around hers.

Xav returned a few moments later to break us from the comparable trance. "I brought you some tea. It would be good if you could eat a little something too."

Taking his seat beside her once more, Xav laid out a tray next to the sofa, signalling for Aurelia to sit up. Taking my queue, I smoothly shimmied my body out from beneath Aurelia's, the anger increased at the missing contact. What was happening to me?

"I'm going to go wash up." I didn't wait for anyone to respond, finding my way upstairs into my ensuite bathroom. I slammed the door, not meaning to, before I grabbed the basin of the sink, willing myself to get my shit together.

We had no idea what Aurelia was or why she was here. An anomaly that may get us killed. I couldn't deny her probable connection to the curse, and to Raithe, went much deeper than we initially questioned. If she could help break the curse, she may not be from this world. Which led me to question where she was from and how that may impact her life.

Vigorously, I scrubbed the salve mixed with Aurelia's blood off my skin. I never wanted to see her bleed again. My mind was too muted to question the continued rising emotions I felt toward our little intruder. What I did know, was if we were going to figure out her part in our lives, we would need to expose ourselves. Composing myself as best as I could, I returned to the living room, gesturing for my brothers to meet me in the kitchen.

As I waited for Fox and Xav to fuss over leaving Aurelia on her own for a few minutes, I leaned over the sink, attempting to exhale the concern mixed with frustration pumping through my veins. Revealing our secrets didn't cause any apprehension in me. What climbed beneath my skin was the reality that Aurelia played a much bigger part in our lives than any one of us had wanted to admit. With the impending threat of her past on our front step, we didn't have much time to waste in approaching the unavoidable.

My brothers shuffled into the kitchen, immediately taking up posts on either side of me, their rightful places. Xav spoke first, ever the mediator, "What is going on, Mads?"

I turned to face my brothers, taking note of the weight of Xav's stare and the clever glint in Fox's clear blue eyes.

"I don't know." I spoke the truth. I didn't have any more information than they did. We would have to approach it together.

"We'd assumed Aurelia fled something more serious than she had let on. It appears we were right."

My tone stayed matter of fact. I held no judgement on what Aurelia kept from us. She had every right to. Just as we had held back information from her.

"We need to tell her." Fox's curiosity resonated through the circle our bodies had erected.

"She was just beaten by her father," Xav's concern bled through Fox's voiced thoughts and my internal ones. "Aurelia needs rest before we chuck a bunch of nonsense at her."

I turned to Xav. "How much time?"

A look of disbelief bled across his face. "Healing from the injuries? Days, Mads. She'll need days."

We didn't have days. Not only because my blood hummed with the need to scour the woods to find the fucker who inflicted the injuries on our golden-haired guest, but also because we weren't going to uncover Aurelia's part in the curse without actually talking about it.

"I'll give you until this evening. Let her rest, eat, then we need to get this moving."

I uncrossed my arms as I moved to step away from my brother's intimate judgement. It was Fox, not Xavier, who stopped me. "I agree on the timeline but maybe we should see how she's doing later before diving into the fairy-tale?"

I turned to survey my baby brother. In surprise, I questioned back, "Are you concerned about our little thief, Fox? That's so uncharacteristic of you."

I let the coy smile build on my face as the red rose on his cheeks.

"Fuck you, Mads. You aren't King here. And for your information, I do care about her. No matter what comes next, she is under our protection. As you, yourself, pointed out."

Having my own words thrown back in my face was always a tough pill to swallow. Having it done by my youngest and most reckless of my siblings was a punch to the gut.

Gritting my teeth, I nodded in agreement before making my way back to the living room. Aurelia shouldn't be left on her own in this state. I settled in the armchair across from the sofa, conscious of keeping my distance, as Aurelia's eyes scanned my face. Careful not to let my expressions give anything away, I kept my voice low, soft. "Get some rest, Aurelia. We will watch over you."

Her body loosened at my words. Settling further into the cushions and blankets, she let her eyelids delicately close. The ache in my chest pulsed in need. The underlying desire lay in wait, but the need I was experiencing was to fiercely protect the woman in front of me. Whatever demons she faced; she wouldn't have to do it alone. Not anymore.

CHAPTER 9

MADDOX

"How is your head, Goldie?" Xav's tender connotation whirled through the tense few hours my brothers and I had sat through.

Aurelia slept away the afternoon as my brothers and I took turns monitoring her breathing and ensuring she was never once left alone. The waiting began to shape into severe impatience on my end. Since I'd set my mind to bringing her in on our secrets, I wanted nothing more to expose everything to her. Well, not everything. A dark part of me still feared the knowledge would push her away from us, not bring her closer.

As the sun began to drift past the tree line and the muted hues of the evening filtered through the cabin window, Aurelia stirred awake. Xav was the first to notice, shifting his seat closer to the sofa to check her head. My palms came down on the tops of my thighs in an effort to keep me from launching towards her.

Aurelia's blue orbs shifted to me before she turned back to address my brother. "Fantastic. Not like I was smashed on the side of the face with a log at all."

The ache in my chest dissipated slightly at her sarcasm. I didn't realise I needed to see that side of Aurelia to know she would be okay.

Xav chuckled as he picked up a small pot of balm from the table beside the sofa. "Well, the good news is you were able to get some rest and hopefully, with these potions, you should be back to your non-bludgeoned state soon enough."

Xav let the short conversation silence as he worked the ointment into the wounds on her head. Aurelia's eyes drooped at the soothing motion.

"Does she need more rest?" My question to Xav was delivered in a whisper, not wanting to disturb the relief Aurelia experienced beneath his movements.

My attempt failed as her eyes snapped open. "I am in the room, Mads. You don't need to talk like I'm not here."

The irritation in her tone would have usually dropped my mood, but I couldn't deny the relief I felt at her back talk. "Fine." I bit, not wanting to show my satisfaction. "Do *you* need more rest, Aurelia?"

A sliver of a smile threatened the corners of her lips. "No. I am kind of hungry though."

Xav finished applying the salve, popping the lid back on with a click before rising from his chair. "That's good to hear. Mads can make you something to eat."

Jaw clenched; I left the living room without another word. He really did know how to dig beneath my skin. Xav may have had the most compassion out of the three of us, but he had a sinister side, as we all did, and he loved to poke the bear.

I prepared a tray of meat, cheese, fruit, and bread while I waited for the kettle to boil. I'd observed Aurelia's tastes close enough the last few weeks to know she favoured a board filled with variety. As the kettle whistled, I paused to consider my small but potentially very noticeable action in the tray I'd prepared. Hopefully, Aurelia was still too focused on what had happened to read into it. If I could keep outwardly denying it, so could she.

When I returned to the living room, Aurelia sat upright on the sofa with Rock settled in next to her. Fox added a few logs to the fire as Xavier sat in quiet contemplation. I set the tray down on the small table in front of her without a word, returning to my seat in the hope she wouldn't comment on my choice of meal.

The room sat in companionable silence as Aurelia ate her food, pausing occasionally to give Rock a bit of cheese and a scratch behind the ears. I kept my hands on my knees to stop them from bouncing in anticipation of what we needed to share. Even with my broad, muscled arms, it was difficult to keep the impatience at bay.

Once Aurelia finished eating, she settled back on the sofa, breathing in the steaming mug beneath her fingers. I looked at Xav who caught my eye immediately. I raised a brow in question to which he turned to Aurelia, keeping his voice steady.

"Aurelia, we have some things we'd like to discuss with you. Are you comfortable doing that now? Or would you like us to wait until you're a bit more rested?"

Fox took that moment to situate himself down on the other end of the sofa, the agitation clear in his jerky movements. Fox was a commander, never one to shy away from the unknown and seeing his unease had my spine straighten.

Aurelia looked to each of us as she contemplated her answer, not showing any signs of nervousness. "I'm okay. What did you want to discuss?"

Xav lent forward, placing his elbows on his knees as he addressed her with his signature kindness, "What we are about to discuss, will not only come as a shock, but it is also something you can never discuss outside of this cabin. Do you understand?"

Aurelia's brow lowered in what I assumed was confusion. Leaning forward, she set her mug down before finding Rock's ears once more. "First, I think you'd be surprised at what shocks me these days and secondly," her head bowed as she let her confession loose, "Even if I wanted to, there would be no one to tell."

The bruised organ in my chest pulsed with a mixture of anger and sorrow. I wanted to pull her onto my lap, stroke her beautiful golden locks, and remind her she'd never be alone again if she didn't want to be. I shook the thoughts from my head. *Focus, Maddox.*

At her words, Xav sat back, giving me the sign to take over. The room turned to me. My throat cleared on impulse as I sat back, letting an ankle rest on my knee in an attempt to keep my demeanour calm and indifferent. *Here we go.*

"Tell us, Aurelia, do you believe in magic?"

The question should have caught her off guard or at least, brought a sense of nervousness to her features, neither of which happened. Instead, an excitement grew on her face, silently waiting for more. I waited for her to answer my question before I continued.

"I've never had any reason not to believe in it."

I studied her, trying to read her thoughts. Aside from the visual excitement growing on her face, she wasn't giving anything away. I shot a glance to Fox and then Xav, both of which weren't giving me anything by their expressions. Aurelia followed my gaze as though trying to decipher the silent conversation she assumed we were having.

"The three of us," she turned her attention back to me, the blues of her eyes electrifying, "aren't from this world."

I paused unnecessarily, but I wanted to allow her enough time for the words to sink in. When she nodded for me to continue, I obeyed.

"Many years ago," I said, then chuckled. I couldn't remember how long it'd actually been. "A curse was placed on us. As part of the curse, we were stripped of our magic and exiled here, to the human realm. We were given this cabin and the land, which are also part of the curse.

"The reason your father couldn't see us," I slowed down, taking a deep breath, "is because the cabin and the surrounding land shouldn't be visible to anybody except for the three of us. Well, and Trix, which is another story. The fact you can see and inhabit the cabin shouldn't be possible. It was why we—I agreed to let you stay."

The lie sat heavy on my tongue. It wasn't the only reason I'd allowed her to stay. I was nowhere near ready to make it known, to her or anyone else. A glimmer of disappointment washed over her features; the corners of her lips turned down while a small crease in her brow formed. I couldn't understand why. I wouldn't question it. She had gone through an ordeal today, and I didn't want to cause any unnecessary panic.

"The curse sealed the remaining portals from this realm to our world, never able to find or open them."

My gaze stayed trained on Aurelia, her expression only laced with intrigue and none of the fear or anxiety I had expected.

"So, how old are you all, exactly?"

Fox chuckled next to her, leaning back and displaying an ease of comfort. I glanced at Xav, his smile large and impressed. Grateful they both appeared relaxed, I turned my attention to Aurelia, trying harder to read her; to understand her thought process and why she wasn't running for the hills. Had I misjudged her?

"Older than we care to admit," Xav announced from the right.

"Time moves differently here in the human world. We age slower in our realm, so although we may not appear much older than you, we have lived a few decades longer."

Unable to keep my attention off of her, I followed Aurelia's eyes as they moved down to her fingers, stained with dirt and blood, as she threaded them together, turning her attention back to me. "Where is it you are from?"

Xav and Fox's silence encouraged me to answer her question. "The world is full of many parallels. Some we know. Some we don't. The three of us," I gestured towards my brothers, "are from the realm of seasons known as Raithe."

"There are four kingdoms, which I'm sure is easy to deduce. Verum is Spring; Aestas is Summer; Havon is Autumn and our land — Hiema, the Winter Kingdom.

Conscious of the amount of information we'd shared, I paused again. I'd lived in the human world long enough to know it was difficult for them to believe the unbelievable, and it wasn't as though we still had our magic to prove otherwise.

Aurelia didn't think very highly of my pause as her hand moved impatiently for me to continue. I was happy to oblige — rather, invigorated to be speaking about our home after so long.

"Hiema was ruled by our mother and father, the King and Queen of the Winter Kingdom. For as long as anyone could remember, the Kingdoms ruled together, and they ruled well. When we were boys, an unrest began to grow, originally stemming from Aestas, dissatisfied with the way things were being run. They wanted access to the human realms to be sealed. They felt noble families should have more power, and they believed non-magical people were beneath them."

Aurelia sat up, trying to hide the wince as her body moved, before pushing her arms to her knees, engrossed in my story. Xav noticed the flinch of pain, too, but she batted him away when he leaned forward to help her.

"The King and Queen of Aestas wanted more. More power. More authority. They felt the counsel of the kingdoms was an outdated way to run our lands. They wanted to rule us all. Leaving territory leaders in each Kingdom, with less influence. The argument continued as they planted their seed of doubt in various lords and ladies across the kingdoms. Then, one day..."

The last three words out of my mouth muted me. I couldn't remember the last time I'd told this story, if ever. I glanced back up and met the determination in Aurelia's blue depths. The orbs held no hints of sadness or pity, and for some unexplained reason, it felt good.

"At our sister's eighteenth birthday party, Aestas had our parents murdered."

The shock hit her face immediately. Fox stayed noticeably silent, growing paler with each word, allowing me to reveal our secrets with no argument. We waited as she assessed us individually. Without noticing, I'd shifted toward the end of my seat, waiting for her to respond. I needed her words.

"Why didn't they kill you too?"

The curiosity in her voice lifted a quick breath of relief from my lips. The fact she continued asking questions instead of offering us her sympathies meant more than I thought it would.

"They'd kept our sister, forcing her to act as the territory leader. Given her age, they assumed they'd have an easy enough time using her as their puppet. Severing our ties to Raithe, our magic, and even potential relationships with humans, given the curse on our land, was a more satisfying punishment than death. Or so they thought."

Sitting further forward, Aurelia clasped her hands together in anticipation. "What magic? What can you do?"

The childlike glee radiating from her was hard to ignore. My brothers and I exchanged silent glances, bewildered by her rapt attention. Xav's brows were furrowed, and Fox's lips thinned, as if they were contemplating her intent. The silence stretched on longer, prompting Aurelia to ask, "What?"

Xav stood, his presence towering over the room. A hint of condescension laced his words. "Well, Aurelia, it's just you don't seem at all surprised we just told you we are from a parallel world and magic is real. You do understand what we are telling you, don't you?"

Aurelia's jaw visibly clenched as she stood on shaky legs, to meet Xav's stance. "Would you be happier if I ran away screaming?"

Xav stepped back, a sheepish look on his face as he recognised his tone wasn't the one she'd grown accustomed to. "I wasn't insinuating you couldn't handle the truth. It's more that we've only told our story a few times and most of those haven't ended well."

I recognised the apologetic tone for what it was, not sure if Aurelia knew Xav well enough yet.

"I think," Fox interrupted, "before we divulge much more, we should hear a little bit more about why you are here, thief. Because it's clear that you being able to see the cabin, and step onto the land, is not a coincidence."

He was right. Fuck. I must've been so out of my own head if Fox was the one talking actual sense here. Aurelia eyed Fox as she lowered herself back to the sofa, holding as much of her weight on her arms to alleviate whatever pain was bothering her.

"Alright. Where do you want me to start?"

I leaned forward to my elbows, eager to know what she was about to offer, "How about we start with why I found you, beaten and bloodied, by your own father?"

We offered our silence, watching as the wheels turned in her mind as she worried her lip and stroked Rock's ears. None of us knew her well enough to know if she'd feed us a lie, especially without Xav's powers, a part of me hoped she could trust us, or at least Xav and Fox enough, to reveal more of herself to us. Whatever happened next, with the curse and her own life, we were going to have to do this together.

"Before I tell you this," she started, her voice breaking on the first word, "I need you to know I don't want pity. I also need you to hold back your judgments. Some circumstances we find ourselves in, mainly the bad ones, can also become all we know."

She had no idea how much all three of us could relate to her statement. Her gaze dropped down to her hands again as her fingers tangled. A tell for the creeping panic she wasn't so good at hiding.

"I was born into a relatively wealthy family. I had an older brother and a younger sister. When I was twelve, my father made a series of bad investments on behalf of our village. We didn't lose everything, but we were thrown from the good graces of the town's leaders. Following the demise of our name, my father moved us to Huxley where he was determined to build trust with a new counsel and new Lords."

Her hand shifted, grabbing the blanket sitting beside her. She proceeded to weave her fingers around the edges. Yet another tell.

"For the next six years, he devised various schemes to get back into the high standing good graces he'd had in our previous village. Some of which were successful. Some of which were not. It was around this time he recognised the value he had in us, in his family, and put us to work too."

Aurelia's fingers found Rock once more, as though his fur between her fingers brought her stability. She took a slow breath before she continued, "After a time, a few of the strategies had gone right, the town's wealthy had begun to accept him into their circles, albeit slowly. The last bid to increase his position, back to what he was in our previous town, Bayford... Well, the bid was me."

A tension blanketed the room. It may have come only from me, yet it was thick enough to cut through with a knife. She didn't let it take over.

"My father arranged for me to marry the most wealthy and high standing Lord, not just in our village, in the county — Lord Shelton. I accepted at first, playing the part of the dutiful daughter, knowing I had no escape. The same role I'd accepted for so long."

Her gaze flickered, trapped in a memory I would pull from her and burn if I could.

"The day of the engagement announcement, Lord Shelton threw a party in our honour. It was then, I just...snapped."

Lifting her head, her cerulean gaze locked with mine. None of the usual softness sat behind her stare. The recognition was back. The need for vengeance and blood. A need I could taste on my tongue.

"I couldn't do it. I wanted more from life. I decided to take my freedom. And so, I ran."

"Into the woods." Fox's voice was almost a whisper, providing a gentle backdrop to her story.

Aurelia looked over. "Into the woods," she confirmed.

The silence in the air was uncomfortable, the underlying tension holding it in an unfamiliar embrace.

The tone of the Fox she knew pumped up, "Well, is anyone going to point out the obvious?"

All eyes shifted to him, waiting for him to answer his own question.

"We were cursed to stay in this cabin. No one is able to see it or know it exists, but, somehow, Aurelia can. The obvious is, Aurelia, you're supposed to be here. I think... I think you're supposed to help us break this curse."

Chapter 10
Aurelia

The silence following Fox's theory sat heavily on our shoulders as well as some added emotions radiating off of each of the brothers. Mads, supplying his ever-constant temper, mixed with Xav's deep concern, and Fox topping off the emotional cauldron with what I could only describe as excitement.

The spool of secrets I'd known existed began to unravel, and though I was eager to learn even more, I held a slight hesitation on what these revelations may bring. I had yet to decide what my next step was, and in the event I was part of breaking this curse Mads described, the choices were not my own.

A loud rapping at the front door pulled us from our thoughts.

"That'll be Trix." With no hesitation, Fox stalked towards the front door, yanking it open with a beaming smile. "My love!"

"Fuck off out of the way, Fox."

A stunning woman, dressed head to toe in draped clothing the colour of a clear night sky, pushed past Fox, stopping as she reached Mads. I studied her. She was the first woman I'd seen since the engagement party. The way her deep brown skin radiated with what could only be described as magic, mesmerised me. And given I now knew magic was possible, it could be magic.

Mads revealing they were from another world full of magic should have urged me to run screaming, as they'd suggested. What I couldn't tell them, at least not yet, was the intuition in my belly flared to life as though it had been waiting. As if it'd already known.

The woman, Trix, Fox had called her, surveyed me with her almond shaped, honey eyes, wariness steady in her gaze. I found it difficult to focus my attention elsewhere, entranced by her stare. Was she a siren? I had no problem answering her call.

Xav interrupted my ogling to introduce us. "Aurelia, meet Trix. Trix is a witch."

Trix stomped her foot in agitation. "How many bloody times do I have to tell you knobheads? I'm an enchantress and my name is Bea."

She emphasised the pronunciation of her name as Bay-ya.

Xav's lips tilted into a smile, "You can tell us as many times as you like. Enchantress is just a fancy name for a witch. Plus, when we met you, you were going by Trix, so Trix is who you are."

"Fuck off, Xav."

"I'd rather be fucked on if you're offering?" The glint in his eye and the playfulness in his tone brought a lightness to my chest.

The banter was refreshing after the heaviness of the day. I couldn't help the slight smile escaping my lips. It was clear Trix, or Bea, had a relationship with the brothers. One I respected, and also somewhat envied.

Bea turned to Mads with a look that signalled she was asking for the eldest brother's influence over his ridiculous younger brothers, "I can't help you Trix. I agree."

Throwing her hands up, she flicked her fingers forcing a small stool to slide through the room, landing directly behind her. My mouth dropped in astonishment, all four of my companions studying my face closely. "She likes to do that. I already told her she'd catch flies."

I didn't appreciate his insinuation and reminder of the day I'd drooled over him at the woodshed. I sent Mads the most lethal look I could muster. I mean I did, but I still didn't appreciate the veiled remark. I reminded myself that while he showed a softer side when taking care of me, he was still the rage filled, cold-hearted brother. It would take a lot more for me to let my guard down with him. That was what I told myself, anyway.

"Well, are we going to talk about why you summoned me here or shall I continue to play the damn guessing game?"

Bea seated herself on the stool as though it was made for her. The black lace and silk of her cape cascaded down to the floor, anchored her in a pool of darkness. I shifted my gaze to each brother. Did they expect me to spill the details to Bea? I didn't even know why this woman, witch, enchantress, whatever, was summoned to the cabin. It dawned on me, "How can you see the cabin?" I directed the question at Bea before turning to Mads. "You said no one else could see it."

"Ahhh, well, buttercup, as my manner lacking friend here advised, I am a witch."

"See!" Fox and Xav shouted in unison. Mads rolled his eyes, clearly annoyed with his present company.

Bea stared down at the two youngest brothers as her voice became threatening. "For the sake of the conversation and our poor dear, virgin to magic, Aurelia, here, I will use the term witch. However," her tone grew deadly, "if I ever hear either of you refer to me as a witch again, I'll turn your bollocks green, watch with glee as they shrivel off and then brew them into a tea I will force you to drink, neither one of you knowing if it's even your own testicles you're ingesting."

Mads feigned boredom while Fox and Xav gulped down their apparent fear. Bea could do it. There seemed to be no doubt. I studied her curiously. Her little display should have birthed some sort of cautiousness or fear. Instead, my heart let off a tingle, yearning to know more about my new acquaintance.

"Now," Bea continued as though she hadn't just threatened to force Xav and Fox eat their own testicles, "to answer your question, given no one else is being very useful here, I can see the cabin because I spelled myself to."

"You spelled yourself to?" I repeated her words in confusion.

"Yes. A task I'm forced to do often given its complexity and lack of staying power. Each time one of these peasants invites me over, I have to work the spell through in order to see the cabin."

"Could you not spell others to see it?"

"A curious buttercup, indeed. I can't. No. The spell is entwined with my blood. Given my blood has connections to the seasonal kingdoms, it's kind of like a loophole to the curse."

"Connections to the seasonal kingdoms?"

Before Bea could continue, Mads interrupted in a huff, "We asked you here, *Bea,* as it seems our guest here may be able to help unlock our curse."

Bea turned her attention back to me, running her gaze over the length of my body, hopefully ignoring the forest floor, blood, and sweat burrowed in my skin and hair. The visual exploration was littered with curiosity as though I was a puzzle she wanted to solve.

"Interesting."

"Interesting indeed," Fox spat. "And it was my discovery," pride beamed out of him as he crossed his arms over his chest, knocking me in the arm with his elbow. On reflex, I pushed back, annoyed at the realisation that the sofa suddenly lacked room. Sensing my growing unease, Xav moved to grab another stool, identical to the one Bea had magically flown into the room.

"So, does anyone want to give me a bit more detail so we can start to unwind this ball of yarn?"

It was then I concluded, I liked Bea. I didn't know her and it was always difficult for me to trust people, yet she exuded a clear ferocity I was intrigued by.

"I ran away from an arranged marriage" — diving headfirst into the situation hadn't been a thought in my mind before I started — "I got lost in the woods before I finally stumbled upon the cabin.

"Those three found me, after I came in without permission, and thankfully agreed to let me stay until I could figure out my next move."

Fox huffed at my recounted version of the break in. I ignored his annoyance to round off my story as quickly as possible. I sped through my agreement with the brothers, pitching in with chores and cooking in exchange for a place to stay and basic training sessions.

When the brief tale was finished, Bea stayed silent for a few moments before going to retrieve a bag from beside the door. I hadn't noticed she walked in with anything. Pulling out a thick and weathered leather-bound book, she sat back on her stool. She opened the tome, quickly finding the appropriate page before reading out loud:

Bestowed upon you is a blight so bare,
one may never see through the thinnest hair.
For to break from the snares of the exile curse,
you may find your key in a common purse.

Bea read out the riddle twice. I did my best to commit each word to my memory, somehow aware this was important. I looked up to find Bea and the brothers sat in silent conversation.

"What? What is it?"

If I was part of this now, I needed the silent words to cease.

"The curse," Mads answered abruptly. The irritation he felt began to seep into the room.

"Look, I've had a bit of a day, what with being chased and whacked on the head, if you'd forgotten. So, if we could quit speaking in riddles and give me a bit more clarity? You know, given my possible concussion and all?"

I'd be damned if I didn't use my injuries to get some answers and stop the silent whispers as they began to grate on me. The words hit their mark, a glimmer of pity shown through the brother's eyes, Mads included. Bea sat back, arms crossed, a smirk on her face as though she was watching a stage drama.

"We blacked out after the events of that day. We woke up here, outside the cabin, surrounded by a few meagre possessions. Like photographs of our parents and a few books. This one," Mads pointed to the volume on Bea's lap before she hugged it to her chest in a protective manner, "is full of riddles. Trix thinks it may be connected to breaking the curse. We have no idea what it means. Trix 'had a feeling.'"

"Oi! You know I'm infinitely connected to the earth, the Mother! My 'feelings' are stronger than the three of you arseholes combined." Bea's fire was both pleasant and hard to ignore. Welcome to a history of constant obedience. I immediately hoped she would be visiting more.

I did my best to break the tension, "So, what now?"

The room fell silent. Each inhabitant thinking on what the potential next steps could be.

"Now, if you give me the go ahead I've wanted for years, I can start digging further into this curse."

Years? Why hadn't the brothers wanted Bea's help? Bea turned to me, silent permission settling in her gaze. I offered a slight nod before turning to the brothers. The curse had affected their lives. It was their decision whether or not there should be more research. Eventually, I resonated, I would also be in a position to make a choice. If I was part of the bigger picture, of breaking the curse, would I offer my help?

"Fine." Mads rose without another word, stalking off toward the kitchen, taking the remaining healing salves with him.

Fox jumped up, bouncing on his toes before leaning down to kiss me on the cheek and then repeating the gesture to Bea who quickly slapped him away. Xav, the cautious one, the one in tune with emotions, gently took my hand, looking into my cerulean depths. "Nothing more has been decided. For now, we just need you to rest up. Let's start there, yes?"

Offering him a smile as gracious as I could muster, I squeezed his hand in reassurance. "Of course. Let's get my head to stop pounding and then we can go from there."

Xav rose, leaving me alone with my new witch acquaintance — correction, enchantress.

"I like you."

Surprised by Bea's admittance, I couldn't stop the beaming smile that grew on my face. "Thank you. I think I like you too."

"No, buttercup. I like you. I know I do. For certain. I have a way of reading people. It isn't always clear but when it is, it's crystal. Got it?"

I nodded, slightly hesitant to offer her any other answer.

"Good. Now, keep those bears on their toes for me while I go figure this out, will you?"

"Bears?"

Bea studied me, not in annoyance, more like she was attempting to understand my secrets. Dig deep into the hole I'd tried so well to hide.

"You've got a lot to learn, lovely. I have faith those arseholes will guide you. And if they don't? You tell your old pal Bea, and I'll come turn one of their limbs green. Sound good?"

I laughed. It felt fantastic. Bea offered an ease I wasn't sure I'd ever felt in my life. Even with Archer, we both had an underlying fear we'd be found and punished for nothing. More often than not, the fear came true. Archer did his best to take the beatings on my behalf, an act which worked for a while. Until Archer was gone and our father felt I was mature enough to handle the punishments myself.

Swallowing down the bitter memories, cursing the little box for deciding to open during a moment of joy, I was pulled from my head to find Bea gently squeezing her arm. "Sounds like a plan."

I did my best to push a lighter tone in my words, immediately recognising my mistake given Bea's apparent talent for reading people. Bea, however, did not offer me a look of sympathy, rather a look urging me to light my own fire and to never, ever let anyone dull it down. The look, although foreign, lit a spark in my chest. Offering a modest smile, Bea left the cabin to start her own part of the journey.

Once the door closed, the aches riddling my body shot to the surface, reminding me of the trauma my father had inflicted on me earlier in the day. I let my eyes drift close, taking a few deep breaths before turning back towards the kitchen, being immediately halted by the moodiest brother. "You can't sleep on your own tonight."

I blinked slowly, trying to silently understand his words. Was he telling me to sleep in his bed? Or perhaps Xav or Fox's?

"You will sleep in my bed. I need to be able to wake you up frequently, given the concussion." He pointed to the side of my face as though I needed reminding of the wound there.

"Let's go."

Without waiting for acknowledgement, Mads stalked up the stairs towards his bedroom. I sat, frozen in the image of laying down next to him, in his bed. A throat cleared, forcing me to turn towards the kitchen, finding Fox leaning against the wall, a smug smile plastered on his face. "Have fun."

With a wink, he turned back towards the kitchen, once again leaving me to process. He wants me to sleep in his room? The idea itself was easy enough to agree with. I knew concussed people should be closely monitored, particularly during sleep.

Recognising this was an argument I couldn't win and did not have the energy to fight, I slowly made my way up the stairs. Each step sent shooting pains across my battered body. The pain began to mix with the sudden onset of nerves, forming a bond, holding me back from managing either. Once my feet stood in the doorway to Mads' bedroom, I hesitated. The room had brought me face to face with the brothers. The bed was so comfortable I still dreamt about it every night as I forced myself to find a similar sensation on the sofa.

Mads shuffled around the room, pulling the bedding down before turning to his dresser to pull out various bits of clothing. He snapped me out of my fog, flinging a clean tunic and loose trousers at me. "You can wear these. You still can't wash as we need those salves to do their job and I'm not rubbing them all over you again."

A pang of hurt pinched my chest at his words. Taking care of me had clearly been nothing more than a burden to him, even now, as I stood at the threshold of his bedroom. Knowing he wanted me to sleep with him for safety reasons, I couldn't understand why he had offered. Xav or Fox could have easily taken the task he so clearly loathed even the mere thought of.

"If I'm such a burden, why don't you just let me sleep with Xav or Fox? I'm sure they wouldn't spit at the idea of me lying next to them."

Mad stalked toward me, powerful irritation hovering around him. "You sleep here."

Refusing to cower in his presence, I held my ground, flaring right back into his autumn littered gaze, "Fine."

"Fine."

Mads walked into the adjoining bathroom, slamming the door shut, leaving me to dress in peace. Ever so slowly, as this was all my body would allow, I began to peel off the tunic, careful not to inflict any more pain than was already coursing through me. I managed to pull it over my head before I was interrupted by the sound of the bathroom door swinging open. I quickly covered my front with the soiled top, my breathing escalated with the knowledge that more than just my fresh wounds were on display. He now had a front row seat to years of visible scars littering my back. The belt. The knife. The torch. The hands. So many items and fists had left their lasting marks on my skin.

Mads moved closer until I felt his heat directly behind me. I stood frozen as I did my best to keep my breathing deep and steady, unsure of what would happen next. At the same time, I felt a thrill at the closeness.

"We —" Mads started, struggling for words. "We forgot to dress your back."

I turned my head towards him, careful not to adjust the rest of my body and caught his gaze moving down my naked back, jaw clenching. "Is it...bad?"

I prayed to any and all higher beings that he wouldn't mention the scars.

Mads shot his gaze to mine, catching the corner of my eye briefly before leaving the room. I stood still. Where in the hell did he go?

The question was answered silently only a few moments later when he returned to the room, carrying a jar similar to the ones he'd used on my front and face earlier. "May I?" He held up the jar.

Asking for permission startled me, once again, as it had when he and Xav cleaned my wounds. I offered a brief nod before he got to work. His hands, slow, calculated, took their time spreading the balm over my back. I winced when he moved toward my kidney, remembering the swift and murderous boot of my father.

A single tear escaped, travelling through the pain I felt in my bones, my skin, and my heart. The level of hatred in the world was not foreign to me. On the contrary, I was very accustomed to the evil lurking the streets, the evil who donned the most expensive fabrics. What pushed the lid of this box open further was the kindness I'd experienced. Not just from the last few weeks in the cabin, but from this man, a man who had initially shown me mainly disdain, but today graced me with a gentle side, filling me with a hope I knew I shouldn't have.

The salve's pungent herbal aroma brought me back to my body, focusing once again on the movement of Mads' fingers over the wounds, old and new. If only he knew he wasn't spreading aid on my physical wounds, but emotional as well.

"Done."

The distance settled between us again as soon as his hands pulled back.

"You can get changed in there," he pointed to the door he'd disappeared behind earlier. Grabbing the clothing he'd thrown at me, I rushed in, slamming the door, taking no time to change into the fresh clothing. Another indecent incident wasn't necessary for the two of us tonight. Especially as the other scars still remained covered. The next step would be the hardest, finding solace in his bed. I'd never slept beside anyone before. Not even my sister.

Returning to the bedroom, I found Mads perched on the bed, as far towards the edge as possible. Determining the other side was meant for me, I rounded the bed and sat down. It was simple yet inviting. It oozed Mads. The comforting masculine aroma mixed with cedar wafted through my nose, sending a shiver of anticipation down my spine.

"You're going to need to lie back. Unless you sleep sitting up?"

Without turning towards him, I scooted back, curling myself away while pulling the plush down quilt over my broken body. My broken heart.

The lights clicked off as I felt Mads shift behind me, being careful not to bring his body too close to my own. The silence trickled by. Not uncomfortably though. I listened to the sounds of our breathing, waiting for Mads' to slow and deepen. It didn't. He lay awake just as I did.

"I'm really sorry about your parents."

The sentiment didn't need to be voiced. It may have been stupid, yet I couldn't stop myself. Trying to pull back the sympathy, I went deeper, darker. "I wish it had happened to my parents, not yours."

Why had I said that? I didn't even know his parents and knew nothing more than they were once the rulers of a magic kingdom. The mattress beneath us shifted. Mads offered no vocal response, letting the silence dance between us.

Knowing I wouldn't be successful in a conversation with him, I let my eyes drift. Before sleep took me, his deep voice filled the space. "They were the best people I've ever known."

Careful not to make a sound, afraid he would quickly shut down again, I waited in anticipation for his next words. They never came. He'd offered me a breadcrumb. It was more than he'd given in all our weeks together. Before I could convince myself against it, I spoke, "For years, my father made continuous attempts to increase his standing. It was always so important for him to climb, socially. He wanted to be more powerful than what his birth afforded to him."

Imagining the rise and fall of Mads' strong chest behind me, he kept silent as I continued, "He tried and failed at many things until one day he realised he had a secret weapon."

"And what was that?" he whispered into the darkness.

I stole a breath before I offered him my response, "Me."

The growl lacing his next words was difficult to ignore. "What do you mean 'you'?"

Steadying my breath, I closed my eyes, not able to even look darkness in the eye as I spoke my next words, "My father realised all the men of our town had one thing in common — release. More specifically, a release through physical aggression. "

I expected him to jump from the bed, yell, scream, tell me what an idiot I was for letting those things happen to me. Any type of reaction would have shown me if he cared about me. I wasn't ready to give him the gruesome details, but it was enough for him to fill in some of the blanks. Mads took a few moments turning so his back was once more to mine before offering, "I should have killed him today."

I stayed still, unsure of how to approach a response. Whether I should even respond. I wanted to understand if it was just because he was a bad man or that he'd inflicted pain on me. Why did he want to kill him? I did too, however beside the point. Mads offered no further explanation, and I didn't have the strength to push further.

"I'll wake you every couple of hours just to check on you. Go to sleep, Aurelia."

My name on his lips, which had felt like a song the few times he'd used it before, now felt tainted. A feeling most unwelcome to me, especially given it came from a man I so desperately wanted to break down. I let a few tears fall silently. I did my best to fall asleep. When

I did meet my dream form, it was surrounded by lingering cedar, glistening in the forest.

CHAPTER 11

AURELIA

A soft breeze pulled me from a very deep and much needed slumber. Shifting slightly, the ache of yesterday's events sat heavily across my body. With great energy, I pulled my protesting eyelids up to be greeted by a sight both terrifying and caused my insides to catch fire.

Mads sat in a chair across from me, dressed in loose fitting trousers and a white button down the likes of which accentuated the strong build of his shoulders, momentarily distracting me from his hard gaze. I gave myself a few moments to appreciate the way he had rolled the sleeves up just enough to reveal the veins in his forearms pulsing from the tension he held. He stared down at me, his eyes full of suspicion, ankle resting on his knee, and fingers steepled beneath his chin.

The sheer beauty of him didn't frighten me, but the storm building in his autumn-coloured eyes forced the hairs on my neck to rise. He was such a contradiction. The way he had defended me yesterday, the care in which he showed my injured body, was the complete opposite of the fury radiating from the man in front of me.

Taking longer than necessary, I moved my feet to push up into a sitting position, careful not to remove my eyes from the predator in front of me. I'd be daft to think sharing one traumatic experience would bond us completely. I'd at least hoped for an ounce or two more respect to sit between us. His hardened stare gave me a completely different answer. Attempting to lighten the mood, I did my best impression of a smile, biting back the pain I felt in my face and my head. "I live to see another day!"

Mads studied me for a moment before rising from his seat. "It appears so."

The disgust laced in his words was clear. I had not yet won him over, and the energy radiating from him made me think maybe, just maybe, he despised me even more.

"Oh great. We are back to the surly, 'I hate you,' attitude. I thought maybe yesterday we had a breakthrough."

Back to me, Mads' breathing intensified. I held my breath, the answer teasing its way down the muscles of his back. Twisting his head slightly, he said, "Don't mistake yesterday for anything more than it was."

With a gulp, I thought carefully on my next words. A big part of me wanted to snap back, to tell him he wasn't the big, bad, angry man he appeared to be. Well, at least it wasn't all he was. The tenderness he'd shown me yesterday told me otherwise, and no matter how much he wanted to deny it, I'd seen it. I knew it was real.

"And what was that?" I asked in a partial whisper.

Mads turned away from me before stalking to his bedroom door. Before he was gone, he threw out, "Necessary."

Necessary. That's all I was to them. They needed me alive, and the careful consideration they'd shown me yesterday was, indeed, necessary. They needed my help to break the curse. I'm just a piece of the puzzle, a key to a lock that would give them a chance to get home.

I wanted the admission to hurt, to crack the last pieces of my shattered shell. That single word should've been a jab, piercing me in whatever was left of my abandoned heart, my bruised soul. But beneath Mads' hardened exterior, I realised the mask he wore so proudly had started to slip. He'd recognised his error yesterday when he showed a tad more vulnerability. Today, he'd thrown his wall back up, reinforcing the bricks.

Mads was an incredibly confusing puzzle. Slowly, I'd find the pieces. The thought brought a smile to my face, albeit painfully. Gently, I pushed myself to stand, ready to get myself in the shower when a second party walked through the door Mads had left wide open.

"Morning, buttercup!"

Bea stormed in, black curls as chaotic as her energy, buzzing with a reassuring tenderness. Throwing down a pile of what appeared to be women's clothing, Bea made her way to the bathroom. "Come on then. I don't have all day. Let's get your bits washed."

My bits? Was this woman seriously suggesting she was here to wash me?

"Umm, Bea, I appreciate your help" — each step I took toward the bathroom was accompanied by a shooting charge somewhere in my body — "I think I can wash myself."

She poked her head out, levelling me with a stern look as I moved at a snail's pace, short gasps of agony echoed with each movement. "I hate to be the one to tell you this, buttercup, but there's no way you can wash yourself. Look at the state of you!"

I turned to the mirror on the far side of the bedroom, getting the first glimpse of the collage of colours now painting my face. I raised my hand to touch the bruising and cuts on instinct before pulling my hand back with a hiss as soon as I made contact with the head wound.

"That prick did a number on you. Don't fret my pet. We will get you squeaky clean and then you get to hang out with me all day. I seriously can't believe they kept you from me all this time."

Bea's animated explanation followed her as she pumped the shower, setting up soaps and towels on the basin next to her. I had to admit, Bea brought a calmness to the room, just as her presence had done yesterday. It'd been nice to have known her sooner, making me my first friend. I had my siblings — one of indifference, always preferring to please our parents more than make nice with me. And Archer? I would have called him my best friend if we'd had more time. Everyone else in my life was there to take, ignoring me when I'd had nothing left to give.

Bea snapped me out of the memory, wasting no time in getting me undressed, tugging at the hem of my shirt and trying, and failing, to get it over my head.

"Ow, Bea! I'm covered in bruises!"

"Right. Shit. Sorry. I don't know if I can get this thing off by myself, and you're in no fit state to lift your arms. How did you even get this on in the first place?"

Mads' face flashed in my memory. The adrenaline had not yet worn off when I'd dressed the evening before. Coupled with the knowledge that I would be sleeping in his bed, leaving the task of donning the shirt either easy — or forgettable. Maybe a bit of both.

Observing the challenge in front of her, Bea tapped her full bottom lip with a long, black polished fingernail and shouted, "Fox!"

I flinched at the high-pitched bellow. "No, Bea. It's fine. We can do this without him," I trembled.

Bea turned back, sensing the apprehension in my voice. It wasn't that I didn't want Fox's help and Bea knew it. I would, never again, allow a man to put me in a position of vulnerability. Bea may not know the details, but her magic pulsed with understanding. Were witches blessed with heightened empathic abilities? Yet another magical question I would need to bring up later.

"Don't worry, he isn't going to see anything,"

Fox appeared in the doorway, a sly smile planted on his face, as usual. "You rang, my love?"

Bea, ignoring his imploring tone, barked her command, "I need you to get me a knife."

"A knife?" Fox and I questioned in unison.

"Yes, a knife. Now, please."

I wasn't fooled by her politeness given the ridge of authority lining the word. Fox darted out of the room, smart enough not to bite back at Bea. Not this particular time, anyway.

We weren't left waiting long before he reappeared with one of Xav's cooking knives. Bea, staring at Fox, jerked her head toward the door, a move he immediately obeyed, pulling it closed behind him.

"Now, Aurelia, I'm going to cut this off of you, okay?"

Bea held up the knife, and I hesitated. "Won't Mads be angry we ruined his shirt?"

Bea eyes widened before she threw her head back in raucous laughter. "Do you think I give a damn if Mads gets pissed off about a scrap of fabric?"

Only knowing this woman for the last day, it was clear she cared little when it came to the brothers' wishes, taking what she needed, when she needed it. I envied the trait. One I'd never known in myself; one I desperately wanted to.

A thorough rip sounded as Bea tipped the knife at the bottom hem, using her hands to rip it clean in half. Instinctually, I wanted to cover my bare chest, quickly — painfully — reminded of why we were tearing it off in the first place.

"Now, shuck the trousers off and let's get you cleaned up."

I obeyed without further hesitation, silently thanking Bea for not mentioning my scars. Stepping into the shower, Bea turned the tap as I moved under the hot spray. At first, the pressure of the water hitting the cuts and bruises turned the pain into agony. After a few moments under the water, the ache turned into an intoxicating twinge, allowing me to release the heavy sigh I'd been holding back. The pulsating injuries blending with the relieving pressure of the water filtered through my body physically and mentally, giving me my first moment of peace since the incident.

Bea kept silent as she gently moved a soap-soaked cloth over my body. Watching her closely, it was then I realised this was the most intimate moment of my life. The closeness, coupled with Bea's eager, calming presence, was enough for me to actually enjoy the shower.

Given the slowness with which I was cleaned, the shower began to lose some of its power, as well as heat. Bea helped spin me around to rinse the remaining suds before flicking the tap back and opening a large, plush towel in front of me. I stepped in, no questions asked, immediately enveloped in comfort, the towel, and Bea's arms.

The warmth surrounding the woman, mixed with the ache in my bones and the new information I'd learned, forced a tear to slip down my cheek. Sensing the sorrow, Bea tightened her arms around me, offering a few moments of peace. The silence broke the dam, tears ratcheting down my face and throwing me into such a fit I blubbered.

"I know we don't know each other, but I can promise you, you're safe now. And whenever you decide to tell us your whole story, we'll be ready. You just feel what you need to feel, buttercup. Sound good?"

Bea let my sobs die down slowly, easing her arms to pull back and lift my chin. Puffy eyed, tear strewn cheeks looked back up at her.

"Thank you." It was all I could offer her.

Bea's lips lifted into a genuine smile. How could I recognise and understand so much of a woman I didn't even know? The last time I'd felt a genuine connection with another person was Archer. I'd tried for years to connect to my sister too, never successfully.

Bea slathered my wounds in balms and herbs before helping me pull on some of the clothing she'd brought. She hadn't pushed me to reveal more than I could, but she kept glancing at me as though she wanted to.

"You can ask me, Bea."

Bea's presence alone brought my mind and body reprieve, and I wanted to grow our connection. In addition, the same sensation that urged me to trust the brothers did the same with Bea.

Standing up straight, she squared her shoulders. "Honestly? I just want to know how you're feeling. Really feeling."

Wiping the last remnants of my tears from my cheek, I carefully thought about the answer. I didn't want to scare her away with the full truth of my past, but I also needed to let the words find life.

Taking a deep breath, I let them fly free, "I need to start healing, Bea. Mentally. Physically. Emotionally. In parallel, I now need to dive deeper into everything I now know about the brothers, this other world, and magic."

Closing the slight distance between us, Bea's honey gaze caught mine, ensnaring it happily in a trap I couldn't escape.

"Would you like to know what I think?" Her voice even, nurturing.

I offered a slight nod in response.

"Well, buttercup, from the little I know, you're already on that healing journey. Escaping and finding this house wasn't even the beginning. With everything that is spiralling through that beautiful head of yours, remember to take a few seconds every once in a while and ground yourself in where you are and how far you've come. You're not alone anymore."

You're not alone anymore.

"How are you feeling?" Xav asked, his gentle hug engulfed me with genuine concern and kindness. The feelings were not unwelcome, but still new.

Allowing myself a moment to process the tenderness, I took a seat at the dining table.

"Sore. Very, very sore," I chuckled, attempting to bring a lightness into the conversation.

Xav flashed me a charming grin before turning to pick up the plates he'd haphazardly discarded when Bea and I had walked in the room. "Just keep rubbing those salves on you and rest. Lots of rest. Got it?"

I nodded, eyes lightening as he placed a plate of pancakes, three slices of thick bacon, and a side of scrambled eggs down in front of me. As if in agreement, my stomach growled. Xav placed a plate down in front of Bea who wasted no time diving in.

"Trix is going to stay with you today."

Bea let out a growl indicating her discomfort at the name.

It was then I'd noticed the silence decorated the fact that neither Fox nor Mads seemed to be in the cabin. A slight emptiness nestled in the pit of my stomach. Thinking it could also be hunger, I put a slice of bacon wrapped in pancake in my mouth, not holding back the moan of joy that escaped my throat.

"We have something to take care of today." His tone was more serious than I was used to. "We will be back tonight and can have a nice dinner to answer some of your questions. How does that sound?"

Mouth filled with more pancake; I offered him a nod combined with some strange noise from the back of my throat.

"Excellent. Trix, you know the procedures."

Bea winked, mouth also full, before Xav walked over to me and planted a soft kiss on the crown of my head. “We will be back as soon as we can. Rest up.” And then he was gone.

I placed my fork down in front of me, a blooming light settling in my chest. One I couldn’t quite figure out.

“Weird, right?” Bea’s voice did nothing to abate the growing warmth in my chest which had started to descend to my stomach.

“Sorry?”

“The feeling that’s making you uncomfortable. That, buttercup, is what it feels like when someone cares for you.”

My eyes shot to where Xav had left the room only a few moments earlier. He cared about me? The light quickly travelled across my body, leaving both my fingers and toes with a welcome tingle, settling in my chest, causing my breathing to heighten. “Cares?”

“Oh yes. And the bears? Well, all I can say is if they are accepting you into their sleuth, you are set for life.”

Trying, and failing horribly, I pushed the foreign sensations aside, folding them into their own mental box. “You’ve called them bears a few times. Why?”

Bea polished off her breakfast, using the last of the pancake to soak up the remaining golden syrup. “I’ll give you the short answer because the long one is really theirs to tell — their surname is Artos, which means bear. I’ve always called them the three bears. Not only is it extremely clever, but it also annoys them.”

She chortled, choking on the last piece of pancake lodging itself in her throat.

I offered her a glass of water, which she gulped down quickly, pounding herself in the chest, once, twice.

"Artos." I repeated quietly. The name was fierce, like Mads. Clever, like Fox. And warm, like Xav. I couldn't deny its beauty and perfection. It suited them.

"Right. Might as well start our day. And lucky you, you get to help me look at this damn book."

She held up the book in question, and I couldn't help noticing it appeared larger than it had yesterday. More intimidating given the answers it may hold. The revelation from yesterday, which hadn't scared me much then, sat heavier today. I nodded as I collected our breakfast dishes and placed them in the sink before following Bea into the front room.

Settling down on the couch was a challenge, as every part of my body was screaming in discomfort. I did my best to get situated. Bea offered me a few pieces of paper and a pen, guiding me to take notes. Pleased with the simplicity of the assignment, I readied for Bea's comments.

The day passed, slowly. We'd sat in silence most of the time, only occasionally making conversation as, and when Bea actually wanted a note written down, which wasn't often. I'd done my best to enjoy the quiet time, knowing my body needed the rest to continue its healing journey. On the other hand, the silence coaxed the tightly bound memories to spring free. Glad they were finally starting to listen to me, if only their timing was better.

Rock had ventured in before lunch, taking the spot next to me on the sofa, thoroughly enjoying the many scratches I provided him.

We devoured a quick, late lunch of sandwiches and tea before settling back down to continue our work.

The sun set, alerting me the brothers had not yet returned home as Xav had advised. I tried not to let it bother me. Instead, I thought of yesterday, of my father, if I could call him that after what had happened, and his words. They hadn't stung as much as they used to, yet their presence still lingered.

Even though something tragic had occurred, I'd met Bea, spent time learning about magic and connecting with the brothers. I'd learnt about why they were really here and the curse —

"Bea, the riddle you read yesterday, can you read it to me again?" I asked, my voice urgent, a thread lingering close to the surface.

Without question, Bea opened the book back to yesterday's page, finding the riddle once more:

Bestowed upon you in a blight so bare,
one may never see through the thinnest hair.
For to break from the snares of the exile curse,
you may find your key in a common purse.

I scribbled down the words as Bea voiced them. Once. Twice. Three times. I lost count. At some point, the front door opened, and I vaguely recognised the brother's return. Ignoring them, I continued to copy the words, over and over.

A pattern beginning to form in my mind, fuelled by the repetition of the puzzle, a few words painted themselves into a picture. I wrote it down again, using the combination of the physical words and those mental images to fuel the fire. Consumed with the mystery in front of me, I didn't hear as the brothers found seats around me.

Faintly, Bea's whispered words filtered in the background. Thankfully, no one interrupted me.

Shutting my eyes from the outside world, the pattern evolved, striking the corners in a variety of colours and movements. I happily descended into the chaos echoing through the chambers of my mind. The words were my only focus as I looked for the hidden meaning behind them. The echoes around me tickled my ears, compelling the hairs on my nape and across my arms to stand on end.

The room gave me space, allowing me to dance through the words, over and over again. The answer was here. In front of me. Darkness and vibrant hues drifting through the riddle welcomed me deeper. With a flash, an image of me popped into my head. In the vision, I placed my right hand on a door before gently pushing it forward. Opening it. A light streamed in, growing more vibrant as the door opened further. Whatever was happening, I couldn't and didn't want to deny the pulsing in my body expanding with each second. It felt—right.

Once the door was fully opened, the luminescent light subsided and was replaced by a number of images passing across my mind. Lands of the deepest autumnal hues, golden sunsets, rushing rivers, and snow-capped mountains blanketed in quiet. The sensations rocking my body glittered with hope, blossoming flowers and gently flickering fireplaces. The vision showed me the key to breaking the curse.

The answer would get the brothers back to their world. The answer was...

"It's me." My eyes drifted around the room, looking from Xav to Bea, then to Fox. My eyes locked on Mads as I said, "I'm the key. I can break your curse."

CHAPTER 12

AURELIA

The room was silent, the only sound the thoughts racing through my head. It was difficult for me to accept the pride in finding a solution when it also brought something I'd never experienced in my life, a true purpose. Wrapping my brain around the idea I was of some importance to anyone was almost too much to bear. It was suffocating.

My hold on the pen tightened, the pain sending pricks of reality into my fingers. I still held Mads' eyes, only broken at the sound of someone taking a rather large gulp of air.

"Explain, Goldie," I couldn't ignore the attempt of lightness in Fox's tone. Too many unanswered questions rose to the surface, the discovery igniting the last shred of hope evident when I met his stare.

My breathing steadied as I tore my gaze from Fox, each pair of eyes focused solely on me. "Well..." I started with a shaky breath, "First, 'a blight so bare,' is you three."

Silence. I looked to Bea who offered a nod of encouragement.

"Your family name. Does it not mean bear?"

Mads nodded, not remotely curious as to how I came to know this.

"And a key found in a common purse. What do you put in a purse?"

"Coin." Fox answered.

Technically correct. The riddle looked for something more specific. Xav, thankfully, pulled the pieces together. "Gold. You can find gold in a common purse."

I nodded while the thin layer of confidence I'd gained from solving the riddle left me, "Adding to 'one may never see through the thinnest hair,' my hair being golden."

Confusion danced across the face of my company. Was I wrong? Was it too much of a longshot? No. I commanded myself. The reason I was here went deeper. I could see the house despite the curse, and there had to be a larger purpose to the horrific life I'd endured.

"Think about it. I can see the house. My hair is golden. You are 'the bears'. I think... I think I can help."

"How?" Mads huffed in a tone laced with accusation.

"That part I haven't figured out yet." I glanced at Bea, silently begging for support.

The look of disbelief on Mads' face automatically triggered a flood of memories, the times I was told I was worthless or less than, but this time, instead of shoving them back in the depths of my mind, I decided to fight them head on. Defensiveness lit a fire in my heart. "Look, I know I'm nobody, I've been told enough how pathetic I am. How worthless. But you said so yourself that I shouldn't be able to see this house and yet I can. There must be something here. If I was some magical being with a hidden agenda, I sure as hell wouldn't have put myself in this world, with the family I have and endured years of abuse."

The confession wasn't meant to spill out. Especially after I'd dropped a few of those last night in Mads' bed. This felt different though. The last thing I wanted was for Xav, Fox, or even Bea to take pity on me. I didn't need their pity. I needed an escape, and I was right in front of securing one.

Bea, intuitive Bea, sensed the indignation in my confession, bringing the conversation back to the monumental task now in front of us.

"This is a big breakthrough, boys." Attention finally strayed from me, and I let out a slow, shaky breath.

"If Aurelia is the key, I just need to find the lock."

"And you think you can do it?" Fox was stoic, almost frighteningly so.

"Yes. I never knew where to start. I can cast some recognition spells with you, Aurelia, see if something will point us in the right direction. If you all want me to, of course?"

Xav and Fox turned towards Mads. Odd to see them submit so heavily to their eldest brother. Then again, he was the rightful sovereign of their kingdom.

A brisk breeze travelled through the front door no one had noticed was left open. Clouded with a sudden anxiety of my discovery, I stood to shut it, needing something to do rather than sit and stew. My body protested with each movement, willing me to continue to rest.

Rest was now the last thing on my mind.

One of my steps, clearly not calculated, more so driven by the stress flooding through my veins, caught my foot on the floorboard, launching me towards the ground. Before I could add further injuries to my already damaged body, strong arms grabbed me around the waist, hoisting my back to meet his front. The smell of cedar hit me. Mads. I sighed as he gently set me on my feet. I tried not to lean into him when he didn't immediately remove his arms. It wasn't quite a hug; however, the embrace lifted at least a fraction of the anxiousness flowing through my veins.

"I'll do it," he said, his voice low as it danced past my outer ear, sending unintentional tingles down my spine. I wanted more of those flutters.

Ensuring I was steady on my own, Mads slowly removed his hand from my waist, moving to shut the front door. With a click of the lock, the room stood frozen, the only movement was the blood pumping through my chest, faster and faster.

The sides of my vision began to blur. Struggling to get a sufficient amount of air into my lungs, I reached out for the arm of the sofa, missing by a few inches, my body torpedoing towards the floor once more. This time, all three brothers came to my aid. Mads gripped my waist, once more, while Fox leapt across the sofa to steady my shoulders. Xav grabbed the sides of my face, bringing my attention to him.

"I think the excitement and your injuries aren't mixing very well. You're going to pass out. Can you sit, slowly?"

"Excitement," I repeated. That's one word for it. Although I didn't have much to compare it to.

The three men helped me into a sitting position on the sofa; Mads was the last to remove his hands, only once a glass of water appeared in front of me. Looking up, I was met with Bea's concerned smile.

"Drink this slowly. We will get you some tea. You're looking pretty peaky right now."

I obeyed as a blanket was draped over my shoulders. An automatic smile spread across my face as I turned toward the bringer of warmth, only to find Mads at the other end. His expression was detached, showing no signs of the comfort he physically provided. Before I could voice my gratitude for the knit relief, Mads stalked off toward the kitchen.

Bea sat down beside me, wrapping her arm around my shoulders. "How are you feeling, buttercup?"

"Alright. A bit dizzy, otherwise fine."

"Fine is how you describe the weather, Aurelia, not how you feel."

I chuckled as Xav entered with a tray of tea, Fox close at his heels. I happily took the warm mug into my hands, inhaling the steam accented with floral notes, letting it seep into my pores in the hope it would fix me enough to withstand the next steps with my new-found friends. Friends? Could I call them friends? Xav and Fox, definitely. Bea was on her way there swiftly. But Mads? His temper still overshadowed all the good bits I'd seen thus far and didn't convince me of anything other than he was a moody arse.

Sipping the tea slowly, I let the sweetness of the honey fill my veins, knocking the wobbly irritation down. The room sat in anticipation, waiting for the next move in the game we'd suddenly found ourselves in.

Fox, thank the stars for the mouth on that man, finally broke the silence. "So, are we all going to sit here and pretend like the last hour didn't happen?"

Instinctively, I looked at Xav. As the second oldest brother, making the assumption he was in charge if Mads was absent.

"We should wait for Mads."

"Seriously?" Bea piped in, annoyance lacing through the question. "If we waited for Monsieur Moody to make a plan in regard to anything, we'd be waiting a very long time."

The words rang true. Mads was the leader, a king, and nothing happened in this cabin without his say. We could either move on without him, filling him in later, or, "Maybe someone should go find him?"

The suggestion should've been obvious even as I voiced the words out loud.

"Are you volunteering, Goldie?" Fox sent me a wink, knowing full well I was in no state to chase his brother.

I clutched the teacup harder as Xav moved to take on the task himself, Fox announcing he would go put together some sandwiches. As they left, Bea settled into the armchair, book open on her lap.

The physical exhaustion began to weigh on me as my eyelids grew heavy. Adding in the emotional and mental spectacle of the afternoon had me growing wearier by the second.

"Why don't you close your eyes, buttercup?" We'll wake you when we are ready to continue."

Without argument, I set the mug down before letting my head slowly drop to the back of the sofa and comfortably drifted off to the scent of cedar and the taste of honey on my tongue.

The sound of soft voices filled the air. Peeling my eyes open, I was first met with soft firelight and a faint residual glow from the setting sun that drifted through the curtain drawn window. At some point,

I must've laid myself down across the sofa. Pushing up, my body still protesting in pain, I situated myself into a more vertical position, the blanket sliding down my arms to rest on my legs.

"Morning Goldie!" I wanted to be annoyed with Fox's cheery greeting. I had become accustomed to his vibrancy, shedding light on my darkness.

"Hi." The lingering sleep crackled through my response.

Additional chairs had been brought into the room, Mads and Bea were hunched over the book now resting on a table. Fox's bright smile radiated toward me from the chair next to the sofa just as Xav walked in with a tray full of pastries filled with meat and something else I couldn't decipher. My mouth watered at the aroma, my stomach grumbling at the sight.

The amount of food I'd consumed in the last couple of days wasn't nearly enough to recover or my general appetite. I liked to eat, something I was never ashamed of. My curves weren't the 'fashion' of our times, but I was proud of every fistful I could grab. When everything you have was stripped from you except the presence and abundance of good food, you take the small victory, and you enjoy every inch of it.

Xav handed me a plate with a steaming meat pie and a cup of tea, offering me a small smile in greeting. "Thank you. This smells wonderful."

At the sound of my voice, Bea and Mads both looked over, Bea holding a smile of her own while Mads lived up to his grumpy nature. I smiled at him. *I will wear you down, mister.* A task even further down the list now, given the light of yesterday's events, but I concluded it was an important one all the same.

"Have you found anything?" I enquired.

The pie now moving to my mouth, I couldn't hold back a soft moan as the buttery pastry met my tongue, the meat tender and perfectly seasoned. Mads narrowed his eyes, an action I wasn't going to even try to decipher while pie was in my presence.

"Better than porridge, eh Goldie?"

Offering Fox a sly smile of my own, I turned back to the two investigating.

Bea tapped her knee as she addressed my original question. "Not yet. There are a lot of translations I'll need to make with books back at my house. And when you're a bit better, we can do some recognition spells, see if we can confirm the connection."

I nodded my head in agreement, mouth still full of delicious pie as Mads' voice shot through the pleasant conversation in irritation. "Aurelia needs to rest."

The way my name rolled off of his tongue, even in the threatening tone, sent pleasured chills down my spine. *What is wrong with me?*

"I know, caveman, which is why I said 'when' she is better." Bea rose in a huff, taking the book with her.

"I'll pop back tomorrow and see how you're doing. In the meantime, I'll get to work on these translations."

Leaning down, she planted a quick, soft kiss on my forehead, a foreign sensation sparking, similar to the one I'd received from Xav.

Fox shot to his feet. "I'll walk you home, princess."

"No." Bea, stern and pointing a finger at Fox's chest, said, "You're not getting under my dress today, boy. So don't even try it."

Fox chuckled, ignored her protest, and followed her out the door. I wondered whether or not there was something between the two of them. A question I could ask at a later date, if the friendship between us continued to blossom.

Finishing off my pie, I hadn't noticed Mads leave the room, but I couldn't deny the air felt lighter. Xav plopped down next to me, offering another pie. An offer I wasn't going to refuse.

"How are you?"

"Fine." I chuckled, thinking back to my previous conversation with Bea.

"Good. You still need to let your body rest." He curled his fingers beneath my chin, gently drawing my face towards him to examine the branch's fine work on the side of my head.

Xavier's eyes softened further as he nodded his head. "I'll get some more salve. I don't think it will leave a scar."

I moved my head down once, still concentrating mostly on the pie.

"And," he continued hesitantly, "what about all of this?"

He gestured around the room. I didn't need further explanation as to what he meant by 'this.'

Swallowing, I looked down at my lap, attempting to muddle through the thoughts I hadn't had much time to think about. The life I'd known had changed drastically over the last few weeks, barely giving me space to breathe. And I hadn't gotten used to being asked my thoughts, my opinions. A courtesy which had never been afforded to me before.

"I—I don't know, Xav."

Drawing courage from the well deep within, the same courage I'd shown when opening up to Mads, I decided to offer Xav the same. Well, maybe not the same, they didn't all need to know my deep dark secrets.

"You have to understand, my whole life, nothing has been my own. Not my freedom, opinions, body, or even dreams. I'm so grateful to have found you all and to be here. The truth is, I'm still wrapping my head around the fact I can do whatever I want, whenever I want. And now there is this whole parallel world I'm somehow connected to? I'm lost, Xav."

Nodding in understanding, he took the plate from my lap, replacing it with his hand. Carefully cupping my hands in his own, he said, "I can't say I understand fully, but I do know what it's like to be lost. We all do. I hope you can find a sliver of comfort in the knowledge that you are no longer alone. We will be patient."

I snorted. The idea of Mads showing patience could've had me on the floor in a fit of laughter. Xav detected as such. "Well, I will make it my job to ensure the other two are patient. How about that?"

I did the only thing I could think of, offering him a genuine smile in gratitude.

"Xav." Curiosity crept in, and I asked, "What is your magic?"

Leaning back, his eyes stayed straight, almost a glazed like look falling over them. "When we were in Raithe, we each had different magic. I was an empath, giving me the ability to sense and feel the emotions of others." He waited a beat, allowing me to process.

Xav's power made sense, even without it here. He was still in tune with the emotions of others, far gentler than the other two.

He continued, "Fox's power allowed him to create ice."

"Ice?" I interjected in awe as my mind tried to picture what that must have looked like.

Xav chuckled. "Yes, ice. And Mads, his magic... Well, as first born in a royal line, his magic is tied to our seasonal kingdom."

Confusion furrowing my brow, I shifted uncomfortably in my seat waiting for him to continue.

"Each kingdom's leader generally holds the magic connected to their season. Earth with Spring, water with Summer, air with Autumn, and fire with Winter."

"Fire? You're saying Mads' magic is fire?"

The ability to form ice had intrigued me, but the capacity to create and manipulate fire? His power made sense given the heat I'd always felt from him, but it also washed a calmness over me. Fire was warm, comforting, but it also had the ability to destroy. Those thoughts alone heated my core.

A fascinated smile grew on his face. "Yes. Well, he used to, in Raithe. Don't tell him I told you, though."

I offered an awkward wink. "Don't worry, Xav, it'll be our secret."

The room was shrouded in darkness, just a breath of moonlight streaming in. The masculine cedar haze surrounding me confirmed I was back in Mads' bedroom. Back in Mads' bed. A shift beside me caused me to peek over my shoulder to find the outline of the man himself. Confirming it was him by his intoxicating scent. "How did I get here?"

A few seconds of silence ticked by. Maybe he was asleep. As I snuggled in deeper, he spoke.

"I carried you."

Taking a deep breath, I asked, "Why did you carry me here?"

"Because your body needs to rest and the sofa wasn't doing you any favours."

I almost voiced my gratitude, the niggling in my gut stopping me. "You didn't ask if it was ok to hoist me up here."

"I didn't 'hoist' you. I carried you. Gently, I might add. I was going to wake you but you —" As if about to unintentionally reveal a secret, he stopped himself.

I pressed, "I, what?"

Clearing his throat and shifting, the mattress dipped, and I knew he faced away from me now, confirmed when his voice sounded further from me. "You looked peaceful."

Shock hit my chest at his admission. The man I had known, for the most part, was unforgiving and heavily guarded, continued to reveal a softer side of himself. Disbelief stopped me from doing an internal jump of joy. The onion had begun to peel.

The silence between us stretched on, surprisingly not uncomfortable. I couldn't deny the warmth I found so quickly in this room, in this man's presence.

"Aurelia?"

The sound of my name on his lips continued to do unthinkable things to my stunted emotions, and I couldn't help my physical response.

"Yes, Mads?"

He inhaled deeply before posing his question, "The man you were due to marry, was he your abuser?"

I knew his curiosity would pique further with every kernel of information I'd shared. I wanted nothing more than to be swallowed by the darkness. Instead, I dug deep, wrapping myself in the safety I'd felt in the cabin and with the brothers.

"He was one of them. Yes."

"What happened to him?" He growled in a way that made me wonder if he was losing his control. The way his body shook, the barely contained rage I knew brimmed at the surface, had me clenching the bed sheets so tightly the beat of my pulse could be felt under each fingertip.

It was the question I'd feared most since the brothers had allowed me sanctuary at the cabin, in their home. I'd known I'd need to share it eventually, but now it was in front of me, and I wasn't sure how to approach it. I hadn't lied to them. Kept back details, yes; however, there had never been anything untruthful in my words.

The beat of my heart echoed through my entire body. Doing my best to practise the breathing exercises Fox taught me, I resolved not to start with the lies now. The stiff air left my lungs, the confession bleeding out. "I st—I stabbed him with his letter opener and then," I swallowed a lungful of air, "and then, I ran into the forest."

Our breathing cut through the dense silence. I felt him shift, and chancing a glance, I turned my head over, lifting it, to see his outline in the moonlight. He lay, staring directly at the ceiling, breathing deep.

"Good."

Good. He wasn't angry? There was no hint of malice or frustration in his voice. Did he not think my actions were wrong? Even if the man in question was the cruellest kind, taking what wasn't his, forcing himself on not only me, but everyone he came in contact with, whether in business or pleasure, I would have at least expected some sort of hostility in Mads' tone.

I repeated in a whisper, "Good?"

Entranced by his silhouette, his tongue skated his bottom lip. After a beat, he said, "Yes. Good."

Finding the pillow once more, I was lost for words.

"And Aurelia?" His voice dropped further, laced with vengeance.

I swallowed down the fear of what may come next. "Yes?"

"I want you to make sure you always carry a blade."

"Okay." I hadn't expected that.

"And if anyone ever tries to touch you again, you don't hesitate."

"Okay." I repeated, not knowing what else to say.

"Because if you don't stab any fucker who tries to touch you, I will." The maliciousness met a crescendo then, transforming into a level of anger I'd not heard from Mads before.

The bed shifted again, taking him further away from me and his threat induced words. A bead of fear found its way moving down my throat. Not the threat itself, more so the fact the layers peeled back didn't just show me more of the man beside me. No, it also forced my attraction to grow. Quickly, this fear mixed with anticipation… I'd never had the freedom to feel this way, and it just may prove worth it.

The next morning, I woke up in an empty bedroom and on the bedside table, I found a small, elegant dagger with a matching sheath.

CHAPTER 13

MADDOX

Sleep evaded me following Aurelia's words. There were hints of the abuse she'd endured, and for some idiotic reason, I didn't want to believe it went as deep as it had. I cursed myself for trying to stay away. I'd thought the barriers I'd formed around myself were smart, ensuring I didn't get too close. The truth was, I was already dangerously close. So much so, I was out of bed before the sun rose, the violence ready to pour out of me.

Xav and Fox joined me in the kitchen a short while later. We weren't only blood brothers, we'd lived in such close proximity for so long we knew each other's movements before we took them, even behind closed doors.

"What's going on?" Fox yawned as he made his way to the kettle, unintentionally becoming the coffee maker for our trio.

I pushed down the rage, knowing I needed to attempt to keep my head straight as I laid out my poorly thought-out proposal. My brothers would follow me to the ends of the earth. I didn't question their loyalty. What concerned me was whether or not they'd agree with the rationale behind my plan.

"We need to find this Shelton cunt." My statement was firm.

Both of my brothers paused their morning routine to turn and face me. Fox's trademark sly smile kicked up one side of his lip. Not many knew, while his given name translated to fox, the reason we gave him the nickname was because of the many similarities he had to the woodland creatures. Xav, I couldn't read. His usual calm sat between us, always difficult to decipher.

"Why do we need to find him, Maddox?" Xav's calm tone broke through, always thinking logically as I knew he would.

I ran my hands through my hair, taking care not to tug too roughly. "When she ran? It was because she stabbed him to escape."

Fox set down a steaming mug in front of me, taking the seat to my right. "Is he alive?"

"Yes," I confirmed, my voice holding a thick layer of determination.

We didn't need to talk about the details. When Aurelia was attacked by her father, a title the bastard nowhere near deserved, we'd gone out the next day to track him down. He was currently being held in a small dungeon we'd built for ourselves when we first arrived in the human world, not knowing whether we'd need to hold someone, or multiple someones, accountable for certain actions. The humans bred an entirely different version of evil in their lands we had learned soon after we'd landed in this damned place.

Against Xav's judgement and my need for vengeance, we'd kept Niall alive. I wouldn't tell Xav, but he'd been right. It wasn't our decision whether or not the man kept his life. I huffed thinking how ridiculous it was to call him a man. He was the furthest thing from it. I clenched my jaw as the image of Aurelia crawling to me flashed in my mind. The things I would do to him.

Until Aurelia's confession last night, I'd made the assumption that the orchestrator of her abuse was mainly her father. The tone in which she delivered her admission told me while he was definitely a part of it, Lord Shelton was the real evil puppeteering her demons.

"We have some things to do this morning." Xav's steadfast tone broke through my thoughts. "We can head out later this afternoon."

I was taken aback. It was a very rare occasion when Xav didn't question things to the end of the earth, ensuring we were making the right decision. He was the responsible one. The logical one.

"We won't say anything to Aurelia yet." I didn't want her having to deal with the emotions crashing down until I knew I had Lord fuckface secure in a cell.

"Agreed," Xav and Fox confirmed together.

The thought of the chase enthralled me, doing nothing to abate the outrage resident in my gut. I nodded to my brothers, both of whom were aware of my temper, before walking out the back door. I needed to release some pent-up aggression. And so, I took to the forest floor without looking back.

Tracking Lord Shelton down was thankfully an easy task. We found him at home. Aurelia had done a number on him when she thrust the letter opener in his neck except she unfortunately missed some key ingredients to complete the death recipe. He'd made a strong recovery by the time we had arrived.

Fox and Xav teamed up to use their incomparable verbal skills on his staff, clearing the way for our impromptu meeting with the Lord himself.

Walking into the study, my lip immediately curled in disgust, not just at the sight of the man we were hunting but at the room itself. It reeked wealth, tormenting anyone who stepped foot in here thinking they were less than this man. The walls were veiled in the deepest shade of crimson that couldn't be ignored even with the many animal trophies surrounding us. Aurelia wasn't the only creature he'd abused.

The good lord was behind his desk, bent over some sort of bullshit he was tangled in. I had to force the bile down my throat at the sight of him. Knowing his hands had touched Aurelia pushed my body into a fury I'd never known before. Xav sensed it immediately, placing his hand on my shoulder to ground me. What I wouldn't have given to tear him apart with my bare hands.

A few moments passed before he looked up from his desk, startled to find three unknown men standing in his study. Fox made himself at home, walking around, touching random objects before a fine cigar case took his fancy.

I studied the man in question. A fine dusting of hair circled his mostly bald head and his glasses sat upon a crooked nose, skin covered in pock marks and ageing spots. He wore his wealth in the cut of his waistcoat and glimmer of the chain in his pocket watch. He was a short, stout man with fingers that had brought pain to our girl. The fury pulsed beneath my cheeks.

"What is the meaning of this? Who are you?" Shelton's face grew a deeper crimson with each word he spat in false courage.

Xav took centre stage. After all, it was his birth right to lead negotiations, whether friend or foe and Lord 'I-can't-fucking-wait-to-see-his-life-leave-his-eyes,' was most definitely foe.

"Good evening. Apologies for the intrusion —"

I snorted. Xav wasn't apologetic at all. He was always a diplomat.

"Get out of my house!"

We were going to start with anger? Good. My fingers clenched, readying my fist to meet this arsehole's smarmy face.

"Now that is something we can't do," Fox chimed in, stepping closer to the lord's desk. He picked up a gaudy letter opener and before any of us could register his next move, the pointed end stuck out of the fair lord's hand, as a shrill scream escaped from his lips.

Fox looked back at me and said, "I can see why she chose this as her weapon."

The screaming continued so incessantly that Fox was forced to rip the lord's tie off and wrap it around his mouth like a gag.

"You see, we really need you to shut the fuck up because we have some business to discuss."

"Business," Xav took over, "which never should have been business at all."

The sweat pooled on the Lord's forehead, a tear leaving his eye.

"You took something which wasn't yours to take. So now, we are going to need repayment."

A grumbled response left the lord's mouth. I wanted to pity the fucker, given we were nowhere near done yet. He didn't deserve it.

"The repayment," I stepped up to the desk, "is not our debt to collect, unfortunate for us. The one you owe will have their chance. We'd just like to have a bit of our own fun first."

I couldn't, nor wanted to, stop the smug grin growing across my face. The nerves in my fingers danced with excitement. Aurelia would have the final say, of course, but for now my fury wanted to dance with Shelton. And what a dance it was going to be.

"Aurelia." I leaned over the bed, my voice ghosting across her cheek, conscious of not making contact with her or the mattress given the condition of my hands and clothing.

It was possible we'd done a bit more than we'd initially planned with Shelton, and we needed to take her to the cells tonight. The bastard didn't have much time given the state he was in.

"Aurelia." I kept my voice low and even.

"Hmmm."

I clenched my jaw at the delicious sound. The noises falling from her lips would be my undoing.

"I need you to wake up and come with me."

Those stunning blue orbs peered up at me from sleep filled eyelids.

"Mads?" A tremor of anxiety bit through the question.

"Yes. We need you to come downstairs now."

"What time is it?" She glanced toward the darkened window.

"Late. Let's go."

I was aware of the sternness in my tone. Not just then, but every time I spoke to her. Just another mechanism I thought would help me keep my distance. I was an idiot.

Obeying, she kicked herself out of the bed before giving me a once over. "Why are you covered in blood?"

"None of your concern."

"It most certainly is my concern. Mads you're hurt."

"I'm not hurt. It isn't my blood."

"Let me look at you."

"No. Come downstairs, please?"

The moonlight dancing through the window illuminated the harsh expression sitting on her face. I didn't have time to process if it meant she cared. I needed to get through the next part of the plan first.

Thankfully, without another word, she grabbed her dagger from the bedside table and followed me to find Xav and Fox in the kitchen. Those arseholes managed to clean themselves up a bit, not looking like they slaughtered a goat, unlike me.

"What's going on?"

The concern laced in her voice cracked something in my chest. I nodded to Xav to take the reins. "We have Shelton and your father."

"What?" The concern grew into a panic as Aurelia's stare darted around us, thinking we'd brought them into our home. "Not here. We have them in a secure location not far from here. We found them," Xav paused, allowing the information to sink in before he presented our offering. "What happens next is your decision, Aurelia."

Her vibrant blues glazed over with what I could only ascertain as fear. I hated it. I wanted to soothe her, to tell her I would go take care of them both and she'd never have to worry about them finding her again. I also knew she wouldn't heal if I took that path. They would haunt her for the rest of her life if she allowed it. Whether or not they were breathing. So, this had to be her choice. Their lives were in her hands.

"Why?" Her one-word question was laced with an emotion I couldn't pinpoint.

Why? Had she forgotten the reason she fled from Huxley and the people within it? The scars strewn across her skin were enough to know the physical aggression she'd admitted were clearly the result of continuous beatings. She still didn't feel safe with us. Understandable yet unacceptable. I needed to prove it to her. I needed to give her my words. "Because whether or not we show it, you are one of us now, Aurelia, and we will do everything in our power to make sure you are never hurt again."

Aurelia glanced toward me, a sheen of something I couldn't place flicked over her eyes. I waited with bated breath. She knew I didn't show many emotions outside of anger. And that anger? It fuelled me to become the monster she needed to hunt the men from her past who haunted her present — who wouldn't haunt her future.

We waited in anticipation as her breathing evened, lightening the tightness in my chest. Our anxieties finding comfort in one another. She took one barefooted step toward me, not paying any mind to Xav and Fox who also awaited her response. Her azure gaze erupted with determination, not fear.

"Take me to them."

The spark was lit. I was ready to stand by her side as she burned the world to the ground.

I led our revenge group through the night covered forest toward the dungeon.

Xav and Fox surrounded Aurelia as we paced quickly towards the makeshift dungeon. The urge to grab her hand and never let go continued to course through my veins. I knew better. This was her redemption, not ours.

Stopping once we arrived at the stairwell, I turned to face Aurelia. She kept her eyes over my shoulder, trying to catch a glimpse of what, I wasn't sure.

The dungeon was basically a dug-out hole with three cells covered in iron bars. Fox took great pride in his masterpiece, and I couldn't fault him for it. Over the years, we hadn't used it much. Standing there in front of Aurelia, I knew the true purpose of why we'd built it.

"Aurelia."

Wide cerulean eyes flashing to mine, her fear was apparent. I leaned forward attempting to remind her she wasn't alone.

"Neither of them are in a good state of health."

Fox leaned forward, voice hushed as he said, "We had to have a bit of our own fun first, Goldie."

He offered a wink before taking his place behind her as Xav moved forward to take hold of her arm in a gentle grip. "Do you want to talk to them first? They're both gagged so they can't say anything to you unless you want them to."

Aurelia kept her eyes trained to mine. I watched in fascination as the fear dissipated, leaving a flourishing storm of rage in its wake. Taking a prolonged inhale, Aurelia pushed her shoulders back, clenching her fists at her sides before breaking our stare to turn her gaze toward the stairwell.

"First, I have a few things to say to them."

I was taken aback by the evenness in her tone.

"Then, I want to make them pay for each time they made me feel less than I was. Less than I am."

Breaking the eye contact, she turned to Fox. "Are there tools?"

Shock flickered over Fox's face. "Tools?

"Yes. Tools. There isn't enough pain in this world I could possibly inflict on them. I'm damn sure going need some support."

Fox was almost giddy with excitement, her words finding the darkness within him. "Oh, I've got tools, Goldie. Whatever you need."

Nodding once to him, she met Xav's eyes and then mine, giving me the signal to move forward. Aurelia was ready to savour the sweet taste of revenge.

CHAPTER 14

AURELIA

Maddox led us down the stairs into a tunnel, the torches Xav and Fox carried illuminating our path. Mads descended empty handed, embracing the darkness as if he greeted an old friend.

The stone hallway stunk of despair and decay, pushing the rising excitement through my veins. Part of me knew I should be terrified to see both my father and Lord Shelton again. The other part, the part nulled by so much abuse in the past, salivated at the prospect of bringing these men to their knees. I didn't know what kind of damage the brothers had already inflicted on them. I somehow knew they'd left the juiciest morsels for me.

We passed the first cell, the door open where I noticed a table pushed against the far wall. As Fox promised, the table was covered with the tools I'd asked about. I only gave them a short glance, knowing in my blood when the time came, I would have no doubt which ones I would want to use.

The sudden need to inflict pain should've concerned me. It didn't. The brothers, nor I, had realised just how much I needed this. How much my broken soul craved it. I couldn't help the slight smile curling on my lips.

The favours these two men provided me were about to be reciprocated. My stomach jumped in anticipation and I felt the temperature in my blood rise. No part of me thought torturing and ending the lives of these men would heal me. Not in the slightest. Instead, it would fulfil my desire to take away their freedom the same way they took mine.

The end of the tunnel was in sight, the scent of blood piercing my nostrils in the most delicious of ways, fuelling my anticipation. I'd never been the squeamish type. I didn't have the opportunity to be. I'd inhaled and cleaned my own blood enough times to grow numb to the gore.

Mads halted a few feet away from the cells on either side of us, my gaze transfixed on his back as his shoulders rose and fell with each heavy breath. Turning, he caught my eyes in the torch light, waiting for my instructions.

"Father first." I responded, voice as steady and even as I'd kept it since I told them to lead me here.

Mads nodded, moving to the left cell, removing a set of keys from his pocket and deftly unlocking the door. He walked in first, leaning back against the iron bars in a stance signalling he would be on guard. A shadow in the background.

Pushing my shoulders back, I followed him through. My eyes didn't initially centre on the man tied and bound to a chair. My gaze landed on the stone and dirt making up the walls of this soul sucking place. I smirked, appreciating the effect, then flicked my gaze down. The fire in my veins pulsed at the sight of Niall covered in a myriad of cuts and bruises, and with blood splatter across his clothing.

Fox stormed in from behind me, chucking a bucket of water over Niall. The effect was immediate as his eyes shot open, attempting to gulp in a large breath, body shaking from what I assumed was frigid water. He looked around in shock-soaked fear before his eyes came to me. Gradually, he lifted his gaze from my knees up my body until he met my eyes. The fear morphed into utter rage, and I chuckled. "Hello, father."

The gag, which appeared to be his own blood-soaked clothing, stopped his words from forming properly as he started to scream.

I tsked. "What a predicament you have found yourself in, isn't it?"

The calm in my voice should have surprised me. As with everything until this point, it didn't. I stood in a moment I never thought I'd see. Surrounded by men who would hand me the torch to set the world on fire. I had the other fucker who marked my body in the cell next door and a table full of tools my fingers itched to touch.

A further mumbled howl left his throat as I began to circle his chair. You would have thought, after all these years, I had a speech rehearsed. If I ever found myself in a moment like this, I'd know exactly what to say. The truth was, I'd lost hope of freedom and revenge so long ago. So, I did the only thing I could. I let my fury take over.

"It appears as though you are now at the mercy of your daughter whom you put through so much. How does that feel?" I relished hearing the fury wrapped around my words.

He began to cough around the gag at the force he used to get his words out. I turned to Fox, signalling I wanted the gag out as I reached beneath my knee length coat to remove the dagger I now kept strapped to my thigh. Fox obeyed, ripping the gag out with such force the room echoed with a pop followed by two bloodied teeth falling to Niall's lap. I kept my eyes on his as I let the smile stretch across my face.

"What are you doing, Aurelia?" Even with the gag removed, his words were muddled, showcasing the earlier beatings he'd received from the brothers.

"Who are these men?" The newly formed lisp mixed with a slight gargle was music to my ears.

I blinked in boredom before turning to the brothers. "These are the men who have brought my redemption. And I have to say, they did a wonderful job, don't you think?"

The venom twisting through my words was refreshing and shocking. The latter I didn't let show in my expression.

"Untie me right now you bitch!" Spittle flew from his bloodied mouth at the eruption. His anger was beautifully laced with a terror I could eat.

I spun the ornate dagger between my fingers, grounded by the weight of it in my hand. "You always loved that word, father. It lost its kick so very long ago.

"You see, I finally managed to escape you, Shelton, and Huxley, finding solace and safety with these gentlemen you see in front of you. And it turns out, family is deeper than blood, something you've never acknowledged."

My sorry excuse for a father surprised me by throwing his head back, a roaring laugh escaping his battered mouth. "You think they want you for anything more than what you are good for? You idiot girl. These bastards are liars. They only want you for your pussy and —"

I leapt forward, slicing the dagger across his throat, pushing my muscles until they burned and enjoying every millisecond the blade dug into his skin. The drops of blood thrashed down faster the further I cut, filling the room with a thick scent of freshly spewed blood.

The sight of the crimson liquid descending down his throat lifted a perverse smile from my lips. My chest rose and fell in rhythm to the dripping noise surrounding us as my hand held steady. I felt Mads shift behind me. He didn't come forward, letting me delight in my actions without any interruptions.

Pulling the blood-soaked dagger back, I stood up straight, balancing on the balls of my feet as I savoured the sight of the life bleeding from Niall Mallory. The gurgling noises filled the room with the sweet sound of revenge. Savouring each of the last seconds of Niall's life, I took one step back, eyes trained on the deadly wound I'd just inflicted without a second thought. A shred of warmth blossomed in my chest with each of Niall's laboured attempts to breathe life back into his body.

The last few ripples of oxygen left him as his eyes glazed over with the sweet blanket of the death he deserved. I'd expected to feel slightly nauseous at the combined sight, sounds, and smells, but nothing came besides the warm satisfaction that nestled itself in my chest.

He was gone.

Dead.

One down. One to go.

I turned to the brothers behind me. Fox stood, hands on his hips with his trademark smirk, a hint of pride glistening in his eyes. Xav stood, stoic, oddly enough for him. I shifted my gaze to Mads, arms crossed, a flicker in his gaze I couldn't decipher.

"I didn't even get to use any tools."

Fox chuckled, stepping forward to take the dagger. I held tight at first, letting go once he held up a cloth, indicating he would clean it for me.

"That was —" Xav started.

Mads' finished. "Impressive. Maybe those lessons with Fox aren't useless."

I caught Mads' gaze again. An energy filled the space as one of his eyebrows lifted in question. He wanted to know if I was alright. I don't know how I knew, but I had too much adrenaline coursing through my veins and another life to take before I could question it.

To answer his silent question, I nodded once. I was better than alright, but we had no time to linger on the euphoria I felt. I had my last act of revenge in my grasp, and I didn't want to wait to take it.

I gestured for Mads to lead us across the tunnel to the second occupied cell. Shelton was positioned similarly to Niall, gagged and tied to a chair. The state of his body much worse than my dead father's. Curiously, I glanced at Mads, raising my eyebrow in question. Scowling, he held up his hands in defence as he explained, "We may have gotten a bit carried away with him."

"He did." Xav chimed in, pointing directly at Mads as a wicked smile teased the corners of his mouth. "Fox and I were on our best behaviour."

The warmth in my chest grew knowing Mads had to hold himself back from butchering the man who had caused so many of my nightmares. The reason I could barely hold my own head up most days.

Fox followed us in with his hands full. Unrolling a piece of leather, he presented me with a number of tools from the table next door.

"Didn't want you to let your emotions get the better of you before you got a chance to use some of these," he said with a smirk.

I looked down at the various pieces in his hands. A myriad of objects I had no understanding of. "I picked my favourites just for you."

I caught his eye just as he gave me a wink. I couldn't help a small snicker escape my lips. How messed up was all this? Though, it was, in no way, as terrible as the pain I'd endured the last ten years and swallowed back the sliver of morality escaping my thoughts.

"Is he asleep?"

"Unconscious. I have an herbal concoction to bring him to." Xav followed his answer by removing a small vial from his pocket, stepping towards the mangled remains of Lord Shelton. "Do you want to keep him gagged?"

I nodded. For now. I pounced on Niall because of the effect his words had on me. I needed a bit more time with Shelton before I took action. Niall may have been the one to hand me over to Shelton, the original orchestrator in my life of captivity and abuse. But Shelton. Well. He held ownership of the majority of my physical and mental scars. Shelton had invited his friends to let off steam by lashing my skin with belts or canes. He was the one who insisted I learn obedience and become wife material. He was the one who built a hidden compartment behind the back bookcase in his office to house the collection of tools he grew over the years, giving himself more than a dozen different objects to flay me.

Taking one step back to let Xav work his herbal magic, I took a deep breath before I felt warmth at my back. Twisting my head only slightly, I met Mads' gaze at my shoulder, nodding once to confirm they were with me, whichever step I chose next.

Xav pushed the tiny bottle beneath Shelton's nose, moving it back and forth. It took a couple of minutes before he started to come to, forgetting where he was before he passed out as revealed by his stunned expression. Similar to Niall, he tried to force his voice through the gag to no avail. I could taste retribution on my tongue. Niall had only been the appetiser. Lord Shelton the main course.

"Good evening, Lord Shelton," I pronounced slowly in the same even tone I'd had in the cell next door.

Eyes widening, he took in my guests, registering just how deep he was. His wrinkled throat contracted as he belted a scream, once again muffled by the cloth filing his mouth. Taking a step forward, I leaned down to his eye level, my tone taunting. "No one can hear your screams." The same words he'd said to me so many times spat right back at him.

The venom in my voice grew thicker with each word as my fingers itched to pick up one of the tools Fox held. Patience. I reminded myself again. Needing some distance, I stepped back. Without a word, the brothers moved towards the walls of the cell, giving me the room I needed to pace. Turning the words over in my head as Shelton continued his muffled screams, I started at the beginning.

"The first time I was forced to spend time with you, alone, you told me something. Do you remember what you told me?"

My eyes settled on the bulge of his eyes as he processed my question, his muffled words filtered into the room.

"You told me," I continued, "my only purpose in the world was to submit to your power and that one day, I would open my legs too. A servant and a pleasure palace. Nothing more. And you told me I should be honoured to be the chosen one."

I paused, waiting for his muddled wails to die down before moving to the next part, not daring to glance at the other men in the room. "You then went on to lay out your plan. You wouldn't touch me. No. I needed to be untouched — the forbidden fruit, pure, a maiden — until the day I would fully be yours. Instead, you took great pleasure in inflicting every kind of pain imaginable. The bow on top was when you invited your friends to let off their own 'stea m.'"

Out of the corner of my eye, I noticed Mads clench his fists at his sides. I didn't have time to analyse it. I knew he'd let me have my say.

"At the time, I didn't believe you. I knew the world offered me more than being just your plaything. I knew I had more to offer."

I continued walking in circles around his chair, the sweat dripping down his cheeks visible even from where I paced.

"Then you did what you do best, didn't you? You wore me down. You peeled every single layer of dignity and respect I had for my body, my mind, and you made me a shell of a human being."

Passing Xavier, my eyes flicked to him to find his trained on Shelton with a fire in them I'd not seen before. They didn't know half of what this man had done to me. And what little I had shared was enough to bring me here, to my vengeance. It tasted so good.

"For years, I'd given up hope of an escape, and I don't know if I will ever forgive myself for not fighting back. What I can do now," I paused, Lord Shelton's breaths came in quick spurts, fury or fear fuelling him I wasn't sure, "is take as much of you as I can."

Shelton began mumbling, his eyes creasing as tears tried to escape. Fucker. One tear wouldn't erase the thousands he'd taken from me. I stopped in front of him, lowering down once more and making my eyes level with his.

"You broke me."

More tears joined the first as his breathing quickened. As did mine.

"You broke me!"

I screamed into the cell, into his face, into my soul. The anger morphed into a deep sadness I'd not let myself acknowledge since those first lashings. It was grief for the loss of myself I'd tightened into a box so long ago. Standing straight, I brought my arm back and threw my fist into his face. As soon as it met his eye socket, the pain shot through my knuckles into my arm. Rather than wincing, I savoured the feel of it. The taste was sweet, and I was hungry for more.

Fox stepped forward, coming to stand close behind me. He didn't say anything or reach out, but I still knew he was there, ready with the tools.

"Take the gag out."

It wasn't what I'd planned initially, but I needed his words before I took his skin. His fingers. His blood. Without hesitation, Xav stepped forward and pulled the blood-soaked cloth from Shelton's mouth. He gasped for air.

"What the hell are you doing? You stupid girl!"

My eyes rolled of their own volition. Of course that scum would pin this back on me.

"You have no idea the war you will start if you don't let me go right now."

Taking a deep breath in, I closed my eyes for the briefest of seconds, confirming my next move. As I opened my eyes, I reached behind me, silently instructing Fox to hand over one of the contraptions. He obliged immediately as I felt the cool metal lay down gently on my open palm. I pulled my hand back around to find a narrow hammer. I'd never purposely caused anyone pain before, so I wasn't sure if the hammer had a specific use. Rather than asking the brothers, I decided I'd make do with my imagination.

"What is the meaning of this, Aurelia?" Shelton struggled beneath his tied wrists as I let the sparkle in my eyes grow at the sight of the hammer.

"You wouldn't dare. You don't have the backbone to hurt me!"

The tremor in his voice told me otherwise. He fully believed I was capable of inflicting pain. Not the same kind he'd put on me for all those years, but close enough.

"It's funny, isn't it? You're on the receiving end this time. What does it feel like to have no choice or say in what happens to you next?"

Before he could respond, I brought the hammer up, his eyes twitched in terror. "You should have never underestimated me."

As the hammer sliced through the air, life slowed down and flashes of my time in the study came roaring back, reminding me of why I was doing this. The crack of his breaking finger bones echoed through the small space, filling me with the need to continue. Ignoring the bellows of agony from Shelton, I brought the hammer down, twice more on the first hand before moving to the second. Once all his fingers were shattered, I stepped back, heaving in prideful breaths as I waited for his cries to die down.

"There," I said, handing the hammer back to Fox. "Now you can't touch anything or anyone else."

"You're crazy!" Shelton babbled between sobs.

A chuckle escaped me, "Crazy? No, Shelton. This isn't madness. This is redemption."

A high-pitched cry left his lips as the sight at his crotch caught my eye. He was pissing himself. I smiled. He'd die losing his dignity.

"She said I had to force it out. You wouldn't give me what I wanted without force."

I let the words circulate through my mind. Shaking my head, confused at what he was going on about, I didn't want this to become an interrogation. Shelton took too much from me and any more of his words would cool the flames coursing through me. His garbled screams tore through the cell again. "She said you would show it if I beat it out!"

Ignoring his nonsense, I turned to my companions. "Anyone else like to take a bite?"

Mads stepped towards me immediately, gently pushing me to the side as he stood in front of Shelton and wasted no time connecting his fist to the prisoner's face. Again and again until Shelton's face was almost unrecognisable through the blood. In front of my eyes, Shelton's health deteriorated. He wasn't going to last much longer. A shame, really.

Mads stationed himself back on the stone wall, a calm settling over him as though he hadn't just beaten a man's face in.

"Anyone else?" I addressed the room in genuine curiosity. Fox and Xav said nothing, silently urging me forward. As much as I enjoyed watching the physical breaking of the man responsible for the majority of my nightmares, I knew I didn't have much time left. Whatever Mads had done when they'd taken him was worse than they'd planned.

"Well, Shelton, it looks to be your lucky day."

Crimson trickled down the sides of his mouth as he gasped, his next words a hopeful gargle through his blood-stained teeth. "You're letting me go?"

Laughter filled the room, and I shared a look with the brothers. "No. Of course not. But your death is going to come much quicker than planned."

The tears now mingling with the blood on his face made him even more of a pathetic mess than he'd already been. He'd held the power over me for so long, yet he was always a sad excuse for a human being.

"You...can't..." He drew out, struggling to finish his own sentences.

"Oh, I most definitely can." I reached once more around my back, indicating to Fox to hand over the next object. Instead of one of the many tools he'd brought into the room, I felt the hilt of my dagger lay on my palm. Looking over my shoulder at him, he offered me only one nod. When training, Fox had taken a lot of time to focus on dagger skills in hand-to-hand combat. He showed me the various places on the human body to focus, of course, always concentrating on the throat. There were a number of places someone could be cut on the throat that would bring upon various lengths of death. I didn't want Shelton to go as quickly as Niall had. He had it too easy. I wanted to walk out of this cell and know he would still be dying when we made our way back to the cabin. The light in his eyes would go out beneath the moon, taking my own internal darkness with it.

"You are a vile, twisted human being. Say hi to Lucifer for me."

Before he could inch out any other protests, I thrust the end of the dagger in with the hope that I nicked the carotid artery. The twist of the dagger meeting flesh filled my body with a warmth I should address later. For now, I was content to watch as his eyes bulged, the blood began to drip out and the gurgling noises began. I waited only a few seconds before turning back to the brothers. He'd be dead within a minute, if not sooner.

Without a word, I walked out of the cell and up the steps with the trio at my back as I left my past in the dungeon, bloodied and broken.

CHAPTER 15

AURELIA

"Buttercup!"

Shifting in my half sleep state caused a hammering to erupt inside my head. It was most likely brought on from the previous night and was quickly joined by a screwdriver twisting into my brain, around and around.

"Buttercup, wake up!!"

Bea. With the events from last night, I'd forgotten the agreement Bea would put me through recognition spells in an attempt to find my potential connection with the curse. An agreement I'd made before a night filled with torture and death. Groaning, I rolled over in the hopes I could bury myself in the bed deep enough to go unnoticed. Although a long shot, I had to at least attempt it.

"Aurelia!" The woman accompanying the voice was in the room, in very close proximity to my attempted burrowing.

"Go away, Bea. I think I fell off a cliff and hit my head, really hard."

Bea sniffed in amusement. "Nonsense. You just expended a lot of physical and emotional energy last night."

I'd felt many types of pain in my life. None of it compared to the explosion brewing in my head. How could revenge taste so sweet and then collide with your insides as though it meant to end you?

"Yes. And I don't plan on doing it again anytime soon. I can't help you today, Bea. If I move, I'm going to either throw up or die. Or both. In that order."

Chuckling, Bea sat on the edge of the bed, gently resting her hand on my head. The coolness of her touch, soothing. "You have forgotten a vital point here, buttercup."

Trying not to move too much in fear of throw up, death, or both, I grunted in question.

"You are now friends with the all-powerful Enchantress Beatrix Bluegrass."

Leaning down to my ear, she whispered, "Who has many magical concoctions for the brain and body."

The statement had me moving. Slowly, as to not disturb the workers in my head, I caught Bea's eyes, a glint of glee flashing in them. "Why are you whispering?"

"Because, sweet golden child, the bears don't know. And if they did know, they'd be pestering me for these teas all of the bloody time. And as an all powerful Enchantress, I don't have time for that."

I smiled. The smile itself was awkward, still conveying the message well enough.

"Now, sit up and drink your tea."

With Bea's assistance, I finally found myself in a sitting position, steaming cup of tea in my hands. The tea smelled of health, like dirt and grass and something else.

"The key is to plug your nose and get it down your gullet. The quicker it's in, the more success you've got of it staying down," Bea said, reading the disgusted expression I was certain was on my face.

Nodding once in agreement, I plugged my nose and tipped the mug back as quickly as I could. The taste was worse than the stench. It reminded me of those hot summer days in the town meetings, sweat seeped seats and humidity assaulting all your senses. If I was offered dirt and grass instead, I would have taken it.

Finishing the concoction, I shoved the mug back into Bea's hands who greeted me with another chuckle. "It tastes like a rubbish heap. I promise you'll feel better in five minutes and want to worship at my feet for it," Bea paused, an eyebrow tilting up. "Just so you know, I don't like people touching my feet, however hand kisses are acceptable."

Bea's humour was already helping the pain subside. I cast her a grateful smile before finding her hand for a quick squeeze. I'd always been in tune with the few emotions I'd allowed myself to have. What I struggled with was conveying those positive ones to other people. I had with Archer. Given those moments were so long ago, my emotional maturity was generally only internal.

"Thank you, Bea." I inserted as much gratitude in the sentiment as I could.

"Don't go getting all sappy on me now, buttercup. You may feel better now but as soon as I start these spells, you're not going to like me very much."

Concern settled in my chest. "Bea, should I be worried about these spells?"

I couldn't hide the panic in my words. Nor did I want to. I had so many grim memories locked away that the idea of digging deep into them terrified me. What if I wasn't ready to face my past in that way?

Bea's features softened as she reached out to squeeze my shoulder, "We are going to be revisiting some memories and some of them may be unpleasant. But you've got me and three ridiculously overprotective bears at your side. I promise it will be okay."

I nodded, unable to form a vocal response in the fear that it would crack.

"Now, get yourself showered and dressed. Xav created a post revenge feast for you."

With a wink, Bea left me alone to rinse off the rest of the night, internally and externally.

The spell circle took up the majority of the living room. The furniture had been moved at Bea's aggressive insistence, the brothers quickly following her orders. She'd created the circle using multiple smooth, white rocks, each about the size of my fist.

Inside the stone circle, Bea traced a triangular pattern with some sort of white paint, none of the brothers protesting at the potential irreversible marks on the cabin's incredible oak flooring. Bea worked quickly, finishing the drawing before moving on to mix various herbs unfamiliar to me.

Cautious not to interrupt whatever the pre-spell ritual may be, I moved around the room quietly, placing myself next to Mads on the sofa. Our thighs grazed and my stomach tightened at the contact. I expected him to shift away, but he made no attempt to move. I relished the warmth and stability it brought me. The way he came to my defence with Niall and Shelton had settled itself in my gut, morphing into something I wasn't yet ready to address.

"Right," Bea interrupted, pulling me from my inappropriate thoughts. "Aurelia, I need you to sit directly in this circle. See the triangle there in the middle? Your arse needs to be firmly planted there. Legs crossed."

My left leg brushed Mads' right as I rose, a zap of electricity difficult to ignore. Making my way to the centre of the circle, I pushed all thoughts of my reaction to Mads' touch and dropped my body to the floor, ensuring my backside was exactly as Bea directed. Unsure of what to do with my hands, I gently laid them on the tops of my thighs.

"Perfect. Are you comfortable if these knobheads are in the room?"

Taken aback that she'd even thought to ask my permission, I shifted my gaze to each of the brothers. Fox had a look of pure excitement plastered on his face. Xav offered me a calm smile, and Mads stayed stoic, showing no emotion whatsoever.

"Now you three," Bea turned to point an ebony painted fingernail at each of the brothers, "you know the drill. You want to be here for this, you don't move. You don't speak. Got it?"

All three nodded in agreement, eager to get one step closer to going home. A thought bringing a mix of excitement and sadness I couldn't quite decipher.

"Aurelia," Bea lowered herself down outside the circle, careful not to disturb her line work. Her voice adopted a soothing lilt as she continued, "I need you to follow each of my instructions. We are going to push your mind a bit, only a bit, but you need to know you may experience some unpleasantness."

Staring into Bea's eyes, I'd reviewed these steps with her in the last week, knowing the recognition spells were ones which would delve deep, filtering through memories that could both be my own and ones that were owned by others but had an effect on my life in some way.

Only knowing Bea for a short time should have made me question the trust I'd already put in the enchantress. It didn't. I felt a deep connection with Bea I didn't want to ignore. I wouldn't ignore it.

"Drink this." She shoved a mug in my hands at the blunt instruction.

Similar to the brew Bea had given me earlier, the drink's odour was filled with earth, although not as unpleasant as the previous liquid. Taking the same approach, I plugged my nose and downed the drink. Fox's faint words mentioned something about wanting the drink for himself, and I saw Mads slap him on the back of the head out of the corner of my eye.

Gently letting my lids close, a tingling sensation began to swim across my skin. A lightness settled over me, almost welcome.

"How are you feeling?"

A gentle breeze drifted through the living room's open window, bringing the cool sound of a robin nearby. My senses enhanced as I opened my eyes, finding Bea's considered gaze trained on me. I smiled.

"Good. Now, I want you to close your eyes, moving away from all of your senses. We need you to focus on your mind."

Following the instruction, I took a slow, deep breath, exhaling as I gently let my eyelids fall once more. Pulling back from the sights, sounds, and scents around me, I nestled into my mind's eye as comfortably as I could. A lot of cobwebs and skeletons sat in this place, unintentionally forcing my eyes to snap back open.

My breathing intensified as I found Bea's eyes once more, "It's okay," she soothed. "You're safe here."

Glancing over at the brothers, at Mads, he offered me a subtle nod, just the encouragement I didn't know I needed. More vigorously, I closed my eyes again, greeting my skeletons with an enthusiastic wave. We may as well get further acquainted.

In the distance, the faint sounds of Bea chanting touched my ears. Whispered words in a language I wasn't familiar with. The letters that blurred together into unknown words were quite beautiful. Almost melodic. A mellow tune joined the chanting. Whether or not it was part of the process or just in my head, I decided to just enjoy it, asking one of my skeletons for a dance. Before I could capture its bone hand and begin twirling, I was catapulted out of my mind's closet. A gasp escaped my chest grounding me enough not to let the panic rise. Bea's voice filtered through in mumbles. I was unable to make out the muddied noises.

I tumbled through obscurity before landing on my feet. Rising, the room before me was one I knew too well. Shelton's study. *Great. We are starting deep then.*

Sighing in defeat, I perused the memory noting nothing out of the ordinary. His office had always been a prison to me. The beatings themselves were horrific. The worst part was never knowing what demented game he wanted to play. Would the belt and cane suffice for whatever sick fantasy played in his mind that day? Or would he get more creative?

I stepped toward his desk, readying myself to shout out to Bea in the hopes she would hear me, when the door to the study flew open, the hinges creaking across the space. Shelton, closely followed by Niall, sauntered into the room. Looking at them even in memory, bile rose in my throat. Even knowing they'd both met their end by my hand, the memory version of them both sent tremors of rage through my body, my hand itching to hold my dagger.

Fighting back the imaginary sickness, I studied the two men, much younger than I remembered them, even in my earlier memories. Was this even my memory? Making no move to pull from the reverie in fear the spell would disengage, I stood frozen as the two men exchanged pleasantries before settling down on the sofa. They'd paid no mind to me, confirming I was a ghost within the scene. As I stepped forward, the conversation took an odd turn.

"The deal," Shelton spewed, "has been confirmed. And you're confident in your part?"

Niall scoffed, "Confident? Yes. It will be done."

"Good." Shelton picked up the glass of whisky I hadn't noticed earlier. "No hiccups."

The ferocity in Shelton's words was vile even in the memory form. His hot breath on my neck was a memory I didn't think I could ever escape. Even with his death.

"No hiccups." Niall confirmed.

"And you will hold up your end of the deal, Shelton."

Shelton's face grew red at Niall's demand. "They will be sent through next week. You go to Bayford, and we integrate them, as per the plan."

As he finished the sentence, Shelton cocked his head to the side, staring directly at where I stood. His eyes may have looked straight through me, but I still couldn't help the unease climbing my spine as his dead eyes were trained towards me.

I should have killed him slower.

My foot moved inches closer just as the images in front of me blurred. An invisible hook situated itself behind my belly button before I was torn through obscurity once more. Thankfully, the journey didn't last long, and I was once again on my feet. This time, I had landed in a small clearing, a fence of trees surrounding me. Dusting off some residual dirt from my trousers, the air surrounding me crisp and even, indicating I'd landed in a memory that had taken place in springtime.

I stilled as a soft breeze brushed along the treetops, a faint sound of birdsong not too far away. The clearing itself felt somewhat familiar with its circular structure and wooden guards. Had I been there before? As I was about to move forward, a rustle of bodies sounded towards my left. Hoping I would stay invisible in this memory, too, I waited.

The song of the birds died out as I stood there, the breeze halting not too long after, bringing an eerie calmness to the area. The anticipation grew, urging me to move toward the sound. Just as I went to take a step forward, the reason for the rustling showed itself in the form of Niall. *Fuck. Him again?*

Almost immediately, he was followed by two men I didn't recognise, one of which pulled what looked like an empty horse buggy behind him.

I stood my ground, waiting to see if I'd be noticed. None of the party had taken any note of a woman standing in the field sending a miniscule sense of relief fluttering over my skin.

"Niall!" A feminine voice shouted from the trees, my blood boiling as I recognised the voice of Leona Mallory, my mother. In the grand scheme of my life, I didn't have any love for my mother. I just forgot about her most of the time. She knew what was happening around her and chose to follow my father, blindly, into whatever plan he'd hatched.

She marched on quick feet towards Niall, an air of irritation following in her wake. "What are you doing, Leona?"

Niall attempted a whisper, yet the angered tone echoed through the clearing. Clutching her fists at her sides with no attempt to shield her volume, she said, "You tell me I'm all of a sudden going to be a mother, so you damn well better believe I'm going to be here for the pick-up."

What? What did she mean? My mind didn't have time to drift further as the group picked up pace towards the other side of the field. Kicking myself forward, I closed the gap to the group, following closely, ignoring the continuous shouts of pain my body liked to remind me of.

As we began to slow at a gap in the trees, I noticed a pathway covered in a natural arch from the overhead trees and surrounding brush. The man pulling the buggy set it down gently before following Niall onto the trail. The second man and my mother went next as I followed on their heels.

The leafy canopy kept the path in almost complete darkness, forcing me to watch each step I took. Thankfully, the path wasn't long, and we soon found ourselves in what appeared to be a circular opening at the mouth of a cave. The entrance to the cave was tall, enough for a man of Niall's height to walk through comfortably yet quite narrow. If we were going into the cave, we would have to go single file and pull our arms in.

What about the comment from mother back in the field? I pushed the thought back down. Bea needed me to find something and confusing myself with thoughts I didn't have the capacity to process or focus on was not what I needed. I shook my head, hoping the motion would shake those damn words straight out of my mind. It didn't work.

As I was about to spiral back into figuring out the deeper meaning in what she had said, voices came from in front of us — from inside the tunnel. The group stilled in unison, waiting for the owners of the voices to show themselves. I felt my heart rate quicken. Was it possible to have heart failure in dream form?

A few agonising moments later, a man appeared, his face mostly shadowed apart from the light leaping from the torch he held in front of him. The shadows dissipated as he moved closer to the opening until he was fully in view. The first thing I noticed wasn't the eyepatch covering his left eye, it was the clothing he wore. It wasn't vastly different from the fashions I knew except they held a regal quality about them I'd never seen before, even from our own monarchs. The dark hair on his head was quaffed, signalling he spent a significant amount of time and care on it while the facial hair he wore was much more dishevelled.

"Are you Blaze?" Niall spoke in a low, somewhat authoritative voice.

The man's face transformed into a scowl before leaning his head back in what I could only describe as a cackle. "You know others who would come through a magical portal to the exact spot you stand in, sir?"

Magical portal? We may finally be on to something. The stranger's voice was rough, not unpleasant. Niall scoffed at the stranger's tone, clearly unimpressed by his sarcasm. "Where are they?"

The stranger yawned, feigning boredom as he inspected his nails, enjoying the sight of Niall squirming under his power. I had no idea who the man was, but I enjoyed watching the silent torture he inflicted.

A minute passed. Niall became more agitated and as he was about to berate the stranger, muffled voices echoed further down the tunnel. "I didn't realise they were so gods damn heavy."

"Shut up. We'll get our money then we can piss off back to Hiema."

Hiema? The bear's Kingdom?

"They can bring them down the path there." Niall pointed toward the leaf strewn path we'd come through. "We have a cart."

The stranger motioned the two men forward, and I finally got a look at the goods they transported. Covered in sheets yet no less recognisable, the first man carried two bundles on either shoulder and the second with one larger heap. Humans. They were humans. Not only humans, by the size of them, they were children.

Stunned, I followed the two burly men as they walked back through the darkened path, the rest of the group unknowingly behind me. My mind raced with the possibilities of who those three children were. In my heart, I already knew. Three children Niall had agreed to 'integrate.'

"Careful of the middle girl," the stranger called at our backs. "She opened the portal. We had to knock her out afterwards. She's fierce, that one."

A silent gasp left my lips as I knew immediately who the middle girl was. That same feeling that had shown itself outside the bear's cabin pulsed deep in my belly, indicating I knew exactly who those three men had dragged from the cave. The larger wrapped figure, my brother. The smaller, my sister. The middle girl had the ability to open portals. She was the one who would get the bears home. She was me.

CHAPTER 16

MADDOX

Aurelia's eyes snapped open with an audible gasp. She lay sprawled across the circle on her back, her chest rising and falling rapidly as she struggled to inhale enough oxygen. Before she could right herself, I was across the room, my hands working their way beneath her knees and neck before I pulled her to my chest and settled us both on the sofa.

The warmth of her form pressed against me seeped through my clothes but did nothing to abate the fear running rampant across my body. Refusing to release her from my grip, I gently wrapped my fingers around her right hand before placing it over my own heart, a trick my mother had taught me when I was a young boy. "Follow it. Breath in. And out."

My eyes moved between her mouth and chest as she worked through the movements, slowing her breathing down to mirror the beat beneath her fingers. Once she was able to take in enough air without convulsing, I snapped my head to Trix. "You said it wouldn't hurt her!"

Aurelia stayed still, hand still on my chest as she focused on my heartbeat. Bea rolled her eyes. "It didn't hurt her, you pillock. She's fine."

Grinding my teeth, I despised her flippancy. "She's not fine. Look at her!"

Before Trix could offer a retort, a squeak of a word left Aurelia's mouth. I glanced down, locking on those stunning, vibrant blues as they concentrated on my face. She said in a whisper, "Fine."

I knew my rage danced across my features, no doubt a matching fire in my eyes. Slowly, Aurelia shifted her hand off my chest to cup my cheek beneath the smooth skin of her palm. My immediate instinct was to close my eyes, to savour the touch in every possible way. The fury that settled deep within my chest, refusing to disband, wouldn't allow that.

"I'm fine," She repeated, never once breaking eye contact.

"Aurelia?" Trix soothed, my gaze breaking from Aurelia to narrow in on the witch.

"Back the hell off, Trix." The ire in my voice would not abate, no matter how many times Aurelia wanted to reassure me she was okay.

"Mads," she enticed again, ghosting her hand across my cheek in subtle movements, sending a shiver of longing down my spine. "I'm okay. I promise."

As if to prove her words to me, she lifted herself up to move off my lap. The absence of her weight an instant disappointment.

She settled down next to me, letting her thigh rest against mine, before glancing toward Trix who had cocked her brow in question. "Aurelia," the witch's tone light, "I think you've been hiding some secrets you didn't realise you had."

The room momentarily fell silent at Trix's comment before Fox's excitement got the better of him as he took a tentative step toward Aurelia. "What is it? What did you see?"

Xav moved closer too, the act of such direct scrutiny causing a shift in Aurelia's posture. Her back straightened, signalling to me she was still trying to process what exactly she'd seen in those visions.

Threading her fingers through her golden strands, her eyes shifted to mine with something akin to confusion flashing through them.

"I came through a portal."

The room fell silent, the echo of Aurelia's breath casting shadows around us all as we waited for her to continue.

"Not just me, my siblings too. Archer and Eva. I think... I think we are from Raithe."

The knot in my chest tightened at the admission. I'd somehow known her ability to see the cabin meant something deeper. That she was connected to us in more ways than one.

"There's something else," Trix stepped forward, her voice even, "Aurelia can open portals."

"What?!" My brothers and I exclaimed in unison, booming with the same exciting concern.

Trix continued, "That is what we have been looking for. The portals. It isn't a revelation itself given most parallel worlds have portals, and we assumed you'd all come through one. What I think may have happened when you were cursed is that the portals were blocked or hidden. I'm not completely clear on those details yet, but there must've been a way to unlock them if Aurelia and her siblings came through."

Shock at the confession paralysed me. It took all the mental and physical energy I had to turn my gaze back toward the golden-haired beauty sitting next to me. Fox leaned forward, a glint of understanding in his eye. "You're Raithean?"

Aurelia and Fox's blue eyes drilled into one another for a few moments before the air in the room shifted and Aurelia's eyes found mine once more. I tried to read the emotion laying behind her stare, but I couldn't move past the very real fact that Aurelia was most likely from our own world.

Xav moved past Fox, taking the seat next to Aurelia on the sofa and engulfing one of her hands in his own. On a whisper, his eyes shone with pride. "I knew I was right about you."

Aurelia's head tilted back in surprise. "Right about me?"

Xav may have lost his magic when we were exiled, nevertheless, he was still highly in tune with emotions. Letting the smile reach his brown eyes, he spoke slightly louder, "I knew you were one of us."

One of us.

Fox catapulted from his bent position, shooting his hands up in the air with excited vigour before prancing around the open space in euphoria.

"Looks like," Trix picked up her explanation, completely ignoring the idiot dancing around behind her, "if we find a portal, Aurelia can just open it and walk right in. Anyone with her should be able to follow her through."

After all these years, we were closer to breaking the curse and returning to Hiema than we'd ever been, but I needed to know more. We couldn't launch into an escape route without knowing what went on inside of her mind.

"How do you know you're Raithean?" I kept my voice as level as I could, not wanting any accusation to seep into the question.

Turning her attention back to me before addressing the room, Aurelia recalled the two visions she'd walked through, connecting Shelton, Niall, and her mother to what brought her and her siblings here. I didn't question how she knew who the children were because a bead of acceptance grew in my chest at her story. I racked my brain for any memory of knowing about a similar type of magic in Raithe. The truth was, we'd been gone so long. Coupled with the fact we had spent many of those years accepting our fate in the human world, our memories of our homeland weren't as sharp as they used to be.

"What I really can't understand," she started, threading her fingers across the hem of her top, "is why?"

Her glistening blue eyes met mine. My first instinct was to frame her face in my palms, making a promise to her that we would get answers to all of her questions. I shoved it down. I needed to stay strong and logical for all of us, not just Aurelia.

Keeping the emotion from my voice as best as I could, my shoulders fell. "That's not something we can answer right now, but we will try."

Nodding gently, she mumbled something under her breath about her siblings as Trix cleared her throat.

"There is a 'but.'"

Whatever Trix was about to tell us, it was clear it pained her to do so. In unison, we offered her our complete attention as the tension rose.

"I don't know if you can come back through." Trix directly addressed Aurelia as I felt Xav shift in agitation from the other side of the sofa. An action I'd rarely seen from my eternally composed brother.

Out of the corner of my eye, I noted Aurelia's brow drop in confusion. "What do you mean?"

Trix glanced between my brothers and I before turning her attention back to Aurelia, speaking as if no one else was in the room. "I think we can find a portal, and I definitely know you can go through it, but there is a high chance the portal will seal once you pass through, meaning you wouldn't be able to come back here. To England. Whatever these portals are, or how they operate, I sensed a very strong magic pulsing through your visions."

I couldn't stay silent any longer. "Can't she just open the portal and let us walk through?"

The annoyance in my tone was clear. I also realised I'd delivered it in a way that came off as if I didn't want Aurelia to come with us. I did, but that would be her choice to make, not ours. I turned to her hoping my delivery hadn't affected her. Aurelia gave no indication of being hurt.

Trix relaxed into the chair behind her and said, "No. It looks like the curse fixer here will be part of the deal. Particularly because we don't know enough about the portal operation. She would need to go back to Raithe too."

Aurelia tensed beside me. "Look." Trix must have also sensed the rising tension in the room. "This is huge. There are a lot of things we need to figure out. What we do know is that Aurelia is the key to getting you boys home."

Did Aurelia want to go with us? It would be a world she wouldn't have any recollection of, but we would guide her. I'd given up on the prospect of home so long ago but now that it was at our fingertips, I salivated at the possibility, and I wanted nothing more than to throw Aurelia over my shoulder and march her back with us.

Her leg grazed mine as she shifted uncomfortably. The idea of showing her the never-ending beauty of a fresh snowfall in Hiema heated the dismantled organ in my chest. An intense urge bubbled up to shout about everything we could give her in Raithe, more than she has ever known in this world. That we could be the family she always deserved but never had. But I kept my mouth shut, I knew that wasn't what she needed right now.

The tension I felt in Aurelia grew into a tremble racing through her body. The movements shot concern through my chest. Aurelia was subjected to a lot in her life. Most of which we may never know the full extent of. Now she had a chance at freedom, of building a life of her own and this new information placed her in a position with little to no choice, as she had experienced too many times.

I wouldn't take away another decision from her ever again. Knowing now that we had the chance to get home, to bring revenge on what happened to our family and Raithe wasn't enough to turn me against her. She was more than just the key to our return; she was now the fire in my blood. A realisation that should have frightened me. If anything, the desire for her I'd tried so hard to bury deep inside me only pulsed more vibrantly.

Her body shook with more force as each second ticked by. I needed to give her comfort. I reached out my hand to rest on her knee but before I could make contact, she shot off the sofa, bounding toward the front door. I jumped up, trailing her without a second thought. She made it through the door before she began to sway on her feet. Her arms floated into the air as her legs gave way, sending her toward the ground. Before her body could crumble completely, I had her in my arms.

I stayed outside, letting the cool evening air kiss our cheeks as Aurelia's eyes move beneath her lids. I counted one, two, three, long breaths before her eyes peeled open, staring deep into my own.

"You don't have to keep picking me up," she breathed.

"I will pick you up every time you fall."

The admission was laced with more than one meaning. As much as I wanted to pull it back, to continue to try to distance myself from this woman, I let it fall between us.

"What about my brother and sister, Mads?"

My heart broke at the despair laced in her voice. "We'll figure it out."

The four words delivered in the most soothing tone I could offer were all I could give her. At least for the time being.

As I carried her back inside, appreciating the feel of her body in my arms again, I inhaled the comforting smell of the lilac soap infused with the scent of her skin. Before I could pause to revel in the moment further, Rock bounded up the porch, trotting through the front door as if he knew he was needed now. Shaking myself out of the intoxicating trance, I walked back inside and set Aurelia on the sofa as Fox shoved a cup of tea into her hands.

Trix stepped forward, bag strung across her shoulder as she looked to each of us before addressing only Aurelia again. "Well, I've got a lot of digging to do but what I need from you right now is for you to rest. Yes?"

From behind the steaming mug, Aurelia nodded in agreement. No chance in hell any of us were going to let her overexert herself again. Rock jumped up next to Aurelia, circling twice before settling down as close as possible. For a moment, I envied the fox, my lip curling in a jealous sneer I directed at him. Rock cast me a swift side eye before laying his head on Aurelia's lap in silent victory. Little shit.

"I'll be back tomorrow." Trix confirmed. "And hopefully with some new discoveries." She addressed the room with a wag of her eyebrows before moving toward the front door. I walked her out just as Fox moved to Aurelia. "You should go lie down."

It was clear both of my brothers were also concerned about Aurelia's current mental and physical state. I said my goodbye to Trix before walking back to Aurelia, my steps sure, and lifted her into my arms. Thankfully, Aurelia didn't protest this time, letting her head rest on my shoulder and keeping silent as I carried her up to my room. The instinct to brush a kiss across her brow shot through me like lightning. Tamping it down, I moved gracefully through the room to her side of the bed. *Her side of the bed? When did that happen?*

Without a word, I waited for Rock to jump onto the bed and settle down at her feet before leaving her alone to discuss the new revelations with my brothers. The urge to stay, to watch her, kept me in the doorway, watching as she snuggled in deeper, pulling the blanket in close. I ground my teeth and shook my head, walking away. I'd come check on her soon. Frequently, if only for my sanity.

Xav and Fox stood in the kitchen already, leaning against the counter, as if they were waiting for me. Fox moved, bringing over one of our favourite bottles of brandy and three glasses as soon as he heard me enter. My brothers worked in companionable silence, Xav pouring the amber liquid into the glasses that Fox held out to him.

We had all lost so much on that final day in Hiema. Not only our loved ones, but pieces of ourselves. The thought that I could offer them that level of healing and redemption pulsed in the back of my throat.

I took the glass Fox offered before raising it. "To whatever comes next."

Fox and Xav clinked their glasses to mine, repeating the words in unison.

Being the eldest, and rightful King of Hiema, I should've led the serious discussion awaiting us, but it was Xav, the ever apparent fundamental diplomat, who took charge.

"Whatever comes next," he started, repeating the toast I'd only just made, "it is her decision."

With no hesitation, Fox and I both nodded in agreement.

"We don't know everything that she's been through," he continued, "but she's one of us now."

Fox chuckled. "It seems, brother, she's always been one of us."

Xav nodded once. "What a twist in our little tale."

A twist indeed. I'd felt the pull to Aurelia since she'd arrived, but my stubborn mind wanted to think of her a thief, a liar, and of little significance to us in this world or any other. The truth was now in front of us, squashing any misconception I'd had about the golden-haired conundrum. The list of outstanding questions was long, but we at least knew the next step.

Leaning forward, I placed my elbows on the table, twirling the glass between my fingertips; the liquid swirled, holding my attention a moment before I spoke, "We need to make it very clear to her that this is *her* choice."

Fox tipped his glass toward me in understanding, before downing the rest of the contents. Shoving back from the table, he left his glass in the sink before turning toward the stairs.

"Where are you going?" I shot toward him.

Craning his neck toward me, a ghost of a smile lingering on his lips. "That's all we need to know for now, gentlemen. We let Aurelia decide and then we go from there."

Then, he moved toward his bedroom. I turned back to Xav to find him smiling behind his brandy. Today was filled with surprises, but Fox being the voice of reason may have been the one to haunt me the most.

"Bea, what the actual fuck?" I didn't try to hide the wrath in my words and only hoped the use of the name she preferred us to call her would snap her out of whatever trance she was in.

The sounds of chaotic movement on the floor below had jolted me out of bed and away from the warm body at my back. I looked out over the railing to find the living room in utter shambles. Books covered every available service, some opened to specific pages while others stayed closed, stacked high. The end tables were littered with unidentifiable potions, pots of ink spilling at the sides, and loose papers covered in foreign symbols.

The light peeking through the front window was fresh, indicating it wasn't too far past sunrise. What was she doing here so early and in such a state?

Taking the stairs two at a time, I stepped over unidentified clutter, gradually moving toward Trix. "Bea?" Xav's concerned voice came from the top of the stairs. He wasted no time in joining the mayhem.

"What's happening?" He addressed us both before hopping over a stack of books to stand directly in front of her. "Are you okay?"

Up to that point, my focus honed in on the disaster coating our living room and not the woman behind said chaos. Shifting my gaze to Trix, I found her already wild hair in further tangles with curls sticking both straight up and to the sides. Her honey brown eyes were wide in severe concentration, pinging back and forth between the books laid out in front of her. Her madness evident as she sat in a chair that was turned over and squatted down on the back at an odd angle.

Xav took Trix's face into his hands gently, pulling her attention to him. "Bea, be with us. What is going on?"

Footsteps on the stairs behind me indicated that both Fox and Aurelia had woken to the commotion and joined us in the dishevelled room.

Trix's gaze was erratic, bouncing through various parts of the room before eyeing me and then settling her stare on the man in front of her. Taking a deep breath, a calculated but victorious smile spread across her face. "I found a map."

"A map? Of what?" Fox hadn't bothered to put a shirt on in his hurry to get down to the action, and I noticed Aurelia giving him a once over. I thought about dragging my baby brother back up the stairs myself and ordering him to remain clothed around her at all times. *What was this alpha male attitude?*

"The portals. I found a map of portals." Trix's voice broke me from the sudden onset of jealousy.

Shifting his hands down to hers, Xav gently pried the book from her hands, guiding her to stand up, taking a more comfortable seat on the sofa. I did my best to clear a path, making it easier to direct Bea towards it.

With her elbows in our hands, Xav and I smoothly guided Trix down to the sofa. "Now, why don't you back up a couple of steps and tell us how you got here." Xav sat down next to her as he attempted to coax a reasonable explanation for her revelation.

"I walked. Like I always do." Trix's matter-of-fact answer brought a chuckle from someone behind me. Given the lightness in the sound, I assumed it was Aurelia.

Xav took Trix's hand in his own. "No, love, tell us how you found the map."

Eyes shifting from Xav to the book he'd pulled from her grasp, she said, "Oh!" Laughing, Trix put her hand to her forehead. "I haven't slept much."

Fox sat down on the other side of Trix, directly on a book or two and placed his arm around her shoulders. "Much? Or not at all?"

"Maybe not at all? I found a lead and couldn't stop."

"Let's start at the beginning, shall we?"

"Don't speak to me like some helpless damsel, Xav. I'm just a bit sleep deprived. Not an idiot."

I shifted some of the books from an armchair, offering it to Aurelia before repeating the action for myself. Kicking off her boots, Trix leaned into Fox's embrace, softly settling her head on his shoulder before shutting her eyes. "Maybe I should get a bit of sleep first."

"Trix!" My bellow delivered more harshly than I anticipated. "Don't you dare!"

Amusement sparked in her eyes as she lifted her head. "Calm down o'grumpy one. I was just joking."

Shifting her head from Fox's shoulder, she leaned back and breathed out her explanation, "When I got home last night, I started going through some of the books I know best, hoping I could find a spell I may have forgotten about. The spell would have to be powerful to break through whatever wards the curse has wrapped around them."

"A few hours passed with nothing standing out, until I remembered you three were sent here with a few things."

"Yes, Trix. You also have to remember those books are useless. We've been through them a thousand times. So have you." I reminded her, temper having cooled slightly.

"Yes, rightful king of Hiema, true. But what if it was actually something right in front of us?"

Leaning forward, I rested my elbows on my knees, soaking in each word leaving her mouth.

"Remember I took some of those books a few years ago when I was in one of my 'I'm going to get to the bottom of this' moods?" I raised my brow as my brothers and I nodded in acknowledgement.

"Well, I randomly had volumes one and four from the Raithe history, leaving two and three here. I started looking through the two volumes I had, finding the repetition of an unmarked map."

"Unmarked map?" Fox questioned. "No Trix, we checked. Every map in those volumes is marked."

Looking Fox up and down without moving her head, she was clearly not impressed with the interruption. "Wrong. There are two — one in the first volume and one in the fourth. The maps are so small it's easy to pass over them, thinking it was just another drawing of the Summer Kingdom, which is where the maps are sitting. So, I rushed over here to look through volumes two and three —" She glanced around the room, noting the absolute chaos she'd created. Shrugging it off, she continued, "Sure enough, the little map is in both of those volumes too."

"I don't understand." Genuine confusion flinted over Xav's face.

Trix let loose a predatory smile as she said, "Patience and you will."

CHAPTER 17

AURELIA

Tripping over scrolls, vials, and what I could only assume was a jar with animal organs, Bea finally had all four volumes under her arm. Fox and Xav rose to clear some of the chaos so Bea could sit in the centre, splaying out the volumes in no particular pattern. "The individual maps, when combined, form a larger map." She placed the volumes to overlap one another, the separate, insignificant maps combining to form a larger design.

Out of the corner of my eye, Mads tilted his head towards the sprawling guide in front of us. "What does this show us?"

Without looking up, Bea continued to pull the pages together as closely as she could, taking care not to damage the almost ancient texts. "It's a map of England."

The room dulled into a gentle silence, the crumpling of the pages the only noise echoing through the cabin. *Why would a magical, parallel world have a map of England hidden inside of it?*

"The map of England, my dear bears, presents the portal locations."

I froze. This was actually happening. A part of me, a large part, had thought even if I could open a portal, I didn't really believe we would ever find them. Especially since we confirmed the portals were magically sealed.

A pang of anxiety flickered across my toes before sending the numbing sensation across my feet, settling at my ankles. Swallowing down the expected fear, I pushed it away as best as I could in the hopes that I could ignore the anxiety. I did my best to mask my face with indifference, not wanting the panic to echo through the room.

"The portal locations? So, you're saying we now know where the portals to Raithe are?" Xav's voice was low and even, showing none of the emotion he may actually be experiencing.

"Correct." Bea still refused to meet anyone's eyes, busying herself with perfecting the fragments of the map. Fox, seeming annoyed with her fidgeting, leaned down to place his hands on hers. "Bea." His voice reflected Xav's calm. "Are you saying you know where we need to go to get home?"

Taking a long, slow breath, Bea finally met his gaze. "That's what I'm saying."

The weight of Bea's discovery hovered over my head, not quite touching...yet. Looking around at the expectant faces, I knew something more should be said. I should be the one to take the next step. I was the very key to get them through the newly found portals. I was the one to unlock the curse.

The beating in my chest intensified as the anxious tingles catapulted through my legs, up my torso, and down through my arms. My fingers needed to move. I grabbed the end of my shirt, twisting it between my fingers while hundreds of scenarios began running through my head, not giving me the time to slow down my heart rate. My breathing.

Standing, I took a step away from the group, attempting to ground myself with the oak beneath my toes. It didn't work. The edges of my sight blurred, my present mixed with my future, and uncertainty ricocheted my body and mind toward the panicked abyss. Going to Raithe would change my life and my world, forever. Was I prepared for something so monumental?

Did I want it?

For so long, the thought of another life was so far away, I'd stopped letting myself believe it was ever possible. Then, I went and stabbed Shelton, found this cabin and its inhabitants, ones who continued to show me more kindness in the weeks I'd known them than anyone had given me in my entire life.

The knowledge that I could be something more wasn't what took up most of the chaos tumbling through my mind. I wasn't from the human realm. I was from this magical world, just as the bears were. My parents, the only two people I'd known to be my parents, even if the way they treated me could never be defined as mother and father, weren't who I'd known them to be.

And then my siblings, if they were in fact my real siblings, came through that portal with me. Archer was already lost to me physically. And Eva? We had our differences, but I still held her in my heart. Did I now have an obligation to inform her of our past?

The weight of the discovery hung heavy, moving back up my arms towards the top of my head, whispering against my shoulders, closing in on my throat. I needed to move away from it. Away from them.

Without another thought, I pivoted on my bare feet and walked steadily towards the front door. A faint bellowing of my name followed me out as I lunged for the handle, wrenching the door open before breaking into a sprint. Running past the oak tree boundary, I didn't even stop to think of any potential danger awaiting me in the woods. With Niall and Shelton dead, at least the main threat was gone.

My breaths were stunted, unable to inhale deep enough. The further I moved into the forest, it still wasn't enough. I couldn't fill my lungs fast enough, full enough, my heart hammering against my chest urging me on. Away. To keep moving. Panic slithered up my spine and throat simultaneously, giving me no room to block it from overtaking my entire body. If it continued, I would lose control physically. The only thought I could focus on was the need to move further, faster, matching the short breaths to the fire in my lungs and the burn in my legs.

My feet continued forward, and as I made it to the river, I ran alongside it, willing it to be an old friend, keeping me safe from predators. Rocks stabbed into the bottom of my feet, and I didn't care if they broke my skin. I was too deep, my mind teetering on the edge of the abyss since I'd stabbed Shelton, and with the realisation I could be someone of importance, I fell face first into the inky darkness.

How could I claw my way out?

Perspiration trickled down my temple, falling in line with my emotional and mental descent. Shifting my focus from my feet to the forest around me, I didn't recognise my surroundings. The trees felt sparser. Less inviting. The trickle of the river felt far behind me. As I turned my head to study where I'd come from my toes caught a camouflaged branch, launching my body to the path beneath my feet. I didn't react fast enough; my hands didn't break my fall until right before my face would've met the forest floor. The impact sent shock waves rolling up my arms, shooting down through my chest.

Breathing heavy, I stared down at the ground now inches away from my face. Tears streamed down my face, my mind full as too many emotions warred inside of me.

You are the key to breaking the curse.

The words echoed through my mind on a loop, the hopeful look the brother's shared etching itself into my soul. How could I, the abused and broken woman, be anything more? I'd spent so much of my life trying to survive the men that broke me, and the numbing, the fear, all bled out on the floor when I'd killed them, nothing remained to hold those memories in their cages. Self-reflection could be a cruel mistress and I wanted her gone.

Unsure of how long I stayed in the position, I was locked inside my head, examining the memories that had surfaced, willing and wanting for everything to quiet down. It was all too loud.

"Aurelia!"

Faintly, I could hear Xav calling my name, the worry laced in it. Opening my eyes, not remembering when I'd closed them, I pushed as much of the little physical strength I had left into my hands, willing my body to comply and at least get me off the ground. I moved into a sitting position before I caught sight of Xavier's feet bounding toward me. My heart sank, hoping for Mads. But I shook my head, thankful it was the middle brother. I didn't need whatever I felt towards Mads to mingle with everything else.

Strong hands gripped my face, pulling my eyes up to meet a very concerned Xav. "Are you alright?" He breathed heavily, most likely sprinting out the door not long after I did.

Not able to muster the energy for words just yet, I let another tear fall as I nodded once. The gesture must've been sufficient as Xav gently wrapped his fingers around my arms to hoist me off of the ground. He guided me back towards a log, encouraging me to sit down with light, soothing sounds. I complied. My heart rate had finally begun to slow down, welcoming a calmness to now wade through the destruction of my mind, my memories. They were still staring at me but were thankfully much quieter.

Rock bounded up to us, taking a seat directly in front of me and scanning the surrounding area. The sight of my furry friend reassured me, my fingers longing to touch the soft fur behind his ears.

"Aurelia, what happened?" Xav's tone took on its usual soothing melody. He sat down next to me, careful not to touch my anxiety riddled body, no doubt thinking it would do more harm than good to offer physical comfort. This was unchartered territory for all of us.

"I —" Speaking took so much of the little energy I had left. I knew hiding from this wasn't going to do anyone good, so I pushed on. "I'm not sure. Everything seemed to just come crashing down. It felt hard to breathe."

Chancing a glance at the man next to me, his gaze was focused on the forest floor as he nodded his head, understanding laced through the gesture.

"You know what that is like?" The sudden urge to dig inside his head lit up my body, pushing small amounts of energy back in.

"I do." His warm, chestnut gaze met mine, filled with a regret I'd never experienced before. Sensing I would lead into an additional question, Xav took a deep, cleansing breath before continuing.

"When we came here, our entire world had just burned. Mads, he was simple. He just closed up. Built us a life here so we could survive. Not thrive, necessarily, more just continue to breathe each day. I don't know if he ever had hope we'd go home. We never spoke about it. Those conversations were always me, Fox, and eventually Bea.

"Fox though, he took it the hardest. Finding a new woman each night, drinking himself into oblivion. He'd always been stubborn and mischievous. Those traits morphed into a completely different persona. It got so bad, we nearly lost him. A few times."

"Why didn't you try to stop him?" I asked, wanting to understand.

"How could we take away the only things numbing his pain? We all dealt with the losses and the curse differently. Not one of us had the energy to help each other grieve or heal. Mads closed off, Fox found a mask, and I..." Xav paused in memory.

"...I pretended nothing happened. My parents were still alive, ruling over Hiema, Orsa safe with them, and Mads, Fox, and I just took an extended trip here."

The hurt I felt for the brothers lodged in my throat. I swallowed it down, just as I had done so many times in my life. The tainted memories were part of me, and I always knew one day I'd have to face them. The bears, too, were haunted by the memories of their past.

Gently, I placed my hand over his. "Xav..."

He gave me a light squeeze. "I don't need your pity, Aurelia. While I do appreciate it. I can't bear it."

Xav brought his hands to the sides of my face, lowering his voice. "What I need — what we need, is you. I truly believe you are the key to our salvation, the bringer or our opportunity for redemption. Whether you believe it or not, you are here for a reason, Aurelia."

Thankful for his honesty, I decided to give him some of my own vulnerability in return. "It's hard to believe in yourself when you have no self left. If everything you've ever been was stripped away from you, leaving only a shell of a human, how do you ever find acceptance of yourself? How do you give yourself any semblance of confidence or respect when all you've ever known is the opposite?"

Xav lowered his hands, digesting each word as I fed them to him. A gentle smile played on his lips.

"I'd say, curse killer, you start by taking yourself back, which is exactly what you've been doing since you stabbed that Shelton prick. You decided, right then, you were no longer going to be used, beaten, broken. The shell could heal and it could grow. Whether you know it or not, you're building back up the belief in yourself. Plus, you now have three amazing magical brothers and one crazy arse witch who believe in you too."

I knew he attempted to bring some light into this darkness. I smiled at the gesture.

"But what of my history? Of being Raithean? My parents, or who I thought were my parents? And my siblings? There is so much to unpack, Xav."

Gentling his voice further, he placed his hand over mine. "There is. But, if you let us, we can do that together.

"No matter what, this is your decision, Aurelia. Whether or not you help us, is completely your choice. All I can hope for is if you do decide to break the curse, in return, we can provide you the one thing you've always been looking for."

Xav was a strong empath, I was certain, but how could he possibly know what my one true desire was? Had always been?

Eyes locked on his, I swallowed deeply. "And what is that?"

Another soft smile graced his face, one with more intent than I could begin to fathom. "A home."

A home. A simple enough thought for most except one thing I'd never had and always craved. There were some aspects of a home with Archer. The comfort and support he brought died when he disappeared. I yearned for so much more. That gentle pull resonated in my belly, urging me to believe. To trust. To open my mind to magic and a better life.

A home.

Quirking my lip into a half smile, the anticipation on Xav's face was almost physical, "Alright then. Let's break this fucking curse."

Xav whooped, sending the birds above scattering as he hopped off his log and pulled me into a bear hug. A laugh escaped me, feeding the fuel in my belly. Mads may be indifferent toward me, Fox provided a light in my dark, and Xav was giving me a shred of something I never thought possible — hope.

The walk back to the cabin was done on unsteady legs, the effect of the panic lingering through me. Mentally and physically I was tapped out but that wasn't going to stop me from hiding the smile sitting freely on my face.

Xav refused to stop bouncing with excitement, relaying to me all the wonders of Raithe and Hiema, it was difficult to hide it. He babbled on, not stopping as he helped me over tricky logs, comforting me in the fact I could still change my mind at any time and reiterating the choice would always be on the table. My table.

When we finally made it back, both Fox and Maddox were on the covered porch. Mads sat in a cloud of anger so thick it was almost edible. It wasn't until he noticed the holes in my clothes along with the various scrapes across my body, did he unfold his arms and stalk towards me, his expression a blend of concern and determination. "What the hell happened?"

Rather than recounting my panic induced escape, I offered him a reassuring smile. "I tripped and fell."

As the words left my mouth, I knew how false they sounded. "I was running and didn't see a large root sticking out of the ground. I caught myself right before my face hit the dirt." I held up my palms to confirm my story with the dried blood littering my hands and wrists.

Mads studied me quickly, cautiously before turning and motioning me towards the house, disappearing inside. Briefly, I glanced at Fox, layers of uncertainty spread across his face. Xav and I had decided I would deliver my decision to the rest of the group, no doubt leaving both Mads and Fox in a state of unwanted suspense. A pang of happiness hit me momentarily. I'd never held power in any situation and it felt wrong to ignore it now.

Mads already waited on the sofa, strips of gauze and hot water sat beside him. I made my way to him as I took in the now clean living room. Bea was nowhere to be seen and all the books previously littering the floor and all other available surfaces were back in their rightful place.

"Where's Bea?" I asked.

"She went home," Fox chimed in from behind me. "She needed to get some sleep. She'll most likely wake us all again tomorrow."

Taking a seat across from me, Fox's expression still showed his wariness. Mads lightly cleaned my hands with a mesmerising combination of precision and care. The ache of the cuts eased with each gentle sweep of the cloth. It amazed me how such a large and beastly man could show so much tenderness. I relished the contact of his skin against mine. An act which always left me with full body tingles.

Xav made his way into the room, sitting next to Fox and nodding for me to make my move. It should have terrified me. The announcement I was about to make would change not only the lives of the men in front of me, but mine as well. Everything I knew would change.

Clearing my throat gently, I spoke the words with confidence, "I have decided I'd like to help you."

Mads froze. A rather strange noise left the back of Fox's throat, almost between a cough and a whimper. Xav sat coolly already knowing my heart and the decision I would make.

"You're sure?" Mads questioned.

I looked at the man next to me, shocked at his soft tone. His words had never been delivered so considerately, as though the answer would bring him immense pain. I realised it wasn't pain that would find him, but solace. He must've dreamt about their return for years, and somehow, I could be the one to lay it at his feet. The power I'd felt surged. Another foreign emotion.

His eyes didn't meet mine as he continued to stare at my open palm on his lap. Letting the power move forward, I gently placed my first two fingers under his chin, lifting his gaze to my own. A thousand unspoken words sat between us. Many of which I wanted to explore more than anything. Whatever was between us, we now had time to figure it out.

"Yes," I assured.

Mads opened his mouth to respond, before he could, Fox launched out of his chair, throwing me over his shoulder and proceeding to dance around the room while hollering an indecipherable song at the top of his lungs. The pure joy emanating from him threw me into a fit of laughter. The pain in my belly was a welcome one.

"We're going home! We're going home!"

Fox danced with me through the living room into the back of the house and outside where he finally relented and set me gently on my feet. Tears of undefined happiness poured down my cheeks as my laughter carried through the trees. Without letting me catch my breath, Fox scooped me back into his arms, this time in a hug, and whispered, "Thank you."

Setting me down once more, he looked behind me, causing his face to drop into a half smile. Without another word, he walked back up the steps to the house. Turning to see the cause of his departure, I found Maddox standing before me, chest heaving, a clear effort on his part to appear calmer than he was.

"This is your decision."

"I know."

"You owe us nothing."

"I know."

"You most likely can't come back."

"I know."

"It will be dangerous."

"I know."

"Everything you know will change."

I paused to contemplate his statement. Part of it was true, yet he was forgetting one thing, "You won't."

He studied me, arms at his sides as his fists kept curling in and back out.

"I will. You don't know who I am in our world."

Huffing, I said, "To be honest, Maddox, I'm not sure I know you in this world." I gave him my back, suddenly self-conscious of the words I spoke.

"In the last month, I've gotten to know you at least a little. Xav and Fox too. And you'll all be there with me."

I turned to face him once more. I needed to deliver the next part directly to his face. "I have to believe it won't be so bad. I have to believe whatever awaits you, them, me, on the other side, it's better than anything I've ever known here."

Mads took one slow, calculated step towards me. His chest still moved heavily, the motions slowing slightly, "I can promise you, it will be."

"There will be a war," I confirmed.

"I know."

"I'm not a soldier."

"I know."

"I can't give you anything other than getting through the door," I paused, keeping my eyes fixed on his. "Am I still worth it?"

Mads took another step towards me, only inches separating us. "Worth it?"

"The trouble. The obligation I will bring to your life there. Because you sure as shit better not abandon me over there Maddox. I may not be a strong fighter, but I'm not afraid to kill a man who deserves it."

A cocky smile grew on his face, a playful lilt sat within it. "I know."

I let my face drop, "I bleed chaos. Everything I touch, I destroy."

Slowly, Mads lifted his fingers to gently brush a piece of hair off my face, drenched in tears and sweat, his smile never wavering, as he tucked it behind my ear "In that case, Goldie, I cannot wait for you to bleed for me."

With the admission, Mads returned to the house, leaving me at the bottom of the steps, burning from the inside out.

Chapter 18

Maddox

"I'm also a Fox you can stroke."

Aurelia chucked a cushion at Fox who had just walked into the living room as she pet Rock on the sofa. She was still getting used to the sporadic visits from the creature, given his affinity for disappearing. Although the ball of fur had been around more often since Aurelia arrived, and with the events of the last few days, the fox refused to leave her side. I knew she planned on taking the animal with us, she just hadn't found the courage to broach the subject with us yet.

She exuded comfort in her body language as she twirled Rock's soft coat between her fingers, as I daydreamed about what it would be like to be on the receiving end of her gentle caress. Before I could dive too deep into my thoughts, Trix and Xav stalked in. "Good morning, buttercup. How are you feeling?"

Aurelia's silent expression told Trix more than I could attempt to decipher. Looking back at the witch, her face softened before she gently nodded once.

"So, are we good to go on with the curse breaking?"

A smile curled on Aurelia's lips. Trix had explained the heavy and intricate detail of the curse bluntly. The witch had a way of delivering words evoking either terror or comfort. For the most part, it appeared Aurelia only experienced the comforting aspect, which I was grateful for. We had a lot of ground to cover over the next few weeks, or months, and the less fear she felt, the better.

Trix took a seat next to Rock, patting him on the head once before addressing the rest of the room, "Alright, let's get started!"

My eyes stayed trained on Aurelia as her smile disappeared. It was clear a thought was running through her head, and silently, I urged her to voice it.

Thankfully, I didn't have to wait long. "Bea, if you aren't from Raithe, does that mean you aren't coming with us?"

"She may not be Raithean, but she's still coming with us," Fox interjected, shoving a small cake into his mouth, no sense of manners trickling through.

Trix rolled her eyes. "We made a gentleman's agreement a long time ago that if they were to go back, I'd go with them."

"And you want to go?" Aurelia scratched Rock behind the ears, his eyes closing in contented bliss.

"There isn't anything for me here. My Mother died a long time ago. I've got no other family besides these arseholes. Plus, I know more about their kingdom than they do," she said as she flung her finger in my direction. "So, they need me."

"And we want you," Fox added with a sultry wink.

I chuckled, catching Aurelia's attention briefly before she shifted back to Trix. "Didn't you say you were connected to Raithe?"

Trix nodded. "My grandmother came from Raithe, back when the portals were more easily accessible. Well, for a witch."

With a wink, she continued, "It will be like going home for me too, even if it's a home I've never known."

I turned my attention back to Aurelia as she processed Trix's answer. Focusing on her spectacular cerulean gaze, I let my mind drift. Aurelia was enchanting in such a way that I never wanted to leave her side. But the deal I made with myself when she burst into our lives still stood, firmer now given I knew some of her past. If she held any attraction toward me, I wasn't going to force it from her. She'd need to come to those realisations on her own. Now she was going with us, I knew keeping her at a distance would grow even more difficult than it already was.

Trix cleared her throat bringing the room's attention back to her and Aurelia's eyes away from me. "A few things, gentle folk. One, we need to decide which portal we want to attempt first. Obviously the closest one appeared to be the easiest option. Given its location, I wasn't sure if we should."

"Where is it?" Aurelia's curiosity flared without worry.

My brothers and I made a conscious effort to keep our eyes from Aurelia, leaving Trix to deliver the news.

"It's in Huxley."

Huxley. The town which took everything from her. The town whose residents felt it their right to break her. Even with Shelton and Niall meeting their ends, the place itself still haunted her. "No."

No further words needed. We'd already agreed to support whatever decision she'd made and I, for one, would walk to the other side of the world for a portal if we had to.

"It is settled then." Xav cut in. His empathetic soul seeped into the room.

"The next one is in Elvesdon. It's about a two day ride from here so we'll need to do some route planning, supplies, the lot."

"Fox and I can handle the supplies." Fox nodded in agreement to Xav's suggestion.

"Great! Number two is, we need to decide when. Timing will depend on how number three pans out."

A growl escaped my throat. "What is number three, Trix."

A command, not a question.

She swallowed, displaying a nervousness at my tone.

"Number three is an Alegra stone."

Silence filled the room, leaving a mixed look of fear and confusion upon Aurelia's face. I hated the combination of those emotions emanating from her.

"Are you kidding me?" The aggression in my words couldn't be ignored.

"Now, before you freak out, oh terrifying one, I happen to know where one is hidden."

"Then why, *witch* don't you have it now?" I was fully aware of the power my body exuded.

"It's in a cabin. My mother put it there and spelled me against it." She rolled her eyes as she tutted.

"What is an Alegra stone?" The curious lilt of Aurelia's voice echoed through the room, trying its best to soothe my irritation.

Bea sighed, "It's just a safety precaution but we will need it to get to Raithe."

"Why did she spell it?" Xav's calm approach brought the room to a more levelled energy.

"Because the crazy woman thought I'd do something stupid with it."

All at once we cocked a brow at her, confirming we agreed with her mother's decision.

Huffing, Trix patted Rock on the head once more before rising. "I'll get you a map. I'm going to get some auto spells going so we are prepared for our journey. Fox, Xav, get to planning and supplies."

She turned first to Aurelia, "You," then to me, "and you can get the stone."

I pulled in a breath as my nostrils flared in frustration. Before we could question Trix further about the imminent plan, she was up and out the front door, offering only a swish of her hand in the air as a goodbye. Storming after her, I let my anger guide me.

"Bea!"

The witch turned, throwing an attempted look of confusion towards me. "Yes, oh frightful one?"

I stopped when the tips of my boots hit the tips of hers. "What do you think you are doing?"

Feigning boredom, she batted off my comment before turning to continue on to wherever the hell she was going. That wasn't going to work for me. The witch was clever and did nothing without a reason. I gripped her upper arm and slowly turned her to face me again, silently waiting for a response.

"Fine." She huffed, irritated at my anger.

"There is something there, Maddox. If I have to force you two to spend time together, then so be it. Plus, I really do need Aurelia to get the stone."

My breathing stayed erratic, in tune to my displeasure. "Why?"

The word left my lips on a growl. She studied me silently for a few beats. "Because I think her being the key to opening the portal is more than just that."

We stood, eyes locked on one another as we both contemplated how much more to share. Trix pulled her arm from my grip, smoothing down her rumpled top.

"That woman has known a lot of pain, Maddox. Lack of choice. No control. All she's known from anyone, let alone men, is people asserting their dominance on her, for their own selfish needs. And I'm sorry she's never known tenderness. What she doesn't know is that she can find pleasure in dominance. Tenderness can be threaded in power. She needs to feel powerful. And the way you look at her, I know you want to be the one to help her understand those things. Those parts of her. You want to help her heal those broken and bruised pieces."

My breathing steadied further with each one of her words. I wanted, badly, to let them fuel my fire. What they did instead was plant a small seed of hope deep in my chest, readying it for harvest. What the fuck was that?

"You can deny it all you want, Mads. I know it. Xav knows it. Even Fox knows it."

Rubbing my hand over my face, the words sank further.

"You're afraid of her."

My eyes snapped back to Trix's. Her audacity to insinuate, let alone speak the actual words, pushed me into a state of shock.

"It's true. You're afraid of what she represents and what she could bring you."

I huffed. "Afraid to go home? Doubtful, Bea."

Stepping towards me slowly, she raised her hand to my chest. "No, Mads. Love. You're afraid of the love and compassion she will bring to your life."

I didn't have any more words for the witch. A sliver of my former self would have consumed her words like air. I had become so removed from any warming emotions; it was all just so hard to process.

"Bea!" The gentle lilt of Aurelia's voice echoed from behind me. I turned towards her. She'd put on boots and a coat, on a mission to go somewhere.

"Can I go with you?"

I turned back to Trix who offered me a smile so warm it sent fear through me. Fear that every single thing she said was coming true.

"Sure thing, buttercup." Trix held out her arm which Aurelia immediately looped her own through. They both turned to walk away before Trix threw me a glare over her shoulder. If what she said was true, I was completely and utterly fucked.

Aurelia and Trix returned to the cabin later in the evening, a number of parcels and satchels in tow. The plan was to saddle five horses, one for each of the travelling parties and then one extra for our packs.

Fox and Xav were spread over the dining table, ticking off items on a rather lengthy list, chatting amongst themselves while I focused on cooking. I knew my mood projected an uneasy film around the pleasant evening. My mind still processed all the things Bea had spewed, constantly trying to find a flaw in her theory. My traitorous brain kept coming up empty handed. I couldn't ignore that everything Bea said was true and burying what I felt for Aurelia would make it worse.

We enjoyed a mutton stew before finding ourselves back in the living room, sipping on a beautifully aged bottle of brandy Trix had decided to bring over. She'd realised it wasn't practical enough for her to bring with her, deciding instead to enjoy it before we departed. As the evening died down, I finally decided to speak, "Where's the map, Bea?"

A mouth full of brandy, she drank it down slowly before barking back, "Sorry?"

"The map. To the Alegra stone. You said you'd bring it."

"Yes, grumpy Gus. I brought it."

Pulling a small, folded piece of paper from her jacket pocket, she tossed it at my head with a huff of irritation. I bent down from my chair to scoop it up. The room waited silently as I studied the map.

"Bea," my ire oozed from the word, "this is a two day journey."

She chuffed, "No dear, it's a two day journey on foot. You can be there and back in a day on horseback."

Aurelia swallowed audibly and loud enough for the room to turn our focus to her.

'What is it?" Gentle Xav to the rescue.

I focused on her fingers as they began threading through the end of her jumper. A nervous tick I'd clocked early on in her time with us. She sighed before continuing, "I don't know how to ride."

Shame coasted through her words. Aurelia hung her head as I crumpled the paper, throwing it into the air before storming out of the room. A gruff, "fuck" followed in my wake.

"Don't mind him. He's in a super sour mood today." Fox chimed in. I hadn't gone far, only to the kitchen where I could still listen in on the conversation.

I hated that she may suffer shame. I hated that I hated it. Her low voice trailed into where I sat. "I can stay here. Help pack up."

"No, buttercup. I need you to go."

"Why?"

Trix explained her mother had not only spelled her against the storage shed, she'd also weaved the spell to keep men from getting in. They could walk in with a woman, but they couldn't open it themselves.

"You can ride double. I don't know what his problem is. It isn't a big deal." Fox voiced before finding me in a tense position, arms crossed. He shot me a look of annoyance before taking out the chair across from me and sitting down.

Trix and Xav did their best to change the topic of conversation, my mood hovering over them almost in a suffocating manner. Even from a distance I could sense it.

Fox leaned over the table, lowering his voice as he spoke, "What is your problem?"

I gave him my profile, refusing to speak like I was a child. I was hyper aware of the way my moods shifted me back to an age where pouting was acceptable.

"Go get the stupid stone and get back in a day. You aren't going to combust riding double with her."

Fuck if I wasn't. Even being in the same building as the woman set my blood on fire and my cock at attention the majority of the time. I looked at Fox from the corner of my eye before giving him a brief nod in agreement. Without another word, he rose from the table to return to the group in the other room.

"All set then. Goldie, you and Mads will make your way to the storage shed tomorrow. I'll pack you a few things just in case you get stuck."

As I stewed in my own irritation, my mind wandered to what Aurelia might be thinking. She may not want to spend an entire day with me either. I groaned just thinking about her arse nestled between my thighs, my cock rubbing across it with each gallop.

Uncrossing my arms, I couldn't stop my fists from clenching. I needed release before tomorrow, and it definitely wasn't going to come from the woman who caused the tightness in the first place. Without further thought, I stalked back into the living room, hooking my arm through Fox's who protested immediately as I dragged him out the front door.

"What the hell, Mads?"

Clenching my jaw, I refused to give him my eyes. If I did, he'd know exactly what I was out for.

"I need to hit something."

As the realisation hit, he let a smile brew on his lips. "You should have said so."

Without another word, we made our way to the training ring.

Chapter 19

Aurelia

"Are you ready, Goldie?"

I stood next to the barn as Fox secured a pack to the back of an enormous mahogany-coloured stallion. Having only been on a horse a few times in my life, dread sat heavily in my gut. Knowing how to ride a horse was a luxury I was never afforded. And now, I was most likely sitting in a saddle with Maddox Artos. A man I could neither love nor hate. The image of my back pressed against his chest was enough to throw me into a hot fit. One which wasn't unwelcome, per se, but was definitely inconvenient given his hostility towards me at the best of times.

Trying my best to gulp down the dread, I slowly approached Fox and the beast of a horse.

"Who is this?"

Fox threw on one of his, now trademark, cocky grins. "This, Goldie, is Ace."

I sniggered, not impressed in the slightest. "Why on earth would you name a magnificent beast like this, Ace?"

Tsking, Fox pulled the pack's straps down. "Mads won him in a card game. Ace seemed fitting."

"Well, a name like Ace is a bit of a waste."

"How is it a waste?" Fox had grabbed one of the grooming tools from a hook in the shed and began to brush Ace's mane, gently.

"If it were me and I had suddenly come into possession of a giant horse, I'd be a bit more creative, is all."

Fox eyed me suspiciously, the cocky grin still pasted on his mouth. "Pray tell, Goldie, what would your creativity come up with you would deem better?"

I thought about the question a moment, running a few names back and forth before finally answering, "Hercules."

Bursting out into laughter, Fox bent over to catch himself from falling in an absolute fit.

"What's wrong with Hercules?"

Trying hard to compose himself but failing miserably, Fox grumbled out something along the lines of, "tell that to Mads."

I didn't let Fox's teasing bother me. His light-hearted banter had become a natural part of our daily routine, and I would miss it if it were gone. I'd miss all three brothers, the first men showing me they did in fact respect me, even if it was in their own way. Xav with his kind heart and gentle approach, Fox with his humour, bringing light to so much darkness, and Mads, always asking for permission and healing my physical wounds. The bears had gotten so deep under my skin I had only just begun to realise they also helped me heal the invisible aches.

Smiling to myself, I took one slow step towards Fox and Ace. Fox immediately noticed the hesitation in my gait. "Are you afraid of horses?"

Looking at the gorgeous, deep brown of Ace's coat, I shook my head. Fox graciously gave me a few moments before he pushed, "What is it then?"

A hint of pity sat within his stare. I hated pity and felt Fox should know better than to offer it. Brushing it off and concluding honesty had thus far been the best policy, I shared, "I have only ridden a couple of times. It was never by myself, and I was very young."

Sensing my trepidation, Fox tried to offer words of encouragement. Before he could voice them, I shook them off. "It isn't so much being on the horse, it's also the fact I will be in close proximity with your eldest and grumpiest brother."

Fox chuckled in agreement, pushing the brush down Ace's right shoulder, offering me only a non-verbal response, I resonated, and I wanted to know more. "Why does he hate me so much?"

My voice, almost at a whisper, was filled with disappointment. Fox could sense it. Maybe Ace could too. The majority of my life I had despised the attention of men. I'd begun to realise that maybe Mads was different and maybe, his positive attention would be worth more than I ever thought I could have.

"He doesn't hate you, Goldie. He's afraid of you."

Fox's facial expression was so matter of fact it threw me off balance, as though it was a secret everyone knew apart from me.

"Afraid of me? Look at me Fox." I motioned down my body. "I'm a woman who has never shied away from a meal, with the muscle mass of a mouse. You've seen how horrible I am in training." I demonstrated my typical footwork which, if anything, had become worse the more we worked on it.

"I can't even tell my left foot from my right. What is there to be afraid of?"

Fox offered the quietest of chuckles before seriousness flooded his face. His eyes grew with concern. "Everything, Aurelia. There is everything to be afraid of."

Opening my mouth to respond in confusion, our brief conversation was interrupted by the arrival of Bea and Xav, with Rock trailing on their heels. He wouldn't be joining Mads and I today, but Fox had promised me he would look after him in my absence. I'd come to rely on my furry friend, and I couldn't help but think he felt the same way about me.

"Hello treacles. How are we doing this fine day?"

Bea, in an extra pleasant mood, walked over to Fox and planted a kiss on his cheek before repeating the action to me.

"Why the hell are you so chipper?" Fox asked in shock.

Bea stroked Ace's mane as she began to hum a tune, clearly keeping us on our toes.

"Buttercup." Still focusing on Fox's words, I hadn't even noticed Bea standing in front of me, seriousness written on her face.

"Take this," Bea grabbed my hand, gently placing a small piece of folded paper on my palm before curling her fingers over it. Looking to Bea for instructions, she simply patted my closed fist and turned to Mads who had joined us.

"Does she have everything?"

Mads' calloused tone lit something inside of me. Putting it down to the heat still simmering from the daydream, I waited as Bea gave him a silent instruction. Without even glancing at me, he patted Xav on the shoulder and barked, "Let's go."

I didn't know how to get on a horse, particularly one of Ace's size. Before the panic could grow, Fox gently nudged me forward, taking my hand in his and motioning to the stirrup, "Put your left foot there, and I'll give you a boost up."

Fox was almost intimately aware of my clumsiness so it comforted me to know he would be the one helping me up. Ignoring the thoughts of what would happen when Fox wasn't with us any longer, I placed my booted foot in the stirrup with a wave of unsteadiness. Fox must have sensed the unease and offered his other hand in support. Waving him off, I was determined to climb the creature even if it saw me on the ground a few times first. Gripping Fox's hand, I stepped firm in the stirrup and threw my right leg up and over with all of the energy I could conjure. "HA!" I shouted as I pulled my hand from Fox's to grip the pommel with both hands, unsure of how long I'd be able to stay atop Ace.

"Well done, Goldie."

Bea and Xav clapped from the other side of the clearing. Beaming, I felt the pride rise within me. Every single day away from Huxley brought new challenges and triumphs of different sizes. And every time I conquered one, the seed of self-worth was nourished.

Before I was able to relish in the achievement further, Mads mounted Ace, seating himself directly behind me. The pull of his weight caused me to slide back slightly, plastering my back to his chest just as I'd imagined. The spark lit, sending waves of heat all over my body. Tempted to unbutton the top of my tunic, I thought better of it. Removing my hands from the only thing that gave me any sense of safety wasn't the best idea at that moment.

"I need to grab the reins." His strong hands circled around me cautiously.

The calloused tone from earlier had disappeared and was replaced with a soothing whisper. Hot and cold.

"We'll be back later. If not, give us two days before you send a search party."

Without waiting for a response, Mads guided Ace forward, the rocking motion forcing my backside to rub against the thin fabric covering Mads' crotch. Biting back a groan, I closed my eyes hoping to rid myself of the physical need my body had in Mads' presence and the nausea I received from Ace's movements.

The first couple of hours of our journey were spent in silence. None of which was comfortable. The growing tension in my body had me on the edge. My two options were to either launch myself at Mads or to shove my hand down my trousers in the hope of relieving at least some of the ache.

Where did that come from?

I'd experienced sex before, always more out of necessity rather than for pleasure. When it had become apparent I would be groomed to be the perfect wife for Shelton, I'd started an affair with one of the local farmer's sons. Sex had been transactional. Nothing more. Self-pleasure was another story; it was one of the ways I'd felt I could hold on to at least a sliver of myself, knowing what the consequences of my impending marriage to Shelton would've been.

I counted Ace's hoof clomps to distract me from my thoughts and from the presence of Mads behind me. It had only lasted a few minutes before his hand had grazed my thigh as he moved the reins from his left to his right. So then, I'd closed my eyes to focus on the sounds of the forest, willing the natural orchestra to pull me out of this haze. My body shifted and Mads let out a tiny growl from his throat, my eyes flying open. The sound itself was sex. I couldn't wipe it away.

After those few agonising hours, Mads made the decision to stop at a stream to have a quick refresh given my inexperience in travelling long distances by horse. Gratefulness for the break was fleeting given Mads' offer to help me down off of Ace. A normal gesture coming from Xav or even Fox. With Mads? I was in trouble.

Following his direction, I slowly pulled my right leg over Ace, using Mads' strong hands as guidance as I slid down the side of the horse. An act of force made my body lightly graze his.

When my feet were finally on the ground, I found Mads' breathing had also deepened, as had the hold he had on my waist. His hands there felt familiar, and our eyes locked in a penetrating gaze. Thankfully, Mads broke our eye contact by clearing his throat, almost in anger. *Why was he angry? He's the one who keeps rubbing against my arse.*

"You can relieve yourself over there." Mads pointed to a large bush a good distance away. I silently thanked him for the seclusion, shuffling away from him as quickly as I could, a difficult task given my legs already felt dead from the short ride.

How would I make it an entire day on a horse with the most beautiful man behind me, the consistent contact making the ache between my legs grow. It reminded me of the barn cat we had as children. who would bump and rub its head on my legs, begging for attention. *Fantastic. Now I'm comparing his dick to a cat? What is wrong with me?*

I took care of private business and walked back towards Ace where I found Mads standing to his side. Slowing my steps as I got closer, it was only then I gulped down the apprehension of getting back up on the horse. A thought which left my mind quickly once Mads offered me his hand. Without hesitation, I placed my hand in his and took the same position I had when Fox had assisted. The difference with Mads was my hand now felt like an inferno. I couldn't help but wonder if he experienced this heat too.

Luckily my clumsiness still hadn't roared its head, allowing me to safely situate myself back on the horse where I experienced only a moment of solace before Mads' thighs caged my own once more.

"We are halfway there," Mads' gruff declaration tickled my ear as he took the reins in both hands this time, caging me against him. I couldn't deny I liked it. I did, however, try to deny I wanted more. Surely no good could come of this. Whatever this was.

Instead of offering him words, I made a strange rumbling noise he must have taken as acknowledgement. *Great. The physical sensation has blown logic and words right out of your head. Keep it up, Aurelia.*

Scolding myself, oddly, was an effective method to somewhat ignore the heat continuing to build between us. Somewhat.

A breeze drifted through as we found ourselves moving deeper into a much denser forest. Each part of the forest brought a new charm and sense of adventure.

What could have been days later with the way my body burned, Mads finally pulled Ace to a stop. Looking across the small glen we'd found ourselves in, I spotted the run down cabin. It wasn't much bigger than the woodshed back at the bear's property. My gut danced in the same way it had when I found the cabin, almost urging me to notice something out of the ordinary in front of me, as though an air of magic surrounded it.

Mads removed himself from Ace before once more offering his hands. I took them, shaking off the zaps of energy tearing through my body every time he touched it.

We made our way to the small building, Mads leaving room for me to lead given I was the one to open the door. Wrapping my fingers around the handle, I turned and pushed with as much strength as I could muster. The door stayed securely closed. I released my hand before trying once more, the second time I pushed my weight into it. I sighed in growing frustration.

"What did Bea's instructions say?" Mads' voice caressed my ear.

Blinking away my confusion, I reached into my inside coat pocket to retrieve the small piece of paper Bea had passed to me. Unfolding it, I gasped at the short line of scribble:

You better fuck him while you're out there.

Bea's presence in my life was new, growing extremely important. Having said that, I was definitely going to kill her for this. How in the hell was I going to get the Alegra stone with this bullshit?

Hugging the anger rapidly building inside of me, I clenched the helpless scrap of paper to my chest. Heat rose on my cheeks as tears of frustration pooled in my eyes. Without another thought, I raised my tightened fists to the door and began to lash out on the inanimate object, as though it would fight back.

Ignoring the pain shooting up my arms, I continued my barrage of blows. Time didn't matter at that moment. The floodgates of my bottled up emotions opened further, and I wasn't sure how I was going to manage them. If at all. The only thing that mattered was beating the door into submission.

Open! What good was a key if it couldn't unlock a door? The burn in my hands built with every crack on the wood. I couldn't focus on anything apart from the rage finding an outlet. I seethed as

I thought through every terrible thing done to me, the inability to get the stone the breaking point.

I was unsure how long I mauled the wood with my fists. It could have easily been hours. Then something brought me through the rage haze, a hand. Soothing, strong, wrapped around my now bloody right fist. The one with the paper clenched inside of it. Then, a second hand over my left. Breathing heavily, the hands brought mine away from the door, slowly as though not to fully disrupt the fury I expressed.

"Aurelia."

The voice, silk and strength, a voice I knew well. One I wished I could wrap myself up in. A cocoon of comfortable breaths and words.

"Aurelia, you're okay."

I wasn't okay. I may have been excellent at pretending I was. The outburst only the beginning. Most likely to be the first of many. A fact I couldn't ignore. The overflowing self-doubt was hard to ignore after so many years of feeling utterly useless. A thousand moments stood in front of me that would allow me to prove all of those thoughts wrong. I wanted to help the brothers get home. I held onto that thread.

Following the guidance of the hands wrapped around mine, I slowly turned to face the man I could obsess over one second and despise the next. His beauty was undeniable as the autumnal swirls locked onto my own blue depths. The expression wrapped around his face would have terrified anyone else. I knew though, it was fear for my safety.

Calmly, Mads raised my right fist to his full lips. Entranced, my gaze followed his movements as he placed a kiss on my first knuckle.

He paused, looking for further permission to which I only offered a brief nod. He kissed the next knuckle, taking a brief moment afterwards to lick the drop of blood off of his full bottom lip. I attempted to gulp down my inadequacy at the intimate moment. Afraid? Yes. Except I wanted nothing more than for him to do it again.

A kiss to the third knuckle and then the fourth before he twisted my wrist to continue to my thumb. Slowly, as though a hunter trying not to frighten his prey, Mads lowered my right fist, applying a gentle squeeze before releasing it. Next, he raised my left hand, my mouth watered at the thought of what came next. Coupled with the intensity of my breathing, the actions spurred a light headedness, not in an uncomfortable way.

Finishing with my left thumb, Mads mirrored his previous movement and released my fist back down at my side. Gradually moving closer, with only inches between us, a small smile tugged on the corner of his mouth. "You're bleeding."

An odd statement given he had just literally kissed the blood off my hands.

"And I don't see any chaos." Relaying what I'd told him outside of the cabin, he moved his head left and right to prove his point.

I followed his eyes, taking in the tranquillity of the wood. A soft hum of birds and insects danced around us, showing no signs my assault on the door had disturbed them.

Breathing in the safety of the wood, I let my eyes close briefly before meeting Mads' confident gaze. A more playful look graced his face, giving me no indication I'd scared him off. No condescension or disappointment passed across his face which was equal parts comforting and confusing.

"What did the note say?"

Unintentionally squeezing my fist, I'd forgotten about the contents of the note. Part of me felt there should be a level of embarrassment flaring as I uncurled my fist, holding the crumpled piece of paper out to Mads.

Hesitantly, he took the note from my hand to read it. I waited, trying to decipher his reaction to the instruction by his facial expression. He let nothing show. Simply reading over the words again, he paused to look at me before rereading it once more for good measure.

Without a response, he placed the paper back in my palm. *That's it?* I couldn't believe the master of moodiness had nothing to say about Bea's clear attempt at pushing us together. Mads turned on his heel to walk back towards Ace.

Shouting after him, I said, "Did she even need the stone?"

"Oh, she needs it." He threw over his shoulder, the underlying tone undetectable.

"What are we going to do now?"

We'd been sent to get the stone. We were going to get the stone. Right?

"Now we set up camp. We both need a clear head to solve this riddle."

Riddle? The note wasn't a riddle. At least not to me.

Squeezing the paper back in my palm, I winced at the sharp ache following. Looking down, it was clear I'd done nothing to get the door open. I had only succeeded in battering my own hands. The blood from a few knuckles had begun to dry as though Mads' kisses magically started the healing process.

CHAPTER 20

AURELIA

Our camp was small, consisting of a fire and two bed rolls. We shared a small pot of stew Xav had packed for us before falling into a companionable silence around the crackling flames.

"You should get some sleep," Mads broke the silence.

The flames danced in my vision, making me wonder what the fire Mads created would look like. "Shouldn't you get some sleep too?"

I felt his eyes against my cheek. What I would give to be inside his head even if just for a few moments. The man was an expert at hiding his true intentions.

"Somebody has to keep watch, and I can't say I trust Ace to do it."

A joke. Mads' humour was difficult to read and continued to stun me into silence.

"I can sit up for a while if you need to get some sleep?"

Mads shook his head and in a surprising turn of events, patted the spot next to him. An invitation. An olive branch. I could've denied his request, lay down, and get some sleep. Maybe I should have. Instead, I chose to follow my curiosity. Grabbing the bedroll from beneath me, I moved over and placed it next to Mads before settling down into a somewhat comfortable position, watching the flames lick the air.

"What happened today?" Mads voice didn't take its usual commanding tone. The question was asked more in interested concern.

I wove my fingers in the quilt on top of my lap in nervousness. What was there to be nervous about? The man beside me knew about more of my scars than anyone had in my entire life.

"When the beatings started happening..." I paused, a bead of unease filled me knowing I was going to voice something I had never said out loud. "I knew the emotional, mental, and physical toll they'd have on me would need to be dealt with at some point. A lot had happened in a very brief timeframe that I knew I wouldn't have the distance from the beatings or the mental capacity to work through them as the events happened. So, I carved out a portion of my mind, one shrouded in darkness, and locked them away, one by one."

"How did you do that?"

I didn't need him to expand on his question. Without making eye contact, I continued, "This is going to sound very strange."

Out of the corner of my eye, I could see Mads watching the flames, giving me the time I needed to tell my story.

"Each time I was called into that study, every object that broke my skin, all those times my parents reiterated how useless I was, I'd take those moments and sort of store them. Some I envisioned locking into trunks while others were small enough to wrap up in a parcel. Each bad memory I have, I'd tuck away, lock it up, and push it into a part of my brain I knew I could access later. If I was ever able to get myself away from that life, I vowed to confront the memories and work through them," I paused, letting the initial explanation sink in.

Mads flicked a twig into the flames. "Your method is incredibly emotionally mature for a girl with no strength."

I turned, catching the swirling ambers and green hues of his eyes as they were focused solely on me. I expected to find a glint of humour. What I found was an intensity burning hotter than the fire at our feet.

Breathing deep, I took a moment to gather the courage to finish my story. I exhaled. "When I came to the cabin, that part of my mind started to open. Some memories on their own, some because I wanted to start braving them, and others triggered by various moments."

Mads tensed at the thought. "Not bad triggers. More like you three, and Bea, guided me into confronting some of those memories. Ones I knew I needed to face and with each day, I felt safer in the house and with all of you."

Nerves shot, I twirled the bottom of the tunic between my fingers as I waited for a response. Anything to prompt me to either move forward or stop the confession all together.

"You are safe with us." The words felt like a promise. He'd taken to staring at the ground in a hushed tone as though he was embarrassed by the admission. One thing I did know about the man beside me was nothing was as it seemed. His infinite layers could never allow anyone to make a firm judgement of him.

"I know."

We sat in comfortable silence for a few minutes before one of the many questions sitting at the tip of my tongue stumbled off my lips, "Mads, how am I from Raithe?"

"I don't know the answer to that."

The popping of the fire filled the gap before I asked the question I was most fearful of. "What if...I'm from Aestas?"

"Then you're from Aestas."

"But they murdered your parents..."

Mads let a chuckle loose. A chuckle! "The kingdom didn't murder our parents, Aurelia, two people did. Their actions do not define an entire kingdom, nor would their actions define you."

I swallowed down the apprehension of what that could mean for me, even with the reassurance of his words.

Before I could explore further, or let my mind riddle my body in worry, Mad suggested I get some rest. We would need our energy to figure out how to get the stone in the morning.

I held a calmness in my shoulders that settled around me from the forest above as I let my eyelids fall closed, hugged by the silent support radiating from the man next to me.

The whispers of birdsong filtered through the tree canopy above me, soothing an ache in my chest. I embraced the dew of the forest morning kissing my cheeks as I followed the path to a private area, helping clear the fog of an uneasy night of sleep. I took comfortable strides towards the river, stopping abruptly when I reached its bank. Heated shock licked up my spine as I found a very naked Maddox, bathing himself in the river. His back was to me, my eyes locked on the strength in his shoulders, muscles clenching with each brush of soap. And his arse. Chiselled to perfection. There were very few times in my life where I had appreciated a man's body, never anything more than a few passing glances. Mads though? Not a day would pass where I would forget the lines of his backside and the intense need to run my hands, my tongue, my teeth over all of it. It was now and forever deliciously ingrained in my mind.

Taking one slow step forward, a moth drawn to a flame, a twig snapped beneath my boot, causing Mads' head to whip around, locking eyes with me. Narrowing his eyes at the realisation of my intrusion, I struggled to find anything to say. I didn't want to apologise for the interruption, but a deep rooted part of me felt I should. Another part of me, sitting quite south, wanted to compliment him on his delectable arse.

Swallowing down the embarrassment, I hoped he would break the silence given my brain and mouth were failing to communicate properly.

"Would you like to join me?" No cocky smile. No deviance sat across his face. He was completely serious, both terrifying and exciting me. Before I could respond, I turned on my heel and ran back towards the camp.

My life had so many moments filled with people taking from me, without permission and I couldn't help the sickness sitting in my gut, knowing I should have turned around as soon as I saw Mads in the water.

Once the shock had worn off, I would apologise. Beg for his forgiveness at my thoughtlessness. I'd seen him shirtless before, but this had gone many steps past that, and I was uncomfortable knowing I could possibly put someone else in the situation I'd found myself in for a large part of my life.

Taking a seat on my bedroll, I pulled my knees up, contemplating how I'd approach apologising. I knew what it was like for people to take from you and Mads still had the right to who saw what and when. It would be difficult now for me not to focus on the lines of his body beneath his clothes. Even if I hadn't spied the front, the back was enough to frustrate me sexually for a good few months.

Mads entered our camp a few minutes later. Before he could say anything, I shot to my feet. "I'm sorry." I almost screamed the words at him. Not the particular tone I'd wanted to use but at least the words were out there. Mads froze, putting his dirty clothing into one of Ace's packs before turning to me. The layers of confusion on his face were obvious but what I couldn't understand is why he was confused. Leaning into whatever strength I'd pulled the apology from, I spouted further. "It was unacceptable of me to watch you." The shame began to fill my shoes, rising up rapidly.

Mads stood to his full height before slowly stalking towards me as the corners of his lips tipped into a mischievous smirk. "Goldie, you can look until the end of your days." The sincerity in his voice pimpled my neck. "I'm not ashamed of my body and if you look at me like that every time you see me naked, I'd die a happy man."

With no further explanation, he walked towards the cabin. I stood frozen in awe and general confusion. Was I finally breaking through the thick shell he'd constructed so carefully? I had gone too long not trusting men, it was difficult to fully trust his barriers were coming down. Could I trust him? Yes. Implicitly? A question I couldn't yet answer.

"Let's try and get this door open."

I nodded, pushing my feet to move towards him, keeping my head down so I wouldn't flush over the way his shoulder muscles contracted beneath his shirt as he walked ahead of me.

I found myself standing in front of the thick wooden door once more. Mads surveyed the other sides of the cabin. There were two small windows, one situated in both the left and right side of the building. The windows themselves were covered in dirt, time, and other forest debris, hiding the inside contents from the outside world. Mirroring his movements, I shifted around the building, looking for any potential loose boards or cracks we could pry open.

"We'll have to try the door."

My eyes rolled back on their own accord. "We don't have a key or any damn clue as to how to open it."

Mads' hands roamed over the door with precision. He followed the door frames, looking for hidden alcoves. Coming up empty handed, he took a long deep breath.

Careful not to ruin his contemplation, I stepped closer to the door. A strange wave of euphoria drifted over me. One I could only compare to a soft breeze on a warm summer's day. It settled lightly in my belly, almost emitting its own heat as my fingers and toes became fuzzy.

Closing my eyes, a memory flashed before me. No, not a memory, a guide. In my mind, a door stood in front of me. Not dissimilar to the one I was in front of. Looking down in the mental image, a soft light peaked through the keyhole, brightening with each second that passed, urging me to grab the handle. Blinking out of the reverie, I found my hand extended to the door handle. On a deep exhale, I wrapped my fingers around the ringed handle, hesitating momentarily before using what little arm strength I had to push. To my immediate surprise, the door opened. Slowly and painfully heavy, a loud creak resonated throughout the forest surrounding them.

"What the fuck?" I silently agreed with Mads' sentiment, standing frozen, the door handle still clutched in my palm.

"What just happened?"

I snapped my mouth closed before finding Mads' intense gaze. "I just closed my eyes and saw a door."

"You saw a door?"

"Yes."

"This door?"

"No, not this door. One similar."

"One similar?"

"And in my mind, a light was coming through the keyhole."

"A light in the keyhole?"

"Are you going to repeat everything I say?"

"I will until this makes sense."

With a huff of frustration, I pried my fingers from the door handle, moving my touch upwards to push the door further open.

"It was like it was telling me to just open the door."

"What was telling you?"

"The light."

"The light spoke?"

"Not explicitly."

"What the hell does 'not explicitly' mean?"

Trying my best to push down my annoyance, particularly because it didn't sound as strange coming out of my mouth as the actual experience had. Mads was no stranger to magic yet it could have dulled over the years in exile.

"I closed my eyes. Saw a door. The light came through the keyhole and the only thought in my mind was just to try to open it. So, I did. And now it's open."

We stared at each other before looking towards the now open door. Both uncertain of what passed between us, the building, and our surroundings.

Mads pushed past me into the derelict building, I followed close on his heels, again doing my best to ignore the close view of his shoulders moving beneath the fabric.

Distracting myself with the contents of the confined space, I gazed around at the many objects now surrounding us. Hundreds of gems and stones of varying shades, all forgotten and covered in what I could only assume was years of dust. Purple gems, thick, tall stones, jars containing any manner of remains, bones, and one I thought looked like marmalade, colour and all. A small space filled to the roof with unidentifiable objects.

"Well, we're in. How are we supposed to know what the Alegra stone looks like? Do you know?"

Mads was also in the middle of looking around, clearly as mesmerised and confused as I was.

"Bea said you'd know."

I huffed, "I'd know?"

"Yes."

"I don't even know what an Alegra stone is. Do you?"

"No."

"She said I'd know?"

Pulling his gaze from a jar holding animal organs floating in a foreign goo, Mads hit me with a gaze of pure confidence. "She said if you concentrated, you would be able to sense its energy."

I laughed. I couldn't help myself. Magic. Parallel worlds. And now this ability to open the door would have indicated to any normal person they were on the verge of a nervous breakdown, yet I couldn't deny that pulsing feeling in my stomach had yet to steer me wrong. I willed myself to continue to trust the foreign sensation.

What else could I do? We were there, in the cabin which only minutes ago had seemed unattainable, within arm's reach of the stone.

I took a deep breath, closing my eyes and doing my best to concentrate, which was a difficult feat given I knew nothing about the stone apart from the fact it would help us on the journey.

As the colours of the room swirled around my mind, I silently chanted *Alegra stone* doing my best to ignore how ridiculous it all seemed. Just as I was about to start another round of mental chanting, my left pointer finger began to twitch. The twitched synched with the words, curling in on Alegra and out on stone. A strange sensation began to crawl up my left leg, similar to the fuzziness I'd felt in my digits. The feeling grew stronger, urging my body towards the left of the room.

Eyes closed, I sensed Mads move out of my way as to not disturb whatever the hell I was currently experiencing. Maybe it was the thought of his blind faith that kept me in the trance.

My left arm lifted, as if on its own, gently grazing my index finger across the top shelf. I didn't want to know what manner of items I caressed and instead, continued to focus on the words A*legra stone* in my mind.

After I'd skimmed a number of the items on the shelf, the word 'there' popped into my head just as my eyes snapped open. My finger had gently landed on a rock, about the same size as my hand, deep amethyst in colour. Covered in the forgotten. A comfortable jab poked in my belly, indicating to me this was it. How did I know?

A question I'd need to bring up with Bea, after I rang her neck for the little stunt with the note.

"This is it."

My voice, almost a whisper, spurred Mads into movement. He didn't even question whether or not I was sure it was the Alegra stone. He simply popped it off the shelf and walked out of the cabin.

I stood with the new sensations coursing through me for a moment longer. Torn between wanting to question them so badly to knowing whatever it was I was experiencing, it felt right. As though I had just been gifted with a limb I'd been missing.

Taking a few deep breaths before walking out of the cabin, I pulled the door shut behind me, gently resting my forehead on it before turning back to camp. Mads wrapped the stone in cloth of some sort, readying it for one of the packs on Ace's hindquarters.

"It looks like a storm is rolling in. We should head out now if we want to make it back before sundown."

Instinctively, I turned my face towards the sky. The image framed by the tips of the large trees, the smell of the near rain tickling my nostrils. My mind was conflicted. I wanted to get back to the house, to see Xav, Fox, Bea, and Rock. The other, very primal part of me, wanted to be alone with Mads just a bit longer. The private trip saw him opening up, slightly.

Quickly residing to the fact I had no excuse to keep him out here longer, I approached Ace. Mads extended a hand, helping me climb back up on the noble steed, immediately followed having had the saddlebags packed already.

Wasting no time, Mads kicked Ace into motion with so much force it flung me back into his chest. His hand found my abdomen, steadying me with the pace before finding its way back onto his knee.

A brief and yet delicious sensation. I tried my best to be happy about finding the Alegra stone, trying not to let the thought of Mads' moods come back into play. Those thoughts left me…empty.

CHAPTER 21

AURELIA

Our trio didn't make it far before the rain came down. First, a light drizzle, enabling us to continue on with just a dash of dampness. It didn't take long for the rain to turn vicious, pelting us with each stomp of Ace's hooves.

I was soaked through in minutes, struggling to grasp the pommel with my slippery hands. With the rain, the temperature had also dropped, bringing the rain and a penetrating cold sending sharp aches through my entire body.

"Mads! We need to go back!"

We weren't too far from the cabin we'd just left. The best course of action was to return there and wait out the worst of the storm. If we continued further towards the house, we'd either be frozen or in an accident. I didn't like that plan.

Mads grunted out what I could only assume was a 'no' before pressing Ace harder. I had terrible visions of the beast's foot getting caught in something covered in the recent mud, sending us all spiralling to severe injury. Angry at his stubbornness, I elbowed him in the stomach, trying my best to get his attention.

"We need to go back! We'll die if we keep riding in this!"

Pulling the reins hard, Ace came to a stop before Mads ushered him to turn quickly back the way we'd come. Mads' anger radiated against my back. I knew he wanted to get back and start our journey to the portal. It wasn't worth injuring ourselves or worse, our lives. Most of the time, I found Mads' hardness intriguing. A puzzle I was determined to solve. And then sometimes, I'd find myself expressing more anger at him and his constant zigzagging than I'd felt towards anyone in my life. The thought popped back into my head — Mads only showed kindness to me only because of the role I played in getting them back to Raithe, erasing any sentiments of him wanting more from me, romantic or otherwise.

Arriving back at our makeshift camp, Mads threw himself off of Ace before motioning him under a tree canopy, ensuring he wouldn't get wetter than necessary. His hand shot out to help me down. Still a bit sick from my treacherous mind, I decided to get down myself.

Grabbing the saddle bags, Mads marched towards the cabin without a word. The anger mixed with the nausea pushed me towards the cabin, the words ready to jump off my tongue.

"What is wrong with you?" Slamming the door after me, Mads had settled our packs on a workstation I hadn't noticed before.

"What is wrong with me? We could have made it back fine."

"Possibly. Was it worth risking our safety, Ace's safety?"

"Yes."

The anger punched the nausea straight in the face, leaving me trembling in fury and confirming what I'd thought, Mads tolerated me only because of what I could do. Nothing more.

"Your stubbornness could have gotten us hurt. Or worse! Killed! Then you would never get to your precious Raithe."

The last words weren't meant to be sent with the venom I expelled. I couldn't hide it. I now wanted nothing more than to help them get home. It was just too damn hard to ignore my part in all of this. Just as I was my entire life, I was only being used in this situation too.

"What did you say?"

Not giving my words time to filter through the logical part of my brain, I continued, "You heard me. Well, don't worry, *Your Majesty,* you'll be back in Hiema sooner than you know and then we can be rid of each other."

Taking the few steps it took to get across the room, Mads was in front of me, fire dancing in his eyes. "What the fuck did you say?"

I wasn't sure when my breathing had escalated. "I said, then we can be rid of each other."

Mads' lip cocked into a wily grin. "Oh, Goldie, you'll never be rid of me."

Before I had time to respond, his lips crashed into mine. Pushing me backwards, my arse hit the worktable. The kiss was rough, claiming, finally being free of its confines after all of these weeks. His tongue grazed my bottom lip, willing me to open for him. Complying immediately, his tongue caressed mine, not allowing either of us a moment to breathe. I didn't care. I'd gladly suffocate.

The nearly consistent ache in my core, lingering since I'd laid eyes on him, erupted into the most vicious need. Wrapping my hands around his neck, Mads gripped my hips, pressing himself further into me before roughly sliding his hands around to my backside. Grabbing, like a man starved, he lifted me up before shoving me onto the work surface. The fact he could lift my weight in such a quick, precise movement drove my need further.

Never once removing his lips from me, he continued his assault on my mouth, devouring every sweet moan coming from my lips. Not knowing whether he was looking for permission, I removed my hands from his neck and lifted my arms. Wasting no time, Mads took the hint and ripped the tunic over my head, leaving me in the thin wrap.

My large breasts were given no lift from the wrap, and unable to let the self-doubt in, I latched back onto him. His fingers tracing the bare skin of my rib cage was enough to make me come or set me on fire. Maybe both. I didn't care. Everything in my life felt like it had led to this moment and nothing was going to stop me from enjoying every second. I could feel the broken pieces of my sexuality knitting themselves back together with every stroke of his tongue.

Mads' hands found the ties of my trousers breaking the kiss briefly to look down at me and then he caught my eyes. "You tell me to stop and I'll stop."

I grabbed the sides of his face, placing a soft kiss on his lips. "Don't you dare stop."

Crashing his mouth to mine once more, Mads wasted no time in tugging the laces with so much force a loud rip sounded through the small space. He bent down to untie my boots, every second I wasn't touching him caused the fire to burn deeper. With deft fingers, he unlaced the boots and pulled them off in seconds before his fingers found the waist of my trousers, gently tugging at first. "Get them off of me."

The prompt pushed him to move quicker, exposing my undershorts. Those and my wrap the last pieces covering me. I barely had time to register. Mads was still fully dressed before he ripped my undershorts clear off. I sat, shocked, before he met my eyes. Gently, he traced a finger from my collar bone, rotating around each one of my still covered nipples, sending shockwaves to my pussy, before he stopped at my stomach.

"I've wanted a taste of you since I found you in my bed." His voice, generally deep, was laced with a new sexy huskiness I immediately needed more of.

"Can I taste you, Aurelia?"

Never once taking my gaze from him, I swallowed hard. The fluttering in my pulse was so rapid I felt like my entire body was going to take flight.

"Yes."

The sense of safety that had grown since meeting Mads pulsed in my chest, reminding me that the moment in front of me was mine for the taking, and by the gods did I want it.

Using the hand on my stomach, he guided me down so my back was flat on the table. Locking his strong fingers around my thighs, he pulled me across the table, my arse hanging just off the edge. As he dropped to his knees, he pulled my legs apart. The need to watch him devour me was primal. I lifted my head up just in time to see Mads lightly touch his nose to my clit, taking an audible inhale, eyes closed. I was wound so tight I thought I might burst into flame, burning the entire cabin down. "I could live on your scent, alone."

Before I could demand he follow through on his request, his tongue found my clit and my world exploded.

CHAPTER 22

MADDOX

Aurelia tasted of everything good in life I'd never thought I would experience again. I had sex since we'd landed in this world. Usually nothing more than a quick fuck. A release. With Aurelia, each brush of my tongue was an out of body experience. Her taste alone could leave me with a lifetime high.

I had never felt so ravenous for a woman before, like the craving could never be satiated. My only goal in life had changed to focus purely on her pleasure from now until the end of time.

My cock strained against my trousers purely from her sweet taste on my tongue, mixed with the soft moans escaping her mouth, was enough to make me come in my trousers with no regrets.

Aurelia's thighs tightened against the sides of my face, cutting off my access to oxygen. I would happily drown right there in her wet pussy. Subtly, I felt her begin to clench around my tongue as it dipped back into her. That wouldn't do. This moment was not going to be stopped too abruptly. "Not yet." A growl escaped with the words. "I will tell you when you can come. Understand?"

I pushed one finger deep inside her, driving the message home. "Give me your words, Aurelia."

And every single noise, sensation, and taste of this sweet ecstasy for the rest of my life. How could I ever think I would actually fight this?

"Yes." The words were breathy, delicious. She gasped when I added a second finger, the additional sensation causing her back to bow off of the table.

Her fingers tightened in my hair, clawing at my head to give her more. This woman, this beautiful, enchanting woman, would learn how to own her pleasure, and I, being the gracious instructor I was, would be there every step of the way. I would show her everything she had missed and with each orgasm I had planned, she would take herself back.

I flicked my tongue over her clit before taking it in my mouth, sucking her swollen, most sensitive spot, letting my eyes roll in the back of my head from the pure, exquisite sensation. I ate her pussy like I was a starved man. And I was.

Reaching with the hand not inside of her, I squeezed one of her fabric covered breasts before moving to the other. Finding her nipple beneath the wrap, I rolled it between my index and middle fingers, my cock pulsing at the knowledge I had her luscious tits in my grasp. The fullness was bigger than my large hand. A groan left the back of my throat at the need to be inside of her. One day. One day, I would completely devour the goddess currently writhing beneath my tongue.

"Mads..." Aurelia gasped. "Please. I need... I..."

Removing my tongue briefly, already needing to taste her again, I said, "What Aurelia? Tell me what you need." The deeper than normal timbre surprised me.

Bucking her hips up, I moved my hand from her nipple to gently push her hips back down, proving to her I was in control and she could trust me with her body. I could sense her difficulty in voicing her needs, knowing it had never been asked of her before. I needed that to change. Tasting her was only that, a taste. This was the beginning, and my dick twitched in anticipation of all the orgasms I would push her body through. If I would have access to her pleasure, she needed to know she was safe.

"Tell me." A commanding softness echoed through my words, less in dominance than before and more in encouragement.

"I need... to come."

Her breathing stilted as her body twitched with need beneath my fingers and tongue.

"Where do you want to come to, Aurelia?"

Panting, I could see her eyes shoot open, finding me in the sexed haze surrounding us. The cabin may go up in flames if I didn't let her come soon. She needed to tell me. I needed her words.

"Tell me where you want to come."

The fire in her eyes sent further pulses to my cock. Her jaw clenched. "On your tongue."

Pulling back slightly, I hesitated. Aurelia's head snapped up, her eyes pinning me with ire and frustration. I don't know why I felt the need to tease her, but I couldn't deny how much pleasure I took from it.

Her hips bucked up again. I pushed them back down. "Maddox, please!"

My name on her lips sent me diving back in. I traced my tongue from arsehole to clit, stopping my ascent only once I reached her most sensitive spot, pulling it between my teeth.

A growl grew in my throat at the immediate sense of rightness of the taste of her on my tongue. I pumped my fingers in and out, curling them slightly to hit the spot, her moans growing with each thrust. I didn't want this to end, but the thought of her sweet release urged me on. Gods damn I would show her what this could be.

Twisting the tip of my tongue against her clit elicited the most delectable sound from her lips. I swiped, back and forth, my fingers pumping deep inside of her. She clenched around my fingers. The haze of her pleasure wrapped around us. I wanted nothing more than to eat her for the next ten hours, but I wasn't going to withhold her release.

Wanting to watch as she erupted on me, I flicked my eyes back up, staring at the stunning, half naked, golden-haired beauty currently being powered purely by my tongue and fingers. Hips pushing upwards once more, I eased my hold on her slightly, wanting to see her come completely undone. A guttural roar built at the back of her throat, releasing into an intense cry of pleasure as she burst onto my mouth, my fingers.

Relishing every single second, I lapped at her until the last of her orgasm had come and gone. Her body shuddered in tune to the low whimpers escaping her lips as the aftershocks coursed through her.

The sight of Aurelia sated echoed in the beat of my heart. Somehow, with everything she had endured, this woman chose to trust me, as she closed her eyes and let me take from her. The visceral ache of what that meant lay waste to whatever doubt I had before this moment.

Leaning back, I basked in the euphoric sight of Aurelia's post orgasm glow, immediately ready for the next time I could make her come apart for me. In my mouth. On my fingers. On my cock. On her own finger while I sucked and tugged on her nipples. I didn't care which way as long as it could happen again. Continuously.

A crack formed in the outer shell I'd meticulously built upon Aurelia's arrival in my life. One I was sure would never break. Except, when my lips touched hers for the first time, I realised the wall was penetrable. With one taste, I knew I would never be able to stop. I knew Aurelia was the beginning, middle, and end. *Fuck.*

CHAPTER 23

AURELIA

I couldn't move. The intensity of the orgasm Mads had just blessed me with pulsated aftershocks through my body. It took a few minutes before I was back in my body long enough to realise I was still bare from the waist down with a sexy, frightening man kneeling in front of me. *I had this man on his knees.*

Before I could say anything or let the embarrassment wash through me, Mads was on his feet, gently sliding my trousers back on. Pushing myself into a sitting position, I followed his lead as his hands gripped my waist, guiding me off the table and onto my feet so he could pull the trousers the rest of the way up. I caught sight of the now ruined undershorts on the floor, thinking briefly how the ride back would be uncomfortable.

Silently, I let Mads put on my boots, placing them one by one on his chest to lace them up with care and precision. Next, he grabbed my top, motioning for me to raise my arms. Obeying, I took the opportunity to search his face, looking for any indication of his feelings towards our...encounter. Trying and failing to ignore the doubt creeping in. Did he regret moving our relationship, or lack thereof, in a sexual direction?

You might as well ask. Otherwise, you are going to drive yourself crazy. Just as I went to open my mouth, Mads lightly pinched my chin with his thumb and index finger, tenderly brushing his lips against mine, letting a coy smile grow from his lips.

"The rain stopped."

I tried to turn my head towards the window, my muscles refusing to budge. Plus, I couldn't take my eyes off the man in front of me, my lips instantly missing the way he caressed them.

"We can head back now."

I offered a nod in agreement before he stepped back, giving me the space to leave the cabin.

Each step was met with a sour thought, all pertaining to the very intimate moment I'd just shared with a man I was convinced hated me. If he did, in fact, hate me, would he have given me such a tender kiss? *Maybe it was his way of saying thanks.*

On shaky legs, I could do nothing to stop the sudden assault of boxes being flung open, pouring out my deepest, darkest memories and fears. My hands shot up to clutch the sides of my head as I willed them to stop. To be shoved back down even if it was just for our journey back.

Unintentionally, my knees hit the dirt as soon as I stepped outside, a pained scream escaping my lips. Instantly, Mads was in front of me, covering my hands with his own, "Aurelia," he said, his voice soothing, "Aurelia, you're safe."

Removing my right hand, he placed it over his chest. "Follow this. Breathe."

The pleasant pumping of his heart kicked off its rhythmic solace, slowly bringing me back to reality. The memories and judgements began drifting back into their respective boxes, lids sealing for the time being. Once my breathing somewhat mirrored Mads', I lifted my head to find his eyes, gentled with concern, ready whenever I was.

"What happened?" I squeaked.

"You collapsed." Confusion laced his face as though I'd had temporary amnesia.

"No. What happened," I pointed behind me, towards the cabin. The oral sex cabin, as I would remember it, "back there?"

Mads took a few breaths, searching my face for something I couldn't distinguish.

"How do you feel about me, Aurelia?"

Hearing my name on his lips sent my heart fluttering. My face grew into a puzzled expression before I blurted out the first words that popped into my head. "Generally? Anger and intrigue with a continuous urge to punch you square in the face. I'd do it, too, if I didn't already know I'd hurt myself more than I'd hurt you."

Chuckling, which was still an odd and incredible sound, he helped me to my feet before pointing to my chest. "No. What do you feel here?"

I glanced down. The sight of his strong, confident hand hovering over my chest sent pricks of desire to my core. What was wrong with me?

"I —" I started, not knowing how to continue. "I don't want to tell you."

Hurt flashed across his face briefly. "Why?"

Sighing, the urge to vomit the truth rose up, impossible to ignore, "If I don't tell you, I can protect myself."

Bringing his fingers to my chin again, tilting my head so I had no choice except to look at him, his gaze softened further, "I know it's important for you to protect yourself, Aurelia. Just one flaw in your plan. You keep forgetting you aren't alone anymore."

Pulling my face from his grasp, I blew out an exasperated breath. "For how long though?"

My brain didn't want to look past his words in the cabin being purely driven by the heat of the moment.

"Give me your eyes."

The firm, dominant Mads was back. I briefly shut my eyes to hold back the tears building before I shifted them back to him.

"I meant what I said. You will never be rid of me."

Deciding to flip the switch, I threw his question back at him. "What do you feel for me?"

Searching for the right words appeared to genuinely pain him.

Before the dread could rise, Mads answered, "Everything. I feel everything about you. It's terrifying and infuriating and exciting. I don't remember the last time I was excited about anything before you turned up. I only remember the anger. The hurt. And then, there you were, in my bed. A beautiful conundrum. And for the record, I've wanted to do that," he pointed to the cabin, "since the day we met."

I couldn't fight the blush rising up my neck and into my cheeks. It may not have been as explicit as Mads, yet I had definitely wanted something more from him since I'd woken up in his bed on the first day.

We stood in comfortable silence for a few minutes. Both of us were lost in our own thoughts. I enjoyed the post storm harmony in the surrounding forest.

"Maybe we should head back."

Offering me his hand, I took it, nodding in agreement. As we walked towards Ace, a lightness rose between us. I tried my utmost not to let the sliver of joy flood me too much in fear of losing it. Once on Ace's back, Mads' arms curled around my waist where his hand rested lightly on my stomach, I couldn't deny the one thing I'd wanted for so long. To not feel alone.

The ride back was uneventful and uncomfortable, given I wasn't wearing any undergarments. Thankfully, the rain held off as well as any further sign of the storm. And as I leaned into Mads, relishing the warmth of him at his back and his hand on my waist, I wondered if something larger might be at work, forcing Mads and I together. As though a cosmic energy had pulled us toward one another, igniting the ember which had popped constantly for the last few weeks.

Just as Ace stepped over the tree boundary to the house, Fox burst through the front door, Rock on his heels as he pounded toward us with severe concern written on his face. "We were just about to form a search party for you two!"

"I told you to give us two days before starting to worry. And I thought Xav was the mother hen."

I giggled as Mads dismounted. *Giggled?* Holding out my hand for Mads to assist me down, Fox shot us both a look of confusion, quickly forming into something else I wasn't sure I wanted to entertain.

Looking between us, Fox huffed before sniffing the air, then made his way back toward the house. A shiver ran down my spine, anticipating the storm about to hit us once inside the house. In silent encouragement, Mads gently pressed his hand to my lower back, guiding me up the steps.

I leaned down to offer Rock a scratch before Xav and Bea joined Fox in the entryway, all three forming a semi-circle of annoyance.

Fox's bemused grin broke the tension radiating from the other two. Once Mads and I stood in front of them, Xav and Bea mirrored Fox's earlier expressions before Bea let out a loud whoop, clapping her hands in front of her.

"What?" I spit out, unable to hide my confusion.

"You two had sex." Fox, the frustrating Fox, had to blurt it out as though it was perfectly normal our sexual encounters should be made public.

"Fox." Mads practically growled at his youngest brother. The threat is more like a promise of terror to come.

"Don't 'Fox' me. I can smell it all over you two."

Resisting the urge to sniff myself. "We didn't —" before I could finish, Mads stepped in front of me, stopping me from exposing more than I wanted to. I didn't owe anyone an explanation or argument. I was grateful for Mads' anticipation.

"What Aurelia and I did or didn't do, is none of your concern. Are we clear?"

"Crystal, oh moody one. Although maybe not so moody anymore."

Fox wiggled his brows before breaking into a fit of laughter followed by Bea. Xav kindly refrained from the noise, instead letting a mischievous grin spread across his face.

"We got the stone."

I moved the conversation in another direction, masking the slight shame building inside me. Mads and I still had a lot to discuss about what had happened and what it meant for us. *Us.* Yesterday, I couldn't decide if I wanted to seduce him or murder him. How had things changed so quickly?

Bea couldn't stop her laughing fit to offer gratitude in retrieving the stone. Mads, clearly fed up with their frightful disrespect, cleared his throat. The first sign he was about to make good on his growling promise.

Gradually, the laughter twins righted themselves, nodding in understanding towards Mads whose anger was quickly suffocating even in the outdoors.

"We need to discuss what's next." Bea did her best to keep a straight face, aiming a continuous 'you did it' look toward me. It was difficult to take her focused attempt seriously.

"Later," Mads huffed. Turning around, he grabbed my arm before bending down to hoist me over his shoulder, positioning my face in perfect view of his sculpted arse. A yelp escaped me, "Mads!"

"First, we are going to get cleaned up. You three carry on and leave us the hell alone."

Fox saluted after us as Mads carried me up the stairs towards his bedroom. Instinctively, I kicked my feet, simultaneously slapping his arse. An immediate mistake given the flex of his muscles beneath my palm.

"Mads! Put me down! I can walk."

With a quick clap, he smacked my arse, sending pain and pleasure through my body. "I know. I just wanted to carry you."

I couldn't argue, remembering the cabin as well as what the near future may bring. Kicking the door closed, he set me lightly on my feet before moving about the room with an indecipherable momentum. My curiosity piqued as he pulled clothing from his wardrobe before marching into the adjoining bathroom, pumping the shower.

Returning to the room, he threw over his shoulder. "Take those off."

I looked down. The forest had indeed cemented itself on and in my clothes as well as my exposed skin. Lifting my gaze back to Mads, he pulled his shirt over his head, my mouth going bone dry. Our experience in the forest and the fact he stripped bare in front of me meant I finally felt like I had the right to ogle him. And ogle I did. So much so I had completely forgotten his request.

"Aurelia." The huskiness in his voice sent electric currents down my neck.

Eyes snapping up, I flushed with embarrassment. The fire could be seen burning in my eyes.

"Take those off." He signalled to my sodden clothing. A firmer tone, not thinking it was possible. One I would have despised coming from any other man. Not this one. I would walk off a ledge if he commanded me to and the thought wasn't met with any fear.

"You want me to shower with you?" My voice was low, confused as to what was about to happen.

Mads cocked a brow. "We don't want to waste water now, do we?"

My mouth gaped as he unlaced his trousers, shucking them off before standing in front of me, only the thin fabric of his undershorts covering him. The flush reared back, catching fire on my neck and rising rapidly to my cheeks. I took a breath, wrangling my current emotions. He had seen most of my naked body and my scars so why was there a lingering hint of embarrassment?

"I still have the taste of you on my tongue and you're worried about me seeing you naked?"

His breaths oozed sex. Coupled with the deep timbre, the words purred from his mouth. The cocky grin returned, making my knees weak. Regular Mads was a force to be reckoned with. Playful Mads? I may as well just lie down and die right there on the bedroom floor.

Internally, I reminded myself I was safe and decided to just go with it. Obeying his command, I shimmied out of the drenched leggings — not an easy task — and removed my top, leaving me with only the wrap covering my breasts. The undershorts were long gone. I paused, waiting for the self-doubt to roar to life. Surprisingly, nothing grew further than the slight niggle of embarrassment I'd had a few moments earlier. I felt nothing. Well, not nothing. It was difficult to pinpoint exactly what the emotion was, concluding the only thing I could relate it to was shoving the letter opening into Shelton. Was that power? Did the beautiful, scarred, broken man in front of me make me see how powerful I could be?

Mads took a slow step towards me, as though he were a predator trying not to scare off his prey. Mads wasn't a predator, not in the literal sense. He had captured a part of me I had thought dead and buried. He'd lit a path for me. It may be much longer to travel than I cared for, but right then, I decided I would very much like to explore it with him.

Reaching behind my back, I carefully untied the wrap covering my chest, removing it with precision, and focused on Mads' eyes locked on mine. Letting the wrap fall to the ground, I took a deep breath before I hung my arms at my side, standing naked in front of him. Mads took the opportunity to drink in every inch of me, pausing only to clench his jaw when he noticed the remaining scars painting my flesh. Not stories which needed to be told yet. When, what felt like years later, his eyes reached mine once more, his chest heaved. He then gifted me with the three most beautiful words anyone had ever spoken to me, "You are spectacular."

Biting back tears, no one in my life had ever looked at me the way Mads did. With complete and undying respect. Although it was sprinkled with desire, the wonder in his eyes couldn't be denied.

He offered me his hand, which I took before following him into the washroom where he proceeded to remove his undershorts. At that moment, my nerves decided to take over my body. In the past, I'd made a point never to look at anyone completely bare. With Mads, I wanted to consume every inch of him. Squeezing my eyes shut in an attempt to build courage, fingers grazed my cheeks. "You can look whenever you're ready."

Eyes still sealed shut, I nodded.

"I'm just going to pump the water a bit more."

Listening to his movements, I counted fifteen pumps before I felt Mads heat in front of me again.

"I've never —"

"You don't have to explain anything."

Timidly, I peeled my eyes apart, conscious of keeping only his face in view.

"I want to." And I did. The fear I felt from divulging my secrets wasn't a result of voicing them to him, more because I breathed life into them when I wanted them all dead.

Mads stared down silently at me, waiting for me to take the next step on my own.

"I've never seen one."

The words sounded ridiculous rolling off my tongue. Given my abusive past with the male sex, it seemed silly I'd never seen a dick before.

"A cock?" Mads' tone was only questioning, not condescending. I silently thanked him.

"Yes. I've had sex, but it was out of necessity, knowing what would eventually happen once I was married to Shelton. I just didn't want to see one."

We stood in silence for a few beats. "Can you say it?"

Quirking my brow in question. "Can I say what?"

"Cock."

The word off his lips sounded delicious, yet it didn't stop me from turning my head toward the window, unsure why I found it awkward.

"Of course I can say it."

"Then say it." Out of the corner of my eye, Mads crossed his arms over his chest in a matter-of-fact sort of way.

"Mads —"

"Say it, Aurelia. You can't take back these morsels of power without taking the steps. I'm not going to push you on anything, but you bet your fine arse I'll have you saying the filthiest things. And you know what? I promise, you will like it."

Gulping down my bashfulness, I let the word leave my mouth on a whisper. Mads' fingers found my chin, coaxing my eyes back on him. "I can't hear you. Give me your words."

"Cock!"

Shifting his hand to the back of my neck, Mads pulled my face to his in a bruising kiss. He didn't tempt my mouth open. He didn't need to. The fierceness of his closed lips on mine made my feet wobble.

Pulling back, he kept his grip on my neck firmly. "You say it so well."

Breathing heavily at the combination of the kiss and the small morsel of power I'd taken back, Mads twisted the shower knob and stepped in, keeping his backside to me, knowing I wasn't ready to see his front yet.

Following in after him, I pressed a chaste kiss to his shoulder, surprising myself. Intimacy was such a new concept to me in both thought and action. Reminding myself it wasn't a race, I needed to savour each second of it.

"Can I turn around?" Mads spoke towards the wall. I couldn't help the smile spreading from the thoughtfulness. The big, bad, unreadable onion peeled his layers quickly.

"Yes. I'm not going to look. Yet."

I added the last word in for good measure. Mads turned, brushing his hand over my eyes, "That's fine. You close your eyes, and I'll take it from here."

I sucked in a gasp as aching anticipation erupted from my core. Sensing it, Mads chuckled. "Not what you're thinking. I'd happily revisit it later though."

How had we gone from hate to this in the span of twenty-four hours was a mystery. If I really thought about it though, we'd never really hated each other. There had always been an underlying fear of what would happen if we admitted our feelings. Now that it was happening, at least somewhat, I couldn't remember the reason for the fear.

"Keep your eyes closed."

The gentle dominance his voice evoked intoxicated me. Listening intently, he picked up a bar of soap, floating a faint scent of lilac through the steam. After a few moments of lathering, his foam filled hands moved down my arm. It felt intimate, and it also wasn't as terrifying as I initially thought it would be.

Meticulously, he washed my left arm before grazing his hands over my collar bone to the right. He repeated the action with slow, gentle strokes before pausing to rub more soap between his hands. My breathing picked up a notch, anticipating the next area to be washed. A gasp left me as both of his hands cupped my breasts simultaneously. Almost a feather light touch, immediately leaving me yearning, my back arching.

"Stop being greedy."

I could hear the amusement in his voice.

"I'm not being greedy."

"Oh yeah? Then what are you doing?"

Unable to keep my eyes shut, I blinked them open, relishing in his beauty through the stream of steam. "I'm making up for lost time."

Mads' amusement faded, replaced by a sensual seriousness I hoped I would see much more often. "Trust me, we will make up for all of it."

Offering him a brief smile of gratitude, I closed my eyes once more, relishing every single touch of his fingers on my skin.

Shifting to my stomach, a hint of reservation bubbled up, ashamed of my thicker stomach, littered with raised scar tissue. When he hit the first one, I gasped involuntarily stepping back.

"Aurelia, if you don't want me to touch you in certain places, you can tell me. You need to know not one inch of you isn't beautiful to me."

I thought Xav was the only one with heightened empathic abilities. Maybe I'd been wrong. With a sliver of courage I held, naked in the shower, I stepped back to him, taking his hand and resting it back on my stomach. Without another word, he continued washing, taking more care with each scar he came across.

I was certain he'd move in between my legs next. I was surprised when I felt him bend down and begin his work on my legs, each stroke of his finger resonating deep in my core. Once he finished the second leg, I braced for the brush of those fingers across my slit excitedly, only to be disappointed when he stood and placed the soap in my hand.

Opening my eyes in disappointment and confusion, Mads had given his back to me once more.

"This part of you that I don't have a right to, yet. So, you'll need to take care of yourself."

I looked down at the soap in my hand, somewhat hurt at the emptiness I felt.

Looking over his shoulder, he said, "But, Aurelia?"

I glanced up at him, unable to hide my disappointment. "Your delicious pussy? It will be mine."

The certainty in his tone had me clenching my legs tighter than I ever had. I didn't even need this man to touch me to send me into a spiral. A madness I would happily drown in.

Silently, we moved around each other in familiarity, washing ourselves before Mads scrubbed soap into my hair. An act orgasmic in its own right.

After Mads turned off the shower, he motioned for me to step out while he grabbed a towel, engulfing my now clean and naked body in its warmth.

"That was nice."

Mads wrapped a towel around his waist before turning me to face him.

"I have so much more *nice* to show you."

I smiled, anticipating everything I would learn and regain. Mads stepped into the bedroom, calling over his shoulder. "First, we have some planning to do."

CHAPTER 24

AURELIA

Fresh from our intimate shower, Mads and I found the rest of the group huddled around the dining table, deep in conversation about something. Fox flicked his head up on our arrival, a sly smirk growing on his face. As he went to open his mouth, no doubt to announce something very Fox-esque, Mads slapped him across the back of the head.

"Fuck off, Mads! I didn't even say anything."

Mads glared down at his youngest brother as he soothed the spot where Mads' fingers met it. "I'm sure you were going to."

Bea broke her concentration on the papers laid out on the table. "Alright, children, Mads and Aurelia are together. That's great. Now can we get to important matters?"

I took a seat as Mads settled down next to me. "We have the stone so please don't tell us there is another bloody object we have to find."

The irritation in his voice was noticeable. Even though the little adventure had broken the dam between us, the anticipation for what was next heightened the tension around the table.

"No. We are good to go. Xav and Fox are picking up two more horses tomorrow —"

"Two?" I interjected.

"Yes, buttercup. One for me and one for you."

"I can't ride."

"I'll teach you." Fox chimed in, always the teacher.

Xav proceeded to fold up what looked to be a map as he said, "We aren't leaving for a few days yet, Aurelia. We will get the horses tomorrow and Fox can have a couple of days to get you comfortable enough for the journey."

Bea and Fox mirrored Xav, arranging their own papers.

"That's it? Then we go?"

Mads' hand slid over my knee, a brief squeeze in comfort. "That's it. Then we go."

In slow motion, the scene played out in front of me. My company's actions were not unusual, yet I couldn't ignore the dread settling in my stomach. Change was now the only thing constant in my life and I had two choices: I could break down, right there at the dining table, reneging on my agreement to help the brothers return to Hiema, claiming what was rightfully theirs, or two, I could embrace the new life I'd stumbled upon, holding each second close to my heart and never forgetting the traumatising events which lead me here were also a part of me. Mads squeezed my knee once more, before he stood to lend a hand.

With the hundreds of questions still looming over me, I also couldn't help acknowledge the flicker in my abdomen. The same one that urged me into this cabin. The one that showed me how to get the Alegra stone. It has been a consistent comfort to me since meeting the bears and now, it may be yet another potential for my future.

Given my connection to Raithe and in breaking the curse, there was a high likelihood that something deeper ran through my veins. Not only that, but I still couldn't escape the image of those three covered bodies. A subtle guilt washed over me at the thought of leaving my sister here, never knowing our true origin. We had never held a relationship like the one I had with Archer, but my mind wandered to the possibilities of what could have been for us, if we were never given over to Niall and Leona. Could we have built a relationship?

I sat in my daze a few moments longer before I felt a light grip on my shoulder. Turning my head, I was greeted by a rare sight, Fox with a compassionate smile lighting up his face. That is when it hit me — no fear ran deep enough to keep me from getting these men home. They had offered me more in the months I'd been with them than any other human being would have even considered. I was far from whole. I may never be. The bears gradually gave me back slivers of myself and of the person I could be.

Straightening my shoulders under Fox's fingers, I gave him a gentle nod, not towards anything in particular just confirming I was all in.

"How about we go get some training in while we have a few hours left of sunlight, Goldie?"

Thankful for the distraction, I stood and with no other objections, mental or vocal, I followed Fox to the training ring.

Our planned travel date loomed as I found myself fetching various salves and herbs from the storage shed as Bea barked orders at me from the kitchen. Xav and Fox had gone into town to pick up the additional horses we would need for our travelling party. Mads busied himself preparing the cabin to be vacant. None of us were sure what would become of the property once the curse was broken and the bears returned home. In my heart, I'd hoped the cloaking of the building would be lifted and someone worthy of this home would stumble upon it. No matter what was to happen next, it was clear the cabin had grown in importance to the brothers, giving them a home and shelter from so much loss.

The day was filled with a to do list keeping us all busy until it was time to prepare dinner. A certain buzz hummed around the brothers no matter where they were. Even with the known fight ahead of them, they'd be going home and I'd finally have the chance to start fresh. Not start over. I would never erase what I'd endured. I could learn to live with it. Manage the boxes. Let them free once in a while. I was comfortable with my decision.

After dinner, the bears, Bea and I found ourselves consuming a great deal of whisky, trading stories of Raithe. I listened intently, consuming as much as I could about the new world I would, hopefully, experience myself in a few days. Bea added in various anecdotes from the time she came into their lives.

Bea had been drinking on her own at The Bloody Duck, a local pub, enjoying a quiet supper when a fanciful Fox had drunkenly stumbled into her and immediately turned on his charm. It hadn't worked, apparently, but Bea insisted she had known something different surrounded the brothers.

Eventually, she was invited back to their table. It only took a few more pints and probing questions for her to confirm they weren't from this world. It was the seed in which the family grew into. A family, Bea added for clarity, which now included me. My heart had swelled immediately upon the confession, but I let my past experiences with family linger in thought. Too much had happened. Too much broken. Still, I let a sliver of it live. The thought of a family.

As I laid in Mads' bed, his body pressed against my back, the way his arm around my stomach and the soft sounds of his sleep in my ear soothed me as a string of lightness burst through my chest. If I concentrated enough, I imagined it could be described as happiness.

"You got up on Ace just fine. Why is this so hard?"

Fox barked his frustrations at my fourth failed attempt to mount my horse, Bandit. They had specifically requested a smaller, agile horse for me. One easy to ride and could keep up with the rest of the tenured group.

"If you'd stop shouting at me maybe I could concentrate." I was just about to concede the horse was impossible to mount.

"I'm not shouting," Fox answered with a cheeky grin. "I'm training."

"Training my arse. I'd have better luck if you weren't here."

Contemplation fell across his face before he turned and walked away, throwing a 'fine' over his shoulder as he did so. I hadn't actually thought he'd leave me. I let him huff his way across the clearing before turning back to Bandit.

"We can do this. Right?"

The horse blinked, inciting no interest in my cool, calm tone. Grabbing the pommel, I put my left foot in the stirrup once more. Taking a deep breath, I launched myself upwards on the exhale, catching myself when I lost a bit of my hold on the horn. I sank down into the seat, immediately finding the stirrup for my right foot. Bandit stayed still as I whooped. "Fox!"

Elation ran through me. A small victory. A victory nonetheless.

"What?" He called to me from the training shed, agitation running through his tone.

"I did it!"

He peeked his head out to find I was, indeed, seated on Bandit, successfully. A proud grin spread across his face as he walked towards me.

"I knew you could do it."

I rolled my eyes. "You didn't imply any confidence when you were getting annoyed with me earlier."

He reached up to take the reins from me. "I wasn't *annoyed*."

"Liar." I smirked. Banter. We were bantering. And it felt good. Normal.

"Right, now the next step."

"Which is?" I looked ahead at the forest beyond.

"Riding."

Before I could protest in worry, Fox began showing me various commands. It was going to be a long day.

Against my initial fears, I took to riding well for a beginner. Fox kept any possible frustrations he may have had fully at bay and focused on praising me when I got something right, also firmly correcting me when I didn't. We laughed a lot, cementing the kinship bubbling up for the last few weeks. My heart warmed thinking about what each of these brothers gave me. Fox, the most hands on in his efforts, brought a lightness to my heart and mind providing a reassuring tranquillity. An odd thought given the calm was brought through tricks and a smart mouth.

Once Fox deemed I was decent enough on Bandit, we tucked him into the stables for the evening. Fox announced he had a few things to get done so I kept myself busy by first showering and then deciding to prepare dinner on my own. The rest of the house's current inhabitants, Bea included, given she refused to go home anymore, would be back soon and given the number of things we needed to do before our trip, I wanted to contribute wherever I could.

As I was putting the pie in the oven, Fox crashed through the back door, breathing heavily, a jilted smile resting comfortably on his face.

"Fox, what the hell?"

Taking no time to catch his breath, he huffed out, "Goldie, you are going to want to see this."

Quickly, his playful grin had faded, leaving a deliberate energy in the room, filled with unwavering support and protection. "Do you trust I wouldn't let anything happen to you?"

"I do."

With those two words, Fox reached out and gently took my hand in his own, giving me only a few seconds before he pulled me back outside with him.

His pace was hurried, as though whatever it was he had found would be scared away. I kept quiet, saving my questions for what may await me in the next few minutes. I was smart enough not to voice any of my curiosities too soon as Fox would easily brush them off or offer only a sarcastic remark in return. He was on a mission and it was best I let it play out.

We kept a quick pace through the woods at the back of the house, not venturing too far before we came into a small clearing with a small cabin in the middle. "What the hell?"

I had toured the grounds enough to know all the buildings contained within it. Apart from this one. This one was new.

"What is this place Fox?"

Fox dropped my hand, staring breathlessly at the building in front of us. "This is the sex cabin."

I gasped, "The sex cabin?"

Turning to me, Fox's cocky grin was back. "Well, you know, we can't bring potential partners to the cabin, curse and all. So, we built this place."

Nausea rose immediately at the thought of how many women Mads had brought back here. A sex cabin. Part of me knew it was reasonable, given they couldn't entertain women at the house. Apart from Bea. I tried to resist the jealousy burrowing itself behind my rib cage.

"Why did you want to show me the sex cabin?" Violence rolled off my tongue.

Fox must have had an ulterior motive. He was a trickster, sure, but he wouldn't be out to hurt me intentionally. "It isn't the sex cabin. It is what is inside the sex cabin."

Pausing, Fox's expression took a grave turn. "I didn't mean it to come out like that."

I nodded, my body beginning to tremble.

"Shall we?"

Fox offered his hand to which I took immediately. Whatever I was about to face, I'd need him on side. Unlocking the door and stepping inside, I followed closely at his heels.

The cabin itself was small, comfortably decorated. A fireplace sat off to my right, framed in various shades of grey stones. A small window sat beside it with a cosy corner ordained with an armchair and small bookshelf not much further along. In the centre of the room, an incredibly large bed sat, taking up most of the room's space. The bed itself was littered with various quilts and furs. An image of a naked Mads, devouring another woman dropped into my head. I shook it off as quickly as it came. Not something I needed to focus on right then because as my sight drifted further to the left, it landed on what Fox had found.

"Aurelia?"

No. No. No. No. No.

A voice I knew well. One with so many opportunities to come to my rescue. This couldn't be happening. Tomorrow I was due to start fresh. In a new world. Where I'd never have to think of my family again. Except I was now in a cabin with a very real ghost from my past.

"Sister?"

Evangeline looked just as I remembered and the complete opposite of me. Eva was shorter, petite build and long flowing brunette locks cascading down her back in the most perfect soft and luscious curls. The one and only trait we shared was our piercing blue eyes. Swallowing the anger down as best I could, I locked eyes with my little sister. Eva's face lit up, tears began pouring down her cheeks as she jumped to her feet and attempted to grab me into a familial embrace. I stepped back instantly. Fox took the hint, pushing himself between me and my sister.

"Sit back down."

An odd tone to hear from Fox's mouth. Commanding, sure, and protective. I was grateful. Looking at my sister, a flood of memories rose to the surface. Although Eva wasn't a direct recipient of the memories now at the forefront of my mind, she assisted in many. Always knowing what had happened and never doing anything to help me. The distance between us had grown swiftly and at a rather young age. I couldn't tell Eva about anything because we'd never allowed each other the opportunity to build a relationship.

"Aurelia, you have to listen to me."

"On the contrary, Aurelia stopped taking orders from anyone and she doesn't have to do a damn thing you say."

A soft squeeze rippled through my chest. I reached out to gently squeeze Fox's hand in thanks and also get his attention back on me.

"Go get your brothers."

I surprised myself at the harshness in my own tone. Fox looked back at me, brow knit, "But —"

"Go. Get. Your. Brothers."

Spending only a few moments studying my potential motives, Fox surrendered with a nod before leaving the cabin, throwing at Eva, "Touch her and it will be the last thing you ever do."

Eva, accepting the seriousness of the threat, began visibly shaking. Fox made to leave before turning back to my sister, ensuring the distance stood.

"Aurelia, it's so good to see you."

"No." I shook my head, taking one further step back. "You don't get to do that."

Confused, tears continued to stream down Eva's face. "What are you talking about?"

"You do not get to turn up in my life, a life I had to take back for myself, and act as if you missed me. Act as if we were anything to each other. Blood does not make us family."

I hadn't realised the tension radiating off of my skin, coaxing the room into an uncomfortable energy. "You had so many chances to help me and you did nothing."

"Aurelia —"

"You stood by and let them take everything from me."

"Aur —"

"Shut your gods damn mouth, Eva."

The tears morphed into a gentle sob, one I thought would've sent something through me. Guilt, sorrow, helplessness. I wouldn't allow myself to grant her pity. We stood in silence for only a few moments more before the door burst open, Mads throwing himself towards me in pure undulated anger. "What happened?"

Wrapping his hands across the back of my neck, he surveyed my face before moving his exploration down my body. "Nothing. I'm fine."

Xav and Fox entered next, neither of which looking any happier than Mads did.

"So," Xav took hold of the room, "you're the little sister?"

His tone was pleasant enough. I now knew him well enough to know the venom sat very closely behind it. Looking between the three brothers, I felt a slight spark of joy knowing I was part of their family now. The protectiveness and kindness they continued to show made it clear enough.

"Y-y-yes. I'm E — Eva."

"Well, Eva, why don't we all have a little chat."

Instantly obeying Xav's request, Eva dropped back down into the chair. Fox stood leaning against the fireplace while Mads motioned for me to sit at the edge of the bed, him at my side. Xav stayed standing, taking the role of interrogator.

"Fox here," Xav gestured at Fox who only raised a brow in response, "This is Fox by the way. Fox told us he found you in the woods and when you asked for Aurelia, he figured it was best to bring you here. What I'd like to know is what, exactly, you were doing in the woods and why you were so determined to find Aurelia?"

Eva thought hard on how she'd approach the initial line of questioning. Her cheeks were stained terribly with tears, and it was clear she was doing her utmost to hold back more from slipping free.

"After father left, well, he disappeared actually. Not long after you left. And then everything went to shit."

Eva toyed with the edge of her skirt. A nervous twitch similar to me.

"How about we start from the beginning?"

Xav's empathetic nature mirrored the fact he was politically savvy and was the exact person who should be running the conversation. I reminded myself of this before scooting closer to Mads who had refused to remove one of his hands from my waist.

Eva looked around the room at each of us before she looked down at her lap, psyching herself up, no doubt.

"Aurelia, you left and everything turned into chaos. None of us know what happened with Lord Shelton. They found him in really bad shape. Father was absolutely livid and Mother just — well, she got really quiet about everything. The town was in upheaval thinking they may lose the most senior ranking councilman and funding for so many of the town's facilities. When Lord Shelton was given the clear, Father packed up a couple of bags and announced he was going out for a while. He made some off-handed comments about trying to find you but I didn't think he would."

I had to interject on this point, "Why?"

At the question, Eva locked eyes with me, a rather severe and unknown look flashed her face. "Because I knew you'd never let him."

A moment passed between us. Foreign yet not unwelcome. If I studied it, it was almost as though Eva had felt something for me. Had she cared for me? I shook my head, I couldn't remember a single moment where Eva had stood up for me, offered me comfort or even spoke to me with any form of respect. Something lay beneath Eva's reasoning to find me. I needed to uncover it.

"Look." Eva's tears halted momentarily. "All I'm asking is you let me explain my side of the story and then you can decide whether or not you want to throw me out."

"Are we not doing that now? Letting you explain yourself?"

I glanced back at Fox, noting a sparkle in his eye. Eva looked around the modest space, before bringing her attention back to Fox, not me.

"Maybe somewhere a bit more comfortable? I can barely breathe in here."

To emphasise she was stifling, Eva tugged on the collar of her pale blue dress.

"You're lucky we are letting you breathe at all." Fox kicked off the fireplace, taking a few steps to eat up the space between him and our new visitor. "You did nothing for Aurelia so why should we do anything for you?"

The room went silent. The deadly side of Fox was enough to make me tremble. It was clear either his protectiveness or his pure dislike of Eva would not be ignored. Xav stepped around Fox to address his brothers directly. "We could get Bea —"

"No." Mads shut down the suggestion before Xav could even finish.

Sighing in frustration, an odd site to see from Xav, he turned to me. "Aurelia, I'm going to leave it up to you, as we all should." He shot both Mads and Fox a look to say, 'she gets the choice, remember.'

Offering a slight smile in gratitude, I looked to my sister. A person I wouldn't have minded never giving another thought to. There she was, barging into my new life with secrets I was unfortunately desperate to know.

"If Bea can, we can move this to the house."

Fox walked out, both in agitation and to fetch Bea for the appropriate spell. I hoped. Mads stood, walking confidently to the door before turning back to me in silent question, was I sure? Not knowing exactly how to answer, I nodded before looking to Xav.

"Alright then. We will see if we can get you into the house and then you can tell us your side of the story."

"Why can't I get into the house now?"

Xav and I exchanged a questioning look. How much were we willing to reveal? We were leaving this world tomorrow so even if Eva knew more than necessary, no one would believe her to even attempt to come after us. Without turning back to Eva, keeping his eyes on me, he said, "We will have to find out if you are worthy of knowing anything."

Eva rubbed her palms together, fighting the visible nervousness still ricocheting through her body. "Okay."

"What do you mean Aurelia's sister?" Bea's booming voice travelled through the clearing, hitting the ears of us left in the cramped cabin. Fox and Bea soon stood at the door, Bea wide eyed as she stared down at Eva and then back to me.

"Interesting."

Bea's curiosity filled the small space as I stood. "Bea, this is my sister, Eva."

The image of the wrapped bodies in a wheelbarrow flashed in my mind. Knowing that both Eva and Archer came through the portal with me made our current situation more complicated.

Bea assessed us silently before announcing she could get Eva into the house with a small bit of her blood, which she took quickly and without asking permission. Bea turned and headed back toward the main house to work her spell. Before the rest of the party followed her, Fox stepped in front of Eva, hatred painted on his face. "If you do anything, and I mean anything, physical or otherwise, to hurt Aurelia, I can assure you I will follow through on my promises."

I stared, gobsmacked at Fox, unable to process the threatening tone while Eva's trembling body almost convulsed with fear. Xav chuckled, as though a hidden joke was laced in Fox's threat before leading them out of the cabin.

Only an hour ago my biggest problem was accepting the fact I was given the opportunity of a new life when now, my old life decided to haunt me.

CHAPTER 25

AURELIA

The spell was completed with the utmost speed, no one in our group wanted to prolong the situation we'd currently found ourselves in. Eva took in the inside of the house in fascination, something I'd done myself not long ago. Mads stayed silent, sticking close to my side wherever I went, acting as my shadow. I was grateful he wasn't making a bigger fuss, letting his youngest brother take on the role of intimidator.

Xav, the ever present host, had made us a tray of tea and biscuits while Bea sat in her favourite armchair, glowering at our new guest. It was clear no one was overly excited Eva had come knocking. I was restless with anticipation of what she had to tell us.

We waited for Xav to pour the tea, which no one touched, before settling down in the seat across from Eva, readying himself to play the questioner. His body language was open in an attempt to draw out a semblance of safety for Eva. I knew the posture well, having been on the receiving end of it so many times since I arrived.

"Eva let's start from the beginning. Can you tell us a little more about what happened before Aurelia escaped?"

Escaped. Not left. Xav knew the reason I fled was the result of things inflicted on me, not by my own choices.

Eva fidgeted, looking for a position to give her the confidence to begin. She took a long, slow breath before answering, "Aurelia and I have never been close. Even before Archer disappeared. It was always Archer and Aurelia. I was happy for them. I had always been the apple of my parent's eyes. I was the pretty one. The perfect one. Well, perfect for the lives they strived to live."

Her tone didn't indicate those judgements brought her happiness, rather they were spat from her mouth in disgust.

"And what life was that?"

Eva's eyes locked on Xav, she said. "A life of power. Influence. One where they would never be the order takers, instead, the order givers."

"It wasn't for a lack of trying, Aurelia and I. There were some points in our childhood where I thought we could build a relationship. Be more than sisters. Maybe even friends."

I shifted, a move Mads recognised. Sensing my discomfort, he shuffled slightly to get closer to me on the couch. His body heat, coupled with the surrounding cedar dancing across my nose, brought me a slight reprieve. I knew he wouldn't offer direct touch, wanting me to face these incidents and memories without physical support.

"Then Archer disappeared," Eva continued, a hint of sadness echoing her words. "Our worlds were turned upside down. I thought our parents would be wrecked over the loss of Archer. All it really did was fuel their fire for more power. The loss meant my father wouldn't have a male heir and ultimately no one to try and overtake him. Mother began living her life even more lavishly. At first, I thought it was a coping mechanism to losing her only son. I realised, not soon after, it wasn't the reason at all."

"Then what was it?" Xav coaxed comfortably.

"It was like she had a new-found freedom and two daughters she could leverage in her journey for influence."

Eva paused, letting the story sink in. I remembered those weeks after Archer's disappearance. I had sunk so low in my own despair, knowing my one and only ally was gone. My brother and the only friend I'd ever known.

"Something else happened with Archer's disappearance."

The room was captivated. I couldn't help the sense of foreboding swirling around me.

"When Archer disappeared, something swept over me. You know when you get really frustrated or agitated and it's hard to find words? How you can get tongue tied?"

Although Eva addressed Xav, the entire room nodded to her question.

"It happened all the time. Whenever I'd tried to talk to our parents about Archer's disappearance or even approach Aurelia, it was like some larger force stopped me, pushed me in another direction. In my head, I knew it was wrong. Nothing I did could fight it. It was as though someone muted me, forcing me to ignore or stay away from Aurelia and any of the horrible situations after Archer."

Looking back down at her hands, Eva twirled her fingers between each other before raising her gaze to me. Both of our breaths had deepened, something silent passing between us. Not long ago, thinking something magical lay beneath my strained relationship with my sister would have never crossed my mind. Now though? Now, I didn't think I could disregard any theories especially given my potential connection with Raithe and the significant role I may play in breaking the brother's curse.

"You mean to tell me," I said as I sat forward, "all those times you didn't fight for me, you wanted to?"

Eva mirrored my movements, untangling her hands from one another and resting them on her knees. "Yes, Aurelia. I tried so many times to talk to you, to our parents, to make it all stop. Physically, I couldn't. I know it sounds impossible —"

"Improbable."

Fox broke his silence.

"Sorry?" Eva looked to him for further explanation, always on alert when he opened his mouth.

"It would be improbable. Not impossible."

The room went silent once more before Eva probed, "I don't know what you mean."

"He means," Bea interjected, "there is something larger at work. You could have been spelled."

Eva sat back, chuckling in resistance. "Now you all sound just as insane as I do."

Every pair of eyes stayed trained on Eva as she began shifting in her seat once more. A silent conversation taking place to ascertain just how much information we would reveal to her.

"Will you excuse us for a moment?" Xav gestured for us to follow him into the kitchen. Everyone apart from Bea obeyed. "Aren't you coming?"

"I trust whatever decision you make. I'll stay here and make sure this one," she thrust her finger towards Eva, "doesn't do anything stupid."

Eva rolled her eyes at the accusation. "I'm not going to burn the house down."

Bea huffed. "You won't with me watching you. I'd set you on fire before you ever had a chance to do it to the house."

Bea crossed her arms, Eva immediately mirrored the action. I looked between the two as each of their stares drilled into one another. Fox nudged me to keep moving to which I obliged. The Eva I'd just seen was one I knew well. I also knew Bea would win if a fight did present itself.

Xav, Fox and Mads stood huddled by the stove waiting for me before they started their hushed conversation.

"What do we think?" Xav started.

Mads let out a slow breath, "I don't like it."

"Look at it this way," Fox chimed in, "we leave tomorrow and even if she did decide to tell anyone, she wouldn't be able to find us again."

My thoughts exactly.

"I agree," Xav muttered. "Plus, there is something more to this story. I know it."

The brothers looked to me for my thoughts. I was having trouble voicing them.

"What more is there?" It was all I could offer. A deep rooted need to connect with Eva pulsed in my fingers.

Xav studied me, quietly, as if trying not to scare off a mouse.

"It does seem strange she felt she couldn't say anything....through everything."

His tone was unsure as though he mentioned something he shouldn't. I reached out to squeeze his upper arm in comfort. None of the three in front of me should be scared of offending me. Did they know everything? Of course not. I wasn't even sure how much more I would share. I did know, in my heart of hearts, they would never purposefully cause me pain. Physical or emotional.

"It is strange. I never read much into our relationship. Or lack thereof. I just assumed she was in line with my parents' way of thinking." I looked back towards the living room as that niggling intuition pulsed. The sensation had intensified since we got the Alegra stone and now, in the presence of my sister, I couldn't ignore the awareness that what Eva told us was the truth. I allowed myself to sit in thought for a moment before turning back to the brothers. "Maybe I was wrong."

Agreeing Eva should be let into the fold a bit more, we made our way back out into the sitting area where Bea and Eva were in the exact positions they were when we had left, scowls covering their faces. Taking our previous seats, Xav took the lead once more.

"Eva, we believe you."

Hope filled Eva's face as she unfolded her arms to clench the sides of the chair. "Really?"

A great deal of optimism sat in her tone and her body language. Even with Eva's slightly miscalculated hope, I believe her and the concept of something larger at play in our lives.

"We do. Only because of what we are about to tell you."

Eva sat back once again, folding her hands, fiddling her forefingers together in discontent.

"What we are about to divulge, will never leave this room. Do you understand?"

Eva looked at Fox, I didn't understand why. Maybe it was his previous threats evoking a fear in her. As my younger sister met the eyes of the youngest brother, someone I had started to see as my own brother, I sensed something deeper. It was too much to dig further into currently, although it was definitely a look I would explore later.

"I understand."

Xav sat back, appearing relaxed. I knew better. Xav was at the peak of his mortal realm power, showcasing a calm demeanour with many underlying motives. I envied him. Admired him. I realised I was also incredibly grateful to have a second brother. Just as I felt with Fox, I'd adopted this family. Every part of me knew, and I had no doubt it would grow deeper.

"We are not from this world. My brothers and I" — he gestured to Fox and Mads — "were exiled here many years ago."

He paused, waiting for the information to sink in, eliciting a reaction from Eva. In another shocking turn, Eva held the same stern look she'd had since she entered the house. No hint of disbelief or worry. Suddenly, Rock bounded into the room, briefly assessing the new company before hopping up onto the couch and curling next to me. On instinct, I began brushing his fur with my fingers.

Eva blinked at the new addition to the room, no hint of surprise on her face, before returning her attention to Xav. Taking it as a sign to continue, "We recently discovered your sister is a key to unlocking the curse and should help us get home."

I wasn't sure what kind of response Xav was looking for. Whatever it was, Eva still didn't offer it. She continued to stare at him. Where was the scepticism? The yelling? The bellows of laughter insisting this was madness? Why wasn't she reacting at all? I, myself, hadn't had a huge reaction to the truth from the brothers but from what

I thought I knew of my sister, the information should have affected her in some way. Therein lies the point. Maybe I didn't know the woman at all.

"We are leaving tomorrow, to return to our homeland and —"

"Where are you from?"

Calm. Collected. The question was delivered with interest. No distaste. No disbelief. Just pure, undulated curiosity. Xav was slightly taken aback although he hid it well. "The land is based upon the seasons."

"So, you have seasonal kingdoms?"

My mouth fell at her sister's intuition.

"We do."

"And which kingdom are you from?"

Xav couldn't hide his shock any longer. Fox, however, was unamused. "Winter."

Eva flicked her head towards Fox, the scowl returning once more.

"You don't seem...bothered by this information."

"Should I?" The retort was spoken with more fire than I thought Eva was capable of.

I glanced between the brothers and Bea, uncertain of how to move the conversation forward. We would have been in the same position should Eva have not believed anything they revealed.

"No. I mean, it makes it a lot easier if you seem to believe us."

"I don't believe him." Eva poked her finger towards Fox who immediately chuckled at the movement.

"What the hell did I do?"

Eva huffed before launching back immediately, "Well first" — she raised her index finger — "You tackled me to the ground, when I had done nothing but ask for your help."

I shot a stunned glare at Fox.

"Second" — her middle finger shot up — "you tied me up, gagged me and then took me to a random cabin in the woods."

Out of the corner of my eye, a slight smile rose on Mads' mouth. I shoved my elbow in his side.

"Third" — her ring finger joined the other two — "You have repeatedly threatened me even though I have done nothing to prove myself a threat."

"Nothing?" Fox stood. "You were an accomplice in the misery she lived through." He jammed his finger toward me, and I instantly wished I was invisible.

Eva launched onto her feet. "I told you, I couldn't do anything even if I wanted to!"

Fox cackled. "How convenient."

"Convenient?" She stalked towards him, shoving her index finger in his chest. "You know nothing about me. So do yourself a favour and stop making assumptions about things and people you don't fucking know."

I stilled in shock. In all the years I'd spent with Eva, profanity would have never left her mouth. It was garish. Rude. And unbecoming of the lady she wished to be. I bit back the laugh I was suddenly desperate to release. So much of what I knew, or thought I knew, began to unravel in front of my eyes, and I would do everything in my power not to look away.

"Eva?" I spoke as calmly as possible, mirroring Xav's gentle approach. "Why don't you sit back down and tell us why you came to find me."

Eva didn't take her eyes off Fox as she backed up to her seat. Sitting back down, a clear tremble of anger radiated through her.

Fox sat down, finally breaking the eye contact he had with Eva who shifted her eyes to me. "I came to find you because I knew I could finally tell you everything I was blocked from saying all these years."

The trigger for my fight or flight response kicked in. I was terrified of what Eva's next words might bring into the world. I needed to hear her out. I did the utmost to prepare myself.

"How?" The question fell from my lips so low it was almost a whisper.

Eva wove her fingers between one another. "It's difficult to explain."

"Try." Fox shot back.

Inhaling a breath, Eva's eyes found mine once more. "It was a feeling, so low in my stomach, as though everything I'd tried to say for all those years needed to escape. Not for the words to just breathe air, but for me to tell you, Aurelia. I needed to speak with you."

My breath felt short at her admission, both because I hated that something else was kept from me. That something being a potential ally. A relationship with my own sister. But also due to the fact that I knew a very similar sensation. The puzzle pieces were slowly coming together. I didn't know how to put it all together, but I wanted to find out.

"And what did you want to tell me?"

Eva shifted her body, "I wanted to say, Aurelia... I want to say I'm so sorry. I tried so many times to step in. The weird, blank, imaginary forcefield stopped me from ever defending you. From helping you. And it killed me, every single day, knowing I could do nothing."

Eva's eyes filled with the tears she was never able to shed. I couldn't stop the strong emotion rising in my chest. At first, the sadness of everything we had lost. The innocence. The opportunity for an ally, a friend. The grief of those losses quickly morphed into pure rage. Everything was taken from me. Not just me, Eva too. Shelton, and our father, played a more significant part in our lives than I initially knew. I couldn't deny it was all tied together. Without taking my eyes off of Eva, I said "Can you all leave us alone?"

Mads let out a low growl to my right. "Is this the best thing —"

"Leave us."

An unexpected power accompanied those two words. I felt it in my soul. The room felt it. Bea stood, gesturing for the brothers to do the same. "We will be right next door if you need us, buttercup."

The tears continued to silently stream down Eva's face. All the hatred I'd felt toward the woman in front of me was a lie. I knew it in my bones. Now we could have a second chance. The distance I'd put between us wasn't going to stop what happened next.

"Alright," I said as I sat back, folding my hands in my lap, "tell me everything."

CHAPTER 26

MADDOX

Leaving Aurelia in the room with that woman set my nerves aflame at the potential threat. I struggled to hold back the need for revenge on her behalf, just as I had with Shelton and Niall. Closing my eyes to take a deep breath, I reminded myself Aurelia's healing could be assisted only when she asked for it. I had to respect her wishes to spend some time alone with Eva.

"I don't like this." The words spilled from Fox's mouth on a grunt.

Thankfully, I was given something else to focus on — Fox's newly developed and intense hostility towards our new guest. The animosity was out of character for Fox, making it hard to concentrate on my own anger. I crossed my arms as an intrigued smirk tipped the corners of my mouth.

"This is unusual for you, brother." Xav busied himself in the kitchen, never able to keep idle, the playfulness in his comment could not be ignored.

"What does she want with Aurelia?" Fox huffed, indignation burning through his next question.

I studied my baby brother for a few moments. The odd behaviour had begun as soon as he announced to us Aurelia's sister was here. He twitched with a clear agitation running through his body as though he didn't know how to manage the emotions he experienced.

My smile grew at the realisation. Fox noticed immediately. "Why in the hell are you smiling?"

Fox's agitation grew as I said, "I'm smiling, little brother, because it is entertaining to see you like this." I plucked a grape from the plate Xav had placed in front of us, savouring the sensation of my teeth breaking through the thin skin, a drip of the juice falling over my bottom lip.

"Entertaining?" Fox threw up his hands. "Why are you not angrier? That's your woman in there being haunted by the ghosts of her past."

Plucking off another grape, I took a seat, ensuring my laid back posture was clear to the room as I spoke, "First, she is not *my* anything. If Aurelia chooses to be with me, it's *her* choice. Second, I think you're experiencing more than anger towards our new guest."

Xav froze, turning back towards me with a look in a silent attempt to shut me up. The idea an unhinged Fox didn't sit well with him while I itched to bring him out to play. Life was dull for so long and then this hidden firecracker appeared bringing us all to our knees, happily.

"I still don't fucking like it. There is something seriously off about the entire thing. The day before we leave, she turns up? Does anyone else find it too much of a coincidence?"

Trix chuckled as she too plucked a grape from the tray Xav had laid out, covered with various meats, cheeses, and spreads. "Everything about our lives is odd, Foxy. This could be a good thing."

"I agree," Xav threw over his shoulder. "Aurelia deserves some semblance of closure before she leaves this world behind."

Fox looked dumbfounded at his supposed support system. I shot him a wink, seemingly adding fuel to his fire.

Lowering his voice, Fox stared directly at me. "She can't be trusted."

Studying him intently, I could see the anger hid something. Whatever it was, Fox was not revealing his whole hand. "Did something happen in the woods today?" My tone was curiously confident. Knowing my baby brother better than Fox wanted me to.

"I don't know what you mean." Fox's gaze moved away from me, suddenly finding the kitchen window interesting.

"It's just a bit odd you — someone who rarely lets themselves succumb to anger — stand in this kitchen with steam coming out of your ears."

On instinct, Fox cupped his ears before throwing me his most dangerous facial expression.

"Nothing happened," Fox confirmed.

"Something must have happened." Xav stepped forward, appearing as intrigued as I was.

Panic began to rise visibly in Fox's eyes. He was being backed into a corner he couldn't talk himself out of. "She ran up to my horse asking for help, when she told me she was looking for Aurelia, I threw her over the back of the horse and took her to the sex cabin."

"That's all?" Trix now stood next to us, arms crossed showcasing she didn't believe him either.

"Yes! What the hell? Why would there be anything else?"

Xav nudged me as a reminder pushing Fox further wouldn't prove fruitful. Deciding to dial it back, I offered some advice, "Just watch how you project your anger on our...new guest, little brother. After all, whether we like it or not, she is Aurelia's family and now, by extension, within our protection too."

Fox bowed his head in defeat, knowing in his heart I was right. He would do anything for Aurelia now. She was one of us whether she was yet to realise it or not.

"So, we aren't going to do anything reckless or insulting." I asked, but it was more of a command.

"I won't if she won't."

"Fox," Xav interrupted, "you're a grown man, a prince, and you know you are better than this. You've never let a woman get under your skin this way before."

His boot slammed into the chair, knocking it on its side. The three of us looked at him in disbelief. Fox had bedded his fair share of women. In full honesty, Fox bedded many people's fair share of women, none of which had caused such a change in his demeanour, his attitude, his tone. I felt a slight twinge of worry. The worry, however, was overshadowed by pure curiosity as to how this dynamic would play out. I had a few guesses as to what they could channel mutual dislike into. I wouldn't dare mention them to my brother now.

Shoving a hunk of ham into his mouth, Fox muttered something about waiting outside to clear his head and we were to call him back in when Aurelia gave the okay.

Xav and Trix joined me at the table. "What do you think that's about then?"

"I have my theories," I answered Xav,

"Theories?" Trix asked in a huff, "You make it sound so intricate and deep. The boy likes the girl. End of."

I loved Trix. She had entered our lives so unexpectedly, bringing a lightness to our dark, constantly surprising us around every turn. It was no secret I was more than glad she had decided to join us in Hiema. Once we'd taken back our kingdom, I would ask her to be on my advisory board. A talented witch and a smart mouth were exactly what I needed.

I snickered. Her blunt approach was refreshing. "I agree."

"Me too. He's really wound up. I do believe what he said about protecting Aurelia. I know this has to go beyond his protective instincts." Xav stood again. I worried about my brother's inability to sit for longer than five minutes. Xav was great at hiding his true level of stress. As his brother, and closest friend, I saw straight through the mask. I wasn't ignorant of the journey, the fight we had ahead of us. More than anything, I wanted to get my brother's back to where their hearts lie. We had made it work in the human realm because we had no other choice. I knew my brothers, like me, had left huge parts of ourselves in Hiema. Some parts even died with our parents.

A feminine throat clearing brought me out of my own head. Aurelia stood under the archway separating the living space from the dining space. I stood, failing at my attempt not to come across too eager. At moments like this, I couldn't help myself. I fiercely wanted to protect her from everything and anything bringing her any emotion other than pure joy. I knew it wasn't possible. Even after everything she'd been through, she was fiercely independent , and I wanted only to stand by her on her journey ahead, bringing forward anyone who hurt her so she could take their heads herself.

"Everything alright?" I did my best to keep the concern from my tone. Not a particular strong suit of mine. Graciously, Aurelia offered me an understanding smile.

"Yes."

We stood, staring silently at one another. So much could be said with a look. Once Aurelia assured me with her eyes she really was okay, the tension in my shoulders loosened slightly.

"Bea," she turned to the witch, "would you be able to tell if a spell or hex was put on Eva?"

Trix looked between us, more just a sign of respect given I knew she would help Aurelia whether I wanted her to or not. I was glad. *Glad?* I couldn't remember the last time I'd thought of the word, let alone felt it.

"I can. She's your sister and therefore has a connection with Raithe."

"What do you need?" Aurelia took one step, slightly closing the distance between them. It didn't go unnoticed her step was slightly towards me as opposed to moving straight into the space.

"Just another small prick of blood. I'll go get my bag."

As Trix hurried from the room, I noticed the faint sounds of Xav busying himself in the kitchen once more, giving us the semblance of privacy. I could have waited for her to take another step towards me. Maybe I should have. I couldn't stand the distance, especially when her past had come back to haunt her in the form of her younger sister. I closed the distance, looking down at her with questioning eyes.

Aurelia tilted her head to meet mine and slowly placed her hands on my chest. "I believe her Maddox. I just want proof for you all."

I lifted an eyebrow, not fully believing her statement. "And maybe a little bit for me too."

Silently, I nodded before gently grazing my lips across her forehead.

"I'm ready!" Trix shouted from the other room. Not wanting to leave the two women alone, Aurelia turned on her heel and moved back into the living room. I gave her a few steps forward before I followed suit, turning to lock eyes with Xav and jerking my head for him to follow.

"What are we going to do if it turns out she was hexed?"

Thinking for a moment, I eyed my brother and voiced the only available option we had, "If she was hexed, then it's Aurelia's choice what happens next."

It would be her choice. Everything in her life would now and forever be her choice.

Chapter 27

Aurelia

"All I need is a small drop or two of your blood," Bea explained as she pulled various vials and tools from her satchel. Eva nodded, immediately holding out her index finger.

The room followed Bea's actions as she pulled out a small glass bottle and a small leather folding case filled with various sized needles. The knot in my stomach tightened as Bea selected the appropriate needle. It was still hard to believe my sister was there, making footprints in my new life. I couldn't deny something about it felt — well, good.

I never remembered holding any hatred towards Eva. Just indifference. I'd always assumed Eva was the perfect image of our parents never considering an alternative judgement. If I had learned anything about my past, it was that I should not hold guilt for how I'd felt back then. Circumstances change and if this was a new opportunity for me and my baby sister, I couldn't pass it up. Not a single part of me thought Eva had lied about a potential spell. The real question now was, what was going to happen once it was proved to the bears?

I'd briefly explained to Eva that we, too, were likely not from this world, only giving her a high level recount of my visions when I was under Bea's spell. Again, my sister had taken the news maturely, even shaking her head in agreement when I revealed Niall and Leona were not our birth parents.

Bea pricked Eva's finger swiftly. She let out a small wince, keeping her hand steady. I glanced over at Fox, who had re-joined us shortly after the others had re-entered the living room and found him watching Eva intently. What an odd effect she had on him.

"That should do it," Bea announced as she dropped the freshly procured blood into the small glass tube. She proceeded to take another glass jar from the table and drop a number of unknown fragments into the jar with the blood.

"Just need to wait a few minutes for this to settle." Bea looked behind her, towards me and the bears. "Then I'll perform the spell. You hovering isn't going to make concentrating any easier so have a seat."

I tossed Bea a wink before taking my previous spot on the sofa, Mads on one side and Xav on the other, forming a protective cocoon around me. The room went mute as we stared at Bea's concoction. I didn't notice anything change in the mixture itself, albeit my eyes weren't always the best from further away.

Fox fidgeted in the corner, folding and then unfolding his arms. Bea huffed before shooting him a look of annoyance which got him moving. Noisily, he settled himself in the second armchair, not once taking his eyes off Eva.

Crossing her arms, she shot him a look of disdain. “I’m not the witch here. Maybe you could remove your eyes from my direction?”

Fox huffed, his eyes narrowing further. “No way, woman.”

The stare off, which had previously been awkward, now turned entertaining. I held back a coy smile. Mads must have sensed my grin, reaching his strong, nimble hand toward my knee, placing it down, gently. I looked to him to find he too held back a smirk. I may not have known Fox for long, but it was crystal clear my sister burrowed under his thick skin.

“Right. We should be ready. I’ll need silence from the room, *please.*”

Bea’s annoyance was apparent, leaving me questioning whether or not I should hold my breath too. She took the jar into her hands and slowly closed her eyes, taking deep breaths, in and out, and began murmuring another language I wasn’t familiar with.

The language was beautiful, enchanting, pulling me in as though it were a spell itself. The room kept silent as Bea continued the chant, over and over again until suddenly, a bright crimson streak flashed within the jar itself, leaving the particles singed. Bea opened her eyes and looked down.

“She was hexed.”

Eva sat back with relief written on her face, the knowledge her story was true had her folding her arms across her chest in victory. Fox huffed in disbelief as I sat forward, Mads’ hand moving up my thigh, sending tingles with each minuscule movement.

“You’re sure?” Xav questioned. I knew better than Xav to ask that question. Even knowing Bea for such a short time, I trusted her magical abilities.

Crossing her arms, Bea rolled her eyes in annoyance before responding, "Of course I'm sure. A pheasant could perform a detection spell. And I am no pheasant."

"So… now what?" Eva looked first to Bea before she directed her attention to me. "Aurelia?"

The room turned to me as I realised they were giving this decision to me. The problem was, I wasn't even sure what the choices were. Relaxing my face to demonstrate at least an air of calm, I needed to speak to the bears and Bea, alone. "Can you give us a minute?"

Without waiting for the others to follow, I shot to my feet and moved toward the stairs. I needed more privacy than the kitchen provided and Mads' room seemed like the best option. The other three followed in my hurried steps. Bea came in last, closing the door behind her before standing to attention, ready for whatever direction I was about to give them.

"What do you want to do, Goldie?" I was thankful Xav was the one to raise the question. His calming demeanour grounded me.

"The problem is, I don't really know what I'm choosing between."

The bears stayed silent as Bea stepped up. "There are two options. She stays and you never see her again once we cross over to Raithe, most likely questioning what could have been for your relationship. Or," Bea paused, but I already knew what the second option was. Meeting my gaze, she offered me a soft smile as she spoke the words, "She comes with us."

"What?" Fox belted. "You can't be serious?"

I looked to the ground as I spoke softly, "Would it be so bad? If she came with us?"

"Aurelia" — hearing my actual name out of Fox's mouth stunned me — "you don't even know this woman and you want to bring her to Raithe? That's insane."

Xav stepped in front of his overly emotional brother. "What Fox means to say is it is all a bit sudden. We could postpone the trip, give you a bit more time to —"

"No." I was fixed. I knew what I would do, and I was grateful to my company for giving me the opportunity to make the choice myself, but I wasn't going to delay their return home for this. I knew blood didn't determine family, as demonstrated by the four people surrounding me. What I did know was that the instinct that had pushed me into this cabin, and in the lives of these brothers and Bea, pulsed at the thought of bringing Eva with us. Eva and I's story was only beginning to unravel and I wanted to uncover it. Looking up and finding Fox's eyes, I said "She comes with us."

Fox groaned loudly. Mads shot him one of his infamous death stares, pushing him to bark out an agitated, "Fine."

"Good," I snapped.

"Great."

"Fantastic."

"Shall we then?" Bea pulled the door open and marched back down the stairs, not giving the deliberation any further consideration. Xav went next, before Fox who shot me a look of disappointment before he left the room. My stomach tightened. I didn't want Fox to be angry with me. I also knew I wouldn't go back on this decision.

"Is this the wrong decision?" I asked Mads softly, training my eyes to the floor once more.

Two gentle fingers found their way beneath my chin as Mads drew my eyes up to meet his. "Aurelia," he spoke in a new, hushed and soothing voice I had only just become acquainted with, "no choice you make is ever going to be the wrong one. Each decision put in front of us will have a ripple effect. We aren't always going to know what those turn out to be. You just have to trust what your gut is telling you."

My gut. I hadn't told Mads anything further about the unexplainable sensation frequently taking residence in me, but I had no doubt he remembered our conversation when we had looked for the Alegra stone. I stepped up to him, placing my hands gently on the sides of his face. "This is what my gut is telling me."

Mads turned his head, brushing his lips against my palm. "Then this is what we are going to do."

Without another word, we made our way back to the group to find Xav doing his best to bring a small level of conversation, failing miserably. Eva sat on the edge of the seat, immediately locking eyes with me as I descended the stairs. The bears, and Bea, waited for me to present my decision to my sister. It was such an odd sensation, being capable and free to make my own decisions. The idea hadn't quite settled with me yet.

"Eva, tomorrow we are heading to a portal to take us to Raithe, their land" — I pointed to the bears — "You're welcome to come with us. If you decide you want to join us, you need to know that we would not be able to get back through the portal and therefore, you would have to stay there with us."

Eva breathed heavily, eyes welling with indecipherable tears.

I continued, needing her to know the full extent of what I laid out in front of her. "Your other option is to stay here. If you decide to stay, we could probably work it out for you to live here instead. The downside is there is still a curse on the house and you would not be able to ever have company here."

Her tears escalated, one trailing down her pale cheek. I was confused as to what emotion they actually stemmed from. "You —-you'll take me with you?"

I glanced at Mads who hadn't removed his glare from my sister. He wasn't going to look at me. He was giving this to me. A sliver of the freedom I had long ago given up on.

"Yes. You can come with us," I spoke confidently, still unsure whether this reaction was one of joy or sorrow.

I didn't have to wait long as a squealed yelp left Eva's mouth before she jumped up and pulled me into a hug. An awkward hug. An unwanted and awkward hug. I stood straight, hoping to show Eva just how much I did not enjoy the embrace. We may have made progress but we were nowhere near cuddling.

Eva stepped back, tears having broken free from both of her eyes. "Thank you. I want to join you."

With no other sound, Fox stormed from the room, his view on my decision clear from his reaction. Mads reached over to softly squeeze my arm, reminding me he would get over it and I needed to trust in my decision. Xav, sensing the exhaustion beginning to plague me, stepped forward and offered to give Eva a tour. She agreed instantly and they walked towards the kitchen, exchanging pleasantries as they did so.

"Wow."

I'd forgotten Bea was still in the room. "This house just went from all dicks to half and half. I'm impressed."

Mads cocked his brow at Bea forcing a giggle from me. "Where is she going to sleep?" Bea examined her ebony nails as she spoke the obvious. Something that hadn't even crossed my mind.

Mads answered for us, "Xav and Fox can bunk together. Bea can have Xav's room and your sister can take the couch."

"So, you're just assuming I'm going to sleep in your bed?" The opportunity to tease Mads was too good to waste.

He turned to me, his eyebrow raised. "I don't care if you sleep in my bed, the bathtub, or in the woods, but you bet your fine arse I'm going to be sleeping beside you.

A warmth blossomed between my thighs. I swallowed and nodded, hoping he'd be doing more than sleeping.

Bea cleared her throat, reminding us we weren't alone. Shaking out of my daydream, I looked in the direction Eva and Xav had gone. "Should I wait to get her settled?"

Stepping towards me, Mads tilted my face towards him. "No. You are exhausted. Go upstairs and I'll bring you something to eat. We can get your sister sorted."

Bea snorted. "From zero to hero, eh Mads?"

He sighed in annoyance. "Out with it, Trix. How we can never avoid one of your opinions."

"It's just, a few weeks ago, you were the maddest Mads and now you're a less mad Mads. It's nice. She suits you."

I beamed at Bea then turned my attention back to Mads unable to hold back my prideful smile. "She suits herself." He looked down at me with a twinkle in his eye. A twinkle! "And one day, maybe I will be worthy enough to suit her."

My insides lit up. How was it possible to be set on fire from the sweetness of his words and the promise of what it may bring? The onion was almost completely peeled and finally, I liked what I saw. Pushing up on my toes, I pressed a nearly there kiss to the corner of his lips, immediately halted by the intense gagging sounds Bea began making from beside us.

"It is cute, I just don't want to see it. I'm going to sort the rooms."

Mads waited for Bea to trudge up the stairs before he pulled my face back to his, a fire burning behind the green and gold orbs. "You should try again."

Wasting no time, I pressed my lips firmly to his. A few seconds ticked by before his tongue teased my lips open. I didn't hesitate to let him in. Since our time in the woods, our physical interactions had only consisted of brief kisses and light touches. I wasn't sure why he hadn't pursued anything further, the thought sliding out of my head as a moan slipped from the back of my throat, his skilful tongue playing with mine. His hands on my face travelled down my neck, meeting my shoulders and skimming slowly down my arms, leaving a plethora of goose bumps in their wake. I lost myself in the kiss. A zing of possession sliding down my spine, both me for him and him for me. With each second tasting him, I felt some of the small, broken fragments slide back into place. Gradually, Mads pulled his lips from mine. Our tandem breathing deep.

A smile tipped the corner of his mouth as he said, "That... That was nice."

I chuckled at the words thrown back at me as I had described our time in the cabin.

"It was nice." I agreed.

Mads planted an affectionate kiss on my forehead before turning me towards the stairs, "I'll be up with something for you to eat soon."

In a daze from our kiss, I stumbled up the stairs dreaming about all the *nice* things I'd yet to explore with him.

Mads returned to the room later in the evening, a tray filled with various foods and drinks. Not wanting to disappoint him, I devoured every crumb available. As I ate, Mads explained they had decided to postpone our trip by a day so we could settle our new travel companion and the supply stock was altered to include Eva. I listened intently, agreeing it was a good idea to wait a bit to be fully prepared. It also meant the sinking in my chest would be planted for a bit longer.

Once I finished eating, Mads proceeded to get himself ready for bed, drooling over the way his shoulder muscles shifted as he moved about the room. How could shoulders be so sexy? The kiss from earlier had haunted me. I was keen to go further. To explore more. The niggling at the back of my mind told me maybe Mads didn't feel the same. He hadn't attempted to further anything between us and it confused me.

"Mads?" Letting the need for transparency take over, I made the decision to discuss it with him.

"Mmm?"

"Why haven't you tried..." my words left me. As soon as the first few left my mouth, I regretted the decision for honesty.

"Tried what?" He looked up from his task in his chest of drawers.

My fingers found the edge of the quilt, nervously weaving it in-between each one as I attempted to find my courage.

"Aurelia?"

My gaze lifted to his, and I was stuck for a moment as he was now topless and any semblance of thought left me. Mads was magnificent. If they hadn't lost their magic when cursed, I would've thought the lines of his torso were put there by sorcery.

Walking to where I sat on the bed, he bent down to be level with me, and gently, he tipped my chin up. "Aurelia, why haven't I tried what?"

Swallowing, my mouth dry, I continued, "Why haven't you tried anything else... with me? Like at the cabin."

Immediately, I dropped my gaze back down to the quilt as the heated embarrassment rose on my neck.

"You mean why haven't I fucked you?"

Given my history with the male sex, the vulgar way Mads' spoke should've offended me. The truth was those words leaving his mouth did the complete opposite. My core began to burn, shock waves pushing down to my most sensitive area, with a sincere hope he would throw me against the wall and rutt me senseless right there.

"Yes," I responded in a whisper.

"Aurelia, look at me."

Blinking slowly, I raised my head back up.

"I want to. More than I've ever wanted anyone or anything in my entire existence. Just the thought of you gets my cock rock hard."

My breathing quickened, his words igniting me further.

"I also know, for too long, your choices have not been your own. I'd like to show you first, if you'll let me."

"What do you mean?"

Mads stood, elevating the view of his chiselled chest and the thrilling warmth in my core.

"Do you trust I won't push anything on you that you don't want?"

"Yes." No hesitation. Even in those initial encounters, I couldn't deny the safety I'd felt with Mads. I always had, even when I couldn't recognise it for what it was.

"I'm not going to touch you."

Disappointment filled me. "Why not?"

Kicking the side of his mouth up, Mads' gaze heated. "Because you are going to touch you."

"I have given myself orgasms before, Maddox," I said, confusion drifting over my face.

The heat in Mads' eyes deepened. "Not like this you haven't."

The promise in his voice pulled my awareness to the wetness pooling between my legs. "Show me." I kept my voice as steady as possible.

Mads stepped forward, placing one of his knees on the edge of the bed as he said, "First, I want you naked."

He gestured his hands toward me, silently asking to remove my top. "I thought you said you weren't going to touch me."

His eyes narrowed at my bold push. "Trust me, I won't."

Pushing my arms above my head, Mads leaned forward and grabbed the edges of the shirt. Without so much as a graze of his fingers, he pulled the top up over my head and discarded it on the floor. I sat in front of him in only my underwear. My chest rose rapidly at the lingering twinge of embarrassment at my nakedness in front of him. The unease quickly faded as his eyes devoured my naked chest, rising upwards before locking his gaze to mine, the heat rising into an inferno. This was going to be difficult for him, not touching me, and a small amount of victory hit me in the chest.

"Now, scoot back up against the headboard there."

Immediately I obeyed, scrambling back in a heap of limbs until my back hit the top of the bed. Mads smiled at my apparent eagerness. The predator had caught his prey.

"Now those." He pointed to the last piece of fabric on my body.

I'd been naked in front of him before, yet this left me more exposed than I had been in the shower. Slowly, I hooked my thumbs in the shorts waistband and gradually shifted them down my legs. When they got to my feet, Mads' hand whipped out to grasp the edge, ripping them off, careful not to make any contact with my bare skin.

He raised his gaze back to mine, and for a moment, I thought he may catch fire. If he was going to burn, I would happily burn with him.

"Lean back and open your legs for me."

I failed to hide my awkwardness from him. A fact which he was clearly aware of. "You aren't going to be ashamed of your body here, Aurelia. Every single part of you is exquisite. What we are going to do...what you are going to do — you will embrace every single part of it. And I promise, you will not be disappointed."

Slowly, I nodded once, not fully believing him although I wanted to, more than anything.

"Now, open for me."

My knees, squeezed so tightly they would likely bruise, parted, gradually exposing everything. Mads sucked in a breath. "I have dreamt of this sight since the cabin. You are stunning, Aurelia."

My cheeks heated as I let him take me all in. This exposure was hard to find confidence in. One side of me wanted to desperately listen to him and the other did its utmost to push any unease from my mind.

"Put two fingers in your mouth."

Taking the first two fingers on my right hand, I pushed them into my mouth, swirling my tongue around them both as I moved them further in. My core tightened with the movement, growing wetter by the second.

"The other hand, put your nipple between your fingers."

I had never been much for breast play. It'd never felt quite right. I'd always just stuck to teasing my clit which in most cases got me off just fine. We weren't here for just fine. Mads wanted me to own my body. Understand it. And hopefully give it to him in the same way.

Filled with apprehension, I took the first two fingers of my left hand, placing them on either side of my nipple.

"Roll it between those fingers."

Obeying, I shifted my fingers, bringing my nipple directly between them and squeezed, a gasp left my mouth immediately. It had never felt that way before. Each roll of my nipple drove pulsing thrills to my pussy. An aching one needing attention.

"Remove your fingers from your mouth and slowly trail them down."

Pulling my fingers from my lips with a slight pop, I began trailing them down between my breasts.

"Slower." His voice grew deep, commanding.

Holding his gaze, I slowed the descent, savouring the goose bumps littering my skin in their wake.

"Keep pinching that nipple, you feel it getting harder?"

"Yes," I responded, breathlessly.

"That's it."

My fingers continued down, slowly drawing circles around my belly button as they passed. I savoured the throbbing in my pussy, building the want and need even further with my fingers' slow descent. When I was near enough to my clit, I paused. Mads shook his head, silently urging me further. I continued down as I salivated at the sight in front of me. One knee still on the bed, his fists clenched and then unclenched, the tension affecting him too.

"Aurelia, are you wet for me?"

My clit was slick with desire. "Yes."

"Tell me."

I couldn't quite process how I could be so aroused by only my hand and his words.

"I'm soaking."

"Good girl. Circle your clit, give it what it's begging for."

I did as I was told and with the first contact of my fingers, my mind and body responded in a way I had never known. I gasped as I felt the orgasm already building.

"You can feel it can't you? Your pussy begging for release."

Gods yes it did. Every part of my body was on fire. I burned with him, and I wouldn't stop until the only thing left was a pile of ash.

"Keep going. That's it."

My circling grew in intensity and firmness as I chased my release. "Not yet. Remember I will tell you when you can come."

I wanted to be mad at him for denying what I wanted so badly, then a thought hit me, hard. I fully trusted the man in front of me. With my body and my heart. A trust I never thought I would know.

"You're going to put your fingers inside of yourself now."

I paused my fingers, apprehension creeping in.

Mads shook his head, the heated stare never once leaving me. "No, keep rubbing."

My chest pushed up hard with each breath. I was aroused by the simple fact that he wanted me to experience something new. But I needed to be honest with him. "I've never done that before." My words were low, almost tinted with embarrassment.

His eyes lowered to where my fingers had stopped. "Good. I get to be the first to ever see those fingers slide into that gorgeous pussy."

With a slight shake of my hand, I moved my fingers down to the opening, hesitating on the edge. Even with the faintest of touches, the wetness began to soak my fingers. Eyes never leaving his, I pushed in. The sensation was odd at first, fading rapidly and replaced by an even deeper throbbing than what my clit had given me.

"Beautiful. You are so fucking beautiful, Aurelia."

His words spurred me on as I pushed in and out, picking up my speed with each thrust of my finger.

"Add a second."

No hesitation this time, I joined my index finger with a second, the fullness pulling a gasp of pleasure from my mouth. Closing my eyes, I revelled in the deep sensation coursing through my body. All of the fear of exposure from before had left me as I soaked up every moment of pure bliss, continuing the assault on my nipple. Fingers pumping in and out.

"Fuck yes. I want to see you come undone, Aurelia."

"Yes!" I shouted unintentionally.

"Give me your eyes, gorgeous."

Snapping my eyes open, I caught Mads' straight away, letting his heat bore into me.

"Use your thumb on your clit. Come for me."

Obeying, the combination of the sensations together forced the magnificent sensitivity in my pussy to hammer with the need for release. I followed it, never letting it settle, savouring every single push and pull of my fingers. In my pussy. On my nipple. The combination was going to be the end of me. And there would be no better end.

"Come, Aurelia."

The guttural command pushed me over the edge. I screamed out his name as my orgasm exploded through me, leaving intense tingles all over my body. My fingers slowed as I gently rinsed the last of my orgasm. Dropping my hands to my sides, I slumped back into the pillows. Breathing heavy, eyes still locked on Mads, I couldn't help as a satisfied smile grew across my face.

The depth of Mads' arousal was clear through his shorts, making me want him even more than I already did.

He made his way to the side of the bed, dipping his head to place a brief and promising kiss on my lips. "You did so good."

"Did I?"

He smiled. "You did. I can't wait to show you more. If you'll let me."

I chuckled at the absurdity of those words. I would give him my complete self. There would be no question any longer.

"I'd happily take you now."

His face grew serious, and I knew he did his utmost to contain his own desires.

"Not yet." He tapped me on the nose before retreating to the ensuite.

I couldn't stop as I asked, "When?"

"You'll get it when you're ready."

The desire wasn't completely sated from my own hand, and as I appreciated his help in learning my body, I couldn't deny I wanted him exploring it too. If not more so. As I settled further into the bed, I let my eyes close, drifting off to images of what it would be like. A smile took up residence on my face for those moments to come.

CHAPTER 28
AURELIA

The day before we were due to leave could only be described as organised chaos. Every single one of our travelling party had a list of responsibilities and tasks to complete, leaving us with barely any time to converse with each other. Xav had graciously taken Eva under his wing, understanding I needed to take this new relationship with my sister slowly. Very slowly.

The best part of the day was that I barely had time to get lost in my own thoughts. Fox threw out jokes whenever he was around, knowing I'd been uneasy about going to Raithe. It also seemed he had accepted the new addition to our group. Well, accepted may have been too strong a word. He tolerated Eva's presence for the most part, ensuring she was rarely in his vicinity. When we finally settled in Raithe, or as settled as we could be before the potential war, I vowed to myself I would question Fox's curious hatred toward my younger sister.

Later that evening, we found ourselves together in the dining room, going through each other's lists and ensuring everything was done. We would leave before dawn the next day which meant we had little room for last minute needs and changes. I was grateful, again, for Xav who'd advised Eva would ride with him, given she didn't know how to and it was too late for us to obtain another horse. Fox snorted to which Eva shot him her best look of annihilation.

"Bea," I said, taking the opportunity to dissuade the potential blow up between my sister and Fox, "can you remind me, again, what I'm supposed to be doing when we get to the portal?"

A hesitation sat heavily on my mind. If whatever I could do was, in fact, magic, the only true experience I'd had with it was when we retrieved the Alegra stone. I couldn't ignore the chance that I wouldn't be able to open the portal once we found it.

Bea dusted her hands off before moving across the room to grab her book. Opening to the page, the source of so much in the last couple of weeks, she found the passage. "You should just be able to open it. What we don't know is if it's a door, a boulder, a bush. That's what we'll have to find out. You'll also have the Alegra stone for protection."

Protection? That's why we had to retrieve the stone before the journey? My heart melted a fraction with the thought of Bea wanting to safeguard me.

"Are you sure that's what it says?" Xav interjected. "Remember what you said once about the spell to remove my nausea and it turned me into a goat for an entire day?"

I burst out laughing, Eva stood in shock. "A goat?"

"Oh you idiot," Bea shot back. "I turned you into a goat on purpose."

With a wink, she announced she was off to bed. Eva followed to the couch shortly after. I followed Fox's eyes as they trailed my sister with every step she took. With Eva and Bea off to bed, I was left with the bears, an odd nostalgia flowing through me at the thought of our first introductions. How, for the most part, I was welcomed into this home when I had nothing and no one.

"I just want to say —" I cleared my throat.

All three bears froze, turning their attention to me and nothing else.

"I just want to say, whatever happens tomorrow, I'm so grateful you took a chance on me. I know part of it was because I could see the house —"

"Aurelia —" Mads started to interrupt. I wasn't going to let him stop me.

I held up my hand. "No. It's true. And that's ok. Because I know a very big part of you, of all of you" — I looked deliberately at Mads — "just wanted to help a scared and broken woman. Which you did. Each in your own way, and I am so thankful. You've all helped me claim back bits of myself I thought I'd lost forever. So...I just wanted to say, thank you."

Silence filled the room for only a few moments before Fox closed the gap between us and scooped me in his arms. I cackled with glee as he whispered in my ear, "Whatever comes next, we will get through it together. You never have to say thank you, Goldie."

Xav joined us in the hug, nuzzling his nose into my hair. Mads stood to the side, letting his brothers appreciate the moment with me, a gesture I was grateful for. The embrace lasted as long as it needed to, filling all our hearts with warmth. Fox and Xav bid their goodnights and walked off to their room, leaving Mads and I alone.

I felt him step behind me, lowering his mouth to my ear. A shiver raced down my spine as he spoke, “You were always meant to be here.”

I sucked back a sob of happiness because part of me, although a very hidden part, believed every word he said.

“Let’s get some sleep.”

I took his outstretched hand and walked towards the last night of sleep I’d have in this cabin, filled with a new sense of adventure. Whatever waited for us on the other side, we would at least have each other.

“If you would’ve listened in the first place, you wouldn’t be standing there covered in mud!”

“If you would’ve spoken your orders rather than brayed like a damn mule, maybe the beast wouldn’t have stomped in the mud!”

“You’re impossible.”

“You’re an arse!”

In the stable, I found Fox and Eva in the middle of yet another argument. Eva was covered, head to toe, in splattered mud and forest floor debris which could have contained all manner of things. Fox stood in front of her, anger radiating off him in waves.

I sighed at the thought of the journey with these two at each other’s throats. The rest of the party would have to take turns playing referee if they continued on this way. “Eva?” I questioned, doing my best to pull them apart and create some distance. “Why don’t you go get cleaned up?”

The two continued to stare each other down, no doubt a variety of insults sitting on their tongues. "Eva?"

Finally, Eva huffed in defeat, turning on her heel and stomping towards me. A cocky grin lifted the side of Fox's mouth. I shot him my best 'I will punch you' look even though it was fruitless at this point. The two were so focused on annoying each other I wasn't sure if anyone could get through to them.

Eva passed me without a word, trudging back towards the house. Sighing, I turned back to Fox once more. "Why do you have to push her so much?"

"She pushes me too!"

"I know, Fox. It's just someone has to be the bigger person here."

Fox folded his arms across his chest in defiance. "Well, it sure as hell isn't going to be me."

I made my way back to the house, bumping into Xav, his brow raised at the look on my face. I ground out, "Fox and Eva went at each other again."

"I saw Eva," Xav said as he huffed out a laugh, "she is really getting to him, isn't she?"

I saw the twinkle in his eye. I knew it was hard to wear Fox down and Eva continued to surprise me. "What do we do?"

Xav handed me a satchel as he said, "Keep them as far away from each other as possible."

Throwing the bag over my shoulder, I knew his advice was easier said than done given we would all be in close proximity on the trip. Not to mention, no one had any idea what would happen if and when they made it through the portal to Raithe.

Xav brought me out of my head with a squeeze of my shoulder. "You alright?"

"I'm fine. Just eager to get going now," I said, attempting to sound confident.

"Aurelia," Xav's tone grew low, what I could only decipher as concerned, "you know you can't lie to me?"

Even without his full magic, Xav's ability to read emotions was astounding.

My eyes drifted to the cabin, a pang in my chest at the only house I'd ever felt slightly at home in, I offered him one of my concerns, "I'm worried Xav. Mads assured me it won't matter where I come from but it's hard to believe. Do you care if it turns out I have ties to Aestas?"

Everything I knew about my life had changed. My parents weren't who I thought they were; the harsh treatment I endured was for what? The last few words Shelton spoke to me echoed through my mind — *"She said I had to force it out."*

A strong hand landed gently on my shoulder as Xav drew closer to my ear and said, "Not even a little bit." His serious tone mixed with his words drew the moisture in my eyes. I was afraid of the sincerity I might find if I was to look at him, although I knew it was there. Deciding we tread in enough emotion for now, I changed the subject. "Is the house ready?"

Xav looked longingly at the structure in front of us. Even though it may not be their true home, I still knew how difficult it would be for the brothers to leave the house and the wood. "It is."

I stepped closer, placing my head on his shoulder, leaning into him as I said, "I know you're going to miss it. I'm going to miss it too." Xav sighed, wrapping his arm around my shoulder. I wished I could tell him they would be able to visit. "It did its job though, Xav."

"I know. I'm just...scared, Aurelia. I haven't been to Raithe in so long. I'm sure it has changed. I know I have."

We stood in comfortable silence as we both said our goodbyes to the house. For different reasons, it means an incredible amount to both of us. Nonetheless, it was a home.

Mads chucked a bag at Xav, bringing us back to the present. His warrior reflexes allowed him to catch it before it hit him square in the face, jostling me in the process. "Ready, brother?"

Chuckling, Xav made his way to the horses, leaving Mads and I alone. "You ready?" A smile tipped his upper lip.

I stared, admiring his beauty as I did every time I took in the sight of him. Nodding, we made our way to the horses together. After I'd mounted, successfully, Mads handed Rock to me. Fox and Mads had fastened a small box seat for him to sit in front of me during our journey. The small creature had dug so deeply into my heart, I would never have left him there on his own. He'd given me comfort in a time of need and so, I would forever protect him.

Once Eva was clean, the horses packed and the cabin shut up, the bears, Bea, and I all took one last look at the house, in the wood, with its protective layer of oak trees, the babbling of the river nearby, and the sound of forest never at rest. It had forever changed us. It brought us together. It brought us all a new life.

The initial part of our journey was uneventful. Xavier had kept Eva occupied enough with the journey itself, seemingly forgetting Fox existed. Fox would grunt occasionally as though he had tried to get her attention and goad her. Rock had settled into his makeshift seat quickly and was asleep within minutes.

Mads led the way with Bea beside him, yammering on about various topics, including but not limited to: Raithe, Hiema, what the men looked like in the Winter Kingdom, where she would be living once they overthrew the Summer rulers, and how much Mads intended to pay her as the kingdom witch. I listened, with no intention of involving myself in such a conversation and instead, enjoyed the sights of the world passing me by with an occasional scratch behind Rock's ears as I took each tentative step towards our new future.

Arriving at Wildhill by late afternoon, there wouldn't be much daylight left for us to easily find the portal. We decided to set up camp for the night. To my surprise, Eva was helpful and didn't complain about sleeping on the ground once. A far different woman than I had come to know from her life of luxury.

The evening progressed without a hitch, each member of the group taking on a responsibility of their own. Eva brushed down the horses with Mads before assisting Xav with dinner. Fox and Bea bickered their way through camp set up, including three tents — one for Mads and I, one for Xav and Fox, and finally, the third which Bea would share with Eva. I was initially concerned about this given Bea had also shown her clear dislike of my sister, but Bea assured me she would be on her best behaviour.

When dinner was served and devoured, the niggle in my stomach returned. A similar sensation I'd had every time I thought about leaving this world. I excused myself to our tent early as I didn't want my doubts to flood through camp. A few minutes after I'd settled on my bedroll and tried but failed to calm my breathing, Bea stepped in.

"Alright, buttercup?"

I shifted, leaving room for Bea to lie down beside me. We turned our bodies instinctively so we faced one another. "Yes and no."

"Okay," Bea said as she pushed her hand under her head, "let's start with no."

I took a deep breath in, my apprehension bubbling to the surface. There was a comfort with Bea knowing she wasn't from Raithe and making the same decision to leave England behind. "I won't be able to come back."

Bea waited for me to continue, when I didn't, she let out a breath. "Is that all?"

"Well, yes."

"Aurelia, what would keep you here? Your family, if we can even call them that, turned you into a tool against your will. You had no freedom. No choice. No life before you found the cabin. You were meant for something bigger. I promise you."

I studied her face, doing my best to find the lies hidden in her words. The thing about Bea though, was she'd never lied to me. I wasn't sure how I knew, but that same nagging feeling in my gut, that instinct, told me she never would. And I clung to that.

"So, what about the yes?" Bea urged.

Running the pros list in my head made me realise, immediately, how silly the fears actually were.

"The yes? Is everything else."

Smiling, Bea leaned forward and placed a kiss on my forehead. "Looks like you figured this one out all on your own, buttercup. Now, let's get some sleep so we can start our new chapter tomorrow."

I nodded as Bea stood and left the tent. The yes was infinite. Getting the brothers back home. A fresh start. Discovering a new world. Seeing the reality of magic. Finally figuring out who I was and what I might become. It was true, I may never be able to return. What has it ever done for me? Only ever taken, including my brother. What would Archer say now?

Mads entered the tent shortly after, making quick work of his over clothes and snuggling down into the bedroll next to me . He leaned over to place us in darkness, his outline stared up at the canvas ceiling.

"Do we need to talk it out?"

Reaching over, I found the lines of his chest beneath my fingers and gently placed my hand over his heart. "Nope. I figured this one out on my own."

The silence ebbed on, the beat of Mads' heart guiding me to the last sleep I'd have in this world.

"It's a tunnel."

"It's a cave."

"Aren't they the same thing?"

"No. Caves don't always have tunnels."

"And do tunnels always have caves?"

Fox and Eva's arguing had morphed into less hostile bickering, and I didn't know which I actually preferred. It was clear the rest of the party also tried to ascertain whether this was progress or not.

"Whatever it is," Bea countered, "we need to go in it. The map says the portal should be at the end."

Mads took the lead, reaching back to grab my hand, a comforting squeeze followed. We each had a lantern given the dimness of the cave even in the daylight. Following in Mads' footsteps, everyone stayed quiet and alert for anything crossing our path. After what felt like an eternity marching through the damp cave, Xav broke the silence, "How will we know what the portal looks like?"

No one answered. I looked behind me at the dimly lit faces of my companions and realised not one of us actually knew what we were looking for. I did my best to quell the panic creeping in, hoping we would know once we saw it. And that's when it happened. A pulsing awareness shot through my chest. Pulling my hand from Mads', I clutched my front. It wasn't painful but the sudden onset caught me off guard.

"Aurelia?"

Mads' panic was clear, and I reached my hand back out, finding his arm in front of me.

"I'm ok." The pulsing continued, similar to the sensation I'd had when we retrieved the Alegra stone. Only this time, it was more intense and there were no visions.

"I think it's close."

"How do you know?" Fox stepped forward, placing his hand on my back to steady me.

"I can feel it." I caught Mads' gaze, who responded with a brief nod, understanding whatever it was I could do happened now. Urging us forward, the tunnel opened to the left into a small alcove and that's when we saw it.

A door.

Not the mental images of a door I'd seen in my previous visions, but an actual door sat at the far end, light beaming through the cracks. It was enchanting in a way that urged me toward it. The design itself was simple; an arch shaped door with wooden slats connected vertically and a round metal doorknob sat directly in the centre. What allured me forward was the faint humming sound that connected to that piece inside of me, causing it to pulse in recognition.

"I think we found it."

Eva's tone was light, forcing a pang of warmth through me. Hurrying to the door, the group followed closely on my heels.

"Now what?" I silently forgave Eva. She hadn't been there through all the planning and was somewhat blind to what lay ahead of us. We were too, except at least we had a theory as to what we needed to do and where we would wind up. Hopefully.

"Now, she opens it." Bea shifted her gaze from Eva to me, the pride already glistening in her eyes.

Setting my lantern down, I approached the door with caution. The vibrations grew stronger as I moved closer, putting me more at ease rather than into my fear. As I stood a foot away, a gentle humming began floating around me, as though the door was purring, urging me to open it. A tingling sensation ran through my hands. This was it.

I turned to Mads and reached my hand back. Without hesitation, he took it, giving one encouraging squeeze. Setting down his lantern, he reached back for Fox's hand. Then Fox to Bea. Bea to Xav. And finally, Xav to Eva. I watched intently as Eva took her other hand to wrap around Rock snuggled into a small pack locked across her chest.

Turning back to the door, my hand moved towards it as though magnetic. Letting the magic flow through me, I turned the handle.

It twisted easily until the echo of a click could be heard through the cave. As I pushed it open, I stood tall as I took my first step into a new world.

PART II

THE KEY

CHAPTER 29

AURELIA

A blinding light met me on the other side of the door. The brightness should have pushed my eyes to ache. Instead, they were a welcome greeting. Pushing forward, I knew I couldn't stop moving until all six of us had passed through the door. Mads' grip on my hand tightened with each step we took. I did my best to keep them on a straight path, not knowing where in Raithe we would actually end up.

A few minutes ticked by before Eva shouted from the back, confirming she had passed through the door. Gradually, the intense light began to die down, allowing my eyes to adjust to the scene around us. Before I could take in our new surroundings, I checked that the rest of the party was safely behind me. Once it was shut, the door vanished, leaving only the wilderness around us. An anticlimactic end to my time in the human realm.

Agonising groans pulled my attention to where all three brothers fell to their knees, stirring panic deep inside me.

"What's happening?" I shouted both out of fear and to make certain my words travelled over the harrowing noises from the bears.

Bea grabbed Eva's hand, rushing to my side before pushing us both a fair distance away from the bears. "It's okay!" Bea shouted over the intense humming surrounding the bears. "We thought this may happen."

"You thought what would happen?!" Everything was so loud, forcing zaps of pain through my ear drums.

"Their magic is returning!" As soon as the words left Bea's mouth, I looked back down at the three men who had taken me in and given me a new life. Mads had his head clutched in his hands, clawing through his dark brown curls. Fox had dropped down to the ground, coiled in a foetal position. The tears escaping his shut eyes sent a heavy ache through my chest. And finally, Xav who was on his knees, clutching his chest in what I could only describe as pure bliss, as though he worshipped a divine power, engrossed in his prayer. I could see a clear irritation in his body language but it didn't stop the smile from growing on his face as if he felt complete. I thought it would never end.

Whole. They were becoming whole again.

Bea clutched my hand and shielded Eva from the light beginning to pour from all three brothers, blinding us once more. The luminous energy forced me to shut my eyes. I cursed inwardly, not wanting to remove my stare from what happened. Before I could think on it further, all went silent and the light blinked out.

Cautiously, I peeled one of my eyes open. Seeing all three brothers back on their feet and examining themselves, I pried my second eye open, taking one step forward. Bea attempted to pull me back, appearing unsure of the safety in our present situation. I wasn't afraid. Not a single ounce of fear could be felt. I unclenched my hand and pulled away, taking another step towards Mads.

Noticing my movements, Mads caught my eye, cocking his brow before raising his right hand and snapping his fingers. As his fingers clicked, a flame rose between them. It was mesmerising. Their magic was back. I knew, right then, Mads was changing. The knowledge didn't scare me, it excited me. I bounded up to him, taking his wrist in my hand and admiring the small flame as it danced above his fingertips. And then it went out.

A gleeful smile rose on my face. "Do it again."

Mads obliged, clicking his fingers twice to create two separate flames, swirling around one another in a dance of heat.

I laughed. A sound still unfamiliar to me. The bubbling ache in my belly was welcome. "This is amazing!"

"You think?" Mads posed the question with caution, as if I was just trying to overinflate his ego.

I was awestruck. How could he think this wasn't incredible? He'd created fire with his hands. "Yes I think! Mads, your magic is back."

A throat clearing behind Mads brought my eyes over his shoulder to see Fox standing behind him. A triumphant grin radiating from him. Fox opened his palm where three separate icicles grew from its centre. Mads turned to find his brother wielding his magic once more.

Closing the gap between them, Mads wrapped his arms around his youngest brother, embracing him in victory. Xav, too, took a few steps to his brothers and threw his arms around them, revelling at their returned magic. I stood, marvelling at the moment, soaking in every fibre of the joy radiating from these men. The journey ahead was filled with unknowns, heaps of danger and a lot of discovery.

What happened in front of me, what gifts fell upon my shoulders, the last few months, it was worth it. I questioned why I'd even hesitated in helping them.

The brothers broke their hug just as Eva decided to ruin the moment by speaking, "Ice magic? Isn't that unnecessary given you're a prince of the *Winter* Kingdom?"

Fox, not letting anything spoil this moment for him, stepped towards Eva. "Be careful, princess, or I'll turn you to ice."

Eva spun on her heel to walk away, throwing over her shoulder, "Well there are worse things than being an ice princess."

Rolling my eyes at their interaction, I turned back to Xav. His magic wasn't visual and I needed him to confirm he too was whole once more. Xav gave me a brief nod as I beamed over at him.

Finally, as the bear's magic returned, I took in our surroundings. We had entered into some sort of glen. The trickle of a stream drifted around us, indicating running water nearby. Bushes of all sizes and shades of greens cocooned us. I inhaled the fresh scent of newly blooming flowers in the fields around us. The air so pure I could taste it.

To our right, in the distance, was a snow-capped mountain range. To our left was a wooded area, filled with trees an equal distance apart. The space was calming in its beauty, as though welcoming us into its fold.

"It's Spring," Fox whispered as he circled around us, gazing up at the rustling treetops above.

"You're sure?" Bea, too, was in awe of the beauty surrounding us.

"Positive."

"We landed in Spring?" Xav's voice was almost childlike, his excitement building.

Mads looked at him, unable to hold back his glee. "We did, brother."

"This is good, right?" Eva stood near the tree line, looking down the path seeming to call to us.

Xav looked toward my sister, addressing us all, "This is perfect."

"Spring is our biggest ally. Our Aunt is one of the queens." Fox added for further comfort.

Eva sighed, letting out some of the tension sitting on her shoulders.

A blinding pain shot behind both of my eyes. A high pitched shriek escaped me as I grabbed my head, attempting to hold back the fast growing agony.

"Aurelia?" Mads called from in front of me, his voice muffled to the ache in my head.

The stabbing pain grew heavier, more frequent as it assaulted the backs of my eyeballs. I cried out in torture. My mouth went dry as bile began to rise in my throat. I tried to breathe in but everything felt too tight.

"Aurelia!" Mads was by my side. I couldn't see him, but cedar drifted through my nose confirming it was him. I tried to focus on that. On him. It was no use.

The throbbing continued to elevate, forcing me to my knees. A guttural scream left my mouth. Raised voices surrounded me but the pain was too much. I couldn't focus on anyone or anything but the continued assault in my head. My limbs grew heavier as I succumbed to the pain. Just as I felt I would throw up, everything went black.

Dreams were such a mystery. Some were so vivid, you could taste the air while others came and went so quickly, you'd never even know they were there. My mind fluttered through so many dreams. Some were filled with strong princes rescuing me. Others were of soft quilts cocooning me. None were particularly memorable. Gratefully, all were pleasant.

I woke, sluggishly, to hushed voices echoing around me. Pressing my fingertips into the material beneath my body, I felt a firmness of a mattress. The last memory I'd had was collapsing onto the ground near where we'd come through the portal door. I could no longer feel the fresh whisper of the outside air tickle my cheeks. Was I inside?

A heavy quilt was draped over my body, and I wore some kind of gown. My fingers traced the sheet beneath me as I gently peeled my eyes open. A room. A rather luxurious one. The bed I was in was large, twice the size of Mads' bed back at the cabin.

My eyes adjusted to the radiating golds and deep, lush maroons decorating the room before flicking my gaze to the left, finding it was filled with vast windows covering the entire wall. The curtains were drawn, keeping me from exploring the view outside.

"Hey." A voice I'd become intimately familiar with came from my right.

Turning my head, I found Mads, situated in a patterned armchair beside the bed. His curls were slightly dishevelled, most likely from running his hands through it repeatedly. A worry filled his eyes I immediately wanted to diminish.

"Hi." I croaked, my throat burning with the effort.

Mads rose, grabbing a glass of water from the ornate bedside table. "Sit up, slowly."

The demand in his voice was clear. I did as I was told, pushing my torso up. Every movement sent flames through my arms and into my back. Ignoring the pain, for now, I was more interested in where we were and what had happened.

Mads brought the glass to my lips before tipping it back, guiding me to take small, slow sips of water. The cool, crisp liquid was heaven, coating the roughness of my throat as it moved downwards. Mads repeated the action twice more before returning the glass to the table and sitting himself next to me on the bed.

"Where are we?" The coarseness of my throat laced through my words.

"The Spring Kingdom palace." Mads' voice was low, guarded.

"We found it then." I tried to smile through the throbbing.

"We did." His tone was anything but light. He was filled with anger and concern. I'd seen this side of Mads more than any other, so it was easy to spot.

Reaching over, I placed my palm on his knee. "I'm okay, Mads."

"You're fucking not."

"Has a doctor been to see me?"

"A healer."

"Sorry?"

"We have healers here."

"Oh, right. Of course." Apart from the fact we were, most likely, going to war, bringing death and bloodshed upon this kingdom, I would have to relearn so much of what I knew. Language being one of them. Something which hadn't actually crossed my mind during the process of deciding whether or not I'd actually come here.

"And yes, you've been seen."

"And?" I squeezed his knee, immediately regretting it due to the pain shooting up my arm. I tried to hide the wince, failing. Mads saw all.

"She said you would be alright."

I sighed, this was good right? "So then can you tell me why you are so angry?"

Mads stood, dropping my hand to the bed gently. Pacing the length of the windows, I gave him the time to process his thoughts. His anguish.

"We put you in danger." The sound leaving my mouth wasn't quite audible, still relaying my belief that what he said was nonsense.

"We did, Aurelia. We should have realised you held some magic given you were the key to breaking the curse."

Shock covered my face as he moved toward the other side of the room, "What do you mean magic? I don't have magic."

Turning towards me, we locked eyes as he said, "Turns out, you do."

Heart dropping into my stomach, my breathing quickened. The same panic I had felt so many times before, slipped through my veins as though an old friend.

Mads noticed the signs of the attack building. Bounding across the room, he sat back down beside me and didn't hesitate to pull me into his lap, pushing my head to his chest with urgency, "Feel it. Follow it."

I wanted to obey his instructions. My body had other ideas. The intake of breath wasn't enough. Wasn't fast enough. My hands grew clammy, needing to grab something, anything over and over again. Mads snatched my hand from my side, pushing it to his shirt. I grabbed on with desperation, clenching my fist around the fabric before releasing it, repeating the action again. Using his other hand, he grabbed the back of my neck, his grip grounding me as he directed my face towards his. "Aurelia, give me your eyes."

I couldn't focus, the edges of my vision blurring in a frenzy. "I can't —"

"You can. Look at me." The insistence in his lilt forced me to seek the outline of his facial features. Gradually, the outline of his straight nose became clear. Resting my gaze there momentarily, I moved to his lips. The full, beautiful lips that had captured mine. Not as often as I'd like, and I couldn't help but hope there would be plenty of time to remedy that. Next, I moved to his eyes where the sheer terror for my wellbeing sat. How could I ever question the way this man felt for me when he looked at me in such a way? When every emotion he'd ever held sat so comfortably in whirlpool of browns, greens, and ambers?

Releasing his shirt from my grip, I lifted my hand, using my finger to gently trace the contours of his face. His lips were silk beneath my touch. His nose the compass of his face, guiding me back up to his eyes. I stroked his perfectly shaped eyebrows before tracing the outline of his eyes, repeating the action as the depth of my breathing eased. Then, no higher than a whisper, I breathed the words which started the attack, "I have magic."

Mads sat still, my finger still on his lips, repeating the words, "You have magic." He let me study his face with only the whispers of my touch until my heart rate calmed to a reasonable level.

"Aurelia, are you with me?"

His voice coasted over my ears, comfortingly. Closing my eyes, I nodded. Another new reality placed on me. One I wasn't sure how to approach. If I had learned anything after stabbing Shelton, I could make my own rules, carve my own path. Magic would have to work around me.

"Good." Gently, he leaned forward, brushing his lips to the tip of my nose. I opened my eyes to find the pained glare had eased slightly.

"She's awake?" Fox and his impeccable timing popped his head through the door.

"You're getting to it already? Can't you two keep your hands off each other for more than five minutes?"

Strutting in, he left the door open behind him as Mads growled his name in warning. Xav strolled in behind with Bea on his heels. She plopped down on the other side of the gigantic bed. "How are you doing?"

I chucked, "Awful." Mads shifted me back to the bed, careful not to let his hands leave me for too long.

"Sounds about right," Fox announced from the other side of the room, plucking a grape off of a tray filled high with food. I still hadn't had the time to properly survey the room I was in. Given my present company, my exploration wouldn't happen for a while.

"How did we get here?" I directed towards no one in particular.

"Well —"

"No." Mads stopped Fox, knowing full well he wouldn't tell the story accurately.

I glanced around to notice Eva was missing from our party. "Where's Eva?"

The panic ebbed again. Mads clutched my hand tightly. "She's fine. She's resting in the room across from this one. Rock is with her."

A sigh of relief left me. The most hateful part of panic was once it was fully triggered, it could pounce on my body and mind with the utmost speed and intensity. Once I fell into the abyss, it was hard to get out.

Xav sat at the foot of the bed, resting a hand on my quilt covered leg. "We didn't know what was happening to you. We should have realised. I'm so sorry, Aurelia."

"I'm not mad at you. At any of you. Maybe we could have guessed at something more to my... curse breaking. Even if we did, we had no idea what effect it would have once we got here."

The room sat in silence. It was clear my companions wanted to blame themselves for the pain. Hating the way their guilt filled the room, I pushed them for more on the journey after I'd become incapacitated.

"We grabbed you and ran. We didn't know where we were going. Good thing we only had to run a few miles before we ran into Kane," Mads explained.

"Kane?"

"My captain of the guard."

"You have a captain of the guard?"

Mads looked down at me and said, "Of course. I was the crown prince of Hiema."

I rolled my eyes playfully. "So, you ran into Kane. If he's from Hiema, why was he in Spring?"

"After our parents were murdered, a lot of Hiemans came to Spring." Mads spoke solemnly as though the words triggered the memory of the day their parents were murdered.

"Were they allowed to?" I questioned thoughtfully.

"Apparently, the Queen of Aestas didn't press the issue. Deserters had no place in Aestas or Hiema. If they left, it meant less disobedient citizens she would have to manage. Confidence is something she has in abundance and I think... I think it will be her downfall."

I looked at each of those in the room, trying to understand their thoughts. My head still caused me pain, making it difficult to read the room. "It is good we are here, right?"

"Very." Fox stepped forward. "Our Aunt has been incredibly welcoming, as we thought she would."

"What if they find out you're back?" The thought hadn't occurred to me prior. The group's focus consisted of getting to Raithe. I hadn't thought about much past the one goal. An error on my part.

Xav chuckled before he said, "No one, and I mean no one, is happy with what happened to our parents. To us. A lot has gone on since we were exiled. A lot should work in our favour."

Fox clicked his tongue from his spot near the fireplace. "Raithe was already experiencing a lot of unrest before we were exiled. Most of that hostility stemmed from Aestas itself. When we were banished, a lot of Hiemans took that as their sign to integrate with other kingdoms, if possible."

I opened my mouth to press further, curious at the state of Raithe now when a knock sounded on the door. Each head turned towards it before Fox stepped forward. "Is she awake?" A feminine lilt drifted through the small crack in the door.

"She is."

"Can I meet her?" the voice enquired with kindness.

Fox turned to Mads for approval who gave it straight away. King in waiting.

Pulling the door open further, Fox stood to the side to let a woman in. A petite woman, donned in the finest fabrics I had ever laid my eyes on. Her trousers were made of the same gold colour decorating the room, a swash of velvet and wool. She wore a crisp white knee length tunic, odd given its simplicity to the rest of the outfit. Her straight, grey and white hair sat just above her shoulders. Kindness radiated from her as she made her way across the room, cautiously.

"I am so glad to see you awake, my dear. You gave us all quite a scare."

Mads stood, "Aurelia, this is our Aunt, Colette Ardath, Queen of the Spring Court."

I went to stand, not sure of the etiquette in meeting a Queen, let alone a Queen of magic. My body protested with each shift. Queen Colette stepped forward, shaking her head frantically. "Oh no. Don't you dare get up. This introduction is more than fine."

Queen Colette's smile hit me like a warm embrace. The sincerity in her eyes was difficult to ignore. I bowed my chin slightly, at least a semblance of respect for the royalty in front of me, although I'd never given the bears that formality. "It's lovely to meet you, Your Majesty."

"None of that, now. I'm only 'Your Majesty' to a few, less than savoury individuals. And my wife. She prefers the more formal title." With a wink, Queen Collette sat on the edge of the bed, signalling for me to sit back down which I immediately obliged. Scooping up my hand into her own, a faint sliver of concern etched around her eyes. "Finding out about your magic has probably given you quite a scare, has it?"

I nodded. A change fluttered through my bones. I thought about my new start in Raithe and the opportunity I had to be the person I was never granted the freedom to be. I also needed to be confident in my inquisitive nature, especially in a new world. And so, I asked the question flickering through my mind, "Are you using magic?"

Queen Colette beamed. "No dear. My magic is elemental. I'm a nurturer. Good for growing things. And very useful in this Kingdom."

"Oh. I'm sorry. I didn't mean to —"

"Nonsense, my dear. You've got a lot to learn. Don't think for one second you should know it all now."

I didn't know how to respond. I was grateful for her understanding, still groggy from the day's events, coupled with the fact I was still very much intimidated in conversing with an actual Queen, I did the only thing I could think of and squeezed Queen Colette's hand briefly.

Shooting me a wink, Queen Colette stood, excusing herself, "Make sure these four don't over excite you and get some rest." She turned at the door, offering one last smile of kindness. "We'll speak again soon."

Offering a silent nod in return, Queen Colette left. Once the door clicked, I breathed out audibly, addressing my companions with a subtle annoyance laced through my words, "I can't believe you let me meet a Queen in this state."

Fox popped another grape into his mouth, "Hey, you met two princes and a king by breaking into their house."

"Thanks Fox. You always know exactly what to say."

He threw me a wink. "Anytime, Goldie."

"She is right though," Xav announced, "we should let Aurelia rest more."

With those words, Bea leaned over to kiss my cheek before following Xav and Fox out the door, leaving me alone with Mads once more.

"Are you alright?" Mads asked, concern laced through his words.

I glanced around the room, "Yes and no."

Mads nodded, accepting that as a suitable answer. "You should get some more rest."

He made toward the door, "Mads?"

"Yes?"

"Aren't you going to stay with me?" I cursed the apparent need threaded through my words. We hadn't yet discussed our future, or whether or not there would even be one. I felt a wave of vulnerability wash over me.

Turning the lock, he looked back at me as he said, "Oh Goldie, I'm not going anywhere."

A subtle smile played on his lips as he settled down next to me, waiting for me to situate myself, slowly. I placed my head on his chest, not fully content, but now calm enough to at least rest my aching body. Closing my eyes, I felt Mads' breath on my head, sighing out a day's worth of concern and revelling in the way my body fit against his. We were going to be okay, I thought. No matter what came next. It was all going to be okay.

Chapter 30

Aurelia

The heat suffocated me, engulfing my mind, body, and soul. The feverish air made it difficult for me to pry my eyes apart. When I finally managed it, I found a hand resting next to my head. A hand that didn't belong to me. A strong hand, featuring long, capable fingers. My focus moved to the tense pressure on top of my legs. It took a few moments to recognise the hand and the weight of Mads wrapped around me, burying me with his body heat. I let out a soft chuckle. For a man I once knew to be filled with anger and lacked the ability to know any other emotion, he certainly did love to cuddle.

Doing my utmost not to disturb him, I delicately shifted his leg off of my own, giving myself some breathing room. Mads stirred, moving his hand to my stomach and pulling my back flush against his chest. The movement brought a new sensation, a very hard one, pushing against my backside.

It wasn't uncomfortable, sending a pang of desire straight between my legs. Now would not be the time, but I still couldn't help my body from wanting it. Badly.

Wiggling with intention, I waited for Mads' response, "Careful." A grumbled groan left his mouth as I continued to push myself back against his hard length.

"You're going to kill me, woman."

Being the death of Mads, purely by his need for me, didn't sound bad at all. Sparkling in triumph, I pushed my hips back once more. A vibration from his chest radiated against my back. Mads shifted his hand to my face, tilting it to look over my shoulder at him. His eyes met mine with an intense desire. "I'm serious, Aurelia. Keep doing that and I won't be able to control myself."

I took my lip between my teeth. "I wouldn't mind seeing you out of control."

A low growl rumbled at the back of his throat, hitting the corner of my ear, the pulsing intensified the sensation between my legs. "One day. Soon."

Just as I was about to continue the assault with my hips, needing this hardness against me once more, a loud rapping sounded at the door. We groaned in unison, sending silent hatred toward the interruption.

"Aurelia?" Eva's voice was a surprising balm to my aching body, dissolving most of the annoyance I'd felt seconds earlier.

Stretching, I pushed myself up, letting my feet hit the plush carpet. Wiggling my toes briefly, I searched the suite for some sort of cover up. My eyes landed on a pale blue silk robe, draped over the chair Mads sat in the night before. With tender steps, given the way my body protested each movement, I made my way toward the door, throwing one last look over my shoulder to Mads, ensuring he was decent.

I opened the door to find my baby sister, freshly bathed and swathed in an elegant off white, silk two piece ensemble. She stared back at me with bright eyes, sending a wave of relief through me. A movement toward the floor caught my eye. Looking down, I found Rock sitting directly behind Eva.

"Fox tried to take him. The little guy refused to leave my side. He's a sweetheart," she confirmed as she looked down at the bundle of fiery fur.

"He is," I agreed. "Are you alright?" I couldn't hide the concern laced through my words, needing Eva to ease it.

Staring back at me, her face descended into seriousness as she spoke, "Absolutely. Are you?"

I offered a reassuring smile. "Come in."

Eva walked into the room as another door slammed, indicating Mads had silently excused himself into the adjoining bathroom. I motioned for Eva to take one of the armchairs near the fireplace, Rock following closely on her heels.

"Did someone tell you what happened to me yesterday?" Not only was it likely I had magic flowing through my veins, but it may also be another wedge driven between the broken relationship Eva and I shared.

Eva stared down at the empty fireplace, refusing to meet my stare. "Yes. Bea. She said you have magic."

I thought back to the panic induced by the revelation and did my best to quell any of the familiar alarms from popping up again. "Apparently."

"How, Aurelia?" Eva's approach was one of pure curiosity, not animosity or disgust.

"I honestly don't know Eva. It seems so odd. Also, not. When Bea discovered I could open the portal, I had visions. Ones indicating we, Archer, you, and I, had a deeper connection to this land than we ever knew."

"It makes sense."

I shot her a look of surprise, "It does?"

Turning her attention to me, she nodded. "I never felt like our home was a home. Not just because of how our parents treated us, although their treatment was definitely a big part. I always felt out of place there. I needed there to be more. There had to be something else."

It was hard for me to accept this new side of Eva. Technically, it probably wasn't new. It was actually who she'd always been, only the hex had held her back from exposing the kind heart she continued to unveil.

"I don't think I ever had the mental capacity to think any differently than what we knew." It was a confession I didn't mean to let slip, truthful all the same. If Eva was finally able to start showing her true self, I resonated, it couldn't be bad if I did the same.

"I know. I'm so sorry." The apology slipped her tongue on a whisper. Without thought, I reached across the space between us, enveloping Eva's hand in my own.

"Can we both agree how incredible it is we are here, together, in a new life and in a new world?"

Eva laughed, a deep cheerful sound hitting me directly in the heart. "And apparently you have magic."

"And apparently I have magic."

I joined my sister in the uproar, savouring every second of the joy I felt. Fear still sat deep, yet the invasion of the new chances and choices gave me a strength I never knew I could have.

"So," Eva's laughter subsided, "what now?"

"Honestly? I have no idea."

"It's kind of beautiful though, isn't it?" she said as she squeezed my hand.

Nodding, I raised our intertwined hands and planted a swift and soft kiss on my sister's knuckles. Capturing this moment in my mind for eternity.

Mads stalked from the ensuite, fully dressed in black trousers, a fresh white tunic, curls still damp from the shower. In whatever state he appeared, he was a beautiful sight. He stopped in his tracks when he noticed the intimate moment between my sister and I.

"We are due to meet everyone in the great hall soon. You should get showered."

Eva stood, taking Mads' words as her queue to leave. Before she and Rock left the room, she looked back at me once more, offering a smile of hope. One I would forever cherish.

I thought the shower back at the cabin was the best thing I had ever experienced, until I stood under the hot stream resembling a waterfall in my guest quarters. Mads leant by the bathroom counter, available if I needed his assistance, as he talked me through the morning's plan. We were due to meet Kane and the Queens before greeting the other Hiema supporters in the great hall later in the afternoon. The Queens would host a more intimate lunch before

Mads and his brothers were to meet with the lords and ladies who had pledged their allegiance to the Hiema Kingdom after the murder of their parents. Mads sounded surprised so many had raised their banners in support of him, the rightful king, especially after all this time. I listened intently as a new Mads revealed himself. King Maddox Artos of Hiema.

Rinsing the last of the suds from my body, I felt it best to address any questions I had before throwing myself into uncomfortable social situations. "Mads, is there anything I should know?"

With his arms crossed, he turned his head toward me inquisitively. "Anything you need to know? Not specifically. Is there anything you want to know?"

I turned the handle to stop the fall of water as Mads handed me a plush towel. I wasted no time in wrapping myself up, thankful for the comfortable fabric against my skin.

I met his gaze as I said, "There is a lot I *want* to know, but I also think I'll learn through time. I don't want to jumble my mind with information before we meet Hiema's supporters."

Mads took a step towards me, brushing the drenched hair from my face before meeting my blue eyes with his own, wrapped in deep golden hues and greens. "What is really bothering you, Aurelia?"

I sighed in apprehension, not in fear of voicing my concerns to Mads, but more so the potential anxiety they may spawn. Placing my palm in his, I spoke as confidently as possible, "It's just that I am prone to episodes of panic, and I'm worried I will get overwhelmed, whether with people or information, and it will cause me to spiral. We only just got you back here. I don't want Raithe's first impression of me to show my weaknesses."

Mads smiled softly. Guiding me back to the countertop, he grabbed my hips and hoisted me up into a seated position, situating himself between my legs. If I hadn't shown my vulnerability at that point, the action would've triggered very different thoughts to flick through my mind.

"First," Mads stated sternly, "not one part of you is weak. No matter what happens, no one will think that. You are the strong, incredible, fighter who got a King and two Princes back in their rightful place."

"But I didn't —"

Mads shook his head, silencing me. Placing his hands on either side of my hips, he leaned down leaving only inches between us. "Second, even if the panic does creep in, I will be there to catch you whether it is in a room of hundreds or just you and I. Understand?"

I didn't have an ounce of doubt toward his words. Swallowing down the tears threatening to creep in, I nodded.

"And finally," he continued, "I need you to promise that whatever questions pop into that gorgeous mind of yours, you voice them straight away. Can you do that?"

I had so much to learn but I knew with the darkness now freely floating through my head and the tangle of recent and future events, I had to give myself space. I offered him a subtle nod in agreement.

I dressed in a simple, two piece outfit, similar to the one Eva had worn except mine was a deep royal blue, the colour of the Winter Kingdom. I had a choice, of course, of various colours but I want to show my support for the bears. Also, I adored the colour and the silk against my body felt sensational.

Mads led the way downstairs. Xav, Fox, Bea, and Eva joined us on our journey, marching as a unit toward our futures. The palace was stunning. The hallways were decorated in the most lavish wallpapers, with just enough detail to envelope you in comfort. The colour palette mirrored a fine spring day, pastels and warming hues promising new life.

Near the front entrance, I caught a glimpse of Queen Colette and noticed another woman at her side. I assumed she was Queen Kendra, the blood Queen of the Spring Kingdom. Colette had married into the Spring Kingdom, and it was purely a coincidence she held earth magic.

Our group made the way to the two women who were deep in hushed conversation. When Colette noticed our party walking toward them, a beaming smile grew across her face, "Good morning, all! Aurelia, darling, it is so good to see you up and about. How are you?"

Queen Colette stepped forward, taking my hand in hers, sending a dash of warmth up my arm. "Much better. Thank you, Your Majesty. I am still quite sore, but I will heal."

"Of course you will. Aurelia," Colette turned, "I'd like to meet my better half, Queen Kendra."

I slide my hand from Colette's before lowering down on one knee, bowing my head in parallel. Next to me, Eva mirrored my movements.

"Oh my." Kendra breathed in surprise.

A finger found its way beneath my chin, lifting my gaze to meet the eyes of Queen Kendra. "You never need to bow to me. You brought our boys home."

Her eyes twinkled with a deep emotion I could only compare to relief. "Stand child."

She gestured to Eva, "You too. I don't want bowing from any of you."

Once I had straightened, I caught Fox's cheeky grin in my peripheral vision. Deciding it was best to ignore him, I waited for the queens to conduct further conversation. Before they were able to exchange any further information, Mads piped in, "There he is."

I looked past the queens' shoulders to see a man, a very tall man, walking towards our group. On reflex, my mouth dropped. The man walking towards me was dazzling — smooth, deep brown skin accented with piercing hazel eyes. I gawked as his full lips tilted into a grin, no doubt noticing my perusal of his many fine features. He wore a jacket I would compare to a military commander. His strides were confident, sexy, and just about knocked the wind out of me. Mads' beauty was muscles and hard edges. This man was elegant with fine lines.

Mads stepped forward, grasping the man's arm before turning to me for introductions, "Aurelia, I'd like you to meet Captain Artemis Kane. He leads Hiema's Queen's guard."

My mouth went dry as this beautiful specimen focused all of his attention on me.

"Whoa." I snapped my mouth shut. I hadn't meant for the word to leave my mouth. Flicking my shocked stare to Mads, he raised a brow in, not jealousy or annoyance, but amusement. The strange pull wasn't sexual attraction, but I couldn't deny his inherent beauty.

"Sorry. Just... whoa."

I'd done it again. A sudden urge to smack myself in the head reared up. Kane chuckled before extending his hand. "You have no idea how lovely it is to meet you properly, Miss Aurelia."

Placing my hand in his outstretched one, I swallowed audibly as he placed a light kiss on the back of my hand.

"Anything other than 'whoa,' Goldie?" Fox shot from my right.

Embarrassment bloomed across my cheeks. Mads had seen me gawk at his captain of the guard and the rest of our group, including Fox who would, no doubt, not let me live this incident down.

Clearing my throat, I said, "Lovely to meet you, Captain. And please, it's just Aurelia."

He bent slightly at the waist, his eyes looking at me from beneath his perfectly manicured brows. "Aurelia. And please, call me Kane."

My name on his lips was a song I could listen to repeatedly. Kane turned back to the queens to offer them a proper greeting as Mads stepped into my space, letting his voice whisper across my ear. "You alright?" The humour in his voice was noticeable.

I placed my hand gently on my forehead. The flush still littered across my skin. "I'm really not sure what happened there."

He laughed, placing a kiss on my forehead before turning back to the group. I took a step back, doing my best to distance myself from the embarrassment. To my dismay, Bea and Eva joined me. "Don't worry buttercup, Eva and I had the exact same reaction to him yesterday. Apparently, his magic has something to do with charm."

A slight relief filled me, knowing I wasn't the only one to react that way. "But he's still —"

"Gorgeous. Sexy. The most beautiful man you've ever seen?" Eva finished my sentence.

Bea giggled, "We're with you buttercup. And don't worry, the initial shock subsides after a while."

The redness in my face continued to project the mess I'd made from the introduction. Bea placed her arm around my shoulder, giving me a squeeze in support. The queens asked our group to follow them into one of the lounges for lunch to which I was grateful for. Anything to move me away from the current predicament.

The room mirrored much of the palace I'd already laid my eyes on, apart from slightly deeper tones than those of the hallways, the room was comfortable, not stuffy, which battled all of my conceptions about what a palace should look like.

The queens took their seats at the head of the long table. I admired the set up. Instead of one seat at the head of the table, the width was altered to enable them to sit next to one another, mirroring the way they partnered in leading Vernum.

The rest of the party sat down, immediately flanked by a number of servants, setting down bowls of steaming, creamy soup in front of us. Freshly harvested tomatoes mixed with cream and cheese drifted from the bowl, enticing me to lean forward and take a further concentrated inhale. The growl of my stomach was drowned out by the rest of the group shuffling their cutlery and diving straight in. I wasted no time doing the same.

"So, Aurelia, I understand you learned about your magic."

I placed my spoon down, not wanting to appear rude while addressing Queen Kendra, "Well, to be honest, I learned I have magic, I'm just not sure what magic it is. We haven't exactly had much time to discuss it."

The queens glanced towards Mads who offered them a brief nod before they turned their attention back to me. "You're a key, dear."

A key.

A key.

Unlocking the doors. The curse.

"A key?" I couldn't hide the confusion lining my face.

Queen Kendra stepped in to explain, "Yes. Essentially it is as it sounds. Keys are very rare in Raithe. I don't actually think we've met another key in a very long time."

"As it sounds?" The perplexed expression seeped into my voice, littering my mind with more questions.

"Apologies, dear. Yes. As a key, you can unlock doors, portals, chains, anything physical. Keys don't open metaphorical or mental locks. Just real ones."

"What we don't know," Colette chimed in, "is why you were in England. It is clear you are of Raithean birth."

"Is it?" Mads had made me promise to ask my questions, and I fully intended to honour that promise now. Whilst the origins of my birth were suspected following the recollection spell, I wanted to doubt it. Too many unknowns sat in front of us. Figuring out my potential and real connection to this realm just muddled things further.

"Well, yes. We may even find if Eva is actually your biological sister, she may have magic too." Silverware clattered against a plate, I looked towards my sister who sat wide eyed, mouth agape. "Seriously?"

Kendra chuckled, "Yes, child. If you are actually sisters, you, too, could have magic."

"But I don't feel like I have magic." Eva denied the claim and from her tone, she didn't want it to be true.

"It may have been suppressed longer than Aurelia's, so it is taking more time to rise back to the surface. Or maybe your magic hasn't revealed itself yet."

"Is that possible?" Bea questioned.

"Oh yes," Colette picked up the explanation. "You can be any age when your magic comes through."

Silence filled the room. The clash of silverware had died, no sips were being taken from cups, it was as though most of the group needed time to process this information. Yesterday, Eva and I were coming to terms with the fact we would enter a new world and a new life. Now, it was confirmed I had actual magic, Eva could too, and our entire lives had not only been vicious, but a lie.

Kendra lowered her voice, taking care with each word she spoke next. "We do understand this is a lot to process, and I hope you know you have so much support here."

I tipped my chin towards Kendra, doing my utmost to offer a smile of gratitude. The truth was, I wasn't overwhelmed nor accepting. I sat in the blank space between the two, willing myself not to tip into a panic and process the information as patiently as I could. I would also need to check in with Eva later. It appeared our new attempt at a relationship would move much quicker than I initially envisioned. Swallowing the void, I filtered through the many questions zooming through my mind, settling on the one I thought was most important. "Would you know which kingdom we came from?"

Kane pushed into the conversation, his voice leaving a thin blanket of comfort above us, "No. Keys are part of the sundry category of magic. Generally, those who fall into that division of magic can come from any kingdom and given we aren't sure what Eva's magic could be, it's hard to say."

Raithe held two categories of magic. Elemental magic connected directly to the four elements of nature — fire, earth, water, and air. Sundry magic contained all other types of magic that did not directly connect to the elements. Even with the two categories, the only differentiating factor was that most rightful kings and queen of the seasonal kingdoms inherited the elemental power of their direct season — fire for Hiema, earth for Vernum, water for Aestas, and air for Havon.

"Is there a spell I could perform?" Bea's constant support filled me with comfort. The witch's intuition was exactly what we needed on our side.

"Maybe?" the queens looked at one another. "We can introduce you to our Kingdom's resident witch and let you both discuss.

"An introduction would be great. Thank you." Bea, appearing more formal than I had ever known her to be, nodded her appreciation.

"Of course, dear, but first, if you are all quite finished, we have some rebels to meet," Colette shot Fox a wink. I brushed it off, realising it was best not to cloud my brain with more unanswered questions.

Mads hung back with me briefly asking me silently if I needed a minute. Gripping his arm in my palm, and ignoring the tense muscles beneath, I proceeded with my question, "Did you know?"

I knew I wouldn't have to specify the 'what'?

Mads shook his head, leaning close enough for our breaths to mingle, and I savoured the scent of him. "I've never known of this type of magic. It's clearly very rare. But it makes sense, given your visions and door opening capability. You came into the cabin, even though we always lock the door."

"You locked the door? It's not like anyone could enter." Was it the necessary time for that question? Probably not but bottoms up to question time.

Mads chuckled, "You're forgetting one mischievous witch in that equation."

Of course. Bea could enter the cabin and no doubt would have been up to no good in the bear's absence.

"We will explore this more. There are a lot of people here, and in Raithe, that I'm sure can teach us about your magic." The corner of Mads' lips tipped up, causing warmth to blossom in my chest. He was a professional at the smoulder but Mads' smile could always find me in the darkness.

"Okay." I nodded, giving his arm one more squeeze before another question plagued my brain.

"Mads?"

"Yes, Aurelia?"

"If your aunt was related to your mother, and ultimately Hiema, why would Aestas not come after her?"

Taking my hand to wrap around his arm, he turned us the way the group had departed. "That's a good question. Given the resistance both Havon and Vernum have shown, they put protections and guards in place to prevent that from happening."

I let the information churn through my mind. "Although it was still a potential threat, they have never been able to get to her."

"And the people that have shown today? How do we know they won't run to Aestas and tell them you've returned?"

Mads nodded in agreement. "Most of those that are here fled from Aestas and Hiema for a better life. Again, there is always a risk involved but we genuinely believe that people are inherently good."

I knew much different to that way of thinking given the people and events of my own life but a part of me, that pulsing sensation, very much wanted to believe that too. If I'd learned anything since meeting the bears, and Bea, it was the knowledge that good existed in this world. Let's hope it was strong enough to persevere.

We met the group back out in the main entryway, trailing the wide, lavishly decorated hallway towards what I assumed with the back of the palace. Given the state of my consciousness when I had arrived the night before, I had no idea what the actual layout was.

I strayed toward the back of the group, doing what I did best, blending in with the crowd. Mads glanced over his shoulder a few times, ensuring I was still with them. What he didn't know was no matter what happened next, I had already made the decision to be with them, always. I knew with these people, this...family, I would continue to rebuild those broken fragments into something spectacular.

Finally reaching a set of grand oak doors I assumed led to the great hall, the queens turned to their guests, Kendra addressed us all, "We will lead you in and make the initial statement, Mads, it would be good for you to speak as well."

He inclined his head in agreement. Two guards stepped forward to pull the doors open. Given I was at the back of the group, it was hard for me to see the full extent of the hall and the individuals within; however, the astonished gasps that left my companions mouths in unison had me pushing up on my toes for a better view.

The queens moved forward, followed by the men of our group. Bea, Eva, and I stayed back for a moment and it was then the room was revealed. I stared in awe at the number of people within the room itself. The great hall had the capacity for at least a few thousand people and was exactly what I saw. I had expected a hundred people to have pledged their support, at most. The sheer amount of people willing to defend Hiema and bring Raithe back to glory was unfathomable. Tears welled in my eyes. Of pride. Shock. Fear. Happiness.

A hand pushed at my back. Eva. The three of us took swift steps to catch up with the front half of the group, trying our best not to focus on the thousands of gawking eyes ensnaring us. Concentrating on the movements of my feet so I wouldn't trip, we were at the dais before I knew it. Mads gestured for me to stand by his side. I hesitated, briefly, before finding my place next to him.

"Welcome friends!" Queen Kendra held out her arms in warm greeting.

"Queen Colette and I are beyond grateful to welcome back the Artos brothers to Raithe!"

A cheer erupted. I scanned the crowd, noticing the hope laced across the thousands of faces in front of them. As Mads stepped forward, he grabbed my hand, taking me with him. "Raitheans, after a very long exile, we are beyond pleased to be home. Along with our new companions here," he gestured to me, Eva, and Bea, "we have come back to take what is rightfully ours and restore peace in Raithe once more!"

A second eruption of cheers.

"Aurelia?"

The room quieted immediately. My chest heaved at the recognition. I searched the crowd in panic, stepping past Mads in an attempt to get a better glimpse at the owner of the voice.

"Aurelia!"

The shock radiating from my name, the depth of the voice. It couldn't be. It was impossible. And then, he stepped into the centre of the room. A man with a head of thick ash brown curls stared straight into my soul.

I stood frozen, unable to grasp the situation in front of me. The ghost in front of me.

"Who is that?" Fox whispered from behind me. Before I could attempt to find my voice, Eva breathed, "Archer."

Chapter 31

Aurelia

Time slowed. The crowd blurred leaving the light to radiate on only the man in front of me. The only man I had ever truly loved. The man who could have changed my entire future if he hadn't disappeared. I had resigned, a long time ago, that Archer was dead. Except he wasn't. He stood, flesh and blood, bellowing my name in agony.

"Archer."

He was alive.

He was there.

"Archer!" My voice squealed at the realisation. I dropped Mads' hand and bounded down the stairs, focusing on Archer alone. Archer burst into a sprint, the tears streaming down his face, a mirror to my own. One second. I pumped my legs faster. Two seconds. He had to be real. Three seconds. We crashed into each other.

I wrapped my arms around his neck as he pulled me off my feet, burrowing his face in my neck. A laugh bubbled up in my chest as I tried to halt the tears, enjoying every sensation. The hold around his neck. His scent. It hadn't changed at all. Every question, every worry, every unknown laying ahead of me, all flew out of my head. All that mattered was the man holding me in his arms.

"You're here." He breathed into my hair.

"You're here." I sobbed back.

He joined in my laughter, swinging my body around in circles in pure triumph. A reunion I never thought possible. Whatever Raithe would be to me, it had already cemented itself with deep meaning in my heart.

Archer placed me gently on my feet, pulling his body back slightly, careful not to let go fully. Studying his face, my chest pounded with questions. "How are you here?"

"I live here."

"How, Archer? You...I thought you were dead."

A throat cleared behind us, bringing us both back to the reality we were in, which was a room filled with thousands of people who had just witnessed a very emotional reunion. I turned to see Mads at the top of the dais, eyebrows raised in curiosity. Turning back to Archer, I felt my insides empty at the thought of leaving him, even if it was temporary. "I'll find you after."

I nodded just as Mads' booming voice filled the room, "Archer, you are Aurelia's family and therefore, your place is up here. With us. Please," he gestured to his side, "join us."

Heart filled with various emotions towards the man, I lead Archer up to the steps, taking my place next to Mads, never once letting go of my brother. Eva shifted left to take Archer's other side, placing her hand in his free one. As the three of us became connected, a unit once more, that familiar pulsing sensation flared to life. I shoved it off as the pure happiness of seeing my brother again. An event I would have never dreamed possible.

Mads straightened, ready to address the room once more. "Looking out at you all before me, I am speechless. Knowing you have all fought on our behalf, on the behalf of your brethren, fills me with so much pride. My brothers and I," he turned to Xav and Fox, "have a lot to catch up on. To relearn. We hope, with your guidance and support, we can be ready to take back Hiema in the coming weeks and to restore our freedoms once more."

A clap sounded from the middle of the crowd somewhere. I wasn't able to make out who, exactly, it was coming from. Then, in a wave of hands, the room erupted in applause, pushing the emotions back up my throat.

"Thank you." Mads' sincerity was palpable. He waited for the cheers to die down before continuing his address, "We want to take the next couple of days and meet with each of your families and groups. Hear from you directly. This is how we will learn. This is how we will strategise, with you by our sides. Now, please, eat and drink your fill. We look forward to speaking soon."

Just as the crowd was about to break towards the service staff and buffet, the double doors creaked from the back, or rather, front of the room. Those on the dais and the crowd paused, waiting with bated breath for whomever had decided to interrupt this most joyous of gatherings.

Stepping through the door was a large man. Dark brown tendrils were pulled together on the top of his head. A gruff beard filled his face. His skin shimmered with proof of his days in the sunshine. When his head finally raised, he locked eyes with Mads, his body tensed beside me, pulsing through our connected hands.

A wicked smile grew on the man's face just before he dropped down on one knee, bowing his head in respect. "Your Majesty."

Mads belted out the most extravagant laugh. It startled me. He had hidden so much of himself from us; new layers of the onion continued to show. Mads let go of my hand gently, making his way down the stairs with swift eagerness. The bearded man mirrored his movements, picking up his pace with each step until they barrelled into one another, arms locking tightly around them both. The two began speaking in hushed whispers, making it impossible for me to understand what happened. I turned to Fox and Xav who were both smiling gleefully. "Who is that?"

"That," Fox nodded once, "is Everett Griffin. Mads' best friend and the leader of the Knights Mara."

"The Knights Mara?"

Fox turned to me, his smile growing. "We have so much to teach you, Goldie."

With no further explanation, the two brothers made their way towards the embracing men, taking turns to greet Everett. I was so enraptured in the reunion I had momentarily forgotten about my own. The one still attached to me by his hand. Turning, I found both Eva and Archer mesmerised by the heart-warming sight in the middle of the room.

Queen Colette approached us from behind, advising we should retire to more private quarters and let the guests enjoy the food and drink while they discussed matters further.

Half an hour later, I found myself back in the suite I, apparently, shared with Mads, Eva on my left and Archer on my right. After a brief introduction with Everett, the bears were escorted to the throne room, which I discovered was different from the room we were in, where they would begin meeting with the Raitheans who had pledged their swords. Bea had stayed with them at Xav's insistence. He wanted her talented intuition to observe and make notes when necessary, which is how I found myself alone with my estranged brother and a sister I had thought indifferent until recently.

The excitement of Archer's appearance still hung proudly around us. After so long, it was clear we were practically strangers. We had lived entire lives apart. Plus the fact everything with Eva was new, the trio felt overwhelming.

"So," Archer decided to break the silence, "should we start with why you're here?"

An odd and immediate sense of anger grew, it wasn't Eva or I needing to start answering questions.

"Wait," Eva interjected before I could, "How about we start with why you are here. You disappeared a decade ago. We mourned you. Even had a funeral."

Shock hit me at the demand in Eva's voice. "So, I'd say, we deserve an explanation first." Eva sat back, crossing her arms over her chest, emphasising her point.

Archer glanced between us, the look on his face indicating the wheels turning in his head. I craved his story. Although a very recent craving, a craving nonetheless.

"I was kidnapped, or so I initially thought I was,' he paused. Neither Eva nor I was going to interrupt.

"Ten years ago, Captain Kane got through a portal to the mortal world, looking for the exiled princes.

"How?" The question came out more accusatory than I planned. "The portals were closed. Sealed. Did Mads know about this?"

Archer nodded his head once, "I believe so. If he doesn't, I'm sure he's learning it now."

I kept my mouth shut, wanting to know more.

Archer didn't hesitate to continue, "Kane did find a Raithean prince, just not one of the ones he'd set out to."

My brain tried to process his words, failing miserably. "What do you mean, a Raithean prince?"

"It means," Archer stood, beginning to pace the length of the fireplace, "I am a Raithean prince, of the Summer Kingdom. It also means," he turned toward us, addressing us both, "you are Raithean princesses."

My mouth went dry as Eva burst into a fit of laughter. A princess? A. Princess.

"You're lying," Eva breathed through a chuckle, eyes beginning to fill with tears.

"I promise you, little sister, I am not lying."

"What?" Recognising I was, again, in a position where I didn't have to stay silent, I lashed out. It felt good. "How are we royalty?"

"An interesting story, and I dare say, one you aren't going to like very much."

"Archer," I pinched the bridge of my nose, "you disappeared. I was used as a pawn in our alleged father's political game for years, resulting in a whole slew of abuse, and Eva," I shot my hand towards my sister, "was cursed from ever trying to help me. Whatever the hell you are going to tell us cannot compete with the dire lives we have already lived."

Archer's face grew grim, the colour leaching out with each breath, leaving him white. I didn't want this. I didn't need his pity or his anger. I needed whatever knowledge he had. "What do you mean abuse?"

"Focus, Archer! You're angry knowing we suffered, blah, blah, blah. Tell us the gods damn truth or we are both leaving this room with no regret we haven't rekindled a relationship with our dear brother."

I knew I was harsh. I also didn't care. This wasn't the person Archer would have remembered me to be. It wasn't even the person I'd allowed myself to be when I'd first found the bear's house. This was the person who was finally taking what I wanted. What I needed to figure out was the enormous mystery otherwise known as my life. Old and new.

"You're right. I'm sorry. You deserve to know everything."

Shifting his now empty armchair to face us, he sat down, placing his arms on his elbows.

"It started when I was five years old, when the King and Queen of Hiema were murdered and the Summer Kingdom took over. Our parents, Queen Carman and King Jolon of the Summer Kingdom, had laid the path for their future, ruling over all of Raithe. As I'm sure you've figured, they still haven't been able to obtain the Autumn and Spring Kingdoms, dividing Raithe in two.

"Back then, they were determined to rule everything. They decided they needed to eliminate the low hanging fruit." He looked between Eva and I, a deep sadness filling his eyes.

"To eliminate their heirs."

Heirs. We were heirs. Heirs to an entire Kingdom. And our parents had made the decision to get rid of us.

"The problem was, they hired the wrong man to do it. Their plan was to hire an assassin to keep their hands clean. Removing them of their three future problems in one fell swoop without having to even lift a finger. What they didn't know was that the assassin they hired was more interested in the potential value of having a prince and two princesses in his grasp."

Leaning back, he began to relax into his story. "And so we went to the highest bidder. Stolen from our family and Raithe but left with our lives."

I looked to Eva who was doing a decent job of appearing to hold it together. I wasn't sure I could say the same for myself. A clamminess grew beneath my palms, my heartbeat erratic.

"Who was the highest bidder?" Eva's voice was a level of sternness one of us needed to have.

"A man, a mortal man, one you remember — Lord Shelton."

Shooting from my seat, the floor seemed to drop from beneath me. Eva jumped up, pushing her body beneath me to hold me upright. Archer, distraught, stood as well. "I don't understand. What's wrong?"

The room began to spin, sending swirls of nausea through my gut. I swallowed down the bile rising rapidly in my throat. Grounding my feet, I leaned into Eva's weight. After all this time. Everything that had happened. It all came back to him. So many questions needed to be answered. First, I needed to grab my panic by the balls and show it who was in charge here. Taking long, deep breaths in and out, I felt my chest lighten slightly. Archer stepped closer as Eva held her hand out. "Shelton was the abuser, Archer. He was the one who put Aurelia through hell the last ten years."

"Aurelia —"

"Don't Archer."

The protectiveness radiating from Eva soothed me. I couldn't properly assess the surprise this brought on, as I used all my energy to hold my body upright and not fall into the pit of panic.

"I'm so sorry. I didn't know."

Patting Eva's arm, I lowered myself back into the chair. Eva kept hold of my hand, just in case I needed the physical support. At any moment, every ounce of respect I thought I'd lost for my sister, grew back, immeasurably.

"Aurelia —"

"Continue, Archer." My eyes bore into his, the grief of my life morphing into pure rage. For everything I'd lost and the reminders permanently etched on my skin. Cautiously, Archer sat back down, taking a few deep breaths of his own.

"We were brought through a portal into the mortal world and handed straight to who we believed to be our mother and father. My assumption is Shelton did not want the responsibility."

I knew that to be true. The vision bubbled up, reminding me of the agreement Shelton had made with Niall.

"That doesn't make sense," Eva chimed in. "Shelton didn't even come into our lives until we moved to Huxley. How could he orchestrate everything?"

"Because he did."

I felt both Eva and Archer's eyes shoot to me on the confirmation. "When we were trying to understand how I may be connected to the curse, Bea put me through a recognition spell."

I paused to shut my eyes, conflicted in denying the memories but wanting to explain it to my siblings.

"The first vision I saw was Shelton and Niall, making a deal of our... delivery. Niall and Leona were to raise us as their own."

I looked to Archer. "What I don't understand is why?"

I squeezed Eva's hand hard, looking to ground myself. If it had any painful effect, Eva didn't let it show, only the slight tremble in her grip showed that she too grew more vengeful by the second.

"I murdered him."

Eva shot her eyes to me. "Who?"

"Lord Shelton. And Niall. The brother's captured them both and then I slit their throats."

My company was silent for only a few moments before Eva blurted, "Way less than they deserved."

Turning my head slowly, my eyes glued to my sister's in agreement as her outrage bore into me. No further words needed to be said on the matter.

"To answer your question," Archer continued, apparently not needing to comment on my murderous rampage, "I don't know why. I have never been able to get close enough to Aestas to uncover their secrets."

Eva huffed, "How is it, Archer, that they never knew you were here? Wouldn't they want to come after you if they'd discovered you were back?"

Steepling his hands beneath his chin, he leaned forward on his knees. "I'm sure they would have, but it was never discovered. The only people that know of my origin are the Queens and Kane. Archer wasn't even my name here. Our names were given to us by Niall and Leona."

Everything I knew was a lie. Even my gods damn name. Processing this information was harder than when the bears revealed their secrets. Accepting these facts was a task I wasn't sure I could conquer.

"Then what happened Archer?" I needed to move forward. The truth was Shelton and Niall's death by my hands had given me nothing but closure. Eva was right, what the bears and I had done to them was less than they deserved.

Fidgeting in his seat, the well of knowledge he held seemed to irritate him. "We grew up. And then, ten years ago, when Kane showed up, he took me back. It was the last time a portal was opened. Well, before you turned up."

"Why didn't he take us too?" I couldn't nor wanted to hide the irritation in my tone.

Archer's gaze shifted to the open window, letting the breeze fill the brief silence.

"All he knew was I was a Summer prince and he could use me against our parents. I wasn't taken willingly. The enchantment Kane put on the portal had a time limit. The sacrifice he had to make for the spell to work was severe. You may already know this, but a Raithean's lifespan is much longer here and Kane... Well, he had to cut some of his short."

The shock hit my chest immediately. For Kane to offer some of his own life just to attempt a rescue of the brothers drove deep into my chest. I would need to address this with Mads at some point, if Kane didn't do it directly.

So many what ifs ran through my head. What if we were taken too? I would have never suffered the years of pain at Shelton's hands and his other preferred tools. At my parent's, or rather, adoptive parent's hands. I could have known love and kindness, possibly moulding me into a better being. A stronger woman.

I shook the thoughts away. As terrible as it all was, the events which led me to the bears, to Mads, to the reunion of my brother and sister, was a chance at a new chapter. Those incidents are what made me who I was. Pushed me to grow stronger, more courageous. I could either hold on to the hate, letting it fester and warp me into the same type of people I had grown up knowing, or I could own it. Accept it was part of me and know I could still be loved, make a difference. I knew I was finally understanding the woman I wanted to be. It wasn't going to be easy. Then again, no part of my life was. The difference now? I was surrounded by people who truly cared about me. Who would give me the love and support I craved and needed for so long. I had something now I never thought possible. Hope.

I knew why Shelton gave us to our adoptive parents, however I wasn't clear on one point, "If you were five, why didn't you remember anything? Why didn't you tell us?"

Archer sighed, "I was spelled from remembering. I did try in my own way. Do you remember the stories I used to tell you?"

"About the faraway lands filled with princes and princesses. The snow, the leaves, the sun, and the land of eternal spring." Eva recounted as I listened to the longing in her voice. I remembered those stories too. Cherished them. It was the only time the three of us were ever truly allowed to be together, hidden under an oak tree behind our house. We would snuggle together on warm, long summer nights and listen to Archer's tales of a better world. A better life.

"I remember," I whispered, twisting my fingers in my lap.

"It was the only way I could. It was all I had."

We let silence fill the space between us. Each caught in our own memories, visions of a simpler time dancing through our heads. Our peaceful daydreams were cut short when a knock came at the door. With no hesitation, Eva stood, finally releasing my hand before moving swiftly to find out who would disturb such a deep moment.

Stepping out of the way, one of the Queen's attendants pushed through a cart filled with cakes and tea. He left it near the three armchairs before excusing himself from the room. The disturbance was welcome, I had needed a few moments to gather the many thoughts erratically buzzing through my mind.

Eva sat back down, shifting towards the cart to grab what appeared to be a fruit scone. "So, what have you been doing here all these years?"

Archer mirrored her movements, pouring us all a cup of tea before collecting his own baked goods and settling against the back of the chair. "I was young, so the Queens took pity on me. Let me tell my story. Kane took a while to warm up to me. Many years into our acquaintance, I can now call him a friend. When they realised I was an innocent child, a child who was due to be executed by my own parent's will, they let me stay."

He lowered his cake, a genuine pang of regret passing his face. "We tried to go get you."

I froze as I lifted the teacup to my mouth, needing something to do with my hands, fearing the panic pit would open up once more. "What?"

"When I told them I had sisters, the Queens went through every possible witch, book, spell, you name it — they tried it. No matter what we did, we couldn't get the portals back open."

Queen Kendra had mentioned the rarity of key magic and explained she'd done her fair share of research on the matter. It made sense now.

"I would have come for you. Both of you."

My eyes stayed trained on our brother, the brother we'd believed dead, the brother I had wondered so many times what he would think or say to me throughout the last ten years, let every ounce of grief pass through him visibly. Not one part of me thought him dishonest. No matter what we'd gone through separately, deep down, I still knew the man in front of me.

I turned to find Eva looking at me, a soft resignation offered in a slight smile. Giving Archer my eyes once more, I gave him the words I felt deep in my soul. "We know."

With the admission, the heaviness of the last hour lifted slightly. As the tension rose, Eva sat back in her chair, her posture and facial features relaxing.

As the tension lifted, the conversation flowed. We shared with Archer most of the information we'd come to know since both Eva and I arrived at the bear's cabin as well as the fact that it was confirmed I have magic. When I told him the specifics of said magic, a look of disbelief washed over his face. Unfortunately, all Archer could tell us about my magic was that it was indeed rare and not something he knew much about.

I let my heart drop slightly at his admission before turning the conversation back to him. I could feel the exhaustion of the day's social interactions begin to sink in.

"What have you been doing since you came to Vernum?" I asked the question before letting my shoulders release some of the tension they'd held.

"I am an advisor to the Queens of Vernum." Archer's blue eyes bore back into mine with pride.

Eva huffed, a clear indication that her irritation had not subsided. "What do you advise on?"

Thankfully, her question wasn't delivered with the ire I sensed radiating from her.

Archer stood, taking a turn around the plush armchair. "Mainly in the human realm. There have been so few connections in the last couple of generations of Raithean leaders. While our day to day lives look similar, there are so many differences in language, culture, and education. I guess you could say I've been more of a teacher than an advisor."

As intrigued as I was about the last ten years of Archer's life, I needed to know something. "Archer, do you have magic?"

Stopping his assault on the same carpeted circle, he turned his attention to me directly. "I do."

When he didn't elaborate, I gestured with my hand for him to continue.

Without a word, he brought his palms together with a light clap. When he pulled them away from one another, a stream of glacial blue water formed between them. My mouth dropped. Even with already seeing magic, the sight of it still brought such awe.

Eva leaned forward, entranced by the sight. "You can create..."

"Water." Archer finished for her. "Generally, offspring of royal lines adopt elemental magic tied to their Kingdom. Fire for Winter, earth for Spring, wind for Autumn, and water for Summer."

Closing my mouth, I tried to swallow the dryness down, still fascinated by the stream rotating between my brother's hands. "What does it mean for you to have Summer magic?"

"It isn't always accurate but usually the eldest child aligns with the kingdom's elemental magic, making them the rightful heir."

Eva sucked in an audible breath. I turned as she grabbed the arms of her chair in a death grip. Not out of anger or resentment, but rather out of admiration. "You're the heir of Aestas."

It wasn't a question, rather a statement that Eva spoke aloud to process fully. I appreciated the gesture given I, too, found it difficult to process the information.

"Apparently." The water vanished as Archer chuckled. "It's been a big day for us, hasn't it?"

Eva and I both nodded, not able to give him a vocal response.

Taking his seat once more, he pulled it closer to the two of us, reaching out his hands. Without hesitation, Eva and I both took his outstretched hands. I revelled in the fact that my brother was alive. He was real.

"Magic powers, royal by birth, a strange new land." He laughed, a genuine sound that filled my heart with wonder.

We let the silence dance around us as we each processed the reunion and the emotions in tow. A new story was ready to be written for the three of us. One we would all be equal authors of. Slowly, the corners of my mouth tipped, lost in the thought. The smile grew as I recognised something I had thought impossible. Family. Whether blood and bone or chosen, I finally had a family.

CHAPTER 32

MADDOX

The tumbler in my hand would smash soon enough. I knew it. I'd done my best in the last two hours to give my undivided attention to the citizens of Raithe who had pledged their allegiance to us. No matter how hard I tried, my mind kept drifting to the scene in the great hall. Aurelia reuniting with her long lost brother should have filled me with joy, not the intense resentment coursing through my veins. He didn't have any claim to her. Nor did I. I had at least offered her sanctuary. Why did the vision of him embracing her in the great hall spark such annoyance?

Xav clinked my glass with his, pulling me from my reverie. He stared straight ahead, listening intently to whatever the man in front of us said. Thank the stars for Xavier. It wasn't just his empathetic magic making him strong, his emotional maturity was leaps and bounds ahead of Fox and I's, combined. I trusted him to pull what was needed from the conversations, at least acknowledging the men and women who sat in front of me. Recognition was the least they deserved.

Bea kept quiet in the corner, observing each of the interactions breezing through. Thankfully, Kane had kept a close eye on his watch, moving people through the room at short intervals. I wanted to meet with everyone who showed up and nothing could change my mind. Except maybe the golden-haired goddess I couldn't get out of my head.

Aurelia had dug into my chest and under my skin so quickly since our first encounter. Initially, I would've assumed I'd want to push it away. My treacherous heart had other ideas. If anything, the lightning that struck when my lips had met hers the first time had done nothing other than push my need for her further. I had to be careful though. Aurelia had too much taken from her already. I reminded myself that slow and steady would win the race. The race, in this case, was her heart. I was done for.

Xav signalled for me to zone back in with another clink of my tumbler. The King mask fell into place without any coaxing. "Thank you for coming today Mr. and Mrs. Carthright. Your dedication to the wellbeing of Raithe and its citizens does not go unnoticed."

With nothing further, the Carthrights offered subtle bows to the group before seeing themselves out. I leaned back in my chair, huffing in exhaustion. I needed to get to Aurelia soon. "How many are left?" Fox dropped down to the seat beside me, fatigue radiating from him.

"We are done for today, gentleman." Kane smiled. I had missed his comradery over the years. I hadn't spent much time in his company since we arrived yet being back with him made me realise just how much I needed him by my side.

"Thank the stars. I need an unnecessarily long bath and the finest wine this palace can offer." Bea stood, walking to Xav to give his shoulder a squeeze before bidding the rest of us a good night.

I turned to Fox, waiting for him to excuse himself. Instead, I caught him in deep thought, the muscles in his jaw tensing. I was about to ask him what consumed him when Xav stepped toward us both. "Well, brothers, we are here. We are one step closer to being home."

My head shifted towards Xav, admiring the silent strength he exuded. I stood, pulling him into an emotional embrace. Xav shot his hand out to grab Fox, hurling him in the triangle of affection. My chest warmed at the vision of the three of us walking arm in arm toward our future.

Once we released one another, Xav and Fox left, leaving me alone with Kane. He offered me a mischievous smirk. "Time for a drink before you retire to your golden angel?"

"Anything for you, K."

Kane poured us both a healthy measure of brandy before gesturing toward the rich, brown leather couch where we both leaned back to stretch out our tired legs. Me much more so than Kane, given he was a hardened soldier, partaking in intense training on a daily basis. We sat in companionable silence for a few moments before Kane took the liberty and spoke, "Where do you want to start?"

A fair but complicated question. So much had happened since we were exiled. Rehashing the events which took us to the human realm wasn't something we needed to be discussed, both of us experiencing loss during those moments. "Shall we start with Xavier?"

Kane turned his head away, a clear indication my brother was not the topic to start with. My parents weren't the only ones who lost their lives. Many innocents were executed as well, including Xav's partner Arrick, who had sacrificed himself to save Kane. The history behind the three's relationship is blurry. What Fox and I had always known was that Xav's relationship with Arrick felt a lot more platonic than what he'd shared with Kane many years ago. Xav had moved on, as he liked to remind us, while Kane's heart has always belonged to my brother.

"You've been back twenty-four hours and you're already treading a fine line Maddox."

I chuckled into my brandy. "That's King Maddox to you."

Kane laughed, sending a wave of joy across his face, forcing my heart to clench. He may not have been blood, nevertheless he and Everett were just as much my brothers as Xav and Fox. "Do you want to tell me about Aurelia?"

Looking anywhere except Kane's eyes, I said, "What is there to tell?"

"How did she find you?"

"Most is her story to tell, Kane. I hope, one day, she's ready to share those details with you."

Kane nodded, "I respect that. How about we talk about how you're in love with her then?"

The brandy had just hit my throat when he spoke, forcing me to lurch forward, doing my utmost not to choke. Laughing at my expense, Kane clapped me on the back, stating the words I knew would follow, "You can deny it all you want. You are very much in love with her."

The cough morphed into a laugh before I smacked him on the back of the head. "Don't go around shouting nonsense about love, you dickhead."

Kane joined my laughter. We let it die down before the silence took hold once more. "I missed you, Mads."

"I missed you too, brother."

So much was ahead of us, and I needed to understand if I was even fit to rule Hiema anymore. I hoped, with the days ahead, I could prove to myself and the Raitheans who had pledged their loyalties that I was worthy.

Kane and I shared a glass or two more of brandy before I finally bid him goodnight, anxious to return to Aurelia. As I opened the door to the suite, the lights were off with only the flames of the fire illuminating her silhouette where she laid on the bed.

Studying the glorious curves of her peaceful form, I gave myself a moment to appreciate everything Aurelia had given us in just a few short months. I will never forgive myself for placing her at such a distance during her initial weeks with us. I was too lost in my own fear of everything she may shatter in our lives when in actual fact, she healed us all. I didn't know if she would ever see it that way, but I promised myself, there in the darkness, I would spend the rest of my life proving to her just how worthy she was of everything she desired in life.

As I let the door click closed behind me, she stood from the bed, confirming she had been awake at least since I walked in. Unable to restrain myself, I bounded over to her, grabbing her ass and lifting her into my arms. Her legs wrapped around my waist. Wasting no time, I pushed her against the wall, nuzzling my nose into the crook of her neck, breathing her in. "I've dreamt of your scent all day."

I could hear the need laced through her tone as she breathed my name. I would never tire of my name on her lips, the way it sounded as she pleaded for me. "Mmmm." I placed a kiss between her neck and shoulder, the taste making my cock stand to attention.

"So much to tell you." I pulled back slightly, noticing her eyes were closed, savouring the sensations just as I was.

I leaned back down, trailing kisses along her collar bone before my tongue crept out, finding solace on her skin. "I love the way you taste."

She pushed her hips further forward. "You feel so good." The breathlessness in her words drove me crazy. I clenched my fists against the wall, on either side of her head, stopping myself from ripping off her nightgown and fucking her senseless right there.

"You haven't felt anything yet."

A seductive smile played on my lips as I pushed my erection into her core, pinning her tighter to the wall. Even through the layers of clothing, I was forced further into the lust filled daze. Aurelia went to roll her hips into me again when I stilled her. My mind travelled across her past and our very real present. I pulled back, "I'm sorry."

Confused, Aurelia reached out, finding my chest beneath her fingers. "What for?"

"That's not how we should be doing this."

I unwrapped her legs from my waist, gently placing her on the floor in front of me. Immediately, she stepped towards me, trailing her hands up my chest until they reached my lips, the harsh breaths tickling the tips of her fingers. "I would have happily let you have me."

The sincerity in her voice mixed with the smile on her lips eased my worry slightly. "Would you, now?

"Oh yes." Gently, she took my hand, moving it between her legs, silently asking me to see for myself how wet she was for me. Through the smooth silk, her desire was clear. Closing my eyes, I took in a deep, steadying breath, knowing now wasn't the time. Soon though. Soon I would show her the most intense pleasure of her life. "You really are going to be the death of me."

Leaning up, she placed a subtle kiss to my lips, not fully removing them as she spoke against them, "But you would die a happy man?"

Throwing my words back at me, I laughed sending a bead of warmth through my chest as I said, "A very happy man."

Turning her hand in mine, I walked us to the bed, doing my best to disguise the firmness of my cock. "Before you go killing me, I think we have a lot to discuss. I spoke to Kane. He told me an interesting story about an attempted rescue."

Aurelia twirled her fingers in her lap. "Interesting indeed, because Archer told us one as well."

Her body language indicated she struggled to take the reins of this conversation. I wanted to push, choosing not to. Aurelia needed to take these steps on her own. "I want to hear everything from you, but I need a shower. How about you sit with me while I wash the day away, and you can tell me all about your conversation with Archer?"

Aurelia nodded. If I put myself in a vulnerable position, hopefully it would ease her fears somewhat. It was amazing how a few short weeks ago, I had tried everything in my power to stay away from this woman and now… now I would die for her.

"So…" I started, once I was in the shower. "I hear you're a princess?"

I left my tone light, knowing the news may bring trepidation with it. It didn't bother me in the slightest whether she was a princess or not. As I told her before, the fact she was from Aestas meant nothing to me. Wherever she was from and whoever gave her life had no effect on who she was. She was Aurelia. Always.

"Apparently." Aurelia situated herself on the counter and quickly found the edges of the plush towel I'd left on the basin, letting her fingers lace through it.

"And? How do you feel about that?"

Letting her chin drop, she pulled the towel onto her lap, "I guess the same way I've felt about everything. Overwhelmed. In disbelief. Angry."

I nodded beneath the hot spray. I would reassure her for as long as she'd let me; for now, I was just enjoying the conversation.

"Tell me about Kane and Everett." Aurelia shifted the conversation while I lathered soap between my hands. The hot spray hit my tired bones, causing waves of bliss. I wouldn't push her too hard yet but we would definitely be discussing her various emotions again.

"Kane, and Everett, are like brothers to me. I've known them both for as long as I can remember. Everett was always more independent, disappearing for weeks a time. When I was a teenager, I began to realise he would never take a permanent place by my side. That's when we created the Knights Mara."

Aurelia twirled a golden lock around her finger, a nervous trait catching my eye. If I could just wrap her hair around —

"Fox mentioned the Knights but didn't elaborate. What are they, exactly?"

I cleared my throat, controlling my need for her, and explained how the Knights were a group of elite soldiers, working across the kingdoms outside of strict Kingdom protocol. The Knights were a specialised unit, containing a number of soldiers of both magic and non-magic kind. They considered themselves misfits, including a stonemason, witches, warlocks, a healer, and a shifter, among the other non-magical members.

Everett, the leader, was a talisman — a good luck charm. Although not one hundred percent predictable or effective, he generally found himself getting out of very sticky situations with relative ease.

"A stonemason? And a shifter? I have so many questions." The lightness in her tone eased some of the tension in my muscles.

"The shifter, Tallen, is an animal shifter, mostly. He can't shift into every animal, but he has perfected a few."

Aurelia swept off the counter, opening the towel as I shut the shower off. "That is incredible. And what about the stonemason? Is it like a human stonemason?"

I took the towel from her, letting my fingers graze hers, savouring the sensation sent up my arms. "A bit. He can manipulate stones, rocks, boulders, and a lot of the earth. It's fascinating to watch."

"Is that not elemental magic?" She stepped toward me, taking the towel between her fingers and wrapping it around my waist, never letting her eyes stray from my own.

"It could be perceived as elemental magic but it's not. Elemental is really pertaining to earth, water, air, and fire, meaning that is what the power is."

Tucking the corner of the towel to secure it, Aurelia's fingers grazed my lower abdomen, causing my eyes to close in response. "So, Fox's magic isn't elemental?"

Letting my eyes find hers once more, the hunger in hers apparent. For knowledge or something more, I wasn't sure. I shook my head in response, unable to ignore her closeness, a level of intimacy living in those moments I'd never experienced before. Not an ounce of fear sat within them though. I was enthralled, wanting nothing more than to experience every level of intimacy with the golden-haired beauty in front of me.

Her eyebrows pinched as she thought of her next words. "And my magic?"

Pushing a golden lock behind her ear, I let my hand trail down her cheek and against her jawline before tiling her gaze up slightly. "We have time, Aurelia. I know the need to know it all now is difficult to ignore but let's take this one step at a time. How does that sound?"

Taking a step forward, Aurelia closed the small distance between us, rising on her toes to press a soft, sensuous kiss to my lips. Pulling back, she nodded before leading me back into the bedroom.

We crawled into bed silently. Once the room was cloaked in darkness, her voice rose in question again. "Were you ever scared, knowing you'd one day be King?"

Running my fingers down her arm in soothing strokes, I moved closer, needing the heat of her body entwined with my own. "Never scared. I had two fantastic teachers when it came to learning about ruling a kingdom. My parents did right by their people. If I can be even half the leader that they were, then I know I'll be doing it right."

The silence stretched between us for a few minutes before Aurelia's words trickled across the space, sending a shiver down my spine. "I'm afraid Mads."

I wanted nothing more than to gather all of her fears and set them ablaze, laughing as they burned away. I knew that wasn't possible. So I gave her the next best thing, I listened.

"What if this is all we ever get?"

The question was whispered in sadness, wrapping a vice around my heart and tightening with each word.

"What do you mean?" I asked.

Her voice was quiet, meek, as if she held back pieces of herself as she spoke, "We've only just let each other into our lives," she paused a moment, wiggling further into my hold, "and now we're here with a war looming over us. And I just..."

"We will win this war, Aurelia. I hear you, but I will come back to you. We still have so much to learn together, and I'm not going to let a little war get in the way of that."

I hoped the humour in my tone showed her how I truly felt regarding the outcome with Aestas. I didn't think it would be easy but nothing would stop my brothers and I from taking back Hiema.

Aurelia snuggled into me as I explained how the number of people who had pledged to support us was thousands higher than we'd anticipated, which was positive for the fight ahead. Given we weren't sure of the potential spies in our midst, I kept the initial plan for battle sparse. As I gave her more information, her body relaxed into mine.

We talked well into the early hours of the morning. She told me every detail about her time with Eva and Archer, lightening my concern around who she would spend time with given my brothers, Trix, and I would be busy with the various meetings over the coming days.

I knew she had a lot of doubts about what the next few weeks would bring us, not just as a kingdom, but as a potential couple. I didn't offer her any additional words of reassurance; instead, I wrapped her in my arms and waited until her breathing deepened before I closed my eyes, dreaming of golden whispers across the snow-capped mountains of Hiema.

CHAPTER 33

AURELIA

Life breathed in from all sides as I strode through one of the many Vernum gardens with Archer and Eva. Rock trailed a few feet behind us, indulging in the vibrant smells of the surrounding blossoms filling the air just the right amount. Never overpowering the combination of sensations the season brought with it.

The colours of the spring season hugged me from all angles. I'd learned that although the seasonal kingdoms experience each of the four seasons, the climate and earth changes were minor, leaving the seasonal Kingdoms' own weather to hold dominance. No matter the season in rotation, the floral festival in Vernum was always on display.

From first glance, Raithe hadn't shown any considerable differences to the human realm, but the more I spent time outside I realised just how different it truly was. The florals of springtime in England were filled with newly sprouted grass and the opening rose buds, always leaving a pleasant aura around the gardens and fields. Those were nothing compared to the Vernum lands. The vibrancy of the roses here, both in their depth and power, was unrivalled. The bluebells and daffodils, appearing as nothing but unruly weeds in the human realm, weaved through the wildflowers with a regality I couldn't ignore. Tulips stood sentry around the lush beds in vibrant reds, yellows, and purples. Lavender wove itself through the dense landscapes enriching the air around us with each step. I wasn't sure how it would appear in the other kingdoms, but if they were anything like Vernum, I was keen to find out.

I admired the new beginnings surrounding us as it mirrored the stage of my life. The blossoming garden's tranquillity filled me with a gentle calmness for a few moments. I absorbed it in my veins before I let the panic of the impending fight creep in.

"What do you both think about some training sessions with me?"

Archer's question caught me off guard, interrupting the brief serenity the garden had graced me with. "You want to train with us?"

Glancing between Eva and I, he let a confident smile spread across his face. "I do. Whatever is coming, it would be good for you both to have at least some basic training."

Eva huffed, lightly grazing her palm over some lavender peonies. "I can't fight, Archer."

"You don't need to fight," he countered. "Just some basic defensive manoeuvres would do you both some good."

The thought of training with Archer brought both promise and trepidation. I was ecstatic to have my brother back, but I also knew that whatever relationship we had no longer existed and the thought of building a new one was daunting.

"I've been training," I mumbled, not intending for anyone to pick up my words.

"You have?" Archer's tone was light with a hint of surprise.

"With Fox. He's been training me for the last few months. I'm not... good, but I have some balance and breathing down."

"Well, you did kill two men so you can't be that bad."

Eva's reaction caused me to grin proudly. I had done that and as she'd said before, it was less than they deserved.

"Well, that's great, Aurelia. Would you still be up for training here?" The hope in Archer's voice couldn't be missed. We may have been strangers for the last ten years but there were still some traits that were the same from when he was a boy.

"I am. Eva?" I asked. I wouldn't be making the choices for my sister.

Looking between us, she shrugged once. "Why not?"

We continued our stroll through the gardens, taking in the beauty in its simplicity.

Although we were on palace lands, the property was left wild, ensuring the plants and earth could breathe freely without the intrusion of gaudy fountains or foot paths. I appreciated the power in its ability to just be. I let the vision of a similar future for myself pass in front of me. I may be attached to royal kingdoms, but I had a sense that Raithe would allow me the same pleasure it did the Spring Kingdom gardens.

"Your breathing is too erratic. Follow me. Again."

I stood on the edge of the training ring situated outside on the Vernum palace grounds. The ring was large, much more so than the one back at the cabin, with a building that contained a variety of weapons and exercise equipment.

Archer took Eva through a few breathing exercises, just as Fox had with me. His patience lacked with our sister, however, as the frustration in his tone grew with each of Eva's incorrect breaths.

"How's it going?" A low voice posed next to me.

I turned to find Kane had joined our small trio, arms across his chest as he observed Eva and Archer intently. Mads had explained that Kane was an allurant. Allurant magic was essentially a physical draw, pulling people to them like a moth to a flame. Since I'd discovered that, the initial power of that magic had dulled. Kane's presence now only brought an odd sense of comfort to me.

"It's going. I'm not sure Archer being her brother puts him in the best position to train her." I chuckled.

Glancing at his profile, Kane's eyes narrowed as though he was plotting something. Thankfully, I didn't have to wait long. "Archer!"

The pair turned to where Kane and I stood. "Why don't I work with Eva, and you can work with Aurelia?"

Archer barely had to think before he motioned me toward him as he strode to the farther end of the ring.

Eva's eyes widened as Kane moved toward her. Catching her gaze briefly, I shot her a wink.

"She was frustrating you," I spoke bluntly.

Archer sighed, letting some of the tension ease from his shoulders in the motion. "She's as stubborn now as she was when she was eleven. Maybe more so."

I laughed at how correct he was. All three of us had work to do on building a new relationship but some things had not changed. Eva's temper was one of them.

"So, where shall we start? What were you doing with Fox before you came here?" Archer crossed his arms over his lean chest. He wasn't the considerable build of Mads, but the muscles he had developed were well toned, complimenting his tall frame.

"Mostly hand to hand but some blade work. No swords though. Just daggers." At that statement, I withdrew the ornate dagger from my thigh sheath to demonstrate against the air.

"That's a beautiful blade." Archer followed it, with admiration in his eyes, as the metal sliced through the space between us.

"Mads gave it to me. His exact words were 'if anyone ever tries to touch you again, you don't hesitate.'"

I hadn't meant for the words to come out so plainly. The fact was, I knew my position now was to never let anyone take from me again, shifting the intensity of my memories — still slow to surface but the impact once they did was gentle, as though they were coaxing me to assess and work through them at my own pace. A high level of anxiety was still haunting me, but more so about the future and less about my past.

Archer put his palms up, ceasing me from shifting the dagger further. His brow furrowed as if he tried to find the right words to say.

"I'm so sorry, Aurelia. I should have been there." The apology was appreciated but unnecessary. I just needed this chance to know him and for him to know this version of me; the one I fought with daily, but so very proud of.

Letting the corners of my lips tip up, I moved closer. "None of that was your responsibility. Just as it wasn't my fault. What matters is that we are here now, and we've been given the gift of a fresh start," I paused to let those words sink in, reaching my hand out as an offering.

Gently, he placed his hand in my palm as his eyes stayed locked on mine.

"How about we just promise to get to know each other? How does that sound?"

With a huffed laugh, Archer yanked my hand forward, engulfing me in his arms as he continued to chuckle into my hair. "After everything you've been through, you are still the strongest person I've ever known."

I hadn't meant for the moment to be filled with such emotions, yet I couldn't deny the tears that filled the corners of my eyes. The air of the Spring Kingdom danced even lighter as I wrapped my arms around my brother, embracing him for who he was now but never forgetting the boy he had been.

Pulling back, I gave him a tight nod, not wanting to let the tears spill down my cheek, before putting distance between us once more, settling in my stance as a signal that the path of our new relationship was before us, but we didn't have to rush.

As Archer and I sparred, I kept my eye on Eva and Kane, and it appeared as though Kane was making much more progress with Eva than Archer had. Content with the knowledge my sister strengthened herself as well, I called it quits with Archer to run through some cool down exercises.

Breathing the spring atmosphere in deep, I let my eyes fall to the sensations around me. The light kiss of a cool breeze as it caressed my cheek. The soft buzzing of a nearby bee. The gentle instructions Kane continued to give my sister. The panic was gone, for now, and

I took the moment to categorise these new memories, keeping them surface level in my mind to pull on them at a moment's notice.

The training area grew quiet, and I opened my eyes, jumping at the man in front of me.

Not Archer, but Maddox.

"Hello, Goldie."

The playfulness in his tone caught me off guard, his presence a welcome shock. I took a moment to appreciate his body in front of me, a pleasant heat radiating through the small space between us. The late afternoon light danced across his chiselled jaw, highlighting the coy smile playing his lips.

"What are you doing here?" I breathed in surprise.

Stepping forward, Mads reached out his strong hand to push a stray piece of hair away from my face as the playfulness turned into a coy smile. "It doesn't seem fair that you three get to have all the fun. We thought we'd join you."

"We?"

Just as the question left my lips, Xav spoke from behind me.

"Up for a little more sparring, Goldie?" Turning, I found Fox and Xav standing behind me, both with their arms crossed and the same smirk plastered on their faces.

"What did you have in mind?" I may have been tired, but I wouldn't miss the opportunity to spend time with the bears. The whirlwind of events since landing in Raithe meant I hadn't seen them much.

"Three circuits, with the three of us," Fox chimed in.

Lifting my brow in question, he continued, "Start with Mads, the hand to hand combo, then to Xav for blocking, and me" — he leant across to snatch the dagger from my holster — "we can work with the blade."

I scanned the training ring to find Eva, Kane, and Archer watching intently. Placing my hand, palm down, I waited for him to place the dagger in my grip. "You're on, coyote."

Sparring with all three of the bears, and at the same time, was physically exhausting but my heart could not have been more full. I was still uncoordinated with my movements and rather slow, but working with them together was an experience I hadn't realised I needed.

Fox finally called time on our little session when I nearly dropped the dagger, blade down, on his toe, for which I agreed. My mental exhaustion mixed with the aches still tearing through my body. Fox and Xav made their way to the water station where the others were engrossed in comfortable conversation leaving Mads and I alone.

Mads' strong form bent down to collect the dagger before slowly sliding it back into the sheath, letting his fingers linger on the outside of my thigh. I wanted him, fully, and the waiting game we were playing caused more frustration than I could manage.

Playing into the touch, I stepped forward, removing any distance between us. "Maddox?"

His gaze bore down into mine as the autumn in his eyes caught fire.

"Yes, Aurelia?"

"I want you."

The corner of his lip lifted before his head gestured around us. "Here? It's a little unconventional."

With my hands on his chest, I drove them upwards until his jaw was placed perfect beneath my palms.

"I'm going to go shower."

With that, I leaned up to plant a swift but promising kiss on his lips before heading back to our room, ready to wash the day off in the hopes of finding a new kind of dirty.

The brazen feelings I'd had in the training ring were washed away in the shower. Mads hadn't immediately followed me back to the suite, and I found myself riddled with nerves. Needing the distraction for my hands, I sat in front of the ornate dressing table, brushing out the stray water from my golden hair when the door to the room opened.

Averting my gaze from the man I knew was behind me, I took in a slow, steady breath. I wanted this. I wanted him.

I chanced a glance up, my eyes locked on those autumnal storms in the mirror, finding a grave sort of seriousness flash across his eyes. "Aurelia, we don't have to do anything tonight."

I was startled, shocked. After all this time, showing me how to enjoy my own body, own myself once more, and he was going to back out? It fuelled an anger beneath my skin, and I turned abruptly. "What the hell do you mean we don't have to do anything?"

Mads unbuttoned his cuffs, ignoring my gaze. "You know, if you're not ready."

Standing, I stalked toward him, shoving my hands toward his chest and pushing with as much force as I could muster. He didn't budge, but it felt good to use my hands on him. "Don't do that. Don't sit here all high and mighty after you denied me all this time."

"Denied you?" he resounded in shock.

"Yes. Denied me. I was ready for you the first time you kissed me. Probably even before then. Don't you get that?"

He fumbled for words, unlike his usually composed nature. "But your past —"

"Does not define my present or my future. Gods, Mads, just looking at you pulls my broken bits back together. I know, for certain, everything you make me feel is right. You would never be anything wrong. You can't think you would ever be like those other men."

His breathing intensified with each word I spoke. "Fuck."

I stared at him for a beat before going with my gut instinct. "Yes, fuck. Me. Fuck. Me. Mads."

He was on me in less than a second, grabbing my face and crashing his lips to my own. I opened immediately, moaning as his tongue danced with mine. My body exploded with the unspent desire I felt for him as I savoured every calculated movement of his tongue in my mouth, on my lips. Pushing my tongue out slowly , I traced his bottom lip before grabbing it between my teeth. I wanted to bite down hard. But this time, I wouldn't. Mads growled, sending a shockwave to my core, the wetness deepening.

Mads' body shifted me backwards, pushing me onto the top of the vanity table with a crash, shoving vials and powders tumbling to the floor without a second thought. As he stepped forward, placing himself between my legs, my thighs clenched around his hips, eliciting a sultry sound from the back of his throat. I wound tighter at the carnal sound. Dragging my mouth from his to let out a breathless moan, hoping it would silently establish how much I needed him. How much I wanted him.

Grabbing the tie of my dressing gown, he pulled the bow apart aggressively as if he couldn't wait another second to have my skin against his own. Knowing I needed the same, I shifted my hands up his firm chest, pushing the jacket off his broad shoulders. The tangle of limbs was hard to manoeuvre, especially given neither one of us wanted to cease our contact. Mads eventually shimmied the jacket off, placing his hands on the back of my calves, squeezing lightly before drawing them further up.

As he placed a shred of space between us, Mads searched my eyes, needing some kind of confirmation. When my eyes bore back into his in a silent plea, he grabbed the gown at my shoulders and pulled, the ripping sound briefly drowning out the sounds of our laboured breathing. Chest heaving, my breasts were exposed, waiting for him.

Thank the stars I didn't have to wait long. Mads took one look at my sizable chest and dove down. His hand encapsulated my right while his mouth met my left. Pulling my nipple into his mouth, he rolled his tongue side to side before biting down, my pussy throbbing. I needed more. His charge continued, switching his mouth to the other nipple, ensuring it wasn't left out. I rolled my hips up, grinding on his very apparent desire.

Reaching out, I fumbled with the buttons, my hands shaking. Mads didn't interject; instead, he let me take my time in freeing his cock.

"Mads," I breathed, gracing the top of his head with my lust filled whisper. "I need you."

Removing himself reluctantly from tracing my nipple with his tongue, he glanced up. "You have me, Aurelia."

He dove back down, needing to taste my skin, spurred on by the sounds emanating from my throat. I had no doubt he would feast on me until the day he died. As much as I enjoyed the thought and the action itself, I needed more.

"No. I need you. Inside me. Now." The voice trickling from my lips surprised me as I let the craving take charge.

I finally managed to get his trousers undone, pushing them down as quickly as possible. His cock sprang free, my mouth watering at the thought alone. I had no idea why I'd denied myself from seeing one before, but I was glad Mads' cock was the only one I'd laid my eyes on. Staring at his cock for the first time made my mouth water in delicious anticipation. I wanted him inside of me, consuming me. I needed him. "Maddox..."

Grabbing his hips, I pulled him closer, relishing the way his naked shaft rubbed against my bare slit. Mads pulled back, a sensual smile growing across his face. "Tell me again what you need."

"You." Frustration built.

"Where, Aurelia?"

"Inside me." I didn't hesitate to give him what he was after. "Deep inside me."

The words spurred him into urgency, wrapping his strong hands beneath my knees, he hoisted me off the vanity and up his body, my legs wrapping around his waist in response. My arms flew around his neck as I found his mouth once more. Lifting me off the vanity, he walked us toward the bed. I savoured the weightlessness of my body in his arms.

"I can feel how wet you are." He spoke against my lips, throwing me deeper into the frenzy.

"I love when you're soaking for me, Aurelia."

Gently placing me on the edge of the bed, Mads' stare bore into mine in a silent question. I offered a subtle nod in permission. Mads didn't hesitate further, grasping my knees in his solid grip and pulling my legs apart putting me on full display.

"Fuck," Mads growled as he took every inch of me in. "I really do think you will be the death of me."

My chest heaved with the powerful feel of his eyes on my centre. Letting the delicious burn of the newly found sexuality course through my blood, I realised he still wore his shirt, having only removed his jacket and trousers. That simply wouldn't do. I made quick work of grabbing the bottom, Mads lifting his arms in response. Before I could question anything further, Mads stood naked in front of me, and I was more than ready to devour every inch of his magnificent body. With my eyes. My mouth. My body. It wasn't nearly as scary as I thought it may be.

Without another thought, I reached out, wrapping my fingers around him. The skin beneath my palm was soft, almost soothing. I flicked my gaze up in time to watch as Mads closed his eyes, his head falling back on a deep groan. "That feels so fucking good."

"Yeah? You've been such a good boy. Waiting patiently for me to take your cock. Haven't you?" The dirty words leaving my lips should have shocked me. Instead, they pushed further fire to my core.

Mads peeled open his eyes to look down at me, a darkness flickered over his gaze, exciting me further. Raising his hand to my cheek, he followed the gentle gesture by diving into my mouth, lavishing the taste of me, revelling in the sensations pulsating through our bodies at the contact and the promise of what was to come.

Pulling back, too soon, he continued to stroke my cheek lightly. "I want to taste every inch of you and know every part of your skin."

"Yes." I whispered back.

"But tonight, I want to fuck you." His voice hit an octave lower, supporting his spoken promise.

"Yes," I breathed again.

"Lie back, you incredible creature."

I'd taken his direction before, knowing how erotic it was. This time, it was deeper. More exhilarating.

I sat on the bed first, before crawling back a few feet, settling myself down on my elbows. "Open for me."

My knees fell apart at his grisly command, exposing my most intimate area to him once again.

Mads trailed his gaze over my pussy for what felt like hours. A tiny bubble of self-consciousness began to rise in me, involuntarily moving my knees back towards each other.

"Don't do that." Mads placed his hands on my knees, guiding them back apart.

"Your pussy is the most beautiful thing I've ever seen. I could eat you for breakfast, lunch, and dinner every day and still be starved."

I took his lead, exposing myself to him once more, inviting him in. Situating himself between my legs, he stroked his cock in his hand once. Twice. My breathing escalated. The sight of him touching himself would send me over the edge if I didn't control myself.

"Are you ready for me?" he asked, his voice impossibly deep.

Was I ever. "Yes."

"Hips up. Let me in."

I reached out to grip his hips beneath my fingers, encouraging him forward. He obeyed, rubbing his cock against my clit, urging my hips forward. Needing him. All of him.

"Stop teasing me." The words left my mouth in an annoyed command. Mads' lip tipped into a smile of defiance before his cock finally teased my entrance. I was so wet. Agonisingly, he pushed in, inch by inch. Each inch brought the most intense shockwaves of pleasure through my body. Then, he paused.

"Why aren't you moving?" I couldn't keep the frustration from my voice.

"Because," he said through gritted teeth, "I don't want to hurt you."

I dug my nails into his hips further. "You're hurting me by not moving."

It wasn't true and Mads knew it. He let out an exasperated chuckle before pulling out. I growled, *growled*, at him. Thankfully, it was only a moment before he pushed back in with an intense ferocity. A man starved. "You're so fucking tight, Aurelia."

I let my eyes close, savouring the sensation of him planted fully inside of me. "You are so gods damn perfect."

I wanted to reciprocate the compliment except all thoughts ejected from my brain with him deep inside me. He began moving in and out, sending blasts of desire through me, nothing I had ever felt in my entire life. I wasn't sure there would be anything that could eclipse this moment.

Mads pulled me out of my desired haze, curling his hand under my full arse, tilting it upwards, allowing him to drive deeper. I wasn't sure, I may have blacked out at the sensation.

"Stay with me."

Mads' breath coasted along my cheek as I did my best to obey. Leaning down further, he captured my lips in his, moving his free hand to my right breast, teasing the nipple between his thumb and forefinger, just as he had taught me not long ago. I moaned in pure pleasure. "Mads!"

"That's it, gorgeous. You are so good at taking my cock."

His words spurred me, I wrapped my legs around his waist to pull him closer. Digging my heels into his back and letting his pelvis begin to rub back and forth over my clit, my core building in rapid response.

"*Fuck*. You keep doing that, I'm not going to last much longer."

Eager victory grew on my lips. "I want to make you come."

I'd never felt the need to please a man in this way, and I reminded myself Mads was one of a kind. He was mine. Whether or not he knew it yet. And I was just as much his.

Mads' thrusts grew more frenzied, pumping deeper, more vigorously as I chased my pleasure much more than he did his own. "That's it. Squeeze my cock."

I wasn't sure I had any control over what I was doing as I felt the orgasm grow closer with each thrust.

"Come with me." His words, coupled with a sharp twist of my nipple, provoked a scream from my lips and an involuntary thrust, needing to be closer to him. Mads took advantage, grabbing one of my hips with his free hand as he continued to pound into me. Harder. Faster. I felt it everywhere, loving the sensation of my release building, knowing I was about to erupt. And then... I did. Without warning, my orgasm shattered through me, reaching the very tips of my toes with the most glorious release of pleasure. On a groan, Mads followed, not long behind, sending a shockwave back through my pussy, pulsing out the last of my orgasm.

Mads slowly lowered himself, burying his head in the crook of my neck, breathing me in. I cherished every throbbing, pulsing, and tingling sensation continuing to jack-knife through my body as Mads stayed seated inside of me. The sweet scent of his sweat soaked skin happily ticked my nose as I relished in the euphoria trickling over my body. The new sensation of being sated was one to appreciate, fully.

"That was..."

"The next word out of your mouth better not be 'nice,'" Mads grumbled into my neck.

I burst into a giggle. "I wasn't going to say nice."

He lifted his head, tracing his nose against my cheek, peppering me with kisses along the way. "Then, pray tell, what were you going to say?"

I thought for a moment, debating between telling him just how mind blowing the sex was or keeping it casual. The thing was, since the day in the forest when I'd been beaten by my father, our relationship had moved somewhat fast. We'd not had a lot of time alone to get to know each other in a more traditional sense but it had never occurred to me to hold back once we crossed that line. A silent agreement sat between us.

"Empowering."

The word rang true in more ways than one, and I couldn't help the happiness spreading across my body. The biggest smile Mads had ever gifted me grew on his face, his eyes lighting up in response. Slowly, he pulled out, leaving an emptiness I hadn't been prepared for.

"We should do that again."

Mads winked at me. "Trust me, we will be doing that a lot."

Pushing myself onto my elbows, I brought my face closer to his, whispering one word, "Now."

Mads didn't hesitate, rolling me on top of him and connecting our lips once more.

CHAPTER 34

AURELIA

The early morning sunlight danced through the window, enveloping my face in a subtle warmth. Stretching ever so slightly, I savoured every ache in my body. Without opening my eyes, I thought back to the night before. After the first time, we became fiendish, taking each other on the bed, again; up against the shower wall, when we'd attempted to get clean; and my particular favourite, when Mads took me from behind, in front of the vanity as we watched ourselves in the mirror.

Squeezing my eyelids tighter, I didn't want to face the day. The looming dread of the coming weeks sat unwelcomely in my gut. Mads shifted behind me, curling his arm around my stomach to draw me closer. There were no fabrics between us as I felt his erection press against the space between my legs. "Get that thing away from me," I joked.

Mads chuckled in my hair, squeezing me once before turning me to face him.

"I'm going to be sore for a week, at least."

Glancing at Mads' beautiful face, a resounding seriousness spread across it, erasing the brief humour I was able to provide. "Will you join us in battle?"

"What?" I gulped.

Adding quickly before he could answer, I said, "I can't fight."

He rolled to his back, taking me with him, draping me over his muscular chest. My fingers instinctively made circles between his pecs. "You wouldn't be fighting. You could take up the rear or stay in the camp. Whatever you'd be most comfortable with."

I tried to come to grips with his ask of me as I blurted, "Why?"

The truth of the matter was, as much as the subtleties of empowerment, confidence, safety, and importance met me every day, it was still very much overshadowed by what I had believed of myself my entire life — that I was average at best.

Shifting his head so we were eye level, he gave me the words I'd given up hope of ever hearing. "Why? Because I always want you beside me. Now. Tomorrow. I want you to rule beside me, Aurelia. I know it's all been fast and you still have so much to process. Healing to endure. I understand. But I know I can't do this without you. For so long, I thought I could. I thought I was the one who was supposed to keep it together. To lead, alone. And then, you showed up, asleep in my bed, of all places, and I'd never felt the extent of my loneliness until then."

Our breathing escalated, pushing us into the most vulnerable position.

"Not now. Not yet. One day, I want you to be my Queen in title, the way you are in my life. If you'd have me as your King."

I couldn't form words. A few months ago, I didn't believe I'd have freedom. Now, here, in this bed, I had my freedom, as well as the promise of a future. One I wasn't certain I knew what to do with yet. I knew in my heart I would stand by him through everything.

"Yes," I whispered.

One word. One word was all it took for the tension to evaporate. Mads excitedly dragged me into his arms, encapsulating me in his warmth and energy. I wasn't sure I knew what love was. If it was defined by a moment, I'd capture this one to describe it. His lips met mine in vigorous victory. Before we could continue the celebration, we were interrupted by a knock at the door, followed by a string of profanities which could only have come from one man.

"If you aren't fucking decent, get fucking decent because we've got fucking work to do."

Fox's irritation permeated the thick doorway as Mads and I did our best to hide our giggles. Fox paused before adding, "I'm glad you two finally got your shit together."

We silently chuckled as the footsteps moved away from the door, fading into the distance, leaving us alone once more. Being the more responsible of the two of us, Mads removed himself from our tangled limbs, moving towards the shower and giving me a fantastic view as he waltzed naked into the bathroom. I sighed in delight before deciding to join him. Best not to waste water, even in a palace.

Archer, Eva, much to Fox's dismay, and I were invited to join the war council later in the morning. I sat beside Mads who made it impossible to concentrate on any of the discussion, given he insisted on drawing sensual circles over my knee. Rock lay at my feet, occasionally raising his head in the hopes of a snack. His presence was comforting.

Fox's voice echoed around us as he addressed the room with no hint of his usual sarcastic flare. This was commander Fox. The general of the Hiema armies. It was both inspiring and intimidating.

"Our main goal is to deal with the King and Queen of Aestas."

Our birth parents.

Leaning forward to rest his palms on the long, oak table we all sat around, he pulled his eyes from addressing the rest of the crowd to focus on his brothers. "Then we get Orsa."

Fox went on to explain that they'd had a few covert messages come through from their sister, only indicating that she was safe but if we were to go after her first, it would alert the King and Queen of the bears return, leaving Hiema and its citizens, at risk.

Orsa's messages had also contained a coded message that Bea performed a spell on to reveal the contents. It had appeared Orsa had a Kingdom witch of her own who had taken great care in protection spells over Hiema, preventing anyone within the kingdom boundaries from speaking a word of the brother's return, if they, for any reason, had discovered they were back.

Bea was assigned a number of tasks over the last couple of weeks. I looked to where she sat next to Xav. Exhaustion sat beneath her eyes. I would need to recommend rest. Lots of it, if Bea was to be any use to us during the battle. Sensing my stare, Bea shot me a wink, indicating her intuition was at work again. I sighed, directing my attention back to Fox who moved on to the battle formation.

Behind him hung a large map of Raithe. As he directed each move to the room, his fingers demonstrated the acts across the map itself.

The squads would leave Vernum in a few days' time, taking the army in three separate groups. Avilore Keep, Aestas' palace, was situated on the south eastern side of the Gold Peaks mountain range, closing it in from only one side and leaving the other three to be approached by the rest of the Raithean forces. Each group would set up camp a safe distance from the palace lands.

According to scouts, as well as many first hand witnesses from the Summer Kingdom directly, the King and Queen had gradually become reclusive in the last few years as their ruling strength diminished. Apparently they were also afraid of potential sieges from the other Kingdoms. The Summer kingdom was suffering. Many who could had relocated their families to Autumn, given it was the closest, however, many could not afford to uproot their families elsewhere.

Everett and the Knights Mara completed a number of scouting missions, confirming the rise in criminal activity through the Summer Kingdom, more specifically, Vara, their capital.

Fox gave orders to each unit leader in the room followed by Xav, Mads' right hand, who outlined the battle plans for each. The middle rank, including Mads, Xav, Fox and a number of squads from various kingdoms, would enter from the Great Woods forest, a direct path to the palace itself.

Given the sea sat to the left of the palace, Kane and the guard would take a few dozen units on foot while Desmond, the naval leader, who had already left the Vernum port, would meet them there. The right side would be led by another man I had not met, Stafford. Stafford used to be a commander in the army when Mads' parents had ruled. He was faithful, Xav insisted, until the end. I only hoped this wouldn't be the end for him.

Fox took a few moments to introduce a number of the commanders in the room, thanking them for their allegiance. Most hailed from Havon, Verum, and even a few originally from Aestas who had deferred their allegiance when the Hiema rulers were murdered. I was also surprised to note the number of female commanders in the room. Something which would not have been acceptable in the mortal world. The sight of strong, powerful women sent a pang of regret through me before I told myself I, too, had the chance to be powerful. I still wasn't quite sure what my power did, but I vowed to myself I would explore it further.

As the rightful King of Hiema, Mads unfolded his body from his seat at the head of the table to address the room at the end of the meeting.

"I know I've said it many times over the last couple of weeks," he said as the room was rapt with attention on the King of Hiema. "But it needs to be said again. Thank you, all, for risking your positions, your lives, your futures for us. For Raithe."

Raising his right fist to cross over the left side of his chest, he inhaled deeply and said, "To redemption or death."

I digested the words as the room mirrored Mads' movements before reciting the four words in a strong, even command. "To redemption or death."

Most of the commanders then excused themselves to their respective quarters or the dining room for more suitable refreshments. The tea and cakes served at the war council were not strong enough for the people taking three kingdoms to battle.

I stood on my own, noticing Xav speaking in hushed tones with one of the female commanders. Before I was able to excuse myself from the room, he caught sight of me, motioning me over. Hesitantly, I stepped towards them. "Aurelia, I'd like you to meet Tora. Tora leads a battalion from Havon."

The woman, Tora, held out a delicate hand. A tall woman, with a lean frame, she held her position with confidence. "Lovely to make your acquaintance, Aurelia."

"A pleasure, Tora." I shook her hand, impressed with the firm grip.

"Tora has volunteered to answer some questions for you, regarding your magic." Xav explained with a glint of anticipation in his eye.

In sudden excitement, I looked to Tora with glee. "You're a key too?"

Tora shook her head. "No. My Grandmother was. I was very close to her and think I may be able to give you some more information about your magic."

Slightly disappointed Tora herself wasn't a key as well, I offered her a grateful smile. "I'd like that. I'm not sure how much time we have before... everything."

Xav, sensing my apprehension, stepped forward to drape his arm across my shoulder. "I think you'd be fine to meet before we have to head out."

Tora smiled. "In that case, I'll call on you tomorrow."

I nodded once before Tora excused herself. "You being able to sense my anxiety is a nice perk, Xav."

I'd spent the least amount of time with Xav and Fox since arriving in Raithe, and as much as I wanted to change that, I knew their time was needed elsewhere. I was interested in learning more about Xav's magic though. He had only given me a brief explanation about how his magic helped him read other's emotions.

Twisting to stand in front of me, he lowered his head, lightly pressing his forehead to mine. "You don't need magic to see your unease, Goldie. It's written all over your face."

I sighed, closing my eyes, savouring our closeness. "It's just, I've never been in a war before, Xav. What if something happens to one of you? Or all of you?"

The thought of losing all of them hadn't crossed my mind until then, sparking another level of panic within me. "Aurelia, we may be out of practice a bit, but you have to remember we have thousands of people behind us. The question isn't if we will succeed, it's when."

Opening my eyes, I was met with a softness only Xav could offer. "I've missed you."

He had never needed his magic to provide me with a backdrop of comfort and support. It was just who he was. "I've missed you too." He planted a kiss on my head before stepping back. "And don't worry, we will have all the time in the world, soon enough."

Leaving me on those words, I looked down to find Rock, who had situated himself back on my feet, providing me the grounding I constantly needed. Leaning down, I gave him a scratch behind the ears before deciding it was time to find where some of the others had scurried off to. It was time to make myself useful.

After a few too many wrong turns through the ground floor of the palace, Rock and I found Archer, Eva, and Bea huddled over a table in one of the spare meeting spaces tucked beside the great hall. The light cascading through the window played with the space, blanketing it in a false sense of security. I joined them around the table to find they'd been surveying a map of Raithe.

"Nice of you to join us, sister."

Archer's sarcasm didn't go unnoticed. No vicious intent sat within it, it just confirmed the boy I knew was still there, making my heart swell. "What are you doing?"

"Archer is taking us through a map of Raithe, looking at Aestas specifically, given we are all riding like blind idiots there."

I looked at Bea, surprised. "You think it's a bad strategy?"

Sighing, Bea stepped around the table, focusing on the light glistening through the window. "Something doesn't sit right with me. It all seems too easy."

I agreed. I didn't believe for one second the Queen and King had become reclusive. The niggling sensation in my gut telling me more was at play here. "I think so too."

All three looked at me, slight shock painted on their face, "You do?" Eva questioned in astonishment. "Have you told Mads?"

A nervous twitch hit me, forcing me to look down at my feet as my toes worked hard not to touch. "Not yet. I think he knows it won't be simple either."

"No," Bea agreed, facing them once more. "I don't think any of them do."

The group hung in silence for a few moments before I broke it, "So, what do we do?"

"We go with the plan," Archer interjected, "the strategy is there for a reason."

"What if there are things they aren't telling us?"

Bea chuckled. I cocked a brow in question. It seemed as though the witch also hid information.

"There is, most likely, something the three of you can do that I haven't shared with you yet."

My mind wanted to focus on the curiosity seeping through but the muddled portions of my brain saw red. I knew that after my visions, coming to Raithe would continue to unravel bits of myself, and my past, which would be heavy and overwhelming. It was difficult to stay calm and focused when the mysteries continued to show themselves constantly.

"What aren't you telling us?"

Eva's ire could be felt in her words. I was thankful she voiced the question for all three of us.

Archer leaned back on the table, crossing his arms to indicate his anticipation.

"When you were all reunited, up on the dais, did anything...happen?"

Bea's question was posed as though she already knew the answer, but I had to scan my memory back to that moment. The flare in my abandon had pulsed at that time but I'd simply put it down to the excitement.

I glanced at Eva and Archer before turning my attention back to Bea. I knew my face painted the look of confusion and insecurity.

"Buttercup?"

Threading my top between my fingers, I looked down. "I have, or had, a feeling."

"What was it?" Archer's question remained low, laced in pure interest.

Squaring my shoulders, I withdrew my fingers to address my company directly. "When I first found the bear's cabin, I got this sensation in my stomach. It was a slight tingling, but it gave me this wave of euphoria, that opening the door and going into a stranger's house was the right thing to do."

My three companions silently urged me to continue.

"It has flared at various points over the last few months. It happened a lot in the bear's presence. When we went to get the Alegra stone. As I went to open the portal to Raithe."

Pausing, I locked eyes with Archer, keeping my voice as even as possible. "When Eva, you, and I locked hands on the dais."

Archer placed a hand on my shoulder in understanding as Bea asked Eva if she'd felt anything like that.

"Well, yes. I did. But I just knocked it up to being content in the fact Archer was alive and we were all there together."

Archer offered Eva a gentle smile before turning his attention to Bea, taking one step toward her. "As did I. It was a funny sort of sensation like peace had washed over me."

Bea stepped back, nodding her head in response before addressing all of us together.

"There is an old blood magic. One that Raitheans believed to be extinct. It was a magic born through familial lines. As much as we know, it was created through shared trauma, attempting to protect the ones who held it from further harm.

"The magic is called the aegis and given the tragic experiences the three of you went through together, it appears to have manifested once more with you. When the three of you held hands on that dais, your auras changed. They shifted, like they're all trying to burrow into one another."

I glanced to Archer and Eva as Bea continued, "After a bit more research, and some discussions with Vernum's Kingdom witch, it became pretty clear to me that you all have this aegis magic."

The room fell silent following Bea's explanation, forcing me to concentrate on the escalation of my heart beneath my rib cage. Understanding I had one type of magic was overwhelming but hearing I was something else pushed me further.

With no other words to speak, I let the confused giggle escape my lips. Before I was able to contain it, my hands found my knees as I bent over in an absolute riot. From my right, Eva's laugh echoed through my ears like music. Archer joined us next, placing his hand on my back to either steady me or himself. I wasn't sure.

I let the euphoria elicited by the laughter bleed through my entire body. Enjoying the sensation of being ridiculously out of my depth, rather than the rising panic I was so used to.

A few minutes went by as the room cascaded our laughter all around us in a tender embrace. Pushing myself upright, the tears fell down my cheeks at the absurdity of the situation. But that was the thing. Wasn't it? That everything that I should have thought and felt to be unimaginable was actually true. And in my heart, I knew that I believed in every single part of it.

"I'm really trying to understand what is so funny right now."

Bea stood tall with her arms crossed over her chest in astonishment at our outburst. I waited for Eva and Archer to come down from their fits before letting my words take over.

"It's just the absurdity of it all, Bea. A few months ago, I was a woman stuck in an abusive life, with a brother who I'd believed dead, and a living sister who was pretty much dead to me too. And now, I'm in a magical realm, with magical abilities of my own, having found the brother, who is not dead, and building a relationship with my sister who I actually adore.

"In all honesty, I should be running for the hills, succumbing to yet another panic attack, but I'm not. I'm here, taking it all in, and sometimes you just have to laugh at these things."

In unison, Eva and Archer moved to my sides, placing their arms around me in solidarity, as though absorbing every single word I'd said.

Bea, nodding in acceptance, moved us forward. "I'd like you to try it. If you're up for it?"

"What do we need to do?" The determination in Eva's voice was clear.

Bea explained and her words whispered over us as we followed her direction, our fingers threading together. The room halted, not even the sound of breathing breaking the silence. After a few moments, a tingle trickled through my palm before blasting its way through my forearm then exploding in my chest. Eva, Archer, and I gasped in unison, our hands tightening further as the pricking grew.

Our breathing deepened as the sensation travelled through our bodies, filling us with an unexplainable power.

"Whoa."

"Whoa, indeed," Bea stepped forward, reaching her finger out slowly to connect with the shield. She pulled back as soon as she touched it, hissing as if a sliver of pain shot up her arm. "Well, I think we can confirm it works."

We released each other's hands, the power subsiding immediately upon the loss of contact. A smile grew on my face. The knowledge that we held this power wrapped around my heart in a warm embrace.

"Bea, does anyone else know?" I spoke in a whisper, hoping she hadn't shared this potential information with anyone but us.

Winking at me, she shook her head. "No way, buttercup. This is your knowledge and if the three of you decide to share it, then that is your decision."

Excusing herself from the room for other, more important tasks, she claimed sarcastically, I stood with my siblings alone.

"Well, if no power of my own manifests, at least I have this."

I turned to Eva to find her face resting in pure content. Although her statement indicated resentment, I couldn't find any of that written in her expression.

"Would you both mind if I shared this with Mads?"

It was our power, not just mine, and they had every right to know how we shared the information.

"Not at all, Aurelia." Archer stepped toward the door, following in Bea's footsteps before shooting over his shoulder, "If we can protect one another, let's use every ounce of this magic to our advantage."

Once Archer was gone, I looked to Eva who simply smiled before stating exactly how I felt, "Well, fuck." Before we burst into a fit of laughter once more.

CHAPTER 35

AURELIA

Nervously, I waited for my appointment with Tora in one of the palace's many sitting rooms. Queen Colette had insisted I take lunch there with my new acquaintance. Although I was sick with nerves, I didn't want to deny the queen. Fortunately, the height of my stress was short-lived as Tora strolled through the door, in her deep crimson, military garb, only a minute after our scheduled meeting time. "Princess."

I was taken aback. Technically true, I was a princess, it wasn't something I had given much thought to. Now that it stared me directly in the eye, I didn't like what I saw. I expelled very little effort in finding more about my birth parents. King and Queen. I thought it was best to keep it that way since the little information I did have, didn't paint them in the best of light. In fact, it painted them so dark their silhouettes couldn't even be made out.

"Please, just Aurelia."

"Well, just Aurelia, where I come from, it is highly indecent to address one of royal blood without their royal title."

The formality in Tora's tone gave me pause. "You'll have to excuse me from the title. I haven't been royalty very long."

Tora strolled confidently to the table laid with food, lifting the teapot to pour herself a cup. "On the contrary, young Princess, you have been royalty your whole life."

I couldn't stop the sweat from springing up on my palms. I had assumed my introduction with Tora went well. Our current meeting may be proving otherwise. I felt like I was on the cusp of an interrogation. I didn't like it. Straightening my spine, I took measured steps toward Tora, "By blood, you are correct. But in mind and heart, I am no princess."

Tora paused her pour, turning her head to study me with a reproachful eye before a smirk spread across her face. Turning back to her tea, she mumbled, "If I were you, I wouldn't want to be associated with those pricks either."

A sudden weight lifted off my shoulders. My guard was nowhere near down, nor would it be with Tora, for a long time. I couldn't deny the lightness at least drifted between them.

"Now," Tora turned towards the plush armchairs, indicating for us to sit, "Aurelia, why don't I tell you a little bit more about what I know about keys."

I nodded, obeying the ask to take a seat and doing my best not to fidget.

Tora took a small sip of her steaming cup before she spoke, "As I mentioned, my Grandmother was a key, although in full transparency, she wasn't a very powerful one."

My heart dropped slightly, I had to push the slight disappointment aside. This was the closest I'd gotten to someone who could give me even a sliver of information about my magic. Whatever Tora could tell me, I would absorb every word of it.

"My parents died when I was very young. I was raised by my Grandmother, Birdy, and she was a stickler for learning. Not just about magic, but culture, influence, other worlds. Whatever information she could digest, she would and she taught me in the same capacity.

"I don't know how much you know about Raithe, most of the magic found in the Kingdoms is in tune with the elements and seasons. There is also a smaller class of magic which includes other versions shall we say. Prince Xavier, as an empath, sits within this class, as do you, as a key."

"Does it not cause a divide that not everyone here has magic?" My only experience of class systems was what I knew from England and if magic existed there, which was likely Lord Shelton's plan, the divide between the classes would have been a thousand times worse.

I shifted in my seat. The excitement of learning and anxiety of the knowledge I may come to hold mixed, leaving a dewy residue on my skin. Wiping my palms on my thighs, I silently urged Tora to continue.

"A very long time ago. Many wars were fought between those of magic and those without. Fortunately for Raithe, those wars died out hundreds of years ago. We don't classify anyone differently, with or without magic. And we generally see those of more noble born blood to exist with magic. It's not black and white."

I nodded, taking in every word just as I told myself too.

"So, Birdy forced knowledge on me for as long as I can remember. When I was old enough to hold a practice sword, she allowed me to train with the junior guard as well, as long as I continued my studies." The dark brown skin around her eyes crinkled at the memory, warming something deep inside of me.

"As I said, Birdy was a key. Most of her powers were literal. She could open a locked door, cabinet, shackles, you name it. She didn't have a strong mental capacity with her abilities."

"Sorry?" If I understood correctly, the other side of this magic I thought impossible was, in fact, possible.

"The mind key?" Tora questioned in surprise. I stared at her blankly.

"Essentially, a key has two sides: the first, and generally most apparent in one who develops the power, is the physical key; the second is the mental key."

"Meaning?"

Tora smirked at my impatience. "Just as it says. A mental key can unlock non-physical things, a code, a language, and even, in some cases I've read about, it can unlock a power within a person."

A power within a person. I couldn't wrap my head around it all. Opening a portal and a door was about as much as I could fathom at this stage.

"It is rare, mind you, but it has been recorded a lot in history."

"Queen Kendra said that wasn't possible."

Tora snorted, "Queen Kendra is brilliant, yes. I assure you, she is no expert on keys."

"Can you give me an example?"

Tora set down her now empty cup, leaning forward on her arms, "Let's take your sister, for example. She doesn't have any indicators that she has any magical ability, right?"

"As far as we know."

"Essentially, if you also had the mental key, you could tap into her mind to unlock her power, if one lay dormant."

Looking towards the window, I did my best to process another load of new and almost unimaginable information. At this stage, I shouldn't have thought anything impossible, but with so much to take in, I was mentally spent.

"Aurelia," Tora coaxed me gently, "I know this is a lot. I know you've been through a lot, and up until a few weeks ago, you didn't even know magic existed. Now, here you are, in a land of magic, filled with magic of your own. We have all the time in the world to help you process that."

Birds danced just outside the large open aperture, as I did my best to keep my breathing steady.

"Aurelia, look at me." The captain in her voice shined through, urging me to move my gaze to Tora's, which I did on instinct. "I'm going to be honest with you, we have time to explore this, you and I, but there are bigger fish to fry right now. That can't wait. None of us wanted you to go into this, in the case you do see the King and Queen, without at least knowing what your abilities could be. Do you understand?"

They wanted to give me something to arm myself with. It may not be learning my magic properly, but knowledge was a funny thing, people never gave it enough power. These people knew just how powerful knowing was. I shook my head once.

"If you also have the mental key, I don't know if or when it would show itself. I do want you to be aware of it if it does."

"When I first opened a door," the memory popped into my mind, "I had a sort of vision."

Tora leaned back, fully enraptured in the tale.

"I was initially angry, thinking we weren't going to be able to get the door open, except when we went back, and my head was clearer, I had this haze gloss over me, sort of urging me to just open it."

Tora kept silent, allowing me to be lost in the thought.

"And then I pushed...and it opened. Do you think..." I sat forward, a spark of excitement radiating through her. "If I have this mental thing too, would it forewarn me?"

Tora thought on this, running her long, slender finger along the side of her smooth, dark cheek. "It's a very high possibility. And it would be helpful too. If the power manifests in your mind first, you could use the premonition to your advantage."

The room descended in an exploratory silence, each of us imagining how it could play out. As long as the visions didn't knock me unconscious or incapacitate me, I hoped the magic, if it was there, came to me that way. It felt like a less shocking approach, especially with the situation we were about to find ourselves in.

My head snapped back to Tora. "What about the physical key? Do I need to do anything to prepare for that?"

Tora looked down at the stopwatch hanging from her captain's jacket before standing. "No, Aurelia. This part of the gift is fully ready and available to you."

My eyes met Tora's, each of us exchanging a comfortable smile. "Thank you, Tora. You have no idea how helpful this has been."

I stood, dwarfed by Tora's tall stature, still more level with her than I had when the meeting started.

"You are more than welcome. I look forward to more of our chats."

"Me too."

"After, you know, we defeat the enemy and all."

We both laughed, filling me with another sliver of confidence. I may still be out of place and sometimes lost, but slowly, ever so slowly, I'd find my way.

"Now, these."

Archer placed a set of thick, steel shackles on the makeshift log table in front of me. Following my conversation with Tora, I'd relayed the new information about my magic to the bears, Bea, Eva, and Archer. Archer had immediately insisted we practise my physical key magic in the training ring at dawn. Which was how I'd found myself with shackles, locked trunks, copper cuffs, and every door to the armoury locked for me to open.

The bears, Bea, and Eva had joined in what was clearly a demonstration, not a training session. I didn't mind the audience. The few times I'd used my physical powers had mainly been in front of others and preparing myself for any possible situation also meant there may be human distractions in front of me.

Once the initial objects were conquered, Archer moved them, particularly the restraints, onto my onlookers, wanting to confirm I could also unlock the items when actually used on people. The pulsing kicked in each time I wrapped my fingers around the object, greeting me, no longer as an old friend, but more as a limb I'd just learned how to navigate. It felt—well, it felt good.

Purposely, I'd left Fox in his cuffs for longer than needed, provoking a whiney complaint from the youngest bear and causing Eva to chuckle in his discomfort. The two's verbal sparring had lessened in frequency but heightened in intensity. When they were in close proximity, no one could predict what kind of disgust they'd spew at one another. Bea had attempted to take bets on whether they'd end up in bed together or murdering each other. I'd refrained from taking a side on the matter.

The bears still spent a majority of their time in strategy meetings, or training directly with the troops who had set up camp in Vernum, but every day, they took time to come to the training ring. The various pieces of a family I'd collected over the last few months became more succinct during those moments. Apart from the hostility between Eva and Fox, but even that started to be comforting in its own, strange way.

Successfully demonstrating to Archer and the rest of the crew that my magic and I were well in tune, I took a few moments in the blanket of night to stand in the ring. I admired the clarity of the sky, savouring the stars that never shined as bright, breathing in the crisp, Vernum air.

No one disturbed those moments, leaving me to sit, quietly devouring the pleasant sensations while they lasted, wanting to deny the fact that war was imminent.

As I let the distant hum of the crickets rock me with their rhythm, I relished in the knowledge that slowly, my tool chest had filled, both physically and mentally. No matter what came next, I would always be thankful for that.

CHAPTER 36

MADDOX

The moon bore a sliver of light through the suite window as I stepped through the door. The stillness in the room indicated that Aurelia was in bed, asleep.

Silently, I undressed before slipping under the blanket to curl my body around Aurelia's. A privilege I would never tire of.

Wrapping my arms around her, I drew her toward me. Just as her back met my chest, her hips pushed back into my cock covered only by a thin layer of fabric.

"You're awake?"

The answering moan sent my blood south. "Why are you awake, Aurelia?"

My words tickled her ear, and I hoped she could read the silent promises in my playful tone.

Shifting to face me, she released a rough breath before she spilled, "In the war council, you weren't telling us everything."

It wasn't what I had expected to hear as the confusion spread across my face, no doubt dancing in the moonlight. "What do you mean?"

We had agreed to be overly cautious on who knew what information. It wasn't that I didn't trust Aurelia. On the contrary, I trusted her more than anyone. I also knew the burdens she held on her shoulders for most of her life and I didn't want to put her in a position to absorb more information than necessary. Thinking it through now made me realise it was quite a dick move. She showed nothing but patience and acceptance of everything thrown her way.

"The plan. Strategy. Whatever you want to call it. You aren't telling us or the commanders everything."

I swallowed my apprehension down as best as I could. The woman was a sorceress. In more ways than one. Before I could respond, she launched into a further accusation which was more fact than anything.

"That feeling, the one that beats from my power? It's telling me that you're wrong. Even if my birth parents turned recluse, this impending doom sits on my chest telling me that they have something else planned. I think we are walking into a hornet's nest."

Attempting to dispel some of the tension rising in her shoulders, I wrapped my arms around her back, tucking her head beneath my chin.

"First of all." I kept my voice at a whisper given the way walls could talk anywhere in Raithe. "You're right. We don't think it will be that easy."

Taking a second to breathe in her sweet, lilac aroma, I snuggled in closer.

"Secondly, walking into a hornet's nest is exactly what we plan."

Her breath fanned my neck as I shifted my cheek down to hers. "Aurelia, there are traitors everywhere. Even with Bea and other witches' spells, Aestas have their own and from what we know, have been using them every chance they get. For now, we are protected. You are protected. As are Eva and Archer."

Aurelia's hand wove through the hair on the back of my neck lightly as her fingers focused on the waves in my hair. The threading induced by her panic had shifted from fabrics to my locks. The way my chest tightened, threatening to burst the more she did that which was the most glorious sensation.

"So, you don't believe they are giving up?"

Her tone mirrored my own, now knowing the risks of being overheard.

"Not at all. And we will share more as the days go on but right now, it's not safe to show all of our cards."

Shifting back, her blue gaze matched my hazel one as she nodded gently. "I trust you."

They weren't the three words I thought would tilt my world upside down, but they were no less important. In fact, they held so much sway in my life, my movements, my decisions, and I don't know if I'd ever be able to voice how much it meant to me that I felt those words deeply rooted in my bones.

Placing a soft kiss on her forehead, I breathed her in once more, never able to get enough of that floral scent.

"Good. Now let's talk about how sexy it is when you worry about me."

Rolling her eyes, she attempted to roll away from me but my strong arms immediately captured her. The giggle that left her mouth cast a smile so wide on my face I thought it would reach my ears.

Burying my nose in the crook of her neck, a spot I'd discovered to be one of my favourites, I welcomed the fluttering growing in my core, needing to savour every inch of her.

With a quick twist of her middle, Aurelia's lips slammed down on mine, taking me by surprise. Rolling me onto my back, she kicked her leg over my waist, aligning our body parts perfectly. Pulling away for a second, she mumbled against my lips, "Let me show you how worried I am."

And with those words, I let her.

The conversation with Aurelia repeatedly played in my mind. It was the reason I had decided to take everyone out to the Laora Valley, disguising it as a training session for my closest unit — my brothers, Kane, Bea, Aurelia, and her siblings.

Aurelia's doubt of our strategy made me realise it was unfair that we'd hidden so much from her, Archer, and even Eva. They were a part of this now. We were a family.

An hour's ride south of the palace, we found ourselves in Vernum's largest open expanse closest to the palace.

We'd visited the valley a few times when we were kids, always appreciating the rich serenity of the miles of wildflower fields. Our aunt had brought our family on annual picnics. The fields were filled with so many fond memories and now Laora valley was the perfect spot to hold confidential conversations.

"Why have you brought us all the way out here, Maddox?"

Archer posed the question sarcastically, not fully understanding that he too was in this with us. We were all connected and we'd need to be a secure unit marching into Aestas. Apart from Fox and Eva, because we didn't have enough time to mend whatever fucked up relationship that was.

"Well, Aurelia has brought it to my attention that the way we've withheld information is unacceptable. And I agree, potential future King of Aestas."

Archer, being the eldest, was naturally in line for the throne once the King and Queen were dealt with. We'd approached this with him and his siblings gently the last couple of weeks. Aurelia and Eva had consistently been supportive of the idea but Archer had refused to acknowledge his rightful place until he knew we'd defeated their birth parents. A trait I found admirable, causing the respect I had developed for him to blossom.

"And why all the way out here?" Bea countered.

Xav pointed to the blankets we had brought, indicating we should sit down. We may have disguised the trip but we also wanted to take the opportunity to share a tradition with our new, extended family.

The group settled down, Aurelia as close to me as physically possible, which I relished as Bea silently ensured Fox and Eva were a healthy distance away from one another.

Kane dished out the packed lunch of sandwiches and fruits as I told the entire story.

Everett and his Knights were working hard the last few weeks, gathering as much information from the neighbouring kingdoms as possible and ensuring we were as prepared as we could be before marching into Aestas.

A few, well trusted sources were able to supply us with the intelligence that, although a lot of the Aestas citizens had fled, the Queen and King appeared to be lying in wait, meaning they may know we had returned. Thankfully, from what Everett could ascertain, Aestas had no indication that their children were alive and well, and all now living in Raithe too.

"The attack strategies we've relayed to you are true. Our approach hasn't shifted. We will need to be flexible on the day we march in."

"How so?" Archer bit into a strawberry around his question.

"Everett and the Knights are in Aestas currently. We won't know if they have learned anything else until we arrive."

Bea leaned back on her arms, threading small daisies through her bare toes. "So, we move in as planned but be prepared for things to change, last minute. Is that what you are saying?"

Fox stood, dusting his palms of crumbs before moving toward the baskets to pull more food out. "That's what we are saying."

Xav cleared his throat, "You are all part of this family now. Whether you like it or not. This fight, it's about all of us, and we don't want you to ride into that camp blind, but we understand if you also can't put yourself in that situation. You have the option to stay back in Vernum. The queens have strong security in place and you would be safe."

"So, we don't have to ride to our doom if we don't want to?" Eva presented her question with stiff posture but I was beginning to understand Aurelia's youngest sister more each day. Not one part of me thought she'd miss the chance to march into Aestas and confront her birth parents.

"You don't. You can stay back. We can send for you once it's over."

Xav's smile indicated he too had a strong read on Eva, knowing she blew hot air with her question.

"Well, I guess I'll go."

The casualness in her decision caused Fox to narrow his eyes suspiciously at Eva. Xav stood, wrapping his arm around our youngest brother in an attempt to keep him quiet and the conversation on course.

"I'm not missing this." Archer confirmed as he grabbed for another sandwich.

We all turned to Aurelia who gazed at us in shock.

"You already know I'm going. I don't know why you'd all think I'd say anything differently."

Reaching over, I laced my fingers through hers, giving her a gentle squeeze.

Bea raised her tin mug into the crisp Spring air. "What's that ridiculous thing you always close the war council out with? Redemption or death?"

In unison, the rest of our unit mirrored Bea's actions before reciting the words that signified the next step in all of our lives. "To redemption or death!"

CHAPTER 37

AURELIA

Units had begun departing the palace the following morning, dividing further into smaller units in the attempt to deter any spies from reporting on movement through Aestas lands. The Royal Unit, a name which I was not fond of, included the king, the princes, the Queen's Guard, Bea, Archer, Eva, and myself, totalling fifteen in our single unit.

Walking out into the bustling courtyard with Eva was yet another surreal moment. Servants scurried about as each member of the unit had a horse brought through by the stable hands and packed carefully under Xav's supervision. Kane and his men put the finishing touches in their packs when Eva and I arrived.

"Good morning, Aurelia, Eva."

"Good morning, Kane!" Eva's enthusiasm spread through the courtyard like wildfire, causing me to second degree blush.

Leaning over, Eva whispered, "He is still the most gorgeous specimen I have ever seen."

I giggled, whispering back, "It's magic, Eva."

"Well, it's not all magic. Look at him!" Forgetting our company, Eva's voice boomed once again.

I shook my head before leaving my sister to find my horse.

"Miss Aurelia?" Jensen, one of the Queen's Guard approached me. His confident stride clashed with the nervousness he held in his facial expression.

"Please, just Aurelia."

"Aurelia then, your horse is over here, next to King Maddox's." He gestured towards a stunning white mare alongside a very large, black stallion.

Still not entirely confident with horses, I approached the mare slowly, gently raising my hand as I got closer. The mare raised her head, sniffing my extended hand briefly before nuzzling me, her hot breath skating over my palm, leaving a trail of goose bumps across my forearm.

I chuckled, scratching the horse's snout. "Well, I think I like you too, beautiful."

"Apples."

Jensen stood a few feet behind me.

"Excuse me?"

"Her name. It's Apples. Not very original, I know. The stable hands said she has always been infatuated with apples and it just kind of stuck."

I turned back to the horse, "Nice to meet you, Apples."

Just as I went to step closer, the courtyard erupted in a buzz, startling me and pushing my heart rate to speed up. Turning, I immediately recognised the reason for such a sudden commotion, the bears had arrived, along with Bea, Archer, and the queens.

Xavier and Mads were in hushed conversation with Queen Colette and Queen Kendra while Bea and Archer laughed between themselves. Fox, however, had immediately pinpointed Eva who was stroking a horse's mane, giggling flirtatiously at something Kane had said. The site obviously threw Fox into an angry fit as he stomped down the stairs. Eager to avoid an outburst, I called out to him in the sternest tone I could muster. It worked, halting Fox on the trail to his rampage and pivoting him toward me. When he was near enough and out of the earshot of others, I knitted my brow, trying my best to appear intimidating. "What the hell are you doing?"

"Me? What is she doing?" He pointed a slightly shaky yet strong finger towards Eva and Kane.

"*She* is talking to Kane. Why has it got you so flustered?"

The last word caught his attention, causing him to straighten himself at the insinuation. "I'm not flustered."

"Fox, why do you care so much who my sister speaks to?"

His voice dropped low, laced with a menacing tone. "I don't."

"Keep telling yourself that."

Attempting to keep the fury from his face seemed to pain him in the way his entire body tensed up. "I don't care who she talks to. Kane only has eyes for someone else, anyways."

Thinking he proved his point was about to backfire, given Maddox had alluded to Xav and Kane's complicated history.

"From what Mads told me, Kane has an affinity for all humans, no matter what is in their trousers."

Fox scowled at my rebuttal before turning toward the pair in question, eyeing Kane. "Shit."

"You know, Fox, you could just confess your feelings toward her and see where that gets you, but for now, just calm down."

I placed my hand on his shoulder before calling out to my sister, "Eva!" I had dismantled a potential eruption constantly brewing between the two. Now wasn't the time for it.

Eva looked over, glaring at my audacity to interrupt her fun time with Kane. "I need your help with something!"

Huffing, Eva shot a teasing smile back to Kane before excusing herself. Her steps were hurried and irritated. "Is there a reason you tore me away from the delightful conversation with the nice man?"

It wasn't until she was in front of me when Eva noticed Fox. "And to be in the direct presence of this mongrel?"

Fox chortled, "You aren't much better, *princess.*" He hissed the title at her in disgust.

"Listen you two, we have a lot going on right now so I'm going to need you to settle your bullshit, at least for now. Got it?"

Fox and Eva exchanged an indecipherable look before nodding in agreement.

"Let's get ready to go, Eva."

"Fine."

"Fox?"

"I'm good."

Eva mumbled under her breath, mocking him.

"Good. Now go get your stuff. Jensen can show you to your mare."

They moved in separate directions, as I let the gratitude wash through me at the fact they had listened to me. At least for the time being.

"You know," a deep, sinful voice arose behind me, "when we free Raithe, those two could easily burn it down."

Turning, my shoulder bumped into Mads. Savouring his closeness, I smiled up at him. "Good thing Fox has ice magic then, huh?"

Leaning down, Mads' lips brushed my own as he tugged my braid, pulling me closer. The kiss was brief but, as always, consuming. "You ready, Goldie?"

A soft smile grew on my lips. It wasn't often he called me Goldie and had done so rarely since we had acted on our greater urges. When he did, it filled my heart, reminding me of the time when I'd just discovered myself, and these brothers.

"As ready as I'll ever be, Your Majesty."

Heat rose in his eyes as he said, "I'm starting to like the sound of that rolling off your lips."

Chuckling, I turned back toward the palace, intent on saying goodbye to the queens. Approaching them, a sudden storm of emotions rose within me. I didn't know either of the queens particularly well. What they'd given me in such a short span of time was something I would never forget. Welcoming me into their home, their family, meant more to me than either of them would ever understand.

"Dear Aurelia," Queen Colette held out her arms, drawing me into a hug. She smelled of roses and gooseberries, encompassing the springtime I had grown so fondly over the last few weeks.

"You have so much life to live, sweet girl. Remember that."

Tears pooled in my eyes as I drew back, staring into the face of a woman who had opened her home to not only me, but Archer and Eva and did so graciously.

"Thank you, for everything."

Turning to Queen Kendra, who motioned me forward. She took my face in her hands and placed a soft, sweet kiss on my forehead. "Go, be happy."

No matter what happened, from that moment forward, those two women were permanently cemented in the family I'd built for myself and I couldn't be prouder of that fact.

"I guess we will see you at the coronation."

Queen Colette laughed and Queen Kendra gave me a wink before I turned to head back to Apples. Spring wasn't my home, just as the cabin hadn't been, but it had come close.

The last goodbye I gave was to Rock as I pulled him into my arms for an embrace before promising we would be sending for him soon. He would be staying in Vernum during the battle, ensuring his safety.

Mounting Apples, Mads handed me the reins before kicking his stallion into motion, indicating for me to stay by his side. And I would. I would always be by his side, just as he would be by mine.

The group rode steady for most of the day, stopping only twice for short breaks to water the horses and ourselves. Eva and Fox, thankfully, stayed as far away from each other as possible.

We made good time and were able to set up camp in the forest clearing the teams had mapped out. The camp was modest, opting for ease rather than comfort. Each member of the group had a role to play and mine happened to be refilling our canteens. Not the most glamorous of jobs, but I was thankful because my task mate was

Bea. Since we'd arrived in Vernum, we hadn't spent much alone time together. I missed her.

"Are you getting on alright?" I uttered to her from my kneeling position at the river, the cool water refreshing as it ran over my hands as we filled the canteens. Glancing at her, I noticed the exhaustion that had settled on her features was still apparent although had reduced greatly from the other day.

"I'm good. I will be happy when this next part is over. I'm going to soak in the Hallow Springs for days."

"The Hallow Springs?" I asked as I hadn't known, or heard, of any springs.

"The Hallow Springs of Hiema?"

I stared over at her blankly, my ignorance to these springs clearly defined on my face.

"We've done a really shitty job of preparing you, haven't we?"

Closing the cap on another canteen, I placed it with the others on the bank. "I don't think of it like that. This has all been such a whirlwind. It's not like any of us have had the time to sit down for a proper introduction to Raithe."

"You're not annoyed."

Midway through filling the next canteen, I stilled my movements and asked, "Should I be?"

Bea thought on my question a moment before she shook her head and returned to her task. "I guess not. It's a lot to take in so we were never going to have a quick way we could help you transition."

"Exactly. So, tell me about the springs."

Abandoning the half-filled canteen, Bea settled back on her knees, resting her weight on her palms as she stared up at the clear night sky. "Apparently, the Winter Kingdom has a network of underground hot Springs. Beneath the palace there are hundreds of tunnels leading to different rooms. The water is heated naturally and it's the perfect way to soak worn muscles."

"They sound amazing."

"Mmmm. I plan on spending at least a week in them when we finally get there. Maybe with a Hiema man and lady companion too."

I smiled. Bea had been working tirelessly since I'd met her. She more than deserved a proper rest. The companions may not be for resting, but she could definitely use the release they may bring. I looked over to Bea. "I'm positive there will be plenty of companions to choose from."

Bea chuckled before sobering, closing her eyes in a memory. Her face fell into a serenity I had not seen from the witch before. My heart warmed and whatever was bringing the contentment to her in that moment.

I looked up, appreciating the sky filled with bright twinkling lights, focusing directly on the one which was the least luminous.

At first glance, I had felt bad for the star, being surrounded by so many dazzling ones, it must have been hard. Then I realised, it wasn't how bright the star shined, rather the fact it sparkled at all.

"Bea?" The breath tickled my lips as her name left my mouth.

"Yes, buttercup?"

Hesitating momentarily, I spoke the question whose answer may terrify me, "Do you think we will win this?"

Finding my eyes with her own, Bea gentled, it was unsettling at first, knowing she was a blazing bright star. "I know we will, buttercup. I know we will."

I wasn't sure if she repeated the answer to soothe me, or herself, but as I looked back up at the sky, finding my sister star, I confessed, "I've missed you, Bea."

Scooting closer, Bea looped her arm around my shoulders. "I've missed you too. Not long now and we'll be able to enjoy each other's company without the looming threat of war."

Just like the star, Bea gave me the words I needed to keep glowing, even if my light was dulled in comparison.

We moved out at dawn, breaking up the camp like a well-oiled machine which was odd given Bea, Eva, and I had never broken down a camp before. I didn't dwell on it for long. We were due to arrive at base camp later in the evening, where we would be meeting up with the other units and getting ready to officiate the battle strategy. The nerves had already made themselves at home in my gut. I was, at least, able to hold back the panic for the time being. I was thankful the journey itself was only two days because every step Apples took those last few hours sent shooting pain from my feet through to my hips. Riding was definitely not something I wanted to do leisurely.

When we arrived at camp, we were greeted by the Knight's Mara, as well as two captains from Vernum and one from Hiema. They'd confirmed all units had arrived and had settled into their respective camps. The horses were unloaded by Hiema soldiers before we were shown to our camp area.

The space itself was made up of various circular plots of open land, surrounded by varying thickets and lush trees. The camp was abuzz with movement but the birdsong still trickled through the voices. When we reached our designated space, I took in the stacks of supplies at the centre. The bears wasted no time in grabbing poles and hammering them into the dirt. My mouth dropped as I studied a King and two princes set up their own camps. Watching them work in sync, seeing a further glimpse of them, made my love for them grow deeper.

As Archer left to find his friends from another unit where he'd stay, Bea, Eva, and I made work of arranging the bags into the corresponding tents before grabbing other supplies from the central camp storage areas. I only grabbed what I felt necessary, including a sleeping pallet, wash basin, and linens. Bea, on the other end of the spectrum, went for full comfort, taking as much as she could carry across three trips. Eva's eyes glittered with curiosity and what appeared to be respect as the brothers erected the canvas tents with speed and precision. A wonderful sight, watching three, strong, and beautiful men work with their hands, just as they'd done back at the house.

Once the tent I would be sharing with Mads was secured, I began setting up the inside. The group was done a short time later and convened around the mess camp to grab a bowl of stew and bread. I observed the brothers as they made their rounds, introducing themselves and holding comfortable conversations with various soldiers. Not wanting to disturb them, I excused myself, returning to the tent to wash the day off my skin before settling on to the pallet in my nightdress.

I must have dozed off, waking when Mads entered the tent, a wide grin spread across his face. Wiping the thin layer of sleep from my eyes, I grumbled, "What are you smiling at?"

Mads removed his jacket, never taking his eyes off me as my anticipation grew. I didn't mind the wait, enjoying the view of his muscular arms untucking his shirt and pulling at the fabric. "I just...I just never thought we'd be here, Aurelia. I gave up what little hope I had a long time ago."

Pushing myself to my elbows, Mads sat on the small stool I'd brought into the tent before taking a clean cloth, dipping it in the still warm water before spreading it across his arms. I wanted to be the one smoothing the fabric over his skin. Standing from the pallet, I moved towards him slowly, extending my hand in invitation. Mads glanced at my hand fleetingly before he raised his eyes to mine, placing the damp cloth in my palm. Pushing it back into the pleasant water, I rung it out only slightly before moving it across his broad back, letting my fingers glide over his exquisite shoulder muscles . Mads shuttered as a tingle sparked between my legs. The moment was intimate and I didn't want to ruin it. "When did you lose hope?"

Mads turned his chin, giving me a slight view of his face as he spoke, "A few years after we were exiled. Fox had a really bad run of alcohol and women. Xav and I lost him for three days before we found him, naked and off his face in the forest. We were able to convince him to stay clean for a while," he paused. "When we got him home, I put him in the bath where he broke down to me. Xav was fixing him some food to soak up the alcohol so it was just him and I. Seeing and hearing the depth of his grief pushed me to realise I couldn't fix it." He raised his eyes to mine, a shimmer glistening over them as he recalled the painful memory.

"Seeing my baby brother in such a state, it broke me. He'd lost everything. We all had. The fire he'd always had? It died with our parents, and I knew I'd never make him whole again."

I rinsed the cloth once more before repeating the washing motions, moving to his front. "But you did. He's healing. Just as you and Xav are. You're back in Raithe, at least. You got him back here."

Mads' hand wrapped around my wrist, forcing my eyes to his. "No, Aurelia. You got us back here."

My breath caught as he continued.

"And you know what?" His grip shifted to my hips, pulling me closer to him, engulfing me in his warmth. "I never needed my magic back because when I met you, I realised something."

His lips ghosted mine, fanning them with his whisky scented breath. The sweet taste of hickory danced with it. "What did you realise?" I raised in barely a whisper.

"You are the fire in my veins."

The words pushed an explosion through my heart as I closed the distance between us, letting my lips dance with his was my favourite tune. Standing, Mads took me with him, lifting my hips up, I wrapped my legs around his naked torso. He walked us to the pallet, gently placing me on my back before yanking the cloth from my hand, tossing it behind him. His hands found my thighs, grip tight, pushing up my dress until I was exposed. I spread my knees in invitation.

Mads stood back, admiring my form as he unbuttoned his trousers, the heat in his eyes growing by the second. "I love seeing you like this. Open and ready for me."

The way the words curled off his lips fuelled the fire between my legs.

"Are you wet for me, Aurelia?"

"Yes," I breathed.

"Show me. Sink a finger into your pussy and show me how wet you are for me."

Trailing my fingers down, I passed the space between my breasts, moving around my belly button before finding that delicious spot, pressing down on it once before finding the target. Pushing my forefinger inside, letting the wet heat drench it instantly. I removed my finger, holding it out to Mads, the evidence of my arousal glistening on the tip. Mads leaned over, taking my finger in his mouth, moaning as he drew his tongue across it. A groan escaped my lips at the sight of this beautiful man, savouring the taste of me. Mads moaned, "You taste so sweet."

Leaning further over me, he dragged his nose along my jaw before moving south, taking my nipple in his mouth, rolling it along his tongue before pulling it between his teeth, eliciting another noise from the back of my throat I'd never made before. His gaze met mine from under his eyelashes, a victorious smirk twitched the side of his lips before he moved to the other nipple, mirroring his actions and at the same time, plunging two fingers inside of me, taking me by exquisite surprise. "Mads," I moaned.

"I'm going to fuck you with my fingers first, then I'm going to taste you, then I'm going to fuck you with my cock, Aurelia. Hard and fast because I don't think I have the patience for anything else."

My eyes rolled back in glorious pleasure. "Yes. That. Do that."

Pumping his fingers in and out, curling them, he found the sweet spot with each thrust. Just as the orgasm crested, he shifted further down, covering my clit with his mouth. On instinct, my hips jolted upwards, and using his free hand, Mads guided me back down, steadying me as he ate his fill. I let the sensation build quickly, squeezing around his fingers, getting perfectly lost in every single lick until my body exploded on his tongue, his fingers. He continued his thrusts, slowing down, brushing his tongue over my clit until my orgasm eased. Then suddenly, he was on top of me, his dick teasing my entrance briefly before he pushed in, fast and hard, just as he had promised.

Thrusting his hips in a methodical rhythm, my legs moved higher and wider, wanting as much of him inside me as possible. "That's it. Open for me. Let me in."

"Mads." His name slipped from my mouth on a gasp.

Just as my body began to clench around him, he pulled out, grabbing my arse to flip me over, pulling my hips up. "Head down. Arch your back. Get that gorgeous ass up."

I followed his orders, quickly, and then he thrust back in, filling me again, bringing new sensations ricocheting through my body. His fingers dug into my hips, bruises forming and I loved every second of it. As his pace intensified, he reached his hand around, shoving his fingers into my mouth, "Give me your tongue and suck."

I did, swirling my tongue around his digits over and over before he pulled them back out, finding my clit once more. As he continued to pound into me from behind, he began rotating sensual circles around my overly sensitive bud. "I am going to march into this fight with your come all over my cock."

The illicit image flicked through my sex hazed brain, pushing further pulses through me.

"Yes!" I couldn't think of the potential volume of my screams any longer and I didn't care.

My pussy clenched around him as I grew closer. "That's it, gorgeous, scream for me."

With my face buried in the pallet, I roared, letting the orgasm rock through me, sending my body into convulsions. Mads let out a deep, masculine growl, thrusting harder into me as he found his own release. "Fuck!"

Pumping a few more times as I rode through the aftershocks of my orgasm, his grip on my hips lightened. After a few silent moments, only broken by the sound of our heavy breathing, he laid his body gently on top of mine. We stayed that way for a while, savouring the way his heartbeat on my back. Reaching up, he stroked my hair away from my face before finding my hand, threading his fingers through it.

"You're really, really good at that."

He let out a laugh, rumbling against my back. "I want to do that everywhere."

I smiled into the blanket. "I'd like that very much."

What felt like hours later, he removed himself from me, taking a quilt from the end of the pallet to drape it over me before laying down next to me. I was immobile, the euphoria of the orgasms still coursing through me, willing me to stay exactly as I was.

"Can we do that forever?"

Mads turned his head to me and said, "I already told you I'd be your always. If you'd have me."

Using what little energy I had, I shifted my body, tangling my legs between his and laying my head on his chest. We stayed silent for a while as the candlelight flickered, pulling the tent down into the night. Just as I was dozing off, I whispered, "Always, Maddox."

CHAPTER 38

AURELIA

The chaotic sounds of the hustle and bustle of the camp outside pushed me into action as I washed and dressed, wanting to offer my services wherever they were needed. Mads had left earlier in the morning given the many duties he had to attend to.

When I left the tent, I ran straight into Bea and Eva who advised they were on their way to pull me from what Bea called 'my sex coated morning.' I didn't correct her, and I buried the thought of an entire portion of the camp hearing our intimacy the night before. My mind already brimmed with a myriad of more pressing concerns.

We made our way to the main part of the camp, immediately swarming with activity. Soldiers carrying various weapons, water jugs, and other supplies, the mess line filled with eagerly anxious soldiers about to move into battle, and the brothers busying themselves with numerous tasks, no doubt ensuring they were both helping as well as being visible to the men who were about to put their lives on the line for Hiema. For Mads' rightful place. I still couldn't wrap my head around the fact Mads would be King. The rightful king who had me bent over in pure pleasure the night before. No matter how hard I tried to fight it, the memory sent a welcome tingling sensation through my body.

Letting the sensual thoughts die down, they were replaced with where I stood in this picture with Mads. He had already told me he wanted me by his side. Before I could spiral into a worry whirlwind of what the near future held, I caught Xavier's eye. He offered me a slow, genuine smile before making his way towards me. "Goldie, how are you?"

Not wanting to come across as unhelpful and lazy, I followed Bea's lead and grabbed a few water jugs, readying them to be filled. "I'm doing alright, Xav. How are you?"

I knew better. Xav would sense my unease, the imminent unknown haunting us all. I did my best to hide it anyways, knowing on top of everything we would face, my fear wasn't going to help the situation. Xav's smile lit up his face as he said, "You're a terrible liar."

I let out a chuckle. "I am when it comes to you. Sometimes you just have to take what I say, Xav."

Halting me from grabbing another jug, he laid his hands on my shoulders giving them a brief squeeze. "Today, one way or another, we will see victory. I know it. You have to believe it too. If not for us, then for yourself. You've fought long and hard to be here today, Aurelia. And I'm not talking about the last month. Your entire life has been a war. One battle after another. This one will be victorious."

Digesting his words, I did my best to press a believable smile to my face. Part of me, one still tucked away tightly, knew he was right. "I know. At least I think I do."

Removing his hands from my shoulders, he tapped my chin lightly. "If you don't believe me, ask Bea. You know she can sense these things."

With a wink, Xav left me to my task and to find Bea. The search for Bea didn't take long as she came tumbling toward me a few moments later, shouting instructions on where to take the water. Scrambling to pick up the jugs, I completed the task first before returning to her. "Bea, can I talk to you for a second?"

A rare irritation flared from her face before she studied my body language, clearly recognising my anxiety. She paused what she was doing, features softening. "What do you need, buttercup?"

Twirling my fingers together, I collected the words I wanted to say carefully, "What do you see happening today? With this...battle?"

Studying me silently, a lightness spread across her face before she wrapped her arm around my shoulders. "What I told you yesterday. Plus, you know I can't predict the future."

I nodded. "I think I just need to hear it again."

Bea offered me a gentle smile as she said, "What I do know is we will be successful. I don't know how, and I can't expect it to be easy, but I don't think we have much to worry about, buttercup."

"Really?" I couldn't hide the hope in my voice. Nor did I want to.

Bea leaned in, her lips almost touching my ear. "Really. I know you're worried. I get it. I really do. We need your strength, Aurelia. The incredible resilience you've shown time and time again. The bears, your brother and sister. Me. You're stronger than you could ever fathom. Trust me. Trust that."

Pulling back, Bea offered me a gentle wink before marching off without giving me a chance to respond. Maybe it was better that

I didn't have the time to respond. No one else needed to hear the chaos running rampant through my head.

Abruptly, a soft tingle vibrated across my fingertips causing confusion. Before I had time to question it, Fox was in front of me. I jumped on instinct as I yelped, "Fox, you scared me."

Fox smirked at me, "I can see you were lost in your own head and it is never a good thing."

He bumped my shoulder playfully, "We have been summoned by the King himself."

Setting down the jug, I silently followed Fox to the meeting tent, letting my conversations with Bea and Xav filter through my mind. I didn't have time to over analyse them before I stood inside a tent, furnished with only a table and a few chairs at the centre. Atop the table was a map of some sort. I didn't study the details as I shifted my eyes to the others in the room. The bears, Archer, Eva, Bea, and Kane all stood around the table. A tension blanketed the space, hard to pinpoint who it was coming from.

I glanced around expecting at least a few of the commanders to be in attendance. Before I was able to open my mouth and question what the meeting was actually for, Mads' deep voice filtered through the space.

"They know." Shifting on his heels, he clenched his jaw.

Who knows what now?

"We knew we weren't able to contain all the spies. The king and queen are expecting our attack."

"Neither of them have shown themselves, but they're expecting us. Today." Kane added.

Dread pooled in my gut, confirming my earlier fears. I trusted the previous reassurances I'd been given from so many in the room, yet I still couldn't stop the nausea from creeping in.

"So, what's their game plan?" Bea stood tall, confidence rolling off her shoulders.

"We aren't sure," Xav stepped forward, leaning over the map.

"They know we are taking a pronged approach. We can't be certain where they'll focus their own efforts, whatever those may be."

"Should we move forward if we don't know what they've got planned?" Eva's apprehension was thick, swirling around the group in a tightening grip.

"Yes." The brothers and Kane responded in unison.

"We continue as planned, each of the three units taking their relative stations. We will push forward on horseback, hoping to draw someone of importance out."

The brothers and Kane turned to me and my siblings. The awkward smile Fox pointed toward me sent an uncomfortable quiver down my spine. Kane and Xav both held an expression of apology on their faces and Mads refused to make eye contact. "We will need your help."

Archer stepped forward, his posture indicating he was ready to pledge his allegiance with no other information. A far cry away from the boy I knew so long ago.

"There is a network of tunnels through the palace," Xav began, bringing our attention to the map below. "We know these three are still in use. We think, Aurelia, you can get through with your magic, if needed."

My breathing escalated, my eyes shifting to Mads, looking for silent reassurance, but he was busy focusing on the map. I knew I would play a part in the plan at some point, just not in one of such importance. "Kane will go with you," Mads confirmed. "He and Archer can cover you."

"And me?" Eva stepped forward, radiating a force I'd never seen from her before. "Why do you need me?"

Fox huffed. The annoyance is clear in his stance as he said, "Aegis, princess."

I turned my attention back to Eva, tears of pride beginning to glisten in her eyes before I turned to Archer who offered me a cocky smile.

"We'd like to see it, just to give us the peace of mind that we aren't sending you to the wolves unarmed."

Xav chuckled at Mads' attempted reasoning. "Mads, don't lie. As much as you don't want anything happening to Eva and Archer, you're most concerned about our golden haired intruder."

Kane and Fox smirked as the room's attention turned towards Mads. Clenching his jaw, you could almost hear the sound of his teeth grinding as he bit out one word, "Fine."

Fox stepped forward, a smile of anticipation flicking across his face before he opened his palm as a tiny ball of ice formed above it.

"No." Eva stomped on the silent idea. "Of course you'd want to test your magic on us. I should've guessed."

"I can assure you, princess, this is purely for experimental purposes. I will take no pride in hitting you with my magic."

Eva rolled her eyes before stepping to my side and placing her hand in mine. I extended my other arm to Archer who immediately took his place next to me.

"Remember," Bea took a step out of the firing line, "connection, breath, thought."

The pulsing took immediate effect, making our audience only wait a few moments before I looked at Fox, giving him a nod in readiness. Not wasting a breath, he turned his palm toward us shooting out a stream of ice. We winced in anticipation, waiting for the cold blast to hit us. I held my breath. Nothing happened. Opening my eyes, I was greeted with the sight of the ice bouncing off the invisible force field and back toward Fox.

"Well, that's something."

The bears and Kane stared in fascination as Fox's ice continued to stream toward our invisible barrier.

"I think we can all confirm, it works." Xav smiled, clapping Mads on the back in glee.

Fox drew his ice back as we dropped our hands. "So," Archer said, rubbing the sensation from his hand, "what is the plan then? We break into the tunnel and what? Kill the king and queen?"

Both Eva and I should have been shocked at Archer's immediate thirst for our birth parent's heads. The only thing we showed was our agreement.

"No. We just need you to contain them long enough for us to get through their defences." Mads spoke to everyone in the group, avoiding me. I noticed he hadn't looked at me since I arrived in the tent. I'd have to talk to him about the way he'd been ignoring me. "And, if necessary, get those doors open for us.

"Kane will go with you. Archer can fight too. We have it on good authority that the king and queen's confidence in their own abilities means they won't have much protection. Only a few guards."

"Plus," Xav joined, "we think they'll be using every available soldier to come at us."

I didn't like the sound of that. I also noticed every time someone said, 'we think' rather than 'we know,' not filling me with a huge amount of confidence in this plan.

Xav sensed it, walking around the table and toward me. "Remember we've been planning this for decades."

I kept my eyes down, my hands finding the hem of my shirt and absorbing each of his words. "Some of this has come in unexpectedly but doesn't mean we are less confident in our strategy. You've trusted us so many times before. We are asking you to trust us once more."

Raising my head, I was enveloped in the power of Xav's eyes. It was true, I had given these brothers, this group, so much of the fractured trust I had in the world. Trust was a gift and one I had rarely given out in my life. As I looked around at the faces of my family, a family I had chosen and never through blood, I resolved myself. Turning back to Xav, I reached out, taking Archer and Eva's hands once more. "I trust you."

He smiled before leaning in, planting a soft kiss on my forehead. "Well then. Shall we begin?"

I slid on the lightweight armour just as Mad stepped inside our tent. I let him have my back, knowing I'd need to be transparent with him, a shyness creeping over me at the thought. "Are you done avoiding me now?"

I tried to keep the annoyance from my tone as I felt him step up behind me, his breath ghosting my ear as he said, "I wasn't avoiding you."

"Could have fooled me." So much for not trying to sound annoyed.

"Aurelia," he said, voice cracking on my name. Terrified of what I'd find on his face, I turned around slowly. I was surprised to see a soft smile, his eyes glistening with an emotion I wasn't sure I could pinpoint. My eyes searched his, unsure if I saw sadness or happiness there.

"The last thing I want to do is put you in direct danger or ever having to come face to face with your birth parents, but if there is a chance of you being captured, the best place for you to be is with your brother and sister."

I let the tears well in my eyes as he continued, "I trust Kane with my life and no matter what happens, I know you'll come back to me."

I stepped in closer, cherishing his cedar scent. "But will you come back to me?" I let the words flutter from my lips on a whisper.

Mads raised his strong hands to my cheeks before leaning his forehead down to mine, his eyes fell closed. For a few moments, we stood in silence, breathing each other in. My mind flashed through the journey we took. It was hard to believe only a few months ago he would look and speak to me with nothing but disdain. Now we are here. Together. A unit. I mirrored him, letting my eyes fall closed to the memories.

Before I could question the unidentified emotion he was radiating, three words rolled off his tongue. "I love you."

As soon as the words breathed air, I found myself struggling for it, my heart rate skyrocketed. Opening my eyes, I found his gaze burning into mine. Throat dry, I did my best to swallow down the emotions I wasn't quite ready to face.

"When there is nothing left of me but ash, I will love you."

It was getting worse as my breaths came in short and fast. Mads continued, recognising my growing panic, his words needing release first.

"I'm sorry for not recognising it sooner. I'm sorry we didn't have more time before this. I love you. I fell in love with you the day I found you sleeping in my bed and it has only escalated in need, desire, absolution. Nothing will stop me from loving you in this life and whatever lives come after."

"Mads —" I croaked, the words sticking in the desert taking up residence in my throat.

"I don't expect you to say the words back, Aurelia. In fact, I know you're not ready. I just need you to know, before we march into battle."

Lowering his forehead to mine once more, he found my lips with his own. The kiss was slow, no less devouring than any other. I let a tear escape, appreciating the way it crawled down my cheek before we tasted the salt on our tongues. I wasn't whole. I may never be. The fragments of who I was, who I am, still sat heavy on my chest. I knew my journey of healing would continue far into my future. Maddox though, he held my heart whether I wanted to admit it or not. He made me feel again.

The kiss ended too soon, sending me into a whirlwind of further confusion. He held my heart, yes. Was I in love with him though? If I had to question it, I was afraid I may already have my answer. Standing on my toes, I pressed a small kiss to the side of his mouth before he attempted to offer me a sad smile, his words hanging between us.

"Be careful. Whatever happens next, I need to know we'll at least have one thing."

I didn't offer him any words in question, I simply drank him in, waiting for him to continue. Pushing a lock of hair away from my face, he studied his own movements intently. "Time. I want more time. And I want to be there the day you are able to share those feelings."

Before I could find the words to respond, he left the tent. Instantly, a pang of regret hit my chest, suffocating the panic. For all those lashes breaking my skin, those words that broke me down, the love I had longed for, I was free. My life was mine and the man who just walked away from me had given me more in the last few months than I had ever known in my entire life.

The panic attacks would never cease fully, and those trunks and chests I'd locked so tight would take years to fully unravel and face, but that man, he would stand by my side through it all. He would pick me up every time I fell until I was strong and able to pick myself up. He loved me. The familiar pulsing reared to life deep in my abdomen, shouting at me to react differently. Better.

Whatever came today, a chance lingered, telling me that what we just shared could be our last moment together. Cursing myself internally, I knew in every piece of my soul that I couldn't leave it that way. I may not be able to fully recognise those words on my own tongue, but I couldn't deny the full truth I felt when he said them.

Clutching my hands to my sides, I focused on my limbs pushing every ounce of energy I had to get my legs to move. The steps quickly turned into a sprint as I shot out of the tent after him, bellowing his name for all to hear.

Mads turned just in time to catch me as I hurled myself at him, my arms flying around his neck and legs wrapping around his middle. Huffing out a breath, he wrapped his arms around me as I buried my nose in his neck, the spot just under his ear. The one where I was closest to him, the trace of the forest dancing through my nose and filling me with comfort.

"Don't die today please. I want time too and confessing my feelings to a corpse isn't in the plan."

Chuckling into my hair, he said, "I promise, Goldie. I'm going to annoy you for eternity."

Pulling my head up, I looked him in the eye. "If anything happens to you, I will kill you myself. You know I'm capable."

Mads kissed me, hard, making my abdomen ache with need. It was the best I could give him right now and it seemed he was willing to accept it. When I pulled away, his eyes grew dark, with love and determination. I smiled. "Let's go get your kingdom back, Your Majesty."

Offering one of those rare Mads smiles that could light the darkest of places, he set me on my feet gently, giving me one last kiss before he walked off to his task, leaving me to do the same. Breathing in the day, the power in my chest radiated, reminding me it was time to go and meet Mother and Father dearest.

CHAPTER 39

MADDOX

I hated walking away from Aurelia, not being by her side in this stage of the fight. I couldn't stop my fists from clenching and unclenching as I put more distance between us, ready to lead my unit to battle. It wasn't because I didn't trust her ability or strength, it was more that she had only just gained her life back and the mere thought of those cunt parents of hers taking it away was enough to send me into a spiral. I wanted nothing more than to serve them up to her on a platter, the way we did with Niall and Shelton.

The battle plan was solid and one our allies had strategised since our exile. A simple, yet effective, three pronged attack strategy. Avilore Keep had the sea to the west, the dense Great Forest sitting at its front and the Gold Peaks around the back and east side of the lands.

The naval units would enter the territory via the beaches, Everett and the Knights had moved to the Gold Peaks to spread out units through the passes, and my brothers and I would lead the rest of the forces through the Great Forest.

Aurelia and crew were a last minute change. Given our intel on Carman and Jolon, their forces, and even palace guards, have been retreating for the last two days, leaving a lot of the territory unprotected. An unknown piece existed in this game that we weren't aware of, and the best course of action was to make sure no matter what, Aurelia would have another level of protection that neither us nor our magic could grant her. Plus, she was the only one that could enter the palace through the tunnels with her power.

I trailed back to those moments before when I'd told her I love her. All of it was true, of course, but I was an arse for laying my heart out right before the shitstorm that was about to go down. I had only intended for her to take those words, that knowledge, with her in the hopes that it would give her another level of strength. What it possibly did was scare her, right before she was tasked with being an active participant in this war. Not only that, but I'd done the one thing I vowed never to do to her — take away her choice. Deep down, I knew she could have said no if this was something she was really against, but even the thought of pulling the decision from beneath her made my insides twist.

"Fucking idiot," I mumbled under my breath.

One thought I held on to was that although Carman and Jolon may have had their own eyes and ears throughout our camp, they couldn't predict the numbers we had in our ranks. The turnout of allies for Hiema filled my heart with hope. Hope that I had abandoned long ago and had first sparked again with the arrival of our golden-haired saviour.

Aurelia was an anomaly none of us had planned for. Especially me. Those blue eyes reached into the depths of my soul, uncovering truths and emotions I didn't think myself capable of. I had always loved my family and my kingdom, but a void remained I hadn't recognised until the day she woke up in my bed. My thoughts had started to get the better of me when Xav's hand came down on my shoulder, squeezing as he said, "She'll be okay, brother."

Sometimes I wanted to beat the empathetic bones in his body, hating how he always knew when I needed comfort. Sometimes I just needed rage. On this occasion, I knew in my heart he was right, it would be okay. Would we all survive this? A question I couldn't answer but if anyone would come out of this fight alive, it was Aurelia. I'd burn the world before anything happened to her.

I sighed out a sliver of my agitation. "I know."

Xav laughed. "You're such a shit liar."

"I know," I repeated, unable to hide the smile rising on my lips.

Savouring the laugh, Xav's eyes sparkled. I never thought I'd see the day where I could get that kind of reaction from him again. The day when we all knew we had something to fight and live for. "Kane will be with them and Aurelia is a fighter. You know that."

I nodded. Of course I knew that. The woman journeyed through hell and back on multiple occasions. She had blood on her hands now and from my vantage point, I think she liked it.

So many unknowns laid between us. Those of our pasts and anticipation of our futures. She would need time. We hadn't given her enough of it to process and adapt. But that was the thing about Aurelia, her agility since escaping her tortured life was an invisible strength. And a mighty strong one at that.

I turned to Xav and said, "I know brother. I just don't trust the king and queen."

"No one does, Mads. Which is one of the reasons we are about to storm their lands."

We looked toward the thick forest looming in front of us. "Xav, what do you think they've got up their sleeves?"

Trailing my gaze, Xav pondered the question a few moments before offering his opinion, "I think there is a silent player. I don't know who, but I do know that Carman and Jolon are not nearly cunning enough to achieve everything they have."

I hummed in agreement. When I was a young boy, the kingdoms worked side by side. Even Aestas didn't cause trouble. No one remembered the exact moment of their pivot, but the tides had turned. Unrest had grown steadily. For all we knew, it was purely the evil of Carman and Jolon themselves. They had very few they trusted around them and no one that stood out to me as a potential threat. But I couldn't deny Xav's observation. We all knew someone played a role in the game that we weren't aware of.

"So," Xav turned his attention back to the forest in front of us, "let's get this thing over and done. Let's get our kingdom back."

Just as we turned on the path to head to our unit, Fox sauntered over to us. "Ready for this, brothers?"

A glint flashed in Fox's eye. One I hadn't seen since our parents were alive. Each second we were in Raithe, was a second we took back a piece of what was stolen from us. We had a hell of a march in front of us, filled with more blood than I cared to think about. Then how we'd get Orsa back, in one sane piece, if possible. We didn't want to comprehend the horrors our sister could've braced during our exile.

First thing was first though. We needed to decimate Carman and Jolon for everything they'd caused us, not just for murdering our parents and so many innocents, but for Aurelia and her siblings too. We were all a family now. Some of us may not like others, but we couldn't deny what we were. What we would continue to grow to be.

Throwing Fox one of his trademark cocky smiles, I wrapped my arms around both of their shoulders, pulling them to my sides. "Let's get Hiema back, brothers."

Each step toward our mounts was one step closer to a dream decades in the making. A dream we had all thought long dead, never to be resurrected. Standing next to my onyx stallion, I tested the weight of my weapons beneath my fingers. *For Mum and Dad.*

The cool steel on my skin breathed a wave of determination through my lungs. I dug the heels of my boots into the mud, riddled with camp debris as I checked the straps of my armour were secure. *For Orsa.*

Pivoting, I wrapped my fingers around the pommel, gliding my left foot into the stirrup and took a long, slow breath in. *For Hiema.*

Hauling myself up, I kicked my right leg over, securing my other foot in its hold. The blood began pounding through me as I felt my erratic pulse against the pommel, coursing through my palms.

Rolling my shoulders back, I allowed my eyes to shut gently one last time. Breathing in the air of forest, the battle ahead, and a hint of redemption, I exhaled out every worry I held, letting the weight lift from my bones. The memories settled around me in silent support. We had been forced out of our world, but we'd built a strong, loving, temporary home. We had lost our parents, but we were given a chance to avenge them, bringing honour back to their name and our kingdom.

We had resigned to the fact we would be stuck in the human realm for eternity, and then our world was turned upside down by an enchanting intruder who searched for their own freedom. Aurelia's vivid blue gaze and beaming smile flickered across my mind, savouring each memory I held with her. *For Aurelia.*

The Summer Kingdom wind whispered through my dark curls as I focused my attention on the path ahead. The birds had long abandoned their perches as if they knew what would come next. I had to hold onto the faith in my people.

With one hand clutching the reins and the other resting diligently on my sword, I silently instructed the steed to move forward. Xav and Fox joined me on either side. Silently, we marched toward a new dream. One where our kingdoms were free of tyranny, a new reign would begin, and a golden-haired woman would be by my side.

For us.

CHAPTER 40

AURELIA

The main cavalry, led by Mads, with Xavier and Fox at his side, shifted forward as my companions and I followed the sight for a few moments. Mads' lithe movements as he grabbed the reins showcased his composure, his eyes staying focused on the task ahead of them. The grace of his strong form entranced me, the way his shoulders filled out his uniform captivated me, while his words drifted through my mind on a loop.

I love you.

My fists clenched as he gracefully led the horse, his brothers, and the troops behind him. My heart filled with the pride it felt, seeing the man who had helped me discover so much of myself take his rightful place in this realm.

I did my best to ignore the coiling dread in my stomach as Kane urged us through the trees, pulling my focus away from the man who just confessed his love for me. I'd never known love like this. What I had with my siblings was strained and broken, something we were working on repairing. And with Mads? It felt as if it was still too early for these feelings. Then again, what did I know? The people surrounding me and those brothers, they were my family, and I would do everything in my power to keep them safe.

Was that love?

Our group remained quiet, conscious we could be ambushed at any time, as both Archer and Kane reminded us before we set off. Kane led the way, with Archer taking sentry at the rear. Bea had insisted she join our small rebel battalion to which no one argued, and I felt safer with the witch, and my friend, walking at my side.

I'd been armed with my dagger strapped in its sheath on the outside of my trousers, as well as two swords at my back. I had argued it was a bit much given my lack of ability with blades, but Fox had insisted. He'd even had two smaller swords crafted out of the lightest steel possible for me. Surprisingly, he had ordered for two to be constructed for Eva as well, who had tried to hide her astonishment when he silently handed them over to her. She was the only one in the group that hadn't had any specific training, but I felt safer knowing she was at least armed.

Bea refused anything other than a dagger, insisting she was armed heavily with various powders and potions which were, in her words, 'much more useful than a blade.' Archer had his bow while Kane had an entire armoury strapped to his body. I was thankful his allurant magic had subsided after spending so much more time in his presence. I still couldn't fully deny his allure though, enjoying the view as he stalked along in front of us.

The forest, in any other setting, would have soothed me, with its canopy of trees bringing me a familiar comfort. The surrounding air crowded us like an omen, leaving a putrid taste in my mouth with each step we took.

Our journey halted when we came to a small clearing. The trees and shrubbery surrounding us were eerily quiet, as though no breeze could filter through it. The variety of greenery mixed with the quiet would've brought a calming presence, but now, my nerves sat in my throat.

Silently, Kane pointed across the green towards a narrow opening, indicating what the map had shown us in regard to the tunnel's entrance. Deciding to avoid the expanse of unsheltered grass, Kane brought us around the outside of the field.

The building anxiety was difficult for me to ignore, the pace of my heart escalating with each breath I took. Sensing my panic, Bea reached out, giving my arm a gentle squeeze, reminding me I wasn't alone. Not here. Not anymore.

Kane gestured for me to join him once we met the entrance of the tunnel, very cleverly disguised by shrubbery. One wouldn't have known it was a tunnel unless standing directly at the mouth. "I'm going to move in first," Kane said in a hush, "and make sure it is clear. I'll signal for you to follow when ready."

We held our breath as Kane moved silently through the mouth of the cave. The darkness swallowed him for a few moments before he returned, indicating we could follow. My feet felt unsteady. Thankfully, the rest of the group crowded around me in unintentional support.

The omen filled air from the forest fluttered into the tunnel, pulling the little oxygen left in my lungs. Each step forward closer to an end, signifying another new beginning. I reminded myself of this as I followed closely on Kane's heels.

We continued along in the darkness, not wanting to attract any unwanted attention from torches, using our hands against the stone to guide our way through the damp cold tunnel. I didn't want to know what substances my hands touched as we moved forward.

What felt like hours later, Kane stopped abruptly, causing the rest of our party to run into the person in front of them. We strained our ears as Kane shuffled his hand across the wall to our right before he paused and said, "This is it. Aurelia, you're up."

I swallowed my apprehension and stepped forward. Kane took my hand and slowly raised it until it met a round metal handle. A door. Breathing deeply, my eyelids fell as my hand closed around it. A vivid image shot across my mind's eye, revealing a premonition that the door would open with my touch. Exhaling, I let my eyes drift open as my hand tightened on the handle. An audible click rumbled through the tunnel, each one of my companions let out their own breath of relief. I smiled inwardly, thanking my magic and becoming more connected to it each time I used it.

Using my shoulder and Kane's strength, we pushed the door open only to reveal another tunnel. This one was lit by small sconces adorning each side. We moved in, taking in the rough and ragged rock poking out towards us from either side. A small alcove wasn't far ahead, revealing a set of three different passages.

Archer filed into the small, circular room last. Just before any of us could voice the question of which passage we should take, a blunt object hit the back of my head, pulling me into darkness once more.

A group of drummers had somehow lodged themselves into the back of my head, pounding out their frustrations. I tried to pry my tongue off the roof of my mouth to berate the drummers, failing at both. Painfully prying my eyes apart, my vision adjusted.

Jagged stone walls, the same as the tunnel we'd come through, boxed me in, with a trickle of water leading down the one to my left. I sat on a wooden chair, my wrists cuffed behind me and another chair leaning against my own. The metal of the bindings dug into the skin on my wrists as I shifted. Twisting my neck, my peripheral showed Eva behind me. Her chin slumped toward her chest.

"Eva?" I whispered, not knowing if anyone was nearby.

Shifting my shoulders forward, I sprang back toward Eva, hoping it would rattle her awake. Nothing happened. Pushing myself as far forward as I could go, I kicked off of my feet, also shackled, before slamming into Eva's chair once more. Thankfully, that time was lucky as I felt my sister stir behind me. I gave her a few moments to compose herself before whispering her name once more.

"Aurelia? What happened? Where are we?"

I breathed a sigh of relief before shushing her. "I don't know. Are you cuffed?"

A clinking sound came from behind me, and she said, "Yes. If I didn't hate our parents before, I definitely hate them now."

Using my, very sore, body, I tried to shift my chair sideways. Eva looked over her shoulder for a minute before deciding to do the same. After a few tries, we settled on being somewhat side by side, at least able to see each other. "What happened to the others?"

I didn't know if we were all attacked at once or if it was more of a domino effect. "I'm assuming," Eva made a gesture of being hit in the head before closing her eyes and sticking out her tongue for dramatic effect.

Rolling my eyes, I did appreciate her attempt to bring lightness to our situation. "Helpful, Eva."

"Maybe not helpful, but true. Did you study any of those tunnel maps?"

I thought back to our time in the tent, I hadn't thought further than getting into the tunnel, a clear mistake on my part. I wasn't cut out for war or espionage, that was at least clear.

"Not enough."

"Well," Eva started as she took in our small, stone cell. "One good thing is we can get out of these restraints. I'm just not sure what our next move should be."

I thought of Eva's words for a few seconds, not immediately remembering my magic. Cursing myself for not thinking about it initially, I did my best to shift myself back toward Eva, close enough so I could wrap my hands around her cuffs.

"Wait!" Eva shouted in a whisper causing me to pause. "We don't want to get out of them yet. We don't have any way to defend ourselves if someone comes back."

I looked at my leg where I realised the dagger had been removed, as had our swords.

"Fuck."

"Fuck indeed." A voice came from our left, where we hadn't noticed a short doorway carved deep into the stone. A man of great height, given the length he had to crouch to get through, stood with his arms crossed, an intimidating smile plastered across his face. From his uniform, it was clear he was a royal guard, but the dishevelled beard and coordinating shoulder length hair gave the impression he wasn't prone to taking frequent baths. The room already stunk of decay and with this man's presence, the smell escalated, singeing my nose hairs and forcing me to breathe out of my mouth.

"What ample treasures we have found today." His voice dripped venom, causing a spike of fear to flash through me. His rotting teeth were on full display as soon as he opened his mouth, adding to the pungent disgust in the air.

"Now, can you ladies promise you'll be on your best behaviour, so I can lead you to your family reunion? Or do I need to beat some sense into you first?"

Eva spat at his feet, missing his boots, still having the desired effect as anger rose through his broad chest. Without a pause, he stepped forward to backhand her across the face, the smack echoing through the small chamber. As angry and scared as I was, I couldn't help but internally praise my sister for not giving him a reaction.

"None of that now, Princess." He hissed the last word before forcefully pulling her to her feet, doing the same to me seconds later.

I swayed on my feet, the residual knock of my head pushing me off balance.

"Let's go meet Mummy and Daddy. They can't wait to see you again." His accompanying sneer should have sent further fear through me. Thankfully, it didn't. I straightened my spine as best as I could, knowing I needed all the strength I had for whatever came next.

I kept with our captor's pace, doing my best not to fight him along the way, knowing it could only cause us further problems. Eva did the exact opposite from the other side of the man, kicking and screaming her way through the tunnels. I didn't agree with that approach but Eva was a firecracker, and I didn't want to dull her spark.

Our captor's frustration grew. A growl left his decaying mouth as he shoved Eva toward me with such force, the twist of her skin beneath his grip echoed through the hallway. I took the chance, gripping her hand briefly, giving it a squeeze in the hope Eva would take the hint. I only needed her to keep it together until I could get us out of the cuffs and find Archer to enact the bond, giving us a level of protection. Thankfully, Eva understood, calming her thrashing, slightly.

We were led through an intricate network of tunnels, up flights of stairs and down hallways increasingly becoming larger and lighter as our journey continued. The gradual openness should have provided me with a bit more breathing room. All it did was thicken the foreboding air with each step we took, and I struggled to breathe. I tried not to let the panic get the best of me. But without Archer, we were defenceless. Our last minute plan was already a shit storm.

I readied myself to attempt a breathing technique Bea had taught me, hoping I had enough time for it to have at least a little bit of a calming effect. We didn't have time. We were thrust into the palace itself. The stone enclosure was gone, replaced with an intricate stone floor, framed by walls covered in blood red. The hallway, littered with long, tall, thin tables, was decorated with sculptures and flowers alike. The ornate pieces were gaudy, screaming of the wealth that resided here. Of who resided here. I wondered briefly if the clay busts were portraying any of my ancestors, and if I wanted to learn more about them.

The colours filled my stomach with dread, knowing this was where we had come from. All of the hatred and desperation we felt had been valid. I tried to capture the images covering the walls as our captor sped up, practically dragging us both behind him.

The skin around my ankles began to chafe, the shackles tightening with each faltered step. Focusing on how we would, hopefully, be out of them soon, if not by my parent's command, then by my own magic, I continued forward. Once they fell away, I imagined what it would be like to throw the chunky bits of steel at the man in front of me, hopefully clocking him square in the skull. The image brought a subtle smile to my face. Maybe all I needed to do was to replace my panic by channelling Eva's anger.

We halted in front of a set of grand double doors. The twin arched entryway stood high in front of us, emanating a warning at what waited on the other side. I gulped down my fear as I stared at the tall wooden structures, unable to appreciate the intricate craftsmanship of the etched designs covering it. The man wasted no time signalling to the guards on either side, who obeyed immediately, stepping forward and taking the circular doorknockers and hauling them forward. The heavy set of doors opened in unison, letting through a blinding light. My eyes adjust to the onslaught of bright colours, revealing what I assumed to be the Aestas throne room. Focusing my sight on one specific part of the room was difficult as the brash and vulgar decor filling the space spun my vision into chaos.

Our feet must've moved us forward without us knowing given our captor grabbed Eva and I's arms in a bruising grip, halting us suddenly. In front of us, two ornate, golden thrones sat, side by side, the back of one lower than the other, both occupied by what I deduced to be our parents.

The queen, who occupied the smaller of the two thrones, sat confidently. She wore a gown of the faintest yellow, slightly off her shoulders. Her resemblance to Eva was uncanny, a fact I'm sure didn't sit well with my sister. Mahogany hair streaked with the softest blond hung in loose curls over her shoulders. Her eyes, a deep, haunting brown, were locked on me.

The king, an older version of Archer with his lean yet toned form, ash blonde hair and striking facial features, sat in contrast to the queen. One of his legs draped over the chair's arm with an air of boredom surrounding him. A beautifully gilded staff leaned against the throne, arm's length away from him. Dressed in regality, his coat hugged his form as if he was sewn into it. In any other situation, being worn by anyone else, I would have appreciated the tailoring of his clothing, but all I could think of was what they would look like as he burned within them.

The years didn't appear to have been kind to him, showcasing around his mouth and eyes of the deepest blue. Both monarchs wore extravagant golden crowns, displaying their power with the number of gems littered throughout.

Shifting my gaze to the side, a wave of relief washed through me to see Archer, Bea, and Kane. All of which were on their knees, bowing. Each of our companions wore the same shackles. To my right, the sound of Eva grinding her teeth met my ears as her anger pumped out so deeply I could almost taste it.

"Thank you, Retch. You can leave them with the others."

Retch? A name suited to the bastard. Retch tightened his grip on our upper arms, throwing us down behind the rest of the group, a crack echoing through the room as our knees hit the stone floor. I winced, trying to hide the pain radiating through my legs and my mind. I chanced a brief glance at Eva whose face was coated with determination as she stared down our birth parents. Her hair had fallen from the singular braid she had fastened earlier in the day, the wildness complimented the ferocity held in her sky blue eyes.

"Well, my dear, this has worked out even better than planned." The queen's cool tone addressed the king, never taking her eyes off me. Feigning boredom, he inspected his nails through his words.

"That indeed, my love."

The queen rose, gracefully walking toward Archer first, an air of arrogance in her posture filling the space with uncertainty, fuelling my anger more. She lifted her booted foot to his chin, raising it just enough for her to look down on him and him up at her. She tsked, "This would have been so much easier if that imbecile would have just murdered you like we ordered."

She dropped her foot, the skirts of her dress shuffling as she moved in Eva's direction. I bit my tongue. Patience was needed to fully assess how deep we were, and how in the hell we were going to get ourselves out of this. Stopping in front of Eva, she glared down at her youngest child in utter disgust, the age on her face highlighted by the downturn of her lips. No sign of remorse when she spoke, "You should have never been born."

To Eva's credit, she didn't take the bait. But by the way her jaw clenched slightly, I knew she wanted to. "And you." The queen's attention turned to me, "I understand you got exactly what you deserved all these years. Lord Shelton really does know how to play."

A faint smile grew on her face, accentuating her callousness, pulling her lines taught with an evil like quality. The evenness in her tone as she casually spoke about those torturous years under Shelton's wrath raised my heartbeat.

The woman had been a core part in the initial orchestration of the demise of our lives. The silence Eva was cursed to, resulting in stunted growth, being forced into a loneliness for so many years. The hardships Archer endured, alone. The lashings I took, over and over again, on my own. The carelessness in her words infused with the memories of what we faced churned through my mind as I watched her every move.

I pushed down the disgust, replacing it with rage. I knew, deep down, as that intuition pulsed to life in my gut, this woman was the decision maker between the two of our birth parents. I had to focus on getting us free and connecting with my siblings. If I could do that, we'd at least have a chance to protect our group.

"Did you ever wonder why?" The queen continued to address me directly.

I wanted to keep quiet. I did. The urge to engage was too strong. I wouldn't be able to free us if I kept my mouth shut. "Wonder what, *Mother?*"

The queen flinched on the word, hating to hear it as much as it felt like acid on my tongue.

"Why, dear *daughter,* you were abandoned. Left to die."

A chuckle fell from me without thought. "Given I didn't even know about you until a few weeks ago, I'd say no. I've never cared about you, never had to wonder why."

The queen rotated, the heel of her boot echoing throughout the room as she moved back toward Archer, unaffected by my words. "It's a shame, really, Shelton couldn't fully break you."

My eyes shifted around the room while she wasn't focused on me. Four guards were stationed around the room, confirming Mads' theory that the dear King and Queen's confidence in their own abilities meant they weren't heavily protected. Retch had left the throne room, thankfully, given he would be the heaviest muscle for what would come next.

"What is the actual shame," I said, shifting my glare back to the Queen, "is how long it took before I slit his throat."

The king let out a hearty laugh from where he still lounged on the throne, making me recoil from the sound. "She's got a bit of bite in her after all, my darling."

The queen stopped in front of Bea, her lip curling in disgust as she toed her with her boot, and a fire erupted in my chest at the sight. "I highly doubt it. She is still a mess, just not a dead mess. Yet."

My eyes narrowed and I cocked my head to the side, studying the immobile and compliant Bea. Even in shackles, I never would assume Bea to be so obedient. My gaze shifted to Kane, noticing his fingers moving ever so slowly. I did my best not to hold my eyes there for too long, not wanting to draw attention. It took a few moments before I realised he was pointing his finger back and then down, toward his boot. The end of a dagger peaked out from his left boot, and I forced my eyes down, catching Bea as she inclined her head, slightly.

They *hadn't* taken all of his weapons.

My eyes widened; I needed a distraction. Whatever Bea and Kane were silently communicating, we needed to buy some time. So, I continued.

"You seem to think I'm so easy to kill. Funny, given you've already failed at it once. Lord Shelton never even had the balls. Now, he's in a dungeon, his body decaying, waiting for the rodents to remove any proof of his existence."

It may have been a lie. I don't actually know if the bears had returned to dispose of the bodies. I also didn't give a shit.

"I'm really thirsty. Do you think you could at least give your children and their companions some water?" I asked, attempting to keep their attention on me.

The queen's face contorted, her lips pursing with surprise as she blinked rapidly at the request. Good. A small tilt of their axis was a win. The king gestured lazily to one of the guards who left the room speedily. I was surprised they agreed to the request. Shifting in his seat, the king draped his other leg over the arm of the chair, his hands resting on his stomach. He really had no concerns about us, wasn't threatened by our presence.

I had to keep them distracted. "It's interesting that your throne, *Mother,* is so much smaller than his."

The queen erupted in laughter, indicating my failure to play their power against each other. "Oh, dear daughter, do you think that will phase me? These thrones are a part of our history. The Queen of Aestas has used that throne," she pointed to her vacated seat, "for centuries."

I pondered my next push, knowing I needed to somehow get to Bea and Kane to at least unlock their cuffs. "It's also interesting you seem to care so much about tradition yet are more than willing for it to die with you."

The king huffed, "There is so much you don't know, *daughter.*" This time, he rose from his seat, the disgust for his children seeping into the room. "You were an abomination. All of you. No magic. No strength. What we did was a courtesy. You would have never survived here."

Interesting. They fully believed the three of us were inadequate and non-magical, even in a world where people of no magic thrive just as well as those with magic.

"And who advised you we were without magic?" Eva's silence broke, ready to join in the ring with me.

"Our witch, of course. She knew you would never amount to anything so the decision was easy. We rid Aestas of you, take Hiema, and grow our power through the extermination of you vile, magic*less* creatures."

Eva hiccupped a laugh. Our father's idiocy was entertaining, but we had to keep our heads straight. I shot a sideways glance to her, urging her to look at our companions as well. Archer had stayed silent, no doubt a part of his own plan. If I could get them all free...

"Fortunate for us that you returned, and we can finally right our wrongs and give you the deaths you should have had all those years ago."

The King added to our surprise. We may not know the two people who held us captive now, who had given us life, but not one part of me would have assumed they would admit to their failures.

I've known a lot of cruel and disgusting people in my life. Not one of them enjoyed being proved wrong. I had many markings on my body to prove that.

I kept my gaze down, appearing the attentive daughter, as I tried to watch the others out of the corner of my eye, strategizing. I didn't notice when the queen walked up to me, her boots now in my line of sight, her yellow skirts shifting in front of me, until she yanked my hair, bringing my eyes from the floor to the malicious smile on her mouth. When I met her gaze, my chest tightened. Her eyes were dead, as though the woman hadn't felt any emotion in years, focusing all of her energy on growing her power and control.

"He may not have been capable of your full demise, but I can see it written all over you. You're broken, girl," she said, her voice filled with ire as she released my hair.

The words missed their mark, flying past me and straight through the gigantic, closed doors behind me. So many had thought that of me over the years. Even I had resided in the fact that everything was taken, leaving only a shell of a woman in its wake.

Until, one day, not long ago, I stumbled upon a cabin, in a wood, where three brothers of magic showed me that I was never broken. I was caged. And even at the feet of the people who gave me life and discarded me with no thoughts or remorse, I was free.

As I honed in on the clacking of boots notifying us that the guard had returned, she moved in front of Archer, arms held confidently at her sides as her terrorising gaze focused on her eldest child. The small action sent a shiver down my spine. As the sound of boots came closer, my gaze shifted as the guard held a tray full of water glasses in his hand.

"Oh, but didn't you know, *Mother*, I was never broken," I snarled. *My timing had to be right.*

She tilted her head toward me as confusion subtly spread across her face. The guard lifted a glass to my lips, and I took the opportunity. Leaning back to accept the cool liquid, I used the cover to grab my ankle restraints. I thought hard about unlocking them, my mind following my magic. Channelling my training sessions with Fox, I planted my arse down, simultaneously shifting my legs in front of me, sweeping my feet through the guard's ankles. He collapsed, the tray of water flying into the air as chaos erupted.

Chapter 41

Maddox

"What the fuck?" Fox gasped in disbelief at the sight in front of us. Our intel had said there would be a number of forces stationed at the front of the castle, both in plain sight and camouflaged. We knew many of their guards had retreated, but nothing had indicated the grounds to the front of Avilore Keep would be completely abandoned.

We'd been prepared, all our forces awaiting our signal. And now that we were here, we stared out toward the castle, which now lay directly in front of us. What we found was nothing. There were no soldiers. Hell, there weren't even the usual palace guards stationed around the front. My mind raced.

The intel was wrong.

Someone wanted us to get to the castle with ease.

It was a set up.

Aurelia.

"What is going on, Maddox?" Fox's concern came from behind me.

"I don't know, brother. But whatever it is, we have to get inside, and fast."

Without a response, Fox turned to the units accompanying us and began shouting orders. To my left, one of the soldiers on horseback took off toward the west, no doubt to deliver the message to our forces there. I turned to Xav and said, "Get a message to Everett and the Knights. They need to hold back."

I swallowed down the fear, coating my throat as I spoke my next words, "And Xav?"

I stared deep into my brother's brown eyes, conveying more with my gaze than with my words. "Tell them to be ready for the worst."

Xav's brows lowered a sliver before he nodded once, moving to find a messenger.

Whatever was about to happen, it had been planned, and Aurelia was the bait. I would get her and the rest of the group out of there or die trying. I may be the rightful King of Hiema, but I would be nothing without my queen.

Boots lined up beside mine as Fox took his place once more, followed by Xav a few moments later. "What are your orders, my king?" The depth of sincerity in Fox's voice filled my heart with pride.

I shot him a brief look before turning back to the front of the castle. The air was stale, as if it were an omen of what we would face. I squared my shoulders, lifting my chin high. "Now, we fight."

Taking my first step forward, I wrapped my hand around the hilt of my sword as the sound of battalions behind me followed suit.

"To redemption, or death."

In voices almost at a whisper, my brothers repeated, "To redemption, or death."

Chapter 42

Aurelia

Time was not on our side, knowing I only had a few seconds to act, I devoured them. Jumping to my feet, I launched forward, grasping Kane's wrist, unlocking his cuffs before moving toward his ankles. Without paying attention to the commotion around us, I slid across the floor to Bea. "Just my hands."

I obeyed, freeing her hands before removing my own, one by one. I then pivoted to Archer. I placed every ounce of trust I could muster into Kane who I saw in my peripheral vision, moving swiftly toward the king and queen.

"Go!" Archer shouted at me as the cuffs clanked to the floor.

With unsteady movements, I rolled backwards to come face to face with Eva, a victorious smile spreading across my sister's face. "We haven't won yet, Eva!"

"No, sister. But we will."

With Eva free, I stood to watch the various scenes unfold in front of me. Archer had backed our parents up toward the thrones, the king with his staff in his hand, ready to inflict pain on my brother.

The queen moved to huddle behind him, not wanting to use her own power due to the decay it caused to her body, her deep wrinkles proving she overexerted often.

Kane had two of the three guards engaged in hand to hand combat. The fourth, who had brought the water, was unconscious on the floor. Not sure what happened there, I turned to Bea. She had, somehow, freed her ankles and stood tall.

With a wink in my direction, Bea tossed a small vial into the air, dancing her fingers around it as she chanted a spell into the ether. The vial shattered, sending a faint powder substance toward the royals. Their eyes rolled into the back of their heads before they dropped to the floor like lead, just as Kane delivered the final blow to the last guard who fell atop the other two.

We looked around, stunned that in mere minutes we had changed our own fate. "It can't be this easy." Archer spoke aloud, a nervous chuckle rumbling behind his words.

"Oh, you fools. It's not." A voice rose all around us, filling the chamber with cold dread. "You think it was those idiots who sent you away and took Hiema?"

The voice laced with poison sent a chill up my spine.

"I can admit, they are fabulous puppets. They aren't, however, strategists with a thirst for power."

At the last word, a woman stepped silently out from behind the throne. At first glance, she appeared young, in her early thirties. It was her eyes which told me otherwise. Within them sat her true age, framed by one black orb and one blue.

A blatant fear struck me as I studied her tall form. Her movements, more serpent like than human, forced the hairs on my arms to stand at attention. The woman was powerful in such a way that my mind and body wanted to do nothing more than get me very far away from the throne room, to never be in her presence again.

A hollowed sensation formed in my chest as the realisation struck me, the king and queen weren't the enemies we were convinced of.

"Fuck," Kane muttered, albeit louder than he imagined.

The woman, bathed in darkness, shrouded in the blackest of silks, raised her mismatched eyes to Kane, a viper's grin spreading across her face. "Such a foul mouth for such a beautiful allurant. Let's change that."

The woman raised her hand, squeezing the air in front of her. Kane grabbed his throat, a bellow of agony leaving his breath before a bloodied tongue — his bloodied tongue — flew out of his mouth toward the woman. She appeared bored as she waited for the tongue to stop in front of her before dropping it to the ground with a small thud.

Bile rose in my throat as the world slowed, and Kane fell to his knees, clawing at his mouth, the most horrific moans flying from the back of his throat. Eva made to move towards him, the woman stopped her. "Uh ah. you stay there, girl. Unless you want me to remove a part of you as well."

Eva froze, the anger still pulsating from her body deepened by the sight of Kane losing his tongue.

"Good girl." Condescension laced the woman's praise.

"What I believe our allurant friend was trying to say, although rather horrifically, was I am the one you should fear." She kicked the king's boot as she slithered, yes, slithered, by him. "Not these useless puppets."

Archer turned as she passed him, his eyebrows moving to his hairline. "You're the witch. The one who told them we didn't have magic."

The woman — witch stopped in front of him, tapping his nose three times with her long, black fingernail. "You're quick. And yes, I am —"

"Lamina," Bea breathed out heavily. Her panic apparent; her eyes wide as she busied her hands with the vial she'd held. I was further unnerved having never seen Bea in such a state.

"Ah yes. A fellow witch. I will have great use for you."

My eyes caught Archer just as he shot his hands out, trying to quickly blast the witch with his water magic, hopefully incapacitating her to buy us time. Without a misstep, she reached her hand out, twisting violently as the crack in Archer's arms rang through the air. I felt his screams echo through my bones, twisting my stomach, and raising the hairs all over my body. Instinctively, I pivoted towards him, stopped by an unknown force. "Same for you, girl. Move and you'll meet the same fate."

Absolute horror filled every inch of my body as Archer squirmed on the ground, his arms appearing boneless, and with each thrust of his body, edges of bones began to peek through his skin. "Archer —"

"Stop! Now!" Lamina's voice froze the room, the tear forcing its way down my cheek. My heartbeat, the only movement from me, fracturing at my brother's broken body in front of me.

"Now, you will all do well to obey me." The darkness in her words reverberated through the throne room.

After a few bated breaths, the freeze gradually eased up, letting the tear resume its trek down my cheek.

"I think it is time for a little story, don't you?" The woman's voice tilted with a taunt.

My mind didn't want to move focus from Archer and Kane, writhing in agony on the cold, stone floor.

I brought my attention back to Lamina, her words reminding me of the fictional villains I had read so many times before. Why did villains always need a monologue? This wasn't fiction though, and we were caught in the trap of a real, powerful witch. One whose sole attempt was to ruin us all, taking Raithe for her own. *The game, Aurelia.* I reminded myself. I needed to play if we had any chance of winning. I nodded my agreement, even if Lamina wasn't paying me much attention directly.

The witch continued to slither around to our remaining group, stopping occasionally to let her gaze linger on Eva or Bea, leaving me invisible for the most part. "When I was much younger, I knew I was due more power than a common kingdom witch would've ever been granted. The constraints of the Raithean structure would never allow such a thing. It was unheard of for a witch to rule any of the Kingdoms, let alone Raithe itself. But I wanted it," she paused, her raven coloured locks drifting lazily behind her as she settled in front of Bea. "You know, in the beginning, witches were equals, not servants. That's what Raithe needed, to go back. Back to much simpler times when the non-magical didn't exist here. The ancestors of the king's and queen's destroyed the true Raithe when they created the portals to the human realm."

Not familiar with the dawn of the seasonal kingdoms, I focused on her tale.

"Since I knew segregation would never be demolished by simple conversation with the pathetic rulers of Raithe, I had to create my own plan. It was simple," she paused, cocking her head to the side. Her eyes, unnerving with the unnatural life they held. "But it required something most do not have."

The silence of the room broke by the faint sobs leaving Archer's broken body. The witch's contrasting eyes didn't miss a thing. It would be difficult, almost impossible, to distract her.

"Patience," she said, turning to me. "My plan required patience. A lot of it. After my initial schooling, I had the opportunity to apply to one of the Kingdoms as an understudy. I knew I needed a Kingdom with leaders I could bend, influence. It wasn't difficult to choose Aestas. Those two," she said, indicating behind her with her disfigured thumb, "are two of the most egotistical people I have ever met. I knew it would work in my favour eventually. And so, I stood by, dutifully, as they married, ruled, and spawned the three of you. I, of course, had to get rid of the original witch, otherwise I would have never been in the position to whisper sweet nothings of the greater good into their ears."

I glanced at Eva, finding her attention fully trained on Lamina's story. The fury had not abated. Eva's outrage filled the space between us thickly, as though I could grasp it. The intuition roared to life with such force that my hands flew to clutch my stomach.

"When the youngest came along," she turned to Eva, "that's you, dear. I persuaded Carman and Jolon to run a few exploration spells on you, enabling them to understand your magic and just how powerful you may be. You can only imagine their disappointment when the findings showed none of you held any magic, nor would you."

Tsking, she patted Eva's shoulder. She held her tongue, trying her best not to relay a response, verbal or physical. "It was such a pity, knowing they created not one, not two, but three failures."

"And so, I assisted them in organising your demise. It was easy to convince them they were better without you once they knew you were useless. The one flaw in my plan was neither of them agreed to my recommendation, instead hiring someone they believed would complete the job for them."

I shot a quick glance at Archer, focusing on the rise and fall of his chest, accepting that was as much as I could do for him right now.

"And Hiema?" I needed her story to move faster, deciding to finally interrupt. Plus I was curious as to why she targeted the Winter Kingdom first.

"See, patience is not for everyone." Lamina let off a chilling smile as she addressed me directly.

"Once I found out the assassin failed at his task, choosing greed instead, I had him put down like the dog he was. I, then, had a little visit to Lord Shelton and your adoptive parents before the portals sealed for good."

My stomach dropped at the mention of Shelton. She knew him? The visions of how we came to be in the human realm had confirmed the connections, I just hadn't realised it was her pulling the strings. The last pieces of the puzzle were finally falling into place.

I shook off the thought, needing to focus on what came next. "They agreed to contain the three of you, if ever you were to show signs of magic. It looks like," she said, her mismatched eyes boring into me with determination, "you were the one who needed more of a rough hand. Lord Shelton was willing to beat the magic out of you if need be, and I was more than happy to provide him with that guidance."

Lamina paused, raising one of her eyebrows in thought before delivering her question, "Whatever happened to dear Lord Shelton?"

Eva took one, small step forward, pushing her chest out in pride. "She murdered him."

Lamina's lips parted in shock and her eyes narrowed on me, setting my blood on fire. If I wasn't angry before, I definitely was now. I could recognise it growing in Eva too. *Good.*

"Maybe you won't be so useless. Blood tastes good, doesn't it?" The question was rhetorical and even if it wasn't, no way in hell was I going to give her an answer.

Resuming her glide around the three of us, her voice deepened an octave as she spoke, "Hiema was an easy first choice for takeover. Barrett and Ariana were always too soft, doting on their children, treating their people as equals. It was going to be their downfall eventually, I just planted the appropriate seeds to make it grow faster.

"I must say, Orsa has been a delight to control as well. Bending her to my will is one of my finest accomplishments."

If the bears were here, they'd find any possible way to rip this woman's head off of her neck. I enjoyed the visual momentarily before I glanced over to Kane, ensuring he was still breathing. I felt a twinge of gratitude at the sight before turning my attention back to Lamina.

"So, we seem to have interceded your plans." I did my utmost to keep my voice steady but the constant chill running across my flesh forced my teeth to chatter slightly.

"On the contrary," Lamina said as she twisted, "you being here now is most opportune. Now that you've managed to find a way back, brought along those bastard Artos brothers, and helped rid me of this dead weight" — she gestured to the unconscious forms of Carman and Jolon behind her — "I can finally rid Raithe of you, your vile siblings and any claim to the Hiema throne as well, giving Raithe what it's always needed — one ruler of all."

"If anything," she said as she stepped closer, twisting a lock of my hair between her fingers, "you've brought the solution straight to me."

I scoffed, "Your *curse* clearly had some flaws, given you didn't anticipate my potential abilities."

Lamina's eyes bore into me, hard enough for me to catch the fire burning through them. "Keys are very rare, child. I knew when I placed that curse there was a likelihood of someone breaking and the Artos brothers may return. It just makes this next part so much more...enjoyable."

The chill that gradually built across my spine sparked at the promise in her words. She wasn't just going to kill us, she was going to annihilate every royal force that stood in her way.

She moved toward Archer, sending a swift kick to his right arm, eliciting a shrill cry, crippling him even further. I stopped breathing as the wail left his lips. With Lamina's attention on Archer, I took the opportunity to move my gaze to Bea. The panic still sat across her face. Noticing my gaze on her, Bea met my stare as I gave a curt nod towards Eva, hoping she would understand my plea.

"Now, we will just wait for the dear Winter princes and then we can get the party started."

Bea coughed, bringing Lamina's attention towards her. Thankfully, it worked, Lamina moved subtly towards Bea, studying her every move. Taking minuscule and measured movements, I kept my gaze on Lamina's back as I shifted closer to Eva. I willed my sister to let the anger continue to flow through her.

"You are an interesting witch aren't you. You're not from Raithe. What is your name?"

I paused at Lamina's clear interest in Bea, her tone sitting odd in her throat. Lifting her chin, Bea stared her directly in the eye as she responded, "The name is Beatrix Bluegrass, remember that when I slit your throat."

On the last word, Bea unclasped her hands from behind her back, sending multiple vials into the air, all popping one after another as she shouted invocations from the top of her lungs. I stepped up to Eva, grasping the sides of her head in my hands. "Aurelia, what are you —"

I shushed her, bringing our foreheads together. Finding my magic, almost immediately, I asked it how I could unlock Eva's power. The magic wasn't who I was, but more a part of me, and I needed to work with it. The realisation had hit me the moment I'd clutched Eva's face in my palms.

Slowly, too slowly, an image arrived in my mind clouded in the deepest reds, shadows and smoke, through it I made out the lock — rusted and decrepit with time. I lunged towards it, reaching out with my mind's eye to grasp it beneath my fingers, pulling with everything I had to pry it open. The colours burned against my skin, not uncomfortably, but enough for me to realise whatever I'd done had worked. I cursed at the door, pushing every ounce of mental strength I had toward it. Just when I felt a scream of frustration build in my throat, the door blew open, pulling me through it. My eyes snapped open to find my hands still on the side of Eva's face. Her eyes wide, her voice cracking as she stared at me. "What's happening to me?!"

I let go just as a blast of magic threw us both backwards. I landed on the stone floor with a bang, my body protesting the impact immediately. It took me a second to realise the noise didn't come from my landing, it came from behind me. The large double doors opened, revealing a large group of people, at the front, in all their battle livery, stood Mads, Xav, and Fox.

I held a shred of relief in seeing them unharmed before the panic rose, knowing they were playing into Lamina's hands exactly as she planned.

"No!" I shouted, ignoring the pain shooting down my legs. I turned my attention back to the fight between Bea and Lamina. Bea lifted her hands to perform another incantation, and before she could finish, she was silenced as Lamina grabbed her by the throat, lifting her feet off the floor, launching her toward the other side of the room. Bea's body hit the wall, letting out a crack that reverberated through my bones. Bea slid down the wall, unconscious.

The sight of my friend, Kane, and my brother, broken did nothing but fan the flames of the anger filling me, fuelling me.

Lamina turned toward the front doors, a wicked smile grew on her face. "Well. This is sooner than expected. But I'm not complaining."

Pushing myself to my knees, a flash of midnight blue moved from the corner of my eye. Eva. My baby sister launched herself at the witch. Composed, Lamina reached out, grabbing Eva by the arm, turning her so her back was parallel to the witch's front. Raising her other arm, she settled a dagger just below Eva's chin.

"Stop!"

Fox stepped forward, fury clearly written across his face as his chest heaved in anticipation. A slight surprise fell over me to hear the cry from the youngest brother.

Lamina didn't even twitch. "Oh, the youngest Artos. My, my you have grown up haven't you."

The way her words insinuated something else pushed the bile further up my throat.

Pointing directly at Lamina, a promise in a gesture, Fox addressed the witch, his voice steady. "You touch one hair on her head and I'll rip your throat out."

Lamina chuckled, digging the dagger in deeper. The room followed the drop of Eva's blood as it trailed down her throat.

"Is that a threat, little wolf."

Fox smiled, one that would have anyone on their knees in fear. He let it stretch across his face. "No. It's a fucking promise."

I expected Eva's face to transform into pure terror; instead, a calm came over her, filling the room with a wary aura. Before I could question it further, Eva's eyes found mine. Something had changed. The instinct that had settled in me flared with the hint of — something. The tips of my fingers began to tingle, the same sensation I'd felt when we'd tested the shield. *Magic.*

Eva's lip tilted into a half smile before she mouthed the words, *cover your ears.* A fresh drop of blood fell from where the knife met her flesh. My eyes searched Eva's, trying to understand what was about to happen. Noticing my hesitation, Eva shouted, "Now!" injuring herself further as the knife dug in deeper.

Without another delayed thought, I launched my body to Archer, dragging his mangled body a few feet to where Kane lay. I screamed to the room, "Cover your ears!" I shot a brief glance toward the bears to establish they heard.

"Xav! Bea!"

Wasting no time to question the request, Xav ran toward Bea's unconscious form, dropping to his knees and pulling her to his body. One of her ears against his chest while he manoeuvred his other arm around her exposed ear and finally cupped his own.

Fox continued his verbal sparring with Lamina, giving us those much needed extra minutes to situate ourselves for what was to come.

I was grateful when the entire party that had entered wasted no time in covering their ears with their hands before following my own orders. Dropping to my knees, the adrenaline assisted me in shifting Archer and Kane's bodies into my own, making sure their heads were nestled into various body parts between the three of us right before I locked my hands over my own ears. Looking up, the sudden force radiating through the room knocked every single standing person to their knees.

With the little strength I had left, I pushed past the forcefield, raising my chin to find my sister. What I saw made my jaw drop, not an easy feat given the strength of the energy pushing me back. I couldn't worry about the unconscious parties in the room as I stared in absolute shock toward the scene in front of me.

Eva now stood over Lamina, her mouth open as she emanated the fury she'd kept locked inside herself for so long. It worked. I'd unlocked Eva's magic. And that magic was pure, unfiltered rage. The same rage currently forced into the witch. I couldn't look away. Hatred morphed from emotion to physical violence, pushing Lamina further to the ground. Eva continued to scream as the radiation she produced melted away the woman in front of us, like wax of a candle.

On her knees with her hands in the air as though some attempt to stop the forcefield emitting from Eva's mouth, her fingers were the first to disintegrate, followed by her wrists. Her flowing, black sleeves were no match for Eva's power as they too fell victim to the force. The most fascinating part of the witch's physical demise was her face. Her chin dripped like hot wax, falling to the floor at Eva's feet, morphing her smile into a horrific frown before reaching her nose. Her eyes seemed to glow red before shrivelling up and pouring down what was left of her chin.

The scream didn't end. Eva pushed and pushed as much as her magic let her, every morsel of anger she had felt over the years fleeing from her. It all made sense now. The spell had not only silenced Eva physically, it had also silenced her magic. Since the spell had broken, fragments of her fire had slipped through, showing the world a side of Eva I was convinced was new. Except it wasn't. This was the real Eva, all along. She was currently dispelling years of pent up ferocity into the witch now physically melting in front of us. It was both gruesome and beautiful.

Out of the corner of my eye, I tracked movement. Turning my head against the force as best as I could, conscious of not moving Kane or Archer from their snug positions against me, I saw Fox moving against what looked like an incredible windstorm, his hands covering his ears as he made his way towards Eva. Every step he took toward my sister was met with such an astonishing force, I couldn't understand how he moved through it.

The journey was slow, but as he reached Eva, his hands left his ears, pushing past Eva's shield, a look of pain wrapped in terror spread across his face as his arms wrapped around her chest. On contact, the pressure in the room stopped, the noise fading as Eva collapsed into Fox's arms having riddled herself unconscious.

The energy dissipated instantly, pushing me to my feet to rush to Fox and Eva. "She's okay," he promised, as he gazed at her with a look I couldn't decipher. "She just drained herself, depleted her magic."

I nodded, the sounds coming in various, odd intervals. I lifted Eva's legs into Fox's hold as he found his way to the floor, rocking Eva's body against his own, whispering soothing words into her hair.

The magnitude of the last hour hit me with full force. Uncertain of where to start, I conceded at rushing towards Bea, ignoring Xav's presence beside her. I batted his outstretched hand away as I focused on my friend. The witch, still unconscious, was breathing, thankfully. "Over here!"

I wasn't shouting at anyone in particular, just hoping our new company had brought healers with them. We were going to need them all. After a few seconds, a hand landed softly on my shoulder. "She's okay," Xav soothed. "We'll get her healed."

The panic I'd hidden in the deepest depths began to surface. I needed to move. I couldn't let my body settle, otherwise the anxiety would consume me. I left Xav to care for Bea, rushing to where Archer and Kane lay. The tear stained cheeks of Kane broke my heart, coupled with my brother's actual broken body, I felt nauseous.

"Aurelia."

I ignored the voice, instead choosing to move to where Kane's tongue lay. Not allowing the panic to get me, I reached down to rip a small piece of fabric from my shirt, carefully picking up the appendage, and scanning the room for a healer.

What did a healer even look like?

"Aurelia."

The voice followed me with each step. I refused to listen. The room was in chaos. Too many injuries. We had to fix them. Kneeling down next to my brother, I checked his pulse, his eyes were open but his vision kept losing focus with each stunted breath. His arms were definitely broken, they needed to be set. I brushed his golden curls from his face, unable to give him any words of comfort as the panic took me in its grasp.

"Aurelia! Look at me!"

No, I needed help. They needed help. I shouted to the room, "We need more healers! Over here!"

Tunnel vision kept me from focusing on more than one person at a time. Why didn't I know any of the healers?

"Please! Help!"

"Goldie!"

I squeezed my eyes shut. We'd won, why had the panic, the memories, all of those ill-fated moments in my life need to resurface now? Strong, able hands wrapped around my upper arms, rotating me on my feet. The tears escaped my closed lids. "Open your eyes, gorgeous."

The voice. I didn't ignore it this time. It was home. Breathing deep through my nose, I caught the faint scent of an aged cedar tree letting it soothe my bruised body. A sliver of understanding passed through me, pressing down the panic. Letting my eyes drift open, I stared into those intense depths of dancing autumn — the swirls of greens and golds calling me home. Emotions came crashing through me from all angles, not slowing my moment of reprieve. The tears escaped faster, the sobs wrapping around me. Mads pulled me into his chest, smoothing my hair down as he whispered, "I'm here. We're safe. We're okay, Aurelia."

Just as he had so many times before, when I could no longer hold myself up, he reached out, picking me up as I fell.

CHAPTER 43

AURELIA

The bright sunlight danced across my face, stirring me from a dreamless sleep. My body groaned with each miniscule movement, bringing my thoughts back to the throne room. My eyes shot open as I flung myself into a sitting position, ignoring my surroundings.

"Fuck, buttercup. You scared the shit out of me."

Looking to my left, I found Bea sprawled next to me on the bed, a large book lay in her lap. "Bea?"

Throat dry, her name was a challenge to get out, the emotion rising fast. The last I remembered… I didn't know if I would see my friend alive again.

"'Tis I, buttercup! You will never be rid of me so easily." She shot me a wink before turning the page of the volume in front of her.

Ignoring my body's protests, I flung my arms around Bea's neck, squeezing with the little energy I had. Bea let out an 'ooph' on impact.

"I'm so glad you're ok," I whispered into her dark curls.

I felt Bea set down her book before she reciprocated, wrapping me in a tight embrace. "We all are. Even Kane's got his tongue back in his mouth. Good thing too as I'm sure it would have made a lot of people upset if he lost such a useful appendage."

I chucked against her, relishing the fact my friend was alive and in my arms. My friend. My family. Pulling back, I took in Bea's face, inspecting it for any physical reminders of our encounter with Lamina.

Bea read the question written on my face. "She's dead. Eva basically melted her face off. I'm so mad I missed it."

The memory of Eva's face between my palms as the images swirled through my mind flew in. Helping my sister unlock her magic, watching her become everything she was forced to mask for so long, was like watching someone grow back a lost limb.

"Where is she?" I surveyed the room. The floral embroidered drapes hung heavy, coordinating with the maroon walls and mahogany panelling covering the bottom half. The bed Bea and I laid in was large, hugged by side tables on either side. The room itself wasn't particularly large, and if we were still in Avilore Keep, I was surprised by the comforting aura filling the space. "And Archer?"

Bea patted my shoulders, indicating the need for calm. "Your sister is resting. As is Archer. The healers had their work cut out for them when they set his bones back. They've assured us he'll make a full recovery, it'll just take some time."

A weight lifted from my chest, one I hadn't realised had burrowed itself so deep. Replacing it was a light, unfamiliar, yet kind emotion. "What about the king and queen?"

"Those two have been stripped of their magic, resting not so easily in the dungeon. Although, not the dingy room as I had suggested."

Turning my attention back to the room we found ourselves in, a faint familiarity passed over me. "And the other three?"

"Mads, the fool, was in here all night with you. He is officially King now, which I had to remind him of multiple times. I sent him to do kingly stuff. The other arseholes by his side."

I couldn't stop the smile from spreading across my face. They'd done it. We'd done it.

Leaning back, I thought through the events in the throne room with one individual haunting my thoughts. "Bea, who exactly was Lamina?"

I remembered Bea knowing her name, somehow, even across the realms, the woman was known.

Bea folded her hands on her lap, sighing in agitation. "As much as I hate to say it, she was a witch of great talent. Even I learned about her in the human realm, from my mother and grandmother. Lamina was highly skilled at witchcraft. More so than that, she kept to the shadows, never bringing too much attention to herself, instead using her 'puppets' as she liked to call them."

Of all the evil I'd faced in my life, nothing had prepared me for the face-off with Lamina. Knowing she orchestrated everything pushed the need to bring her back to life just so I could slit her throat. I smiled again. The second best option was for Eva to burn her face off.

"And she's really dead?"

Bea's eyes softened, noticing my internal battle. "She's really dead."

"And we really won?"

Leaning forward, the side of Bea's mouth kicked up. "We really won, buttercup."

I launched at her again, this time letting our bodies roll across the gigantic bed, both of us falling into a fit of giggles. I allowed myself those few moments of peace, the panic sitting idly, deep down as I held her in my arms, cherishing her closeness. I wanted to see Mads and the bears. I wanted to see for myself that Archer and Eva were okay. For once, though, I just let myself be, in Bea's arms, in a fit of laughter.

Bea righted us a few moments later, bringing me back to reality. "Right. We've got a meeting to get ready for."

"What?" I'd only just woken up from my panic and exhaustion induced fit.

"It's all go now, buttercup. You can rest later. The princess is arriving today."

I let my heart fill with joy, knowing I would be able to watch the bears reunite with Orsa. The selfish side of me was excited to add another member to our growing family, a concept I would've never thought possible a few months ago.

"Bea, are we still at Avilore Keep?" I threaded my fingers through the blanket covering me, not due to anxiety, but comfort.

Bea confirmed that we were still in the Aestas palace, supporting each other as we bathed and dressed, ready to greet the new day and the rightful leaders. Queen Kendra and Queen Colette would also be arriving, along with the Autumn King as an act of solidarity to mark the new era of Raithe.

First, to prepare us, we were ushered into a small sitting room where Eva and Archer awaited us. I searched them both for visible injuries, noting the dark circles beneath Eva's eyes before I moved toward her, pulling her in for an overly sensitive embrace. "I'm so proud of you," I whispered into her hair before we both moved to envelop Archer in a similar, albeit, gentler, hug. The cast on his arm concerned me, but other than that, there weren't any visible signs of his injuries. He assured us, multiple times, he was heeling well thanks to the healer's magic.

The party grew, first with Kane who was pestered with concern from Eva, Bea, and me. He gave us all an awkward pat on the back, ensuring us he was fine by clicking his tongue.

Fox and Xav arrived next. Eva paid Fox's presence no attention as he kept his distance from her following their intimate moment the day before. He pecked my cheek before whispering his sincere happiness that I was unharmed.

Once Fox found his seat, I turned to find Xavier standing in front of me. Without a word, we fell into each other's embrace, letting our actions do all the talking. I threw everything I couldn't yet voice into that embrace, soaking in his woodsy aroma as it wrapped around us both in comfort.

A throat cleared behind us, forcing Xav to the side, revealing Mads in all his kingly glory. He stood confidently, clothed in the regal deep, vivid blue of Hiema. The colour accentuated his dark curls and highlighted the hazel flecks in his eyes. The King of the Winter Kingdom. My Maddox. A slight smile tipped the corner of his lips before he stepped toward me, raising his hand to my cheek, unspoken emotion glistening across his eyes flecked with greens, golds, and browns. I swallowed down the tears. "You didn't die."

A laugh escaped his throat, deep and meaningful. It consumed me. Leaning down, he whispered against my lips, "I guess I'm safe from your wrath."

Quirking my brow, I let an unassuming smile paint my face. "For the time being."

He placed his finger below my chin and tilted my face up, and I cherished his strong hands on me once more. He lightly brushed his lips against mine, pouring every emotion of the last twenty four hours into the most subtle of touches. I sunk into it, disregarding our company, happy to get lost in his lips for eternity, whether grumpy, sad, mad, happy. I didn't care. This was my home.

"Alright, lovebirds. Enough of that. We have important shit to sort out."

Fox brought us back to the room, somewhat. I would happily stay lost in Mads for the rest of the day. I had to remind myself there would be plenty alone time in our future.

"Are we waiting for Vernum and Havon?" Kane's voice was just as sultry as before his tongue was removed. If anything, the reattachment worked too well. I side eyed Bea, catching her with her mouth open.

"No, we'd already agreed to speak to you all first." Xav gestured for us all to take a seat. I took the couch, a beautifully upholstered piece, swirling with stitched peonies of varying muted tones. Too bad it felt tainted with the memory of my birth parents. Eva took my right side while Mads took my left, both taking one of my hands in their own, sending a pang of warmth through my chest.

"First, I want to start by saying, we are all here together. The highest victory on the list."

"Stop it, Xav. This is a serious, political meeting where important matters need to be decided. You can spread your fluff later."

Xav laughed at Fox, knowing all too well his baby brother didn't want the waterworks.

"Fine, baby brother. We will cuddle later." Xav sent Fox a wink, pushing his clear ire higher.

"First things first. How do you want to deal with the Manus duo."

Manus. I had heard our birth name in hushed conversations throughout the planning process, but it was that moment where I recognised it, not as one I was attached to but rather one that never had and never would mean anything to me.

The group turned their attention to Eva, Archer, and I. I hadn't realised this would be our decision given it wasn't something we had actually discussed. Without a word, Eva and I turned to Archer for guidance. He had lived in Raithe the longest, with more of a connection to what our birth parents had done. He was also the rightful leader now that they were removed from their positions.

"They deserve a trial. We should do it the Raithean way."

I nodded in agreement. The judicial system here was another mystery. I was happy to agree to his proposal but noticed Eva shifted uneasily beside me. Her voice filled the room with three haunting words, "They should hang."

The room fell silent momentarily, Fox's attention on my sister. "Didn't realise you were so bloodthirsty, Princess."

Eva shot Fox a glare which would have ruined a normal man. Fox, however, wasn't afraid of Eva. Even with her new found magic, he wasn't shying away from her, a conclusion I found both comforting and terrifying.

"They may end up that way, Eva, but they deserve a fair trial," Archer countered.

Eva scoffed before agreeing with a stiff nod. She wouldn't go against Archer, I knew that. I also knew the repressed part of her also needed to have her voice heard.

"It's settled then. Do any of you want to...speak with them?" Xav approached the question with caution. Smart.

"No." All three of us bit out in unison. We had nothing left to say to the people who brought us into the world. As far as we were concerned, that was all they were.

"Well, if you change your mind, the offer is there."

Xav looked down at his stack of papers, the agenda clearly sitting on top. "Next item is the ruling of the Aestas. We all have an opinion on this topic, and we've discussed this previously, but now is the time to make a decision."

Gesturing toward my siblings and I, his voice cut strongly across the room. "Ultimately, it is up to the three of you."

I turned to my siblings, intending to discuss the matter but was immediately interrupted by Eva, "Archer. There's no question."

Nodding in agreement, I knew in my heart the throne belonged to Archer. Not just because he held the sovereign water magic in his veins. Archer was a leader, whether he wanted to admit it or not. The Summer Kingdom needed his guidance and gentle hand. The rebuilding of Aestas would be a long road ahead and the people would need someone they could trust. The question was, did he want to rule?

"If that's what you want, Archer?" I voiced, needing him to know the choice was also his.

He studied Eva and I, tears glistening in his eyes. We'd not known him in this life for long, yet none of us could deny our new bond was strong, neither of us doubted it was a job he would excel at. Summer belonged to him.

"I appreciate your faith in me. I don't know how to rule." The confession was one of truth, not unease.

"We'll help you. As will Vernum and Havon. The question is," Fox said as he leaned forward, "is that what you want?"

Archer stood, slowly, given his arms were still far from healed, tilting the top half of his body, he bowed to Eva and me. "I would be honoured, if you'd have me."

Dropping Mads' hand, Eva and I stood in unison, approaching our brother slowly and gently engulfing him in a light embrace. We pulled back when his body twitched in pain.

"I'll stay with you," Eva announced, planting a look of shock on Fox's face. He held his tongue, most likely not wanting to portray any further emotion.

"Well, this is going a lot smoother than I anticipated. Final point is, Hiema."

Xav looked at Mads, silently encouraging him to take the conversation. Standing, he surveyed the room, his most trusted companions.

"Trix..."

The witch shot him a disdainful look, eliciting a chuckle from me.

Rolling his eyes in a manner not suitable for a King, he started again, "Bea, it shouldn't have to be said but we'd love you to join us in the Winter Kingdom."

Bea folded her arms and said, "Like you arseholes thought you could be rid of me so easily."

The room laughed. I knew Bea wouldn't leave the bears' side. They were her family too.

Turning to his Captain of the Guard, he took on his role of leader once more. "Kane, again, I shouldn't have to say it, but I hope you'll return to your post as Captain of the Queen's Guard."

Kane stood, honour radiating from his body. "Of course, my King."

Mads grasped his shoulder before Kane returned to his seat. "And finally," Mads said as he turned towards me, "Aurelia, you have a choice, and I would never want you to think otherwise. You can reside in any Kingdom you wish with all of our blessings. But you would make me a happy man if you came to Hiema with us. In turn," he added without waiting for my response, "I will do everything in my power to bring the light to your life that you bring to all of ours."

Not wanting the tears to overtake the moment, I jumped up, launching myself into Mads' arms. "How could you ever think I'd want to be anywhere else? Thank you, though, for never taking the choice away."

Mads squeezed tighter in response, ecstatic I would be by his side.

"Before this gets too intimate," Fox said as he stood, throwing his arms around the two of us, "we are happy you'll be joining us, Goldie. Now, on to the next order of business."

I let one tear fall, enjoying every moment of its journey down my cheek. I wiped it away before looking at Fox. "And what's that?"

Fox smiled down at me before his gaze drifted to Xav and Mads. "Reuniting with our sister."

CHAPTER 44

MADDOX

The ticking of the ornately carved clock above the vast open fireplace broke the silence that had descended on the room. Kane, Bea, Archer, and Eva had left, giving us the privacy of a reunion many years in the making.

Aurelia sat uncomfortably since we'd insisted she stay. Fox had sternly advised it was one choice she wouldn't get to make, given she was part of the family now. The golden-haired goddess had tried to argue but all three of us refused to hear it.

My chest felt lighter in her presence and given the last time we'd seen our sister was also the day our parents were murdered, Aurelia's calming presence was welcomed.

The three of us were different men than she'd known, and I had no doubt she would've changed too. Who had Orsa become? The knowledge that she was thrust into such a substantial role following the curse, made me want to turn back time just to squeeze the life out of Lamina's dead eyes myself. Watching Eva melt her into nothing was deliciously satisfying, but the rage of the last couple of decades still sat in the shallow beneath my skin.

The few messages we'd had from Orsa and Hiema since arriving in Vernum were nothing more than temporary bandages. I needed to hear the story — Orsa's story, directly from her lips. To apologise for failing as her older brother and for not trying harder to get back to her.

With everything that had changed, with everything we'd overcome, I still needed to remember the ways I had failed. We were taking Raithe with us into a new era, but those reminders would help build me into the leader I wanted to be. The king I needed to be.

My brothers and I paced through different ends of the room, waiting in anticipation as the ticking appeared to grow louder. Each time the second hand moved signalled another moment closer to Orsa.

Deciding to fill the time with counting those beats, six hundred and eighty seven seconds later, a soft tapping sounded at the door. We all froze in our pacing stances as our gazes locked on the periwinkle panels decorating the wooden door. An unexpected tension swirled around us, mixing with the anticipation and fear of the next few moments and what they would bring.

"Come in." Xav's voice broke on those two words, failing to hide the nervous joy in his throat.

The handle turned before the door creaked open, revealing a tall, slim woman, dark hair coiled around her head in a snake like braid. She wore a simple trouser and tunic combo, perfectly encapsulating the colours of the Winter kingdom.

The twinkle in her eyes, glistening with tears was all I could focus on. Afraid to let out a breath, I contemplated whether I should wait for Orsa to move first or if I would take the leap myself.

The apprehension sunk into my bones, paralysing me to my spot as though I'd seen a ghost. Orsa was just as I remembered her. Even with the years now living in her, the beauty and confidence she'd always exuded was still there, front and centre.

Swift footsteps met my left before the blur of Fox's body bounded straight to Orsa, wrapping her into an embrace decades in the making. without another thought, Xav and I followed suit.

The tears welled in my eyes as my arms wrapped around my siblings. Bound in love, the unwanted tension dissipated, leaving only the thrill of our family being brought back together.

My brothers and I took turns kissing Orsa's cheek, head, touching her face to confirm she was actually real. Actions she didn't allow to last long, swatting us away like flies before bursting into laughter. The joyful sound wrapped around my heart, filling my eyes with further tears. Tears I had no intention of hiding.

Orsa's gaze danced around the room briefly until it stopped on the person responsible for this reunion. Steadily, Orsa made her way to the couch as Aurelia stood to meet her, a smile widening on her face with each step Orsa took. "You must be the goddess who brought my brothers back to me."

Laughing through tear streaked lashes, Aurelia held out her hand in greeting. "Just Aurelia."

"The golden one, indeed. And you, my dear, are not 'just' anything."

Pushing Aurelia's hand away, Orsa pulled her into a hug, whispering what I could only decipher as the words 'thank you.'

Aurelia's shoulders physically loosened, as though the gratitude gave her a reprieve from the anxiety and apprehension she held onto for so long. I knew Aurelia's battles would never fully dissipate, but she would learn to manage them and accept that they were part of her. Not who she was, but what made her so strong.

Orsa pulled back, lifting her thumb to wipe a stray tear from Aurelia's cheek. "Welcome home, Aurelia."

With the initial influx of emotions settling down, my brothers and I spent some time individually saying our greetings to Orsa. My eyes followed every movement she made with Fox and Xav, trying to pinpoint any of the abuse she may have experienced in our absence but sensing nothing of the sort.

Making her way to stand in front of me, she let her face fall into the same one I'd known so long ago. The look she gave me whenever my actions proved overprotective. All those times I'd taken on the burdens of others, and Orsa had to remind me that wasn't the job of a strong King.

"You can stop worrying now, Mads. We're back together."

The sweetness in her words drew us back into another embrace. Breathing in the warmth of Hiema around her, I closed my eyes to the sensation. "We should have been here. You had to face that on your own."

Pulling herself from my arms, she punched me in the chest, right above my heart.

"Ow!" Orsa had definitely gained a strong right hook.

"I wasn't alone. And it isn't as bad as you think."

Turning toward the rest of the group, Orsa signalled for me to sit down as she took the chair to the right of the lounge sofa. "One thing I can definitely thank Mum and Dad for now is that incredibly rigorous education they'd forced on me for so long."

Taking the seat next to Aurelia, she placed her hand on my thigh where I immediately laced my fingers through hers, waiting for Orsa to continue.

"We didn't know about Lamina. No one did. We thought it was Carman and Jolon's moves the entire time. The mistake on their part was that they always thought they were controlling Hiema through their hold on me."

"How, though? How did you manage to mislead them?" Fox sat on the edge of his seat, literally, soaking in every single word Orsa would give us.

"Do you remember Sienna?" The distant look in her eyes sent an immediate question of Sienna's relationship with my sister.

I did remember her. She had known our family since she was born. "Sienna the stable master's daughter?"

Orsa nodded. "The same one. Sienna is a witch. A very smart and powerful witch."

"And from what that look on your face is telling us," Fox interrupted, "she's more than that."

Orsa winked at Fox, giving no further explanation on his theory.

"Sienna and I, along with a band of merry outcasts, managed to mimic obedience through her spell work. It was hard and took so much effort, but we managed to keep the heart of Hiema beating as Mum and Dad would through everything the king and queen did."

I bit my lip in an attempt to keep the pride from bursting straight out of me. She hadn't needed us. In fact, it became clearer that our little sister was the most capable of keeping the Kingdom whole during our exile.

"You're amazing," Xav whispered as pride glistened in his eyes.

Orsa laughed. "I just did exactly what any one of you would have done in the situation."

Glancing between the three of us, her face fell serious. "I knew you'd come back."

Turning directly to me, she said, "Every fibre of me knew that you would return, and I had to do everything possible to keep that seat warm for you."

Aurelia's voice danced across my ear as she addressed Orsa, "Are you happy to step down?"

Orsa turned her attention to Aurelia, relief flooding her face. "I was never meant to rule Hiema, nor did I want to."

Flicking her gaze to me, she offered me a soft smile, no doubt attempting to rid me of any remaining guilt I held. "Mads, the throne is yours. And I would be thrilled to serve you however you see fit, but I'm ready to retire. I have a hot girlfriend I'd like to actually court."

Orsa winked as Fox boomed, "I knew it! When do we get to meet her?"

"When we get back to Hiema. Speaking of which, what is the plan now?"

Xav stood, holding out his hand for Orsa to do the same. "We have a few official things to take care of here, but we can be on route home in the next few days."

"Did Scrapefoot find you?" Orsa asked as she trailed Xav's footsteps toward the door.

"Scrapefoot?" The bears asked together.

Turning back toward us, Orsa raised her eyebrows. "The fox."

Startled by the information, Fox stood. "Rock came from you?"

The look of disgust on Orsa's face pushed a bubble of laughter up my throat. "You named him Rock? What the hell kind of name is that?"

"How did you get him to us?" Xav countered, doing his best to keep the conversation on track.

"I'm an etholim, aren't I? Communicating with animals is my gift. When we discovered Kane was going to attempt to rescue you, I sent Scrapefoot after you, hoping he could watch over you. I would have gone myself, but I couldn't leave Hiema."

Regret washed over Orsa's face as Xav reached for her hand giving it a reassuring squeeze.

"He's here. In Vernum. The queens will be bringing him," Aurelia added.

The remark brought a smile back to Orsa's face. Brushing off the brief regret, she clapped her hands together excitedly before turning back to business and me. "Well, my King, we should move. We can't welcome the king without a king."

Aurelia and I stood, following them through the door and toward our new reality. Just as I passed beneath the archway, I took Aurelia's hand, the coolness of her skin radiating through me as I promised myself to leave the guilt in that room. We were in Raithe, with Orsa, and we'd stand together, whether we were facing our demons or moving forward.

CHAPTER 45

AURELIA

We met the Vernum Queens and the King of Havon on the grand steps of Avilore keep. I hadn't given myself permission to visit more of the palace than I needed to. The events of the previous day still sat heavy, even though our victory was sweet, the air around the palace held a bitter taste. I knew Archer and Eva would turn the atmosphere around, and one day, in the near future, I would return and make new memories at Avilore. Memories worth savouring.

Our party stood in a line as the royals addressed us individually. I was greeted by Queen Colette first, a beaming smile across her face as she pulled me in for a warm embrace, whispering in my ear, "We are so very proud of you, my dear."

I planted a swift kiss on her cheek before she moved on to speak with Eva. Something rubbed on my legs, forcing my gaze down, and I was delighted to find Rock, or rather Scrapefoot, curling his auburn body around my legs. I lent down to cuddle my friend before Queen Kendra stepped in front of me, taking my hands in her soft fingers. "Well done, child. I had no doubts you would be successful."

She shot me what I had come to know as her trademark wink before she followed Colette. Next, a tall, muscular man stepped in front of me. I wasn't a particularly short woman, but this man towered over me. He was even taller than Mads. His amber eyes were framed by dark locks streaked with grey. The bottom of his face was adorned with a beautifully kept beard. The slightest smile sparked beneath his moustache as he extended his hand to me. Without hesitation, I took his palm in my own, surprised at the gentle grip. "You must be the golden-haired saviour I've heard so much about. I am Roux, King of Havon."

The deep timbre in his voice sent soothing whispers down my neck as I returned his subtle smile. Given I was in the presence of another King, I bent my knee to offer a bow in respect. The grip on my hand tightened, pulling me straight. "You should know by now, you bow for no one."

I couldn't hide the tears forming in the corners of my eyes, nor did I want to. On the briefest of whispers, I offered my thanks to the King of Havon. He let out a chuckle as he shook his head. "It is us who should be thanking you."

I couldn't process the intense gratitude his two statements offered. I had grown a lot in the last few months but a very distinct part of me still believed I was only average at best. King Roux gently released my hand before leaning closer as he said, "You don't have to believe it right now. We will believe in you until you're ready to take on that job yourself."

With nothing further, he stepped toward my sister, and I stared after him in disbelief, wondering how he knew what I'd been feeling before I remembered where I was and that magic danced all around us. I felt grateful for his words, tucking them into a new corner of my mind. One that savours and protects all of the good memories I've managed to experience.

After the line of greetings completed, Archer led our party back through the main entrance. Even with the staleness permeating the air around us, I couldn't deny the palace held great beauty in its bones. The stone structures adorned with intricate carvings held stories of times before the rule of Carman and Jolon. Stories that, one day, I would learn and respect. If I'd learned anything from my life, it was that not all family trees were filled with bad apples.

Archer brought us into the throne room which was, thankfully, completely transformed following yesterday's scuffle. No trace of Lamina, Carman, Jolon, or the evil that they exuded. The two thrones had also been removed, leaving the dais empty of anything but the hanging emblems of Aestas, a detailed sun, encased in a band of sunflowers. A symbol both simple and powerful and I had to admit, one that I liked very much.

"I'd like to go through tonight's proceedings, before we do the more official stuff. Then we can show you to your respective rooms for some much needed rest after your journeys," Archer addressed our party in a calm and direct manner.

"We will welcome all units from yesterday as well as the people of Aestas. We've sent out word to the other Kingdoms with the news of what had happened here yesterday and invite all of those who fled to return to Aestas if they so choose."

"We will then officially declare Carman and Jolon's charges against the Aestas crown and Raithe as a whole. The trial is confirmed to take place in a fortnight."

Archer looked at Eva and me. I took my sister's hand in my own and gave it a brief squeeze. We had already agreed that neither of us wished to be present, unless they needed a statement. Archer and Everett, who had agreed to stay in Aestas while Archer got up to speed, assured us the charges held strong without our involvement.

Archer then gestured for Mads to join him as he continued, "The final and most exciting portion of the evening will come last. The members of the Raithean counsel who are here will then formally announce Maddox as King of Hiema."

Queen Kendra's voice boomed as she addressed Archer directly, "Shall we get your swear in sorted then?"

Eva and I looked at the queen whose face beamed with pride. The swear in was going to happen now? Internally encouraging myself to voice the questions that filled my head, I stepped forward. "Do we not need to do that in front of the Aestas citizens?"

Archer shook his head. "No. We will eventually hold an official coronation but a legal swear in as King Regent is enough for now."

"Right then, Archer, you first." Queen Kendra announced before turning to Maddox, "And you later." With a wink, she stepped forward in silent instruction.

The other royals joined Archer on the platform as the doubled doors opened behind us to reveal a group of people I'd never met. I could only assume this was the Raithean counsel. Bea had explained earlier that they were peacekeepers amongst the Kingdoms. Most of which were sequestered by Lamina, freed last night by Everett and Kane's teams.

An older, bearded gentleman with delicate features climbed the steps to stand next to Archer. He held a bronze sceptre in his grip and a genuine smile on his face. "Young Manus, it's so good to see you in your rightful place."

The tone of his voice matched his appearance, soft and inviting. "Thank you, Sir Ansley."

Raising the sceptre above Archer's right shoulder, he uttered one word, "Kneel."

Obeying immediately, Archer lowered onto one knee as the queens, Roux, and Maddox formed a semi-circle around him.

"Do you, the rightful rulers of the Raithean Kingdoms bless Archer Manus as King Regent of Aestas?"

In unison, the ruler of Raithe spoke surely, "We do."

Ansley lowered the sceptre to Archer's right shoulder before moving it above his head to the left. "It is my honour to crown you, Archer Manus, the King Regent of Aestas. Rise and reign."

With a beaming smile, Archer rose before extending his hand to Ansley who took it quickly before pulling him into a tender embrace.

The other Raithean rulers followed suit, offering their congratulations and words of gratitude to my brother. A sniffle came from my left where I found Eva in the throes of emotion. I wrapped my arm around her shoulder just as Bea stepped to my other side, looping her arm through mine.

Raithe was far from what it was. It may never be. But what it had now was a new beginning. One that would be shaped by rulers worthy and ready for the challenge.

I stood in front of a floor length mirror in the room I'd woken up in that morning, staring at the woman in front of me. I'd spent the last hour in the suite, bathing and readying myself for the evening's festivities and found that, gradually, some of the thick hatred I'd felt toward the space had dissipated the more time I spent there.

Staring back at myself I was stunned. The deep green gown hung off my shoulders, accentuating my full breasts tastefully. It nipped in slightly, given the size of my waist was almost the same as my breasts, it was fascinating to see it more defined. The dress draped off my hips, falling in silky heaven to the floor.

For a few quiet moments, I stood in front of the mirror. The heavy part of me assumed I wouldn't recognise the woman staring back at me. However, what I found was I knew exactly who this woman was. A survivor. A warrior in mind and soul. A woman who had fought for an unattainable freedom, only to build herself a family.

Hundreds of unknowns sat in front of us, but the darkness of my past continued to surface, breathing, not attacking. I may never know what feeling normal was. The least I could do was like myself and love the woman staring back at me.

The door creaked open behind me, breaking me from my own thoughts. A few seconds went by before I felt his heat at my back, his after shave and cedar scent wrapping around me. A warm, welcome sensation I didn't know if I'd ever tire of.

"My golden-haired saviour."

The deep beat of his words circled my ears like silk. I let the smile tip on my lips before looking up to meet his eyes in the mirror. "Your Majesty."

A low growl rumbled at the back of Mads' throat as his hands circled my waist, bringing my back against his chest. I took a moment to appreciate Maddox in his regalia. The Hiema blue complimented the myriad of colours.

"What are you thinking?"

The sensuous tone was replaced with concern as he rested his chin on the top of my head. "I am thinking a lot of things, Maddox."

"Tell me two thoughts of concern and two of happiness."

I kept eye contact as I let my thoughts release. "I'm afraid of what comes next and that I'm abandoning Archer and Eva here."

His hold on me tightened as he spoke into my hair. "Good. Now two good thoughts."

I had given him my two concerns and he wasn't giving me solutions. He was simply asking me to make them real by speaking about them. I sunk into his embrace.

"One is this, right now, with you."

I hesitated on the second, not ready to say the words myself, but wanting to acknowledge their importance between us. "And the second is what you told me yesterday."

Mads kissed my hair before releasing his grip, turning me to face him. "Do you really love me?"

The question was laced with a vulnerability I didn't want to run from. A smile broke on his face, lighting up his features in the most sensational way. "I love you more than I did yesterday."

Without letting me respond, Mads' lips met mine in a bruising kiss. I couldn't say it back, but I channelled everything I felt for him in that one kiss, needing him to know that I was there. I was with him, whether or not I could voice my gratitude in that.

Pulling away abruptly, I tapped him lightly on the nose three times. "What happened to the moody man I met only a few months ago?"

"Oh, he is still here."

"Yeah?"

"Definitely. He just met a woman who showed him there is more to life than holding on to anger."

I wrapped those words up tight, holding them at the forefront of my memory to grab onto frequently.

"Shall we go get your crown, Your Majesty?"

The low growl rumbled through his chest once more, indicating how he felt about that title rolling off my tongue. I giggled, grabbing his hand and leading him toward our future.

CHAPTER 46

MADDOX

"Rise and reign, King Maddox of Hiema."

The weight of the crown Sir Ansley placed on my head settled comfortably. It was modest as per Hiema tradition. We were not a Kingdom of decadence or grandeur, but strength and unity. The circlet was made of bronze, detailed with the vines of ivy, having been in the Artos line for generations. Beneath the Artos crest on my chest, two bears facing one another, crossing swords centred behind them, all enveloped in a shield of ivy, beat heavily as Sir Ansley moved his hands from above me. The crown and crest reunited once more, echoing in my heartbeat.

Orsa had the gracious thought of bringing the crown with her. My heartbeat escalated at the sight before me as Ansley took a step away.

The hall itself wasn't lavishly decorated, but it had erased all the pain and anguish that had littered the walls just a few days before.

The pledges were much more detailed than what we'd experienced earlier in the day, given that Archer was sworn in as King Regent, but I was granted the reign of Hiema, officially.

Aurelia stood behind me, with Fox and Xav close. From the corner of my eye, I glimpsed out at the tremendous crowd. I forced my mouth to stay shut in the slight view of the thousands of Raitheans kneeled just as I rose. A sight to sear into my mind for eternity.

I faintly caught Fox instructing Aurelia to kneel as well. Turning, I caught the sight of her chin dropping toward her chest as her knee bent, about to make her way down to the floor.

Before her knee could kiss the stones, I placed my hand beneath her chin. Following my guidance, I met the vivid blue storms I'd looked deep into so many times before.

Using my hand to manoeuvre her back to standing, I let my lip tilt into a grin before I sealed my lips to hers. Her eyes widened in shock before she let herself lean into the kiss, not understanding what was happening. My smile grew wider beneath the caress as she finally gave in and kissed me back.

Aurelia's arms wound around my neck, careful not to disturb the ornament on my head, focusing solely on the man in front of her. A man she had once believed hated her. A man that would continue to give her patience, guidance, and choice.

I broke the kiss reluctantly before turning to our audience, my voice cascading through the space. "Raitheans, I cannot tell you how pleased we are to be back, ready for a new era of our kingdoms. Thank you for welcoming me as the King of Hiema."

Turning to Aurelia, I addressed her directly, "We all owe our deepest gratitude to the reason we are standing before you. The woman by my side."

Her face contorted in a mix of horror and disbelief before continuing, "Without her, we would not be here. Our saviour, our key. Aurelia."

Her name sang from my lips before the crowd erupted in a fit of cheers. Clapping hands met whistles that echoed across the large chamber, raising the hairs on my body in happiness. Aurelia kept her eyes on me, shooting me a disdainful smirk.

Lowering my forehead to hers, I said, "I think you've been advised already, you do not kneel, Goldie."

With a sultry wink, I took her hand, guiding her to face the thousands of Raithean faces before us. The tears filled her eyes freely before peeking out at the corners. Her own gratitude radiating out before her.

Once the praise settled, the throne room quickly transformed into a celebration of a new era of Raithe. The Raithean leaders gracefully moved around the space, greeting guests with an excitement that warmed me to my bones. I stayed by Aurelia's side, sensing the unease she couldn't keep hidden, giving her my hand for grounding frequently.

Waiters circled the room, dressed in the gold and maroon livery of the Spring Kingdom. The queens had travelled with an extensive entourage given Aestas was in disorder.

We met with various people, many of which reminded me that the rightful King of Hiema was home and a new era of Raithe bloomed. I couldn't deny how right it felt each time I heard the words.

Once the initial meet and greet concluded, a band set up, shifting the festivity and encouraging many Raitheans to share their dancing prowess. As I finally let the joy of the moment seep through, I noticed a little girl twirling on the makeshift dance floor with her father, glee radiating from her every move. That is when Aurelia turned toward me. "It just hit me."

"What did?" My brow furrowed in confusion.

"Everything we have accomplished was so much larger than I initially envisioned. We are all healing, Maddox. This is just another symbol of the healing journeys we all take in our lives."

With only a beaming smile on her face, Aurelia skipped away from me, joining Fox, Xav, Bea, Archer, and Eva as they danced to the new era of Raithe. I hoped she knew that although it would never be forgotten, her past was long gone.

With a smile secured on my face, I watched the blue eyed beauty laugh and dance with the people who meant the most. I thought about the first moment I laid eyes on her and how I had always thought I would fight the connection between us. Aurelia fought so many battles in her life, and I was going to spend the rest of mine reminding her that she was, and would always be, a warrior. Our golden-haired saviour.

Happily exhausted, I carried Aurelia to bed, kissing her gently as I laid her down on the plush mattress. I whispered a thank you in her ear, hoping her dreams were filled with the memories of a cabin, in a wood, light shining through a tree barrier, casting it in the most beautiful glow.

CHAPTER 47

AURELIA

My toes danced a few inches away from the plush, maroon carpet as I breathed in the Aestas breeze trickling in through the open window. I wanted to feel hatred of the place I came from, knowing so much of the horror my birth parents inflicted on the people of the Summer Kingdom. Everything Aestas symbolised should have driven me straight toward that fury, but I had faith in Archer and Eva, knowing they would gently guide Aestans into a kingdom of safety and pride once more.

A hand pulled tight on my stomach, pulling me back into a hard, warm, and naked chest. I squeezed my eyes, holding back the tears of joy at being in Mads' muscular hold.

I love you.

The words weren't ready to leave my lips yet, but I could finally acknowledge the feelings were there, floating inside of me in blissful madness. And I was going to take every opportunity to appreciate the man surrounding me.

Mads breathed into my hair, letting a moan of pure content flutter from his lips and the promise of other things, one of which pushed into my lower back, proving difficult to ignore.

I didn't want to ignore it.

The weight of our journey to this moment, and the events of the last few days, had me wanting nothing more than to get lost in the King of Hiema. Or, rather, have him get lost in me. Twisting in his arms, I didn't hesitate to capture his lips. My tongue danced with his as he pushed it deeper, shifting his hand from my back down to my arse, giving it a thorough squeeze, eliciting a noise from my own throat, inviting him to play. And I could play all day.

I pulled back slightly, giving slight distance to our lips. "Good morning, Your Majesty."

"*Fuck.*"

I pushed forward, smiling into his lips. "Yes please."

Before I could say anything further, I was thrown onto my back, a firm grip pushed my night dress up high, exposing me to the hungry bear above me. Grabbing my thighs, Mads pushed my legs apart, evidence of my lust dripping between my legs. A raw sound reverberated from his chest. The noise alone pushed the fire higher. Needing his skin on mine, I reached up with clumsy hands, attempting to undo the buttons on his shirt. Clearly needing me to move quicker, Mads took initiative and ripped it off, exposing his sculpted torso in all its glory. Salivating, I wrapped a hand around his neck pulling him on top of me, moulding my mouth with his.

Our bodies existed as a tangle of limbs, ravaging each other to the knowledge the war was over and we could finally move on. Mads nipped at my lower lip, a growl rumbling through him.

"I need you." My voice was breathy, needy.

"Aurelia."

I reached down, looking for the ties of his trousers, frustration building quickly at my inept fingers. Taking pity, Mads unlaced them before allowing me to help push them down over his chiselled arse. Unable to help myself, and why should I, I dug my fingers into both cheeks, directing his cock towards my entrance.

"Aurelia," he whispered on my lips again.

"What Mads? What do you need?"

Pulling himself back, his eyes bore into mine, a hunger flashing in a way I'd never known. "I need to be inside of you."

I gave him a nod in recognition. I needed him inside of me, too.

"Hold on, Goldie."

Reluctantly removing my hands from his arse, I grabbed onto his shoulders. A spot I had grown to appreciate the last few times we'd had sex. The muscles shifting beneath my hands drove me into a deeper arousal, knowing those movements were the result of Mads thrusting in and out of me.

Once my fingers dug in, anchoring me, Mads drove his cock into me in one solid thrust. My pussy expanded, allowing him in, as I cried out at the sudden invasion. Mads didn't waste any time, pulling himself out before thrusting back in, the rhythm and depth quickening with each drive. The burning in my core grew, my orgasm building at full speed.

"Can you feel that? Your pussy squeezing my cock?"

Before I could answer, he bent his head to my breasts, taking my right nipple in his mouth. As his teeth closed down around it, he flicked his tongue over the centre, the sensation causing my vision to blur at the edges.

"Mads! Don't stop."

Looking up at me through his lashes, a smirk formed on his lips, still surrounding my nipple. He kept his savage pace as his mouth shifted attention to my other nipple. "Don't want this one to feel left out."

I was going to catch fire. The pleasure rolling through my body was cresting, about to reach its peak. As much as I wanted to tip over the edge with him, I didn't have the capacity to stop, nor did I want to. "Maddox."

Lifting his head, the autumnal heat of his eyes bore into mine, never once slowing the tempo of his thrusts. "Come for me, my King."

Releasing a growl, Mads reached his hand behind me as he grabbed the headboard, his other latching to the back of my neck, tilting my lips up to capture them with his own, drilling his tongue deep into my mouth. With little air pushing into my lungs, I let the sensation take over, climax thundering through my body as I exploded around him. A guttural roar ripped free as Mads peaked with me, pumping his come inside of me as deep as possible. Both the knowledge and sensation adding to the satisfaction or my orgasm. With one last thrust, Mads lowered himself, resting his head between my breasts.

Letting our breathing even, I stroked my fingers through his mussed curls, letting the light in my chest grow brighter. "Mads?"

"Mmmmm."

The intensity of this intimacy wasn't in the length of time, change of positions, or filth leaving our mouths. No. This signalled a new era for us both. Together. Alive.

"I can't say those words yet. Even though I can't, I want you to know..." Fighting a magical King and Queen, bringing down a witch, slitting the throats of men who wronged me? They were all easy compared to vocalising how I felt.

"I want you to know, you've shown me there is a life worth living."

Shifting his head, Mads rested his chin on my breastbone, needing eye contact. "You gave yourself that life, Aurelia. And I'd happily worship at your feet for however long you'd let me."

I couldn't hold back the tear that escaped. Pushing himself up on his elbows, Mads leaned in to kiss the tear away. "I'll always be here to pick you up when you fall. I'll always kiss away your tears. And I will always, always make damn sure you have a choice."

Speechless, I whispered a thank you before pulling his head back down, twirling his hair around my fingers once more. The next part of the journey we'd endure would require a lot of effort, learning, time apart, and healing. None of it sent a fear through me the way it would have. Knowing Maddox would be by my side was enough.

A short time later, Maddox removed himself from me, although with complaint, leaving to go and assist our travelling group in preparing for our journey. I took my time getting ready, exploring the room of Avilore Keep further. I may have found comfort here in the last twenty four hours, yet I was eager to leave it. Hopefully, Archer will bring warmth to it when I visit.

Just as I finished braiding my hair back, a soft knock sounded at the door. "Come in."

Eva walked through cautiously, whispering faint words about what may haunt us here. I experienced it too. It unsettled me. Refusing to let it ruin the moment and the little time we had left together, I rushed to her, throwing my arms around her shoulders, channelling every hug we missed into one embrace. The years we spent as ghosts to one another, the possibilities of what we could have been haunting our every move, all died. Those versions of us would never hold us back, make us less of ourselves. Whatever happens next, knowing Eva, bringing her here with us, it was the right choice. The only choice.

Letting our tears fall, we sobbed into the embrace until our cries turned into giggles, the giggles turning into gut throbbing laughter. "Aurelia?"

"Yes, Eva?"

Pulling back, my sister's tear streaked eyes took me in. "Thank you."

There were so many words left unsaid between us. Years of talking would never be able to undo the damage those cocksuckers brought to us, individually and together. I did the only thing I knew I needed to. "Eva, I am so proud of you."

It was true. The journey Eva was on wasn't identical to my own, but no less important. The healing we had done and would do, together and separately, was ours to own. To navigate. And I was so very proud of the woman she was. Not what she could be but what she was. Right then.

Eva started crying once more, and I pulled her back in, letting us both live in the moment.

Eva and I strolled hand in hand through the halls of the Summer Kingdom palace, eventually finding ourselves on the front steps, ready to say our goodbyes. The Hiema King, Princes, and Princess were going home.

I dreaded this part, saying goodbye to people who had grown more important to my life in such a short span of time. I knew one day I'd see them again, but not knowing weighed me down, my emotions brimming on the surface. The sadness threatened to pour over, tears welled in my eyes, but I forced them back. I started my farewells with the Spring Queens, expressing my deep gratitude for everything they'd done for me since arriving in Raithe. Both women waved me off, insisting I needed to stop fussing over gratitude when we were family.

"That is what family does," Queen Colette had said.

Archer and Eva were last. Most of the group had moved away, giving us time to say goodbye without an audience. I pulled Archer to me first, hugging him tight. "I'm so proud of you brother. I will be here whenever you need me, but I think you're going to do just fine."

Pulling back, he kissed me on both cheeks, the said, "Thank you Aurelia. You know I will be calling on you as soon as I screw up. Which will most likely be next week."

I had every faith in the man who stood in front of me. We still had a lot to learn about each other, as did Eva and me. But we were a unit, whether in this world or another. We always were. Always would be.

Stepping up to Eva, I was thankful we had some time alone before this moment. Crying with her was more therapeutic than I would have guessed. "We didn't have enough time, Eva."

Placing her hands on my cheeks, Eva rested her forehead against mine, mirroring what I had done when I unlocked her power. "We have all the time in the world, sister. I'll come visit soon."

"Fox would like that," I said with a smirk.

A conflicted laugh left Eva. "If we don't murder each other first."

"I think he likes the chase." I winked at her, and she fought the blush threatening her cheeks.

I stood back, taking in my blood family once more. It was hard not to think of the lost times, the abandonment. The past would never be forgotten, yet the future was ours to mould. Mouthing the words I never imagined I would, I turned to the bears, ready to start the journey to my new home. I glanced at Fox, who struggled to leave without a word, resisting his own stubbornness not to give Eva anything she could use against him. Instead, he offered my sister one brief nod. An understanding, perhaps? How would their future unfold?

Xav and Mads offered both Archer and Eva a quick embrace before leading us to our travelling party. Bea was already mounted, next to Kane, batting her eyelashes at him in continued attempt. Climbing on my own horse, I waited for Mads to hand Rock to me so I could situate him into his travelling seat before I allowed myself one final look at my family home. Not Carman and Jolon, but Archer and Eva. They would create something in Aestas. Something incredible. I couldn't wait to see what awaited them.

Mads kicked his stallion into gear, indicating for us to follow suit. The journey to Hiema was fast and hard, only breaking when the horses needed a brief rest. The bears were eager to get home. In all honesty, I was ready to settle again. The palace would never give me the comfort the cabin did. I was still determined to find solace there. To explore my magic. Continue my journey of healing. Learn the histories and customs of Raithe. Watch Mads take his rightful place as leader and above all, be by the brother's side as they take back their life and their happiness.

As our travelling group crested the final hilltop, Xav waved me forward, indicating for me to join the brothers at the front. With a gleam of something I couldn't quite recognise in his eye, he delivered a question I would never forget, "Ready to go home, Goldie?"

I glanced from Xav to Fox and Maddox as triumphant smiles spread across all three of their faces. I silently thanked them for changing everything I had ever believed, showing me how magical life could be. "There it is." Orsa called from beside us, pointing down the hill.

Steering my horse a few steps forward, the scene came into view. My jaw dropped to the site in front of me. The palace, although indeed the stature of a palace with a backdrop of snow tipped mountains, was the mirror image of the cabin in the woods. Apart from the apparent variation in size, the similarities to the one home I'd ever known were uncanny. A wooden structure, surrounded by a sea of forest, invited me in.

"What do you think?" Mads coaxed, as he stepped his stallion to my side.

My eyes filled once more as I took in the Hideaway, the structure in which they had mirrored the cabin. The only home I had ever truly known.

Xav and Fox steered their horses next to me as they too gazed down the hill.

"Not too big," Xav added.

"Not too small," Fox echoed.

The tears burning my eyes dropped down my cheek as I looked towards the next chapter of my life. In the slightest of whispers, I smiled as I said, "It's just right."

EPILOGUE

AURELIA

The signs of a new Winter in Hiema dusted the grounds of the Hideaway in the form of freshly fallen snow. The gathering of the white powder had always brought me comfort in its quiet. Once, not long ago, I would have compared it to a bird in its cage, a blanket being draped over to signal a time of silence. Now, the expanse of Hiema lands covered in a blanket of snow resembled freedom. The cage was no more. I was able to fly free.

Almost two months had passed since the events at Avilore Keep. The bears, Orsa, and Bea were occupied with the day to day running of the territory. Orsa had done such a fantastic job of managing during the curse that the main focus was for the new King and returned Princes to build the trust back up with the citizens of Hiema.

By order of the King himself, and his three very pesky siblings, I enjoyed my freedom and stayed mostly out of the spotlight. I visited Invern, the central town, daily, to acquaint myself with the people and merchants of Hiema, always introducing myself as just Aurelia.

Everyone knew of my close relationship with the king, but I was never treated any differently, always welcome with open arms.

The time neared for Maddox's official coronation. With the other seasonal Kingdoms arriving over the next few days, I assisted with the preparations as much as Leonada, the Hideaways main house-keeper, would allow. She was a stern, older woman who had served Maddox's parents before him but with a heart of gold she liked to keep hidden from most. She let me see those caring sides of her more with each day.

While I was nervous for the large celebration and standing by Maddox's side in front of not just Hiema, but the other Kingdoms as well, I was also fraught with anticipation. Archer and Eva would be arriving along with the other leaders, and I couldn't wait to see them. We'd kept in close correspondence since I'd left Aestas, with Eva giving every possible detail of the rebuild of the Summer Kingdom. The people of Aestas were in good hands.

"Goldie!" Fox's frustrated voice echoed across the throne room as I assisted Leonada with the floor plan for the big event. I rolled my eyes.

He had become my shadow in the last two days, hiding the real reason for his need to be near me with 'official royal business.' He was just as eager, if not more, to see Eva.

The two hadn't kept in touch since we left Avilore Keep but it was clear his potential attraction to my sister had deepened with her absence. Either that, or they really would murder each other upon the reunion.

"Yes, dearest Fox. What can I do for you now?" Leonada chuckled at my mocking tone as I turned to face the youngest bear with my hands on my hips.

Fox held a piece of parchment between his hands, yet another tactic to lead me away from thinking he had any interest in seeing my sister.

"I'm organising the arrival schedule. I need to know when Aestas is arriving to make sure we have room in the stables." He stared down at the parchment, refusing to make eye contact with me.

We both knew if he did, I'd see right through his lies.

"Fox, I already told you what time we should expect them." I stepped toward him, raising my hand to his chin and forcing his eyes toward mine.

He held a slight resistance before giving in, letting his magnetic blue gaze capture my own. "Are you going to admit your feelings toward seeing my sister?"

Fox shook my hand off, ignoring my question. "You're right. I've got it written down already. Thanks."

Without another word, he stormed away.

Leonada stepped to my side. "I cannot wait to meet the woman who has Fox up to ninety-nine."

She chuckled. I couldn't resist joining her. Whatever would happen during the solstice coronation, I could only hope they wouldn't burn the Hideaway to the ground.

The time had come later that afternoon. My heart fluttered in my chest to the beat of my footsteps, taking me closer to the siblings I had only recently let into my heart. I bounded down the wooden steps toward the carriage just as the door swung open. In true Eva style, she didn't even wait for the footman to help her down the steps before she bounded toward me.

We collided, letting out a breath before we both burst into laughter.

Holding Eva in my arms felt like I'd grown back a missing limb. An odd sensation given my very recent indifference toward my sister.

"You're here," I whispered into her ash brown locks as they tickled my cheek.

"I'm here," she cooed back.

We held each other in a tight embrace for a few moments before she pulled back from me. "Let me look at you then."

Eva studied my face first, the smile glued on it most likely infectious, before she held me at arm's length to examine my clothing, my visual health. I did the same, needing to know she was, indeed, in one piece and mostly that her and Archer hadn't caused each other any physical damage.

Before we could say anything further, Archer was in front of me, pulling me to his chest. "Hello, sister."

I breathed him in, relishing every beat of his heart against my own.

"I've missed you both." I tried my best to keep the growing emotion from my voice, but to no avail.

A throat clearing behind us had our arms pulling away from one another. I looked over my shoulder to find the Artos siblings standing on the top steps.

Mads took a step toward us and said, "It is wonderful to see you both."

He reached Eva, wrapping her in a brief, yet awkward hug before making his way to Archer. The embrace he offered my brother was much more believable than whatever he gave my sister.

Xav and Orsa stepped down next, offering their welcoming to my siblings. Fox stood back, surveying the situation. I tried to read his face, looking for the frustration I thought would show on it at the sight of my sister. I couldn't deny the lightness filling his eyes as he watched my baby sister, as though what he saw wasn't real.

Taking one step toward Eva, he offered her a slight bow of his head. "Eva."

Folding her hands in front of her, she mirrored Fox's posture "Fox," she said. "It's good to see you."

Was it? The tension between the two was thick, yet I couldn't understand if it would burn them both separately or if they would ignite together. If Fox had thought Mads' and I's initial sexual tension could fill an area, he and Eva's could take over the entirety of the Raithean realm. I would definitely need to speak to Eva about how her feelings may have evolved since Avilore Keep. But first, I needed a proper catch up with my brother and sister.

Looping my arms through theirs, I lead them back into the Hideaway, needing to first give them a very brief tour before pouring us all very large glasses of brandy.

"So, it's been a while, has your hatred for Fox declined? Or did seeing him bring it all back?" I chucked a grape in my mouth as Eva and I sat in my personal library. A gift from Mads not long after we'd arrived. It was modest, cosy, filled with deep emerald green couches and walls lined with bookshelves.

Eva paced the shelves, keeping her focus off of me directly. "I never hated him, Aurelia. He just never gave me a reason to particularly like him."

I wrapped my feet up tighter in the throw across my legs. "Is there someone in Aestas that's taken your fancy then?"

Eva laughed, "No. There hasn't been time for romance, sister. It's a lot of work rebuilding the Summer Kingdom."

My eyes softened as Eva finally met my gaze. "I can't even imagine Eva. I'm so proud of you."

She offered me a gentle smile before taking the seat next to me, burrowing her feet beneath my blanket. I took her hand in mine. "And how has training been going?"

Since Eva's chaos powers were released, she'd been working with some with similar abilities in honing her magic.

"Really good. Tiring. But good. It's nice to have an outlet for this anger that is always coursing through me."

I let my head fall to her shoulder, breathing her in.

"Are you ready for the coronation?" She asked, changing the subject.

I let out a huff and said, "I'm ready for it to be over. I don't like all the pomp and circumstance, Eva. You know that. Plus Xav has asked me to give a speech at the dinner. The spotlight isn't my favourite place to be."

Eva stroked my hair as she spoke, offering comfort. "Everything you've done since you left Huxley has been outside of who you thought you were. This is no different. Plus," she added as she motioned for us to get up, "it's Mads."

I sighed. "It's Mads." I welcomed the smile that grew on my face at the mere thought of that man.

"Well then," Eva said standing, "shall we go get ourselves ready?"

With no hesitation, I took her outstretched hand in my own, buzzing in happiness at being with her once more.

"To King Maddox!" Xav raised his glass to the crowd.

"Here, here!" The crowd responded.

The coronation ceremony, thankfully, wasn't as long winded as I'd expected. It was little more than what took place at Avilore Keep a few months ago.

We now delighted in the merriment of the celebration in the throne room, eating and drinking our fill.

Xav had gracefully started with his speech, congratulating his brother and wishing him a long rule before it was my turn.

With trembling limbs, I stood next to Mads, bringing the small piece of parchment to my eye level. Mads reached out briefly to give my hand a squeeze before I cleared my throat, addressing the room.

"Although I've been Raithean all my life, most of that time I didn't know it. Unfortunate events, mixed with fate, and three men's belief in me is what brought me back here, with both my blood family, and the family who had taken me in as their own."

I paused momentarily to glance at Eva, Archer, Bea, and the bears.

"Many of you might not know this, but your King wasn't the most hospitable host when we first met. In fact, he was rather miserable."

That gained a few chuckles from around the room, easing the tension in my shoulders slightly.

"The Artos family has given me more in the last five months than I've ever known in my entire existence. I will forever be grateful for their unwavering support and belief in me. I have no doubt that King Maddox will be a fair and prosperous ruler with the citizens of Hiema and Raithe at the heart of everything he does."

Setting the paper down on the table, I replaced it with my glass, raising it to the crowd before looking into the captivating eyes of the man beside me and said, "To the man I love, King Maddox!"

Mads' eyes locked on mine as the room shouted, "King Maddox," around us.

Mads swallowed deeply before I raised the glass to my lips. He sat frozen as his eyes stayed locked on mine. Placing my fingers under his glass, I tipped it to his lips. When the liquid was successfully down my throat, I addressed him, "It's bad luck if you don't drink after a toast."

The trepidation grew at his silence. After another moment without a response, my fingers found the hem of my sleeve, weaving through with unease before Maddox knocked his glass back in one go, threw it down on the table and rose. Without a word, he pulled me to his chest and slammed his lips against mine, giving me all his words in that one action. Without a care of the thousands of faces on us at that moment, I kissed him back and let a smile grow beneath our lips.

Mads pulled back slightly, letting his words dance between us. "You love me?"

"I do." No hesitation.

He kissed me again, this time pulling me right off the ground in his strong arms.

The crowd behind us bellowed out cheers of triumph as I kissed the man I loved. And who loved me right back.

Acknowledgements

Well, fuck. I did it.

The first acknowledgement must go to YOU. Yes, you. You've made it this far and I cannot even begin to describe how much that means to me.

To the Bookstagram community: whether you've watched my journey from the beginning, or you've joined the chaos along the way – you all got me here. The comments, the DMs, the shares, the support – that is why you are reading these words today. This community is the reason I blossomed and there is nothing I can do to show the magnitude of gratitude I have for you and this space.

The Book Mafia – how lucky am I to have found a group of women who have become my found family, who do nothing but uplift, love, and support one another. Momo, Courtney, Soph, Jess, Eliza, and Vanessa, I adore you all so very much.

Vanessa, my internet wife, my beautiful goth flower – The Golden Key simply wouldn't exist without you. Your unconditional support from the moment I told you about this crazy idea will never be forgotten. Thank you for never letting me settle. For all the dick jokes. For being a soul mate.

Brit, I may be the hugger in our relationship but the way you embraced this story and supported me on so many steps of this journey is more affection than I could have ever asked for. I cannot wait for our in real life Star Wars marathon together. You will never be yeeted from my life now, I hope you realise that.

Fitzgerald, my catitor – you may have been useless at grammar and sentence structure, but keeping my legs warm on those cold winter nights of writing was everything to me.

Moussa, for always wagging your tail and giving me snuggles even after I locked myself away to write for hours on end.

My extended tripod – Lorien, Luke, Elspeth: nights in the vortex and your constant words of encouragement never went unnoticed. You're unwavering belief in me is something I don't know if I will ever feel I deserve but I love you all so very much.

Mom and Dad – it hasn't always been easy for us over the years but you were the first to ever tell me the one thing I needed to hear, "You should be a writer, Cass." I did it.

To every indie author I have read, spoken to, admired – YOU have all been more of an inspiration than you will ever fathom. Being able to watch and/or be a part of the journeys you have taken gave me the confidence to put in this work. To all of you who answered random questions, gave me encouragement to keep going, and for just being your amazing, badass selves. Continue to be the firecrackers you are. Let's take over the world.

Samuel H. – I wouldn't be here without you. That isn't an exaggeration. You may never read this story in full, but you're the best smut consultant and cheerleader a girl could ask for. Thank you for believing in me every step of the way and never letting me give up. And for being you. I know it's been a weird and wonderful year and you never once complained about my absences, always pushing me forward with a gentle hand. I really got lucky that day you walked into the hostel in Amsterdam and I can never imagine my life without you by my side. All three of the bears are a combination of you. Fox's talent for banter, Xavier's kind heart, and Mads, well, not just in physical features but in his grumpiness too. I couldn't have found a better muse. I love you, Poodle.

Last but certainly not least, to my younger self – Cass, you did it. You fought tooth and nail with your doubt and you finally got here. You wrote a book. You published it. And I am so fucking proud of you baby girl. Let's keep making up stories.

About the Author

Enthralled by fictional worlds for as long as she can remember, Cass prefers to be stuck in a book over most things in life. Originally from the US, she found herself (and her husband) in London and has lived there since 2010, taking on a transatlantic accent she didn't ask for.

She loves things that start with 'w' including (but not limited to) wonderland, whisky, wine, winter, wit, and writing.

You can follow along with all her shenanigans on Instagram – @wonderlandandwhisky

Printed in Great Britain
by Amazon

38450768R00324